HOME IS NEARBY

HOME IS NEARBY

Magdalena McGuire

First published 2017
by Impress Books Ltd

Innovation Centre, Rennes Drive,
University of Exeter Campus, Exeter EX4 4RN

© Magdalena McGuire

British Library Cataloguing in Publication Data

A catalogue record for this book is available from the British Library

ISBN 13: 978-1-911293-14-9 (pbk)
ISBN 13: 978-1-911293-15-6 (ebk)

Typeset in Plantin
by Swales and Willis Ltd, Exeter, Devon

Printed and bound in England
by Short Run Press Ltd, Exeter, UK

For Anton and Miro,
my loves

A note on Polish pronunciation

Readers can be rest assured that pronunciation, in Polish, tends to be consistent (unlike English, which has many exceptions). For this reason, the pronunciation of Polish words is not as formidable as one may think.

In the Polish alphabet, certain letters are conditioned by accents:

ą   on, as in long (nasal)
ć   ch, as in cheek
ę   en, as in sense (nasal)
ł   w, as in wet
ń   ny, as in onion
ó   u, as in push
ś   sh, as in sheep
ź   zh, 'g' as in Niger (soft)
ż   zh, 's' as in pleasure (hard)

Special letter combinations include:

ch   h, as in Loch Ness
cz   ch, as in chip
dz   ds, as in cads
sz   sh, as in shoe
rz   s, as in measure (hard)

The characters' names are pronounced as follows:

Ania – Ah-nya
Dominik – Dom-ee-nik
Małgorzata – Mau-go-zha-ta
Krzysio – Krshi-shyo

Polish surnames can have different forms for the genders. Skowrońska is the female surname and Skowroński is the same surname for a male.

Pan and Pani are the basic honorific styles used in Polish to refer to a man or woman respectively. Państwo is used to address a group of men and women.

One leaves Poland today with the impression that the most beautiful flowers sometimes bloom on the edge of the abyss.

Czesław Miłosz, 1981

'Sculpture', a fourteenth century word from the Latin *sculpere*, means to carve, cut, cleave.

Martin Herbert, 'The Broken Arm',
Thinking is Making

Poland, December 1981

It was eleven days before Christmas and an orange-tailed carp swam in the bathtub, opening and closing the slick tunnel of its mouth. It gulped at my fingers, releasing a stream of bubbles which vanished in the murky water. I withdrew my hand, shaking it dry. The fish returned to circling the tub. Its fins were translucent and stumped, as though someone had cut off the ends.

I joined my friends at the kitchen table. Seven floors below us, tanks were lined up on the streets. Soldiers gathered by in green uniforms and fur-trimmed caps. They held out their hands to cages of burning coal.

Martial law was for our own good, the government said. They said we all had to make sacrifices. And we would all be safer as a result.

'Bullshit,' Dominik said. 'This is complete bullshit.' He darted between the laminex table and the bench, rearranging newspapers and books, the cracked cup we used as an ashtray. He stopped at the window, pulled back the curtain and scrutinised the dark street. When I rested my hand on his back he twitched under my palm like one of Father's rabbits as I tried to pull it out of the hutch.

Dominik lifted the telephone off the hook and pressed it to his ear. 'Still dead.'

At the table, Krzysio massaged his temples and then checked his watch. His movements were unhurried,

1

smoothing the edges of my fear. 'Well, folks. One hour till curfew.'

Yesterday we learned there was a new set of rules we had to live by. From the stroke of midnight there were to be no public gatherings, no travel between cities without permits. No one was allowed on the streets after ten at night. So now the four of us were holed up in Małgorzata's apartment, trying to figure out what it all meant. This was the first time I would be spending Christmas without Father. The thought of being apart from him unnerved me almost as much as the news of what was happening to Poland.

Dominik ran a hand through his hair. The ends stood up, electric. 'Let's go out. Show them we're not afraid.'

'And get arrested?' I dragged a jar of honey wine across the table and poured it into cups. Pools of amber liquid glowed by the lamplight. 'Here.' I handed one to Dominik, then Krzysio and Małgorzata. I took a sip and savoured the sweetness that came before the burn.

Małgorzata dipped her hand into the chest-pocket of her overalls and pulled out some hashish. 'If they treat us like naughty children, that's exactly how we'll act.' A wave of dark hair fell over her cheek as she rolled a joint and dabbed it on her tongue to seal it.

Dominik threw himself on a chair. 'This improves things.'

When Małgorzata passed him the joint, their fingers touched.

'*Na zdrowie*,' Krzysio said. His words released a white cloud from his mouth.

I held up the joint in return, 'To your health.' I filled my lungs with the dank smoke and counted to ten before breathing out. There was a haze in the kitchen. By the time we rolled a second joint, all the hard edges were soft.

Next to us in the living room, the television was on. All the regular programs had been taken off air and we were stuck with a recording, on loop, of the grey-faced General Jaruzelski reading from a piece of paper.

2

Great is the burden of responsibility that falls on me at this dramatic moment in Polish history. I announce that today a Military Council of National Salvation was formed. This is the last chance to pull the country out of crisis and save it from disintegration.

A spasm in his upper lip as he intoned, 'Let no one count on weakness or hesitation.'

'God, he's like a cadaver,' Małgorzata said. 'Couldn't they pick someone more charismatic to send us to the gallows?'

The announcement faded to black and after a brief pause, started once more: *Great is the burden of responsibility that falls on me ...*

Dominik took two strides to the living room and punched his fist against the television to switch it off. 'There's no point in listening to that junk.'

He was right. For the real news we had to rely on word of mouth and the underground press. Already we'd heard that hundreds of people – maybe even thousands – had been arrested the night before. At midnight, militiamen had knocked on their doors and taken them away.

Krzysio flicked through Małgorzata's tapes, the plastic covers knocking gently together. He selected one by Deadlock. 'Now *these* are some great performers. Jaruzelski could learn something.'

My laugh was too high; the sound pressed against my bladder, my bones. Melting limbs made their way to the bathroom. As I left, Dominik turned up the sound. 'Let's be real. No one's sleeping tonight.'

The frenetic sounds of Deadlock followed me to the bathroom. Laughing silently, I stretched out my arms and spun around, wobbling to a stop when I noticed the doleful pair of eyes. Though we ate carp every Christmas, the thought of millions of fish floating in bathtubs and buckets, waiting to be killed, was unsettling. I leaned over the tub, dangling in the line of my plait. The fish gaped in the shallow water. It came to me that what I needed to remember from this night wasn't the tanks or the thin-lipped General. It was this.

I forced my legs to take me back to the kitchen, where I picked up my satchel.

'You okay, Ania?' Dominik asked. I gave him a wave of assent.

Inside the bathroom, I took out my drawing pad. The chipped tiles dug into my knees as I sketched a fish, which soon assumed Dominik's features: his unruly hair and ironic smile, the strong lines of his cheeks. I startled when a set of hands clamped heavy on my shoulders.

'What are you doing?' Dominik crouched by my side.

Biting back my laugh, I tore out the page and handed it to him. The title of the picture was scribbled at the top, *Portrait of Dominik as a Carp*. I held my breath while Dominik assumed a serious expression: narrow eyes, slight frown.

'You've captured a good likeness.' He tilted his head to the side. 'So Ania, are you going to serve me on a platter on Christmas Eve?'

'I'm sure you'd be delicious.'

'Cheeky girl.' Still holding the picture, Dominik scooped me up and dangled me over the bath. 'Do you really think I look like a fish?' He lowered me to the water. 'Do you?'

As I screeched, the picture floated to the bath. Ink bled into the water.

'Now you've seen what your fish-man is capable of …' Dominik carried me to the kitchen, my heart thumping against his chest.

'Ten o'clock.' Krzysio interlaced his fingers and he stretched his arms before letting them collapse by his sides.

We stepped onto the balcony. The smell of burning coal cut through the air. People in the opposite apartment block were flashing their lights on and off, on and off. Some blew whistles. Others simply stood on their balconies or at their windows. Dominik cupped his hands around his mouth and yelled, 'We're still here!' He wrapped his arms around me, shielding me from the cut of the wind.

In the opposite apartment, two storeys above us, a man in a dressing gown waddled onto his balcony, carrying something bulky in his arms. A television. 'Enough!' he shouted. 'They're playing that clown over and over and I've had enough.'

'That's a fair reaction to Jaruzelski,' Małgorzata said. She huddled closer to Krzysio and warmed her hands in his.

The man heaved the television onto the iron rail of his balcony, nearly tripping as he did. The television wobbled before he pushed it over the edge. There was a sharp explosion when it hit the ground. The streetlight cast a glow on the broken glass.

'That's what I think of their lies!' the man yelled.

From another apartment, someone called back, 'Okay fine, but don't come running to us when you want to watch the football!' Laughter in the cold night.

Shortly after, three militiamen rushed down the street, rifles slung across their shoulders. One crouched by the broken television. He stood and pointed at the apartment block opposite us, then at ours. The other two men raced off, ready to search the flats.

'Party's over.' Krzysio kicked a bit of ice from the balcony and we went back in.

'We need to get rid of this.' Małgorzata slipped the remaining hashish under a piece of lino on the kitchen floor. She turned down the cassette player and the scream of the punk music drained to a whisper. No one spoke as we waited for the knock on the door.

Fire

1

Poland, September 1980

In the early afternoon, Father and I crouched by Mother's side, clearing the golden leaves at her feet. We had come from church, where we'd listened to the sermon with plastic fertiliser bags rustling in the pockets of our coats. I held one open now, scraping leaves into its belly as Father updated Mother on the village news. He told her about the latest feud between neighbours after one accused the other of being a slattern who hung her underwear on the front line for all the world to see, about the local boy who was engaged to an American woman ten years his senior, and the rabbit Father had traded for real cigarettes with the priest. (*The French ones have flavour. Not like the sawdust they pass off as tobacco here.*) I had my own news, though Father didn't know it.

He reached across the granite for a portrait of the Virgin Mary, her hands clasped beneath her burning heart.

'Let me do that,' I said. With my sleeve, I polished the frame, its silver colouring edged with rust. I replaced it and then traced the inscription Father had carved on Mother's headstone: *Peace is thine/Remembrance is ours.* Yet I had no memories of a time when she was alive. All my recollections came from photos, from the stories Father told, or here in the cemetery. I remembered how she looked in springtime, when I laid globeflowers and branches studded with berries across her granite shoulders. In winter, when she wore a cape of white. And on autumn afternoons like this, when the birch trees formed cradles above her head.

Nearby, a statue of Jesus looked at me despairingly, a crown of thorns piercing his head. I patted the letter in the pocket of my coat. Now was the time to do this. Holding the letter out to Father, I said, 'This came the other day.'

He brushed the dirt off his hands and took it. His nose made a sharp whistling sound as he breathed out. Then he smoothed the corners of his dark moustache.

All this started as a private game of 'what if'. When I told my teacher I was joining Father in the family trade, she encouraged me to apply for university instead. Incredibly, she thought I could make a portfolio from the little pictures I drew, the figurines I made from straw and wood. To get into art school, I didn't need to sit any exams. I simply posted off my portfolio and forgot about it. Until the other day, when the letter of acceptance arrived.

Father turned his attention to the stones around Mother's grave. Each one was the size of a fist and had a smooth dark surface, like a river at dusk. He picked one up, stroked it, and then put it back down.

'Wrocław isn't so far away,' I said. 'Just under two hours by train. And think of all the things they have in the city. I could bring back sausages ... and cigarettes.'

The letter rested on the foot of the grave. Father wrenched some weeds from the ground and tossed them aside. 'You hear that?' He ran his hand down Mother's side. 'Our daughter wants to leave us.' He shook his head. 'To go study art.'

'I was lucky to get into the Academy. And it's a generous scholarship, see?' I held out the letter but he didn't take it.

'Sausages and cigarettes,' he said under his breath. He kissed the headstone, crossed himself and stood up. 'Come, *słoneczko*.' No matter how old I got, Father still called me his little sun.

We left the cemetery and I walked behind him, kicking my way through the leaves.

2

Inside the shed, dust motes floated golden in the dim light. Father stood at his workbench, chiselling a hunk of black granite. A dust mask hid the lower part of his face. Working quickly, he carved the perfect circle of an 'o'. The commission was on behalf of Olgierd Obuchowski, a retired militiaman who had died of tuberculosis.

Without pausing to remove his mask, Father said, 'Small chisel.' I handed it to him and he rounded off a 'g', releasing clouds of granite as he worked.

On a table next to the workbench was a child-size headstone. Father had given it to me when I was small; my introduction to the family trade. That year, a boy in the class above me had stolen my pencils and as revenge I carved his name in the stone. The letters were crooked but prophetic. Two months later he ran across a lake of ice, a shortcut on his way to school. It was the beginning of winter and the leaden days were yet to turn clear and bright. Apparently when he reached the middle of the lake, the ice cracked. He plunged in and drowned. The thought of it made me shiver.

'We should get rid of that thing,' I said to Father, pointing at the miniature headstone.

This time he pulled down his mask. 'Your first masterpiece? Over my dead body.' He grinned and raise his eyebrows emphatically. Unlike me, Father wasn't superstitious. He maintained the headstone had nothing to do with the boy's death.

He wiped his brow and then rolled up his shirt sleeves, revealing the tattoo on his left forearm; a wobbly outline of a heart and dagger that he'd got during his time in the army. After replacing his mask, he selected a chisel with a diamond-shaped point. He held it in his fingers the way a conductor would a baton. With a swift, decisive motion, he lowered the chisel to the stone and hit the end with a hammer. In Father's hands the tools became living things that danced and sang at the same time, with a chip chip, tap tap tap.

A lamp illuminated the plane of the stone. I moved closer. 'Can I?'

Father stood back and handed me the chisel. I fitted a mask over my face and bit my bottom lip, the chisel hovering by the stone, the hammer at the ready. The first hit always set a jangle to my nerves. I breathed in, steadying myself, and brought the chisel down to the stone. *Clink.* Then another. Soon the rhythm took over and the less I thought about it, the easier it became. As though someone else was doing the carving and I was standing by their side, watching.

'Olgierd' appeared on the stone in neat, even letters. Father said, 'Where am I going to find someone else who can carve like you?'

We took turns chiselling 'Obuchowski'. When we were done, Father added a scroll underneath the lettering and then looked up and said, 'A coat.' He tugged off his mask and pointed the chisel my way. 'If you're going to Wrocław, you'll need a new coat. And some socks too. Seeing as you won't have your old man to light you a fire at night.'

'Oh *Tatuś*' I kissed him on the cheek. 'It was just an idea.'

'You remember Olgierd.' He jerked his thumb towards the headstone.

'How could I not?' Olgierd used to sit on the porch, a bottle of homemade vodka by his side as he yelled at his family: *Feed the pigs, weed the garden.* His wife went to town with her headscarf pulled over the bruises on her eyes and cheeks. When she mumbled a greeting, people looked anywhere but at the marks on her face. Behind her back, they said, *That's why you don't marry a drunk.* Apparently Olgierd was one of the first men in the village to sign up for the militia force that the Russians set up after the war, helping them secure their power over Poland. He rose quickly through the ranks and his wife always bought the best cuts of meat at the Peweks department store.

'Now that Olgierd is gone, his wife and children are free,' Father said. 'I don't want you to have to wait for your old *tatuś* to die.'

A shiver travelled down the back of my skull. 'Maybe it's not a good idea.' Until now, leaving Father had been a fanciful notion, like taking a trip to the moon.

He gave a hard laugh. 'Here's what his wife wants on the headstone.' He dusted off a paper and read in a mock-serious tone, '"We envy the angels, who have the good fortune of living with this man and his heart of gold."' He tossed it aside. 'Some people are easier to love from a distance.'

I squeezed his arm. 'It's time for dinner. I'll make us *bigos* and potatoes.'

I walked towards the door and then glanced back at him working by lamplight. By his side was a row of headstones, their smooth surfaces waiting for names.

3

As Father and I edged forwards in the post-office queue, I said, 'I don't have to go to university – not yet. I could defer it.'

He took the envelope from me and muttered, 'Academy of Arts, Plac Polski, Wrocław.' He tucked it under his arm. 'You know, your mother and I wanted to live there.'

'In *Wrocław*?'

'It's true,' he said, catching my expression. 'That was her dream. To live in the city, where she could go to galleries and Chopin concerts in the park. We always talked about moving there but we didn't have the money.'

It never occurred to me that Father would want to live anywhere but here. For perhaps the first time, I looked at him as someone with a past that was independent of my own.

'Who'll help with the business?' I asked.

'To be honest, it's not much of a business,' Father glanced around the post office and then lowered his voice. 'People aren't dying fast enough!' He gave a snort of laughter. As we neared the front of the line, he composed himself. He prodded the envelope towards the clerk, a pale man with a dark freckle on the tip of his nose.

The clerk licked a stamp and then said, 'Pani Ania's leaving for Wrocław?'

'My daughter's going to university,' Father said. 'She's going to be an artist. A sculptor, like Michelangelo!'

Behind me, someone clucked. There was a loud whisper as the news passed on to someone else.

'A sculptor,' the clerk said, as though Father had announced I could fly.

I wished Father had lied and said I was going to study something normal like bookkeeping. 'Thank you,' I said, my voice firm. I dropped some złoty on the counter to pay for the stamps.

On the way home, we walked past the abattoir. The front of the building was fixed with the sullen face of a cow, two black axes crossed beneath its neck. Just as I thought we had passed by unnoticed, the glass doors opened and Pani Wedel, the manager, advanced towards us. Her apricot lipstick creased under the weight of her smile.

After exchanging some comments with Father about the weather, she turned her attention to me. 'You like this place, do you, Pani Skowrońska? Instead of going to Wrocław, you should come work for me.'

I couldn't help but shake my head. How was it she knew already? 'Maybe after university, Pani Wedel,' I said. All lies – there was no way I was working in the abattoir.

Pani Wedel had a faint red line across the width of her forehead, probably left behind by one of the plastic caps she wore for work. As though sensing my gaze, she touched it. 'You'll miss your daughter very much,' she said to Father. 'I've been lucky with my boys, both of them staying here in the village. They don't like to be too far away from their mother.'

'We can't keep our children forever,' Father said. 'We might as well try to hold on to fistfuls of water.'

'True enough,' Pani Wedel said. 'Even so ...' She gave us a nod and disappeared inside.

Father and I parted at the roadside Madonna, a wooden effigy that sat in the hollow trunk of an oak. 'Come home before dark,' he said. We kissed goodbye.

In truth, I felt safe in the forest. It was a second home

to me. Each summer Father and I came here to pick wild mushrooms that sprouted from the moss-covered earth. Or raspberries that bled onto the tips of our fingers. But the best days were like today, when I was alone.

Branches cracked underfoot. I made my way further in, to the place where I liked to sit and make things. Here, pine trees grew dense around a bunker that was set deep in the earth. I sat on its outer edge, the grass tickling my calves. My fingers rested on a flat piece of branch on the forest floor. As I lifted it an ant edged towards my foot and then backed away.

Now that the letter had been sent I could no longer deny it: I was moving away from home. My chest pulsed with excitement before I let myself feel the undertow of guilt. Father's life would be easier if I were like Pani Wedel's sons, content to stay in the village.

My satchel, a canvas bag with a green and red ribbon stitched across the front, was lying next to the bunker. I retrieved a pocketknife from it and then scraped away the outer layer of bark from a piece of pine. I pushed the knife into the wood, etching the straight lines of a triangle, its three points branching into swirls. Around this, I carved a circle, completing the triskele.

The triskele was one of the symbols that women in my village inscribed on their front doors with consecrated charcoal or chalk. From a young age, I understood that these drawings had the power to divide the world into good and evil, to designate safety or harm. Father said it was all a load of nonsense of course; he dubbed it one of the silly wives' tales I inherited from Mother. Even so, I would hide the carving in his work shed, just in case.

4

The tram rattled down Nowy Świat, by the River Odra. I pressed my face to the window, taking in the majestic red-brick buildings, their reflections doubled in the water. At home we had a lake and a few half-hearted ponds but nothing like the Odra. Its blue veins looped through the city, creating little islands that could be reached from the mainland by bridge. The presence of all this water gave the city an enchanted feel, as though it were floating.

The tram took a sharp corner and I lost my grip on the rail, bumping into the girl beside me. She rolled her eyes and shifted away. I had been at university for four months but still felt like a newcomer. Especially now, after a trip to the village to see Father for Christmas. On my return, I was struck once again by the beauty of Wrocław, by a sharp desire to belong here.

The screech of metal against metal pulled me from my thoughts. The tram stopped outside the university and, with the other students, I got off. They bolted ahead while I paused to look at the enormous pale-yellow building with its elegant turrets and spires. Every time I saw the university, I was taken aback by its grandeur. *Baroque*, was how I'd heard it described. I would use that word in a letter home to Father.

The university dormitory, where I now lived, was my first glimpse into the lives of girls. Six of us shared a room, our narrow beds lined on either side of the walls. It was winter and we kept the windows closed. The room marinated in the smell of stockings drying on heaters and bedsheets pressed by female flesh, together with the alpine notes of the deodorants that the richer girls dabbed under their arms. My roommates were always doing things to their bodies: rubbing creams onto their skin, crimping their hair, doing star jumps in the hall to lose weight. I would sneak glances at them as I lay on my bed with an art book, wondering, is this what it takes to be a girl?

The dormitory was unlocked. My roommate, Basia, was sitting on her bed, filing her nails, an open book before her. She brushed away some nail dust that had sifted onto a page. 'I'm bored,' she said. 'Want to go to the park? We can watch the boys play soccer.'

Of all the things I wanted to do in Wrocław, watching boys kick a ball wasn't one of them. 'I've got class,' I said. 'Art history.'

Basia gave an exaggerated yawn and then picked up a small mirror. She primped the ends of her fair hair. 'Do you think I would look better as a brunette?'

The entrance to the university was through a set of heavy wooden doors. These opened onto a long hallway that was crowned with a high dome ceiling. The effect would have been monastic if not for the hundreds of pairs of feet beating against the wooden floor. As I made my way towards the coat counter, snippets of conversation whizzed past me. 'Do you have Kowalski for history? He's a killer.' 'I need another holiday.' I caught sight of a young man, perhaps a little older than me, sporting a denim jacket and John Lennon glasses. 'Look at these first-years,' he said to the guy next to him. 'So fresh faced. Give them more time ...' He slid his glasses down his nose, looked at me and grinned. My cheeks prickled with heat and I turned away.

Students waited to deposit their coats. On my tiptoes, I made out the attendants, middle-aged women with faces untouched by smiles. Obviously the term break hadn't brightened their moods. I slipped off my coat. Father had

18

got it *na lewo*, from a friend of a friend who imported goods illegally from Berlin. The coat was the colour of moss and just as soft, with dark green buttons down the front. It was the first coat I had owned that was new. When I reached the front of the queue I offered it to an attendant. She yanked it from me and then slapped down a slip of blue paper with a number on it, 999. The symmetry of the digits was appealing. I ran my thumb over the paper before fumbling with my satchel, trying to unzip the inner pocket. The attendant gave me a dark look: I moved away.

A single lesson in art history could cover everything from the Renaissance to Modernism to the Polish avant-garde. These were movements I knew little about, but the other students approached the topics with a knowing air. I dubbed them city types. Their clothes were far nicer than anything the village seamstress could come up with, and they spoke casually about holidays they'd taken in places like East Germany or Czechoslovakia. I didn't tell them that I had never left Poland. When the lesson commenced, I said little, sitting at the back of the class and nodding frequently in a bid to disguise my ignorance.

After class I dashed to the baggage counter to collect my coat before heading over to the Academy. As I neared the front of the line, I unzipped my satchel.

'Yes?' said the attendant, a different one from this morning.

'Sorry.' I fumbled inside my bag. 'I can't seem to find my number.'

'Unless Pani gives me her ticket, I can't give her a coat.' She turned to another student who was waving a ticket in his outreached hand. After taking it, she swung her gaze back to me. 'Don't hold up the queue.'

Fine. I pushed my way out and sat on a nearby bench where I upended my bag, rummaging through the books and pencils and sheets of paper.

'Hey.' A fair-haired man towered before me, his thumbs wedged in the pockets of his trousers. I struggled to place his familiarity before realising I'd overheard him this morning, making smart remarks about first-years. Perhaps he wanted to taunt one of these fresh-faced kids.

As though sensing my wariness he removed his sunglasses. Without them he looked younger, more sincere. His cheeks jutted out as he smiled and said, 'You okay?'

I brought my palm to my forehead. 'The number for my coat. I can't find it.'

To my surprise, he sat next to me on the bench and helped me sift through the contents of my bag. There was no sight of the ticket. He retrieved a pouch of tobacco from his jacket and commenced rolling a cigarette. His fingernails, roughly cut, were stained with ink. 'Where did you last see it?' he asked.

I thought back to that string of nines, recalling the way I'd held the ticket at the coat counter and then … 'I can't remember.'

If I didn't leave soon, I was going to be late for my next class. My professor at the Academy was brilliant but strict. On the first day he'd told us, 'If getting here on time is too much of a challenge for you, I won't expect you to rise to the occasion of making art.'

I crammed my belongings back in my bag. 'I'll have to worry about the coat later.'

'If it's a good coat it won't be there later.' He leaned against the wall and closed his eyes. Despite my anxiety, I found myself wondering what it would be like to draw him. How best to capture the decisive slant of his nose and the inviting bow of his lips? He opened his eyes and I snapped my head the other way.

'Can you remember the number?' he asked.

Three nines, I told him.

'Easy.' He got up from the bench and offered his hand. 'Dominik.'

Slightly startled, I gave his hand a brief shake and said, 'Ania.'

'Ania,' he repeated. He tucked his rollup behind his ear and strode away.

A headache nagged at my temples. I watched the other students charge in and out of the front doors. The hallway quietened as the last of them disappeared. Was Dominik even coming back? Maybe he'd bumped into someone – a pretty girl perhaps – and forgotten all about me. Or, more likely, he was pretending he was going to help. I slung my satchel on my shoulder.

Just then he reappeared. Jogging towards me with another guy in tow. 'Are you going out like that into the cold?' Dominik asked.

'That woman ...' I gestured to the coat counter. 'I'll deal with her later.'

'Not later.' He slipped me something, his thumb resting warm against my palm. I let my hand linger before pulling away. He'd given me a piece of paper with a number on it, 999. He smiled at my bemused expression and said, 'It's amazing what you can do with an old stamp set.'

We went to the counter and Dominik nodded at the coat woman. She set down her crossword and heaved herself up from her seat with a groan.

'Looking lovely today, Pani Rachocka,' he said.

'Pan Duwak, are you here for a coat or do you want to talk nonsense?' To my amazement, she honoured him with a smile.

'No coat for me. But my friend would like to collect hers.'

I offered her the forged ticket, trying to keep my expression neutral.

The woman humphed. 'The young lady found it. Maybe next time she won't be so careless.' She unhooked my coat and tossed it to the counter.

On our way back to the bench, Dominik said, 'So what are you here for, Ania?'

'You mean what am I studying? Art.'

'I'm in my final year of journalism. I write for the student paper. Other papers too.' We reached the bench where the other guy was waiting and Dominik clapped him on the back. 'This is Krzysio. He's our resident historian. He also knows a bit about art.'

'Hardly,' Krzysio said. He was a little shorter than Dominik and broader. His mustard jumper had a hole at the shoulder. Krzysio slowly pushed his dark fringe out of his eyes. When it fell back, he left it there. He said, 'I know someone who's having an exhibition on Friday night at the Pod Moną Lisą. You should come.'

The invitation might have come from a sense of pity – they probably guessed I was new to Wrocław. Nonetheless the offer was tantalising; I had never been to an art exhibition before. 'Maybe,' I said. I glanced at the clock in the hallway. 'I have to go.'

'Friday night,' Dominik said. 'I'll hold you to it.'

Our eyes met and I forced myself to look away. The wooden doors folded behind me as I stepped into the crisp air and buttoned my coat. My palm tingled in the place where he had touched it.

5

For the rest of the week I tried to forget about Dominik.
Yet I couldn't help but look for him whenever I lined up
at the coat counter or wandered the university corridors.
He wasn't like the boys from my village who shot rabbits
and held peeing competitions on the bridge. This was a
boy who attended *art exhibitions.*

I mentioned the Pod Moną Lisą to Basia and Ewa, who
studied bookkeeping together. They encouraged me to go
and even decided they might join me. 'I didn't know you
like art,' I said.

'It's okay,' Basia said.

It was Ewa who enlightened me: 'Exhibitions are a good
place to meet men.'

As the sun set behind the pillars of the gothic town hall,
we walked across the city centre. I was still getting to know
Wrocław, with its narrow lanes, its bridges and medieval
churches. My favourite buildings were the gingerbread
houses that stood shoulder-to-shoulder in the old town
square. They were tall, narrow structures with a jumble
of pointed and flat tiled roofs, attic windows peeking out
the tops. I looked at them as I waited for my roommates,
whose heels kept getting stuck between the cobblestones.
Ewa wrenched her shoe from the ground and gave an exasperated sigh. She slipped it back on, her hand on Basia's
shoulder for support.

We located the gallery behind an office block and as I
opened the door to go in, Basia stopped me. She pulled
out a small mirror and touched up her lipstick. 'Want

some?' she asked. On a whim, I said yes. The corners of her eyes puckered with concentration as she dabbed lipstick on my mouth. The smell was luxurious, like cherries and American soap. 'There.' Basia stood back to assess her work. 'It's called Red Heaven,' she said. 'The colour really stands out with your black hair.'

I checked my reflection in her pocket mirror, studying the shine of my disembodied lips. I decided that the lipstick looked good. Perhaps with a bit of saving my next scholarship payment would extend to a tube of Red Heaven.

When we entered reception my roommates fixed their sights on a couple of men in suits. 'There are two of them and three of us,' I said. 'You go on.' Their objections faded as one of the men invited them over with his smile. I watched the four of them standing together, laughing. Part of me hoped that Dominik wouldn't turn up. It would make things simpler; I could absorb the art by myself.

I went upstairs, to a large white room that was lit with fluorescent bulbs. I spun around, taking in the bare walls. As far as I could see there was no art.

There were about twenty people in the room and, to my relief, they looked equally bemused. Heads turned from side to side. A man in a bowler hat snickered. 'Things are tough for artists these days, hey? Maybe we should start a collection.' He tipped off his hat and held it in his outstretched hand. 'Anyone feeling generous?'

The woman beside him joined in. 'Clearly it's a comment on Gierek's so-called prosperity measures.' More laughter. A flask got passed around. When it reached a girl in bellbottoms, she took a swig and then met my eye, gesturing for me to come closer. She passed me the flask and I took a sip. A homemade concoction, it left my tongue slick with the flavour of turpentine. I coughed, alcohol dribbling down my mouth. When I wiped it my hand came away smeared red. I'd forgotten I was wearing lipstick. I edged away from the group and dug in my bag for a tissue. All I came up with was a scrap of newspaper.

As I was trying to clean my smudged lips, Krzysio ambled towards me. Alone. Smiling through my disappointment, I dropped the soiled paper in my bag.

Krzysio's jumper slipped from his waist and he stopped to retie it. Then he kissed me on both cheeks. 'Ania. You made it.' His voice had the soothing quality of a bedtime story and I had to strain to hear him over other people.

I said, 'It's my first exhibition in Wrocław.'

'What do you think?'

'Not what I was expecting ...' I motioned to the empty walls.

'There's more,' he said, rubbing his hands together. 'That way.' He pointed me down a corridor.

When I reached the end, I pushed my way through a set of heavy curtains. Blackness dropped over me, as swift as an execution hood. I took a sharp intake of breath, struck by how rare it was to be plunged into darkness. Without the stars or the moon or the glow from apartments and flashing neon signs.

Someone prodded me as though I were furniture. There was a giggle. 'I touched a person,' said a woman's voice. Her shape moved away.

Fumbling in the dark, I located a space where I could press my back against a wall. There was a murmur in the room. The sound of communal discomfort, perhaps? It got louder, rolling into a boom. *Repeated greetings from fallen snowmen,* came the announcement over a loudspeaker. A flash of light, then a projection of a face on the wall, its mouth stretched into the shape of a laugh or maybe a scream. Everything went black again. Then a female newsreaders' voice penetrated the room: *People of Wrocław are cautioned to avoid going to the old town square today, where there is a disturbance.* Another illumination, this time of dwarves in red caps marching in the square. Behind them loomed a fat man dressed as Snow White. I laughed.

'You're enjoying this?' said someone close to me. I breathed in the smell of newspapers and cigarettes.

My voice opened up in the dark. 'Yes.'

A high-pitched whine came over the loudspeakers: *I am the King of England.*

It was Dominik's turn to laugh, the sound deep in my ear. The smell of him closer now. His shirt brushed against my hand, the fabric so thin I could feel the heat of him. Without thinking, I reached my mouth to his. His lips met mine. He held my face in his hands before resting the tips of his fingers at the base of my throat.

6

Some of Poland's best artists had studied at the Academy and I could feel their presence in the studio. I could hear them in the creak of the floorboards, and smell them in the remnants of acrylic, turpentine and glue. I could see them in the dribbles of paint on the floor, and in the traces of clay on the handle of the door. They were all here.

Perhaps this was why I found it impossible to work. The studio was a place for artists and I didn't know how to make art. I wasn't even sure I knew what art *was*.

By way of procrastination, I volunteered to make drinks. When the electric kettle screeched from its place on the floor, I ripped the cord from the socket. Beside me, the stiff bodies of tea bags lay on the gas heater. At the Academy we tried to get two or three glasses from each one. By the end of their lifespan all they offered was the memory of tea.

Glasses in hand, I edged my way to a girl who was sketching an urban landscape. 'That's really coming along,' I said.

She blew on her tea, steaming her spectacles. Then she turned, foggy eyed, to her picture. '*This*. This is what I want my piece to look like. As though I'm staring at the city through a haze. Half asleep, half awake.'

The bottom third of her picture depicted a strip of land in charcoal with yellow highlights. Above this, factories exhaled black breath into a pink sky. The overall effect was sombre, but lovely. 'You've done it,' I told her. 'That's what you've captured.'

'You think so?' She removed her spectacles and polished them on her shirt. 'What about you?' Craning her neck to my corner of the room.

'Oh, you know ...' With my glass in hand, I retreated.

As I worked on my sculpture, a current of awareness sparked through the studio. People readjusted their canvases. We gave each other nervous glances as Professor Jankowski sauntered in, a corduroy jacket slung over one shoulder. 'How's everyone today, good? What have you got to show me?' He surveyed the room, his gaze amplified by his enormous black-framed glasses. He wandered over to the picture of the factories. As he examined it he traced the perimeter of his receding hairline with his finger. The artist stood behind him, her hands buried in the front pocket of her smock. The other students put down their pencils and brushes, their scissors and knives.

Professor Jankowski tossed his jacket on the table. He lifted the picture and held it at arm's length. 'It's pretty.' He said the word *pretty* as though referring to a small girl in her Easter dress. With one hand, he returned the picture to the easel.

'So you want it to be ugly?' the artist said.

'I want it to be *true*.' The professor turned to address the room at large. 'Beauty without truth is empty. Remember that, everyone.'

He moved on to an abstract painting in black and red, which a student from Warsaw was working on. 'Better. Just watch this corner of the canvas, right here.' His hand hovered at the bottom of the painting. 'What you're aiming for is a type of complicated simplicity, you understand?' The student nodded slowly, his frown betraying his confusion. 'I'm talking about compression,' the professor continued. 'The viewer has to see the whole world in your painting without realising at first glance that it's there.'

I returned to my sculpture. The clay was cool beneath my hands. I was attempting to make the sort of thing that would be displayed in a museum: a naked person with their arms and legs hacked off. But I wasn't sure if it was working. I had no idea what they expected from us at the Academy.

To my relief the professor strode past me. Then, as if he'd planned it all along, he turned around. 'What's going on here?'

I wiped my muddied hands on my overalls and stood before him. 'Well. I'm working – that is I'm *trying* to work on – a realistic study of the human form.'

The professor's lips pinched together.

'It's classically inspired,' I said, echoing a phrase I'd learned in art history.

He circled my piece, examining its unfortunate shape from all angles. 'You're taking the middle of the road, are you? Many students do. Just remember that the purpose of making art – indeed the only true obligation of the artist – is to have a vision, to follow this vision through and present things as you really see them. If you can do that, you're onto something. Of course, not many people can manage that.' He gave my sculpture a pat. 'Still, it's a perfectly adequate piece of work. The sort of thing a rich lady with artistic pretensions might put in her boudoir because it matches the décor.'

My neck flushed with heat at the laughter in the room. The girl who had drawn the urban landscape made her way towards me. 'Would you like another tea?' There was too much kindness in her voice. Her eyes avoided mine as she reached for my glass.

'No,' I said, and moved the glass away.

Outside the studio I waited for Dominik, my portfolio tucked under one arm. Wind lashed against my face, making my eyes water. I wished I could go back to the dormitory. The professor's ridicule of my work had left me drained. Besides, I looked a mess. My skin was stained with clay and my stockings had twisted around my thighs. I reached a hand under my skirt to rearrange them, composing myself as Dominik appeared from behind an apartment block. His upper body leaned forward as he walked and the sheepskin collar of his jacket was raised high against the wind. When he saw me he hurried his step.

Ever since we kissed at the exhibition a few weeks ago, we'd become something of an item. In spite of this, each time I saw him afresh I had to get to know him all over again. It was as though I had to reconcile two Dominiks. There was the one in my mind, whose face I could never quite picture. (What colour were his eyes, were they brown or grey? Was he really so tall as I imagined?) Then there was the other Dominik, the one who was approaching now. I stood rigid as he neared. But when he pulled me close and I inhaled his tobacco-ink skin, I remembered how things were between us. The soft intensity of his kiss made me forget we were standing on the icy street.

Dominik ran his lips over my knuckles and I took a moment to study him. *Yes, that's right.* His eyes were the colour of a pre-winter lake and when he wanted to kiss me he had to stoop to bring his lips to my own.

'Aniusieńka.' His breath was white-cold. 'Come to the country with me.'

'What, and stay in your villa?' I stamped my boots on the concrete, trying to keep my sarcasm at bay.

'I don't care – let's pitch a tent in the snow. Anything to get you to myself.'

We'd only been alone a handful of times and never a whole night. There was nowhere for us to go. Boys were banned from my university dorm, and Dominik lived in a tiny apartment with his cousin and her husband and child. He assured me it was fine for me to spend the night but I was too embarrassed to do so. Who knew how long I could hold out. Dominik was tired of waiting and so was I. Every time we kissed, or even held hands, desire surged through my stomach and chest and left me unsteady on my feet.

This was all new to me. I'd only been with one boy before; he was from my village and didn't get the grades to go to university so was conscripted to the army instead.

Perhaps this was why I chose him for my first time: there was no risk of falling in love. Afterwards he said, 'You used to look like a boy, with your strange clothes and short hair. But you're pretty now.' As I retrieved my things, he told me he was taking me to the end-of-year dance. 'We don't need to dance,' I said. To myself, I added, *We've already done what all the boys are trying to get the girls to do.* Afterwards I congratulated myself on the way I'd handled the affair, telling myself that I'd been mature. In fact, I'd simply been cruel, striking him with a blow in a bid to protect myself.

Now, with Dominik, I could feel myself opening up.

He looped my scarf around my neck. 'I'm dying to be alone with you.'

'It will be easier in spring,' I told him. 'There'll be more places for us to go.'

'Until then we suffer.'

We walked to Krzysio's place, Dominik carrying my portfolio. It was late afternoon and the ash-coloured sky echoed the dirty concrete of the apartment blocks. In a small courtyard, a girl in a red jumper stood on a metal swing. It creaked as she swung back and forth. Dominik squeezed my palm. 'When do I get to see this sculpture of yours, the one that's stealing you away from me?'

I let go of his hand. 'The teacher hated it.'

'What an idiot. I'm sure it's brilliant.'

'It's not.' There was a whine in my voice and I took a breath to steady it. 'Professor Jankowski knows what he's talking about.'

'Maybe, maybe not. You need to trust your own instincts when it comes to your work – you know it better than anyone else.'

A car slowed down to let us cross the road. 'What about your writing. How's that coming along?' I asked.

He gave a shrug. 'I'm supposed to be working on a paper about Hemingway's influence on Hłasko, but that'll sort itself out in time.'

31

Krzysio lived with his parents in an apartment on Stanislawa Worcella, a wide road that turned off Kazimierza Pulaskiego. Dominik and I let ourselves into the dark foyer. 'Just wait,' Dominik said. He fumbled in his jacket and pulled out a lighter. A couple of flicks released the flame. He lifted it to reveal a bare cord dangling from the ceiling. 'Bulb's gone,' he said. 'Stolen, probably.' They were impossible to find in the shops these days. Holding out his lighter, he led the way to the lift. The metal gate clanged shut. The lift thunked and creaked to the third floor. Krzysio's mother was waiting for us, her back pressed against the open door. Her apron was printed with purple and orange psychedelic swirls.

'Pani Burak.' Dominik reached for her hand and kissed it. On the way over, Dominik had told me that Krzysio's mother was a poet and she could be almost as good as Miłosz if she put her mind to it.

'Dominik, you have the good manners of my grandfather,' she said, sounding amused.

We removed our shoes and followed the laughter and punk music to Krzysio's room. He sat cross-legged on a woven mat, shuffling a pack of cards. When he saw us he gave us a wholehearted smile that rippled down to the line of muscle in his neck. He reached over to the cassette player and turned it down. 'Ania, we've missed you.'

'It's only been a few days,' I said. But I was pleased that one of Dominik's friends had noticed my absence.

Next to Krzysio was a girl with dark wavy hair. Unlike my roommates, who didn't leave the dorm without colouring their lips and eyes and cheeks, her face was bare of makeup. She leaned against the bed, her arms stretched on the mattress, her legs extended on the floor. The girl said hello, but didn't make space for us in the small room. I folded myself down and rested my hands in my lap. Dominik positioned himself between me and the girl, whom he introduced as Małgorzata. I remembered Dominik telling me about her, she was a photographer who'd had her work exhibited abroad.

'So you made it back from Łódź,' Dominik said to her. Turning to me, he said, 'Her husband's making a movie about – what is it, again? A female alien who has sex with men and then kills and eats them?'

'That's right.' At last she pulled her legs in, freeing some space. 'The film ridicules old-fashioned ideas about female passivity.'

'Female passivity,' Dominik said with a laugh. 'That's not something Małgorzata here has a problem with.'

'No.' She cocked her head to the side. 'Thank goodness for that.' One of the straps of her overalls slid down her shoulder, giving her a casually sexy air. I glanced at Dominik, wondering how well he knew her.

Krzysio dealt the cards for a round of *ogórek* – a game I sometimes played with Father at home. Part of me was satisfied when Małgorzata lost the first hand. She should have got rid of her ace during the first five tricks when it was the highest scoring card. Instead she held onto it until the end, when it was worthless.

'This game is stupid.' Małgorzata tossed her cards to the floor. 'What's that?' She reached a long arm towards the bed, where I'd placed my portfolio.

'Nothing.' I put down a Queen of Diamonds. 'You don't want to see that rubbish.' But the portfolio was already in her hand.

She untied the string that bound the cardboard folder and opened it. I threw down a card, barely looking at what it was. The idea of someone – a stranger – poring over my sketches was excruciating.

Krzysio scooped up the cards. 'Ania, are you trying to lose? We should've been playing for money.'

'Or vodka at the very least,' Dominik said.

'Best out of three.' I pushed the deck towards Krzysio.

Małgorzata examined a design for the sculpture that had been giving me grief, the so-called classically inspired human form. She sighed and then selected a drawing of an abstract rectangular face with long eyes, nose and mouth. She turned the picture this way and that, her frown lines getting deeper and then said, 'Yes.' She shook the page. 'This one I'm interested in. I haven't seen anything like it before.'

'That's nothing,' I said, fanning my cards.

Dominik flicked an ace to the floor. 'I told you she was good.'

'Fine taste as always, Dominik,' Małgorzata said. Her voice was honey and ice. She and Dominik held each other's gaze as they smiled and discomfort slivered through my skin.

Krzysio glanced at me. He threw a card in Dominik's lap. 'Come on,' he said. 'Get on with the game.'

7

White cubes, each the size of a television, were stacked in piles on the floor. Each cube was printed with images of body parts. A section of an eye, a foot, a ... what was that? I leaned in close. What had at first looked like a woman's genitals turned out to be two hands pressed together. I smiled, appreciating the joke.

As I shifted away from the cubes, Dominik rushed towards me, his cheeks high with colour. 'Małgorzata's done it again.' He grabbed my hand. 'Come see. I'm going to have a ball with this one – she wants me to write about it for the next edition of *Sztuka Dzisiaj*.'

He led me to the adjoining room, where Krzysio was waiting. 'I can't believe they paid her to do this,' he said with an amused shake of his head. He tugged at a skein of wool that was hanging loose from his jumper.

The wall behind him was covered with black and white photographs. When I examined them I recognised parts of Wrocław: the town square with its jumble of gothic and art nouveau buildings, the dark entrance to the Rura Club, the congested street leading to Krzysio's apartment. Małgorzata was in all the photos but she was often captured in the distance or out of focus. In one photo she was depicted from behind, her curls haloed by a street lamp. In another she stood outside a kiosk holding a match to a cigarette. The photos had a voyeuristic quality; somehow they felt intimate and anonymous at the same time. I checked the title of the exhibit, *This Experiment Has Been Done Before.*

Małgorzata was a few metres away, talking to an older couple. When she saw me she hurried over, a bottle of beer in her hand and a pair of old-fashioned pilot goggles perched on her head. 'What do you think of the photos?' Her words came out breathy and fast.

'They're good,' I said. 'Really good. But there's something odd about them ...'

'Yes?'

I took in her look of anticipation and paused, figuring out how to phrase my discomfort. 'These photos ...' I started. 'Well, they make me feel like I'm intruding on a private moment. Does that make sense?'

Małgorzata clapped her hands together. 'That's exactly it.'

'Go on,' Dominik said. 'Tell her.'

'I put myself under surveillance.' She sounded inordinately pleased. 'For two weeks I was followed by complete strangers. I didn't know who they were or what they looked like. But as you can see, they knew where to find me.'

I considered the photos in this new light. It was a bold concept for an exhibition – and it worked. 'Did you catch any of your stalkers in the act?' I asked.

'A few times.' Małgorzata pointed to a photo in which she was sitting on a bench, running her fingers through her hair. She was clearly aware of being watched and seemed to enjoy it. However, another photo caught her looking vulnerable, about to cross the street with a loaf of bread threatening to topple out of her grip, her mouth open.

'I wanted to document the effects that being watched has on the citizen,' Małgorzata said. 'All of us are under surveillance all the time. We know it and we get on with our lives. But how does it affect our psyches, how does it shape our sense of self? That's what I'm interested in.'

Dominik chuckled and clamped a hand on her shoulder. 'I told you that you don't need me to spin that arty bullshit on your behalf. You're quite capable of doing it yourself.'

She grinned and bowed, one hand in a mock salute by her pilot glasses.

'And the censors?' Krzysio asked.

'I told them it was an allegory about the so-called Cold War. You know, I'm Poland and the photographers are the United States.'

'They believed that?' I asked.

'Our Małgorzata knows how to get things done,' Dominik said. Just as I was bristling at the use of this familiarity – *our Małgorzata* – he looped his arm around my waist. 'It's your turn next, Ania. You'll be exhibiting here soon.'

I tilted my head to meet his kiss. As we broke away, a middle-aged man strode towards us. He wore American-style jeans and a brown pressed shirt and tie. Beside him, the rest of us looked particularly scruffy. Except Małgorzata. For some reason, her rumpled clothes enhanced her beauty.

'Janusz,' Małgorzata greeted him.

He kissed her on both cheeks and then briefly on the lips. 'I'll be at the Poza Nawiasem later tonight. Join me for a drink.' He smoothed the parting of his hair and gave the rest of us a well-practised smile. 'Your friends are welcome too.'

When he was out of earshot, Małgorzata said, 'Darling Janusz. I love working with him.'

'He's her favourite censor.' Dominik jerked his thumb towards the departing Janusz. 'Lets her get away with murder and then buys her drinks to celebrate.'

'Poor man never made it as an artist,' Małgorzata said. 'For him this is the next best thing.' A few metres away, Janusz was standing in front of a sculpture made of tin cans. He was talking to a young woman and gesturing to various parts of the sculpture, as though explaining it.

The tin can sculpture, the cubes, Małgorzata's photos – these were far from traditional. And yet here they were displayed in a gallery. I was beginning to see that being an artist didn't mean I had to copy the masters. What

I did have to do was create something that belonged to me – something that no one else could make. I got a jolt as I realised that this was what Professor Jankowski had meant when he said we needed to acquire our own artistic vision.

There was one thing I didn't understand about the photographs. I pointed to the piece of card on the wall. '*This Experiment Has Been Done Before*,' I read. 'What does it mean?'

'I'm not quite sure,' Małgorzata said. 'That was Janusz's doing. I wanted to call it *Police State* but he said absolutely not. Anyway his title is better, isn't it? More enigmatic.'

I had always thought of artists as a breed of people who were different from me. People who, through a combination of talent and hard work, created things that had the power to move you, things that altered your perception of the world in some fundamental way.

Now that I was surrounded by them, the awe I'd felt in their presence was starting to shift into something else. I was starting to think: if they can do it, why can't I?

Whether she knew it or not, Małgorzata was teaching me as much about art as I was learning at the Academy. Through her, I could see how I might carve out a life for myself as an artist. And for the next week, Małgorzata's life – or at least, her glamorous apartment – was within my reach. She and her husband were travelling to Łódź for one of his films and she'd given Dominik the keys to their place.

He was already there, waiting. Eager to see him, I stuffed clothes into a satchel while my roommate Ewa watched on. She was leaning against the dresser, painting her nails a creamy pink. 'Be careful,' she said. 'You know how to protect yourself against babies, don't you?' She screwed the top back on the polish and then shook it, the steel ball clicking in its pool of varnish.

'Of course.' I selected a pair of plain white underwear, wishing I had something fancier. What I did with Dominik was none of her business. Besides, he was going to make things safe for us. It was all about timing, he said. 'I'll see you in a week,' I told her. 'And if the dorm supervisors ask–'

'You've gone home to visit your father,' Ewa supplied.

'Exactly.'

The city was fragrant with the overtures of spring. I walked through Wyspa Słodowa, a small islet near the old town, where the acacia trees were in bloom. The cool smell of water was all around me. I walked over an iron bridge, emerging on a busy street, and located the salmon-coloured building where Małgorzata lived. She was lucky. Her husband, Ryszard Wiater, did a lot of work for the State. While most other married couples I'd heard of had to wait ten, even twenty years, for their own place, Małgorzata and her husband had apparently acquired one straight away.

A muffled hello from the buzzer and the front door unclicked. I didn't bother waiting for the lift, propelling myself up the seven flights of stairs instead.

'Aniusieńka.' Dominik kissed me as we stood on the landing. He then pulled me inside. 'What do you want to do? We could go to the Rura Club, see who's there.'

'Is that really what you want?'

'No,' he said with a chuckle. 'But I have to be a gentleman, don't I?'

Our bodies pressed together and I slipped my hand under Dominik's jumper. Traced the cool xylophone of his ribs.

That night we took a bath, indulging in the luxury of hot water. Our legs intertwined and Dominik massaged my feet as he told me about his childhood in Warsaw. His father was a civil servant who took Dominik and his younger brother to concerts at the National Philharmonic and to Berlin for summer holidays. Despite these privileges, his childhood hadn't been happy. His father was strict, Dominik said. Sometimes violent. He and his brother couldn't wait to get away.

40

'And your mother?' I asked.

'She's gone.' His fingers went still and then he resumed massaging my foot. 'She took off with another man when my brother and I were young. We were tying her down, apparently.' There was a tightness in his lips as he smiled. 'She used to visit, from time to time. But then she started a new family, and ...' He felt around the edge of the bathtub. 'Where's the soap?'

'My mother's gone too. She died when I was a couple of months old. Her heart wasn't getting enough blood.' I trailed my palm through the water and said, 'It was the pregnancy that caused it.'

There was a heavy exhale from Dominik. He cradled my face in his hands. 'I bet that as soon as she saw you, she fell madly in love. I bet that she wouldn't have given up those two months with you for anything in the world.' With his thumb, he wiped the inner corners of my eyes.

Something shifted inside me and I drew him closer, kissing the soft mound of his lips and the rough stubble on his cheek, my knees knocking against the sides of the bath.

9

Dominik stretched out in bed. I rested my hand on the taut skin of his stomach, the narrow dip of his chest. A warmth flowed through me, reaching down to my toes. He gave a loud snore, the noise startling him awake. When he caught me watching he blinked and gave me a sleepy smile and then drew me into his arms.

'I have to go to the studio,' I said, kissing the line of his jaw.

'And I have to work at the paper.' He shifted, dislodging his arm from under my back before resting his body on mine.

The easy weight of him weakened my resolve. It didn't matter. Things in the studio weren't going well and it would be good to take some time out. I caressed the back of Dominik's shoulders. 'Be careful,' I reminded him. 'We don't want to end up with a baby.'

'Don't we?' His mouth wandered down to my stomach, the top of my thigh. 'We're going to get married anyway, aren't we?' he said. 'I'll be a proper writer and you'll do your art and we'll have three – no – four children.'

A light slap on his back. 'You're fast.'

'Why not?' He propped himself up, resting his elbows on either side of my thighs. 'I don't believe in all this existential bullshit. There's no point in worrying about the meaning of life when it's always been the same: get married and have children. Enjoy good meals and good sex. Get drunk.'

'And I thought you were a revolutionary.'

'I am. But I'm also a good Polish boy.'

I laughed and told him I would guard his secret. Despite my teasing, I let myself imagine it. Dominik and me. All the things we would make together: the home and the children. The books and the food and the art.

When I finally returned to the studio, my hands fumbled with the clay. I'd been away for too long, and I was inert and out of place. My jaw tightened as I contemplated my piece. After going to exhibitions of other people's work, I understood that what I'd made was no good. What's more I understood why. I was trying to be an Artist instead of being myself. I took a few steps back. Heavy with the realisation that it couldn't be saved, I gave the sculpture a shove. It toppled over. With my knuckles, I pounded out its human shape.

There was a low whistle in the room and one of the boys approached. Legs splayed in his corduroy pants. 'I guess that's a woman's prerogative – to change her mind.'

'And now that you've painted a pair of breasts, you know all about women?' I glanced at his painting of a Picasso-esque female nude reclining in a bath. One green breast bulged by her chin and a yellow one pointed in the direction of her shoulder.

He sniffed. 'I know enough.' He returned to his canvas and dabbed some paint on the woman's thigh.

That afternoon, Professor Jankowski wandered in for one of his tours. My heart skittered as he drew near and I wondered how to explain my lack of progress. I straightened up, preparing for another round of humiliation. However, when he saw the unshapen clay he simply nodded. 'You're taking a new approach? That's good. It means you're learning from your mistakes.' He adjusted his glasses. 'This time don't think so much.'

'I'll try. Or maybe it's better that I don't try?' My laugh was unbearably girlish.

'You know how to do this. I was impressed by your portfolio. Your sculptures had a certain rawness to them.'

How awful that he could remember my early attempts at art. 'Those weren't any good.'

'That's where you're wrong. They had something in them,' he said. 'Go back to that. Follow your instincts.'

For the next couple of weeks I went to the studio every chance I could, often staying until two or three in the morning. Much of my time was spent looking at the clay or out the window at the meagre square of sky. When I began to work in earnest, the clay took on a form I hadn't expected. It became a tall, narrow block and assumed the features of stretched-out eyes and lips. I kept moulding it, shaping it. Listening to what it had to say. In time I realised it was Mother. My dream version of her, pieced together not from memories, but from vague sensations and smells, from Father's stories and our visits to the cemetery. My hands worked quickly. It was as though I had discovered a hidden language – bolder and more eloquent than the one I used in everyday life.

Although it was late, I didn't want to go back to the university dorm, to the chatter about clothes and exams. I fetched a withered teabag from the heater and dipped it into a glass of hot water. The bag had been used so many times that it browned the liquid without giving it taste. I squeezed it, trying to extract more flavour. As I did so, footsteps reverberated in the room, releasing fast shallow creaks in the wooden floor. It was the sound of Dominik. I recognised the way that, in his haste to get where he was going, he pushed forward on his toes and put little weight on his heels.

'Aniusieńka, what are you doing here, sitting by yourself in the cold?' He crouched beside me.

'It's not finished yet.' I smoothed the outer edge of the sculpture, trying to obscure his vision.

He moved my hand away. There was an uncharacteristic stillness in him as he examined the piece. Finally he said, 'It's her, isn't it?'

I nodded.

'I thought so. When I look at it, I can feel how much you care for her. You've put everything into this – all your sweetness and longing and sorrow.' He traced a smear of clay on my wrist. 'I love how fearless you are in your work.'

My whole body loosened with relief.

We contemplated the sculpture, his hand warming mine. Then he said, 'You won't believe what Małgorzata's got up her sleeve.' With a laugh, he told me what she had planned.

Surely he was joking. 'Isn't that illegal?' I asked.

'Probably. But if anyone can get away with it, she can.' Dominik helped me up from the floor. Standing close, he bent down to kiss me and I reached up to meet him, pulling at the shoulders of his jacket. 'I'll walk you back to your dormitory,' he said in a low voice. 'Unless you want to come home with me?'

'Your family ...'

Dominik sighed and picked up my satchel from the floor. Lights out in the studio, I locked the door behind us. Leaving Mother in the room, her clay heart beating in the darkness.

10

This was the first time I'd been back to Małgorzata's place since Dominik and I had stayed there, and I had to remind myself the apartment was no longer ours. Dominik was also readjusting. He wrapped his arms around my waist as I rinsed a glass in the sink. 'Remember?' He pointed to the bathroom. 'The night we ended up on the floor and that tile cracked under our weight.'

I shushed him. If Małgorzata had noticed the broken tile she hadn't said anything about it. 'Pour the vodka,' I said. Though it was only morning, we needed fortification for what Małgorzata had in store.

Today was May Day, the international day of the workers. Anyone employed by the State had to march in a parade to show what a perfect socialist society we lived in. It was a chore that Father and I always escaped as he had no employer but himself. Dominik assured me that the parades were as tedious as they sounded. He told me that, like most people, his father would sign a paper at the beginning of the parade to prove he'd been there. Then he would sneak off to enjoy the rest of the holiday. As I picked up another glass to dry it, Dominik explained that Małgorzata wanted to ridicule the May Day tradition by staging a performance on her balcony. While the workers took part in the parade, she was going to indulge in two leisurely acts: reading and self-pleasure.

'I know we've been over it, but I still don't understand the point of this,' I said.

He poured the shots and then licked some vodka off

his thumb. 'You're not supposed to understand it. It's avant-garde.'

'If you say so.' I placed a shot glass in each of his palms and one in my own, then we joined Krzysio on the balcony.

Seven floors below, the preparations had begun. Banners were unrolled and placards handed out. A news crew emerged from a green van. They set up a tripod and a video camera with a square eye.

'Aren't you glad we're not workers?' Dominik said, leaning on the railing.

'Look at that guy.' Krzysio pointed to an overweight man who was giving orders to a couple of people in caps. I could just catch the fat man's words, *Hold it straight. Straight, I said!*

A man in aviator sunglasses plonked himself on the kerb and shaded himself with a portrait of Lenin. He balanced the black-and-white print on top of his head, his fingers clutching Lenin's ears.

'What do you think?' Małgorzata hovered outside the balcony in a blue shift dress. It was the sort of thing worn by shop clerks, but while theirs typically reached the middle of their calves, Małgorzata's, roughly hemmed, skimmed her thighs. 'Will this do?'

'That's just the right look.' Krzysio twirled her around and her dress billowed, tulip-like.

She picked up a camera from the kitchen table and glanced at the clock. 'Do you want to document the proceedings, Dominik?' She cocked her head to the side and gave him a conspiratorial smile.

Again, I wondered what had taken place between them. Whatever it was, having Dominik take the photos of this 'performance' would lock them in an intimacy I couldn't bear. I grabbed the camera in a bid to steer things in another direction. 'I'll do it. I'll take the photos.'

'Now this is a development I like,' Dominik said.

Małgorzata straightened the hem of her dress. 'Thank you, Ania. It will be good to have your artist's eye on this.'

That was one way of putting it. I couldn't believe I'd volunteered to do this. 'I'm not going to get arrested, am I?'

'It'll be fine,' she said. 'If they do want to cause a fuss, it'll enhance the performance. The worst that'll happen is we'll get a night in prison.'

'Having a prison record's not so bad anyway,' Dominik said. 'It gives a person a certain *mystique*.'

I breathed through my nerves. Normally one shot of vodka would have warmed my veins but today there was too much adrenaline in my blood for the alcohol to take effect.

After we'd had another round of drinks, Krzysio dragged a plastic chair onto the balcony and then stepped back into the kitchen, which allowed a view of what was taking place out here. Małgorzata seated herself. As I adjusted the settings on the camera, Dominik wafted about, arranging a cushion on the ground, then shifting an ashtray and dead plant so they would be out of shot. 'You sure you don't need my help?' he said with a mock-innocent raise of his eyebrows.

'Out.' I nudged him in the direction of the kitchen, still hoping that we weren't actually going through with this.

'Whatever you say …' Dominik retreated, leaving Małgorzata and I on the balcony. The breeze cooled my face as I leaned over the rail. The parade had now commenced.

From the kitchen, Krzysio called, 'If you're going to do it, now's the time.'

I rechecked the film while Dominik said, 'Remember, let me know if you need an assistant …'

Ignoring his laughter, I took a couple of photos of the parade, the camera trembling in my hands.

On the chair, Małgorzata lifted one leg so that her foot rested on the balcony rail. My throat went dry. She wasn't wearing underwear and I glimpsed the parting of her legs. I quickly moved away, facing her side-on. She picked up a copy of *Ulysses* and glanced at me. 'Thank you for this, Ania.' As she flicked through the pages of the book, the shouting of the parade got louder.

Long live the workers.
Unity over anarchy.
Praise to the Polish-Russian friendship.

Małgorzata tucked her hand between her legs. I shielded my face with the camera, felt for the large button and pressed. She threw her head back. Eyes closed, one hand moved back and forth, with her other hand holding the book, she read out loud.

Yes because he never did a thing like that before …

To my relief, being behind the camera gave me more confidence than the vodka had. It offered distance from what was happening and, through the eye of the lens, I could aim to give the proceedings an artistic bent.

Małgorzata stopped reading and let out a deep sigh. Below us, someone yelled, 'Three times yes, for the Polish People's Republic!'

She began reading again, quicker now, her hand moving in time with her words.

They do yes he came somewhere I'm sure by his appetite …

Another click. I stepped towards the balcony rail and, leaning over, took some photos of the parade. Then I switched my focus to Małgorzata. Her words were slower now, more languid. Her hand kept moving between her legs as she said *Yes, yes, yes.* In the apartment across from ours, a large man trundled onto the balcony and gaped at us. I pointed the camera in his direction and clicked.

As I loaded a new film, my attention was distracted by a thumping sound from inside the apartment. A knock on the door, perhaps. I could hear Krzysio say something. I glanced at Małgorzata, who was now resting her hand on her knee. More voices from inside – male voices. When I turned around I saw the militiamen. A cold sensation rippled through my chest and I guarded the camera behind my back.

'There's been a report of a disturbance,' said the older of the two men. Incredibly, the edges of his moustache twitched with amusement.

'Yes,' echoed the younger one. 'A disturbance.'

Małgorzata took her leg down from the balcony rail. 'If you call *reading* a disturbance, then yes.'

'*Ulysses*,' said the older officer, craning to get a look. He stepped onto the balcony and I squeezed past him, returning to the kitchen. 'My wife tried to make me read it.' He took the book from Małgorzata and turned it over to examine the blurb. 'It's certainly experimental.'

'I heard it's smut,' said the other one.

'You heard right,' Małgorzata said. Beside me, Dominik coughed in a bid to disguise his laugh.

The older man glanced at Dominik. He snapped the book shut and said, 'As you know, May Day is an important public holiday for the People's Republic. It's an opportunity to show our appreciation of the workers.' He handed *Ulysses* back to Małgorzata. 'You're not workers, are you.'

'Students,' I said, from the kitchen.

'*Artists*,' corrected Małgorzata.

'Right,' said the older man. 'I must warn you that there have been complaints about your conduct and if the conduct in question continues, I'll need to take you all down to the station. You understand?'

'Perfectly,' Małgorzata said.

The younger of the two rested his hand on the gun in his holster. The tips of his ears, poking out from under his policeman's hat, were bright red. 'Aren't we going to book them?'

'I think we've reached an understanding,' said the other officer. He nodded towards *Ulysses*. 'You didn't just skip to the end, did you? Apparently most people do that, but it's important to read it all the way through. So my wife says.'

As they were leaving I was overcome with a streak of daring. I grabbed the camera and snapped some photos of the men from behind. The door closed and I threw myself on the sofa, exhausted.

Dominik leaned against the door, laughing, his forehead resting on his arm. Then he turned around and said, 'I told you they wouldn't care – they don't believe in that socialist bullshit any more than we do. I'm not even sure the Russians believe in it, and they're the ones who've forced it on us. If anything, this little performance will brighten their day. I know it did mine.' He joined me on the sofa, his hand on my thigh. 'Good job, Ania.'

There was a seedy look in his eyes and I nudged his hand away.

'You're a brave woman, Ania,' Krzysio said. I checked his face for signs of lewdness but there were none. For some reason Małgorzata's performance didn't seem to get him all het up the way it did Dominik. Krzysio gave me a glass of vodka, then clapped his hands. The others joined in. 'And another round of applause for the star of the show.' Krzysio turned to Małgorzata, who was leaning against the balcony railing, the bottom of her tunic fluttering in the breeze.

That evening we watched the parade on television. The newsreaders praised the record turnout, which was a testament, they said, to the workers' heartfelt commitment and loyalty to the Polish People's Republic. There was of course no mention of the incident on Małgorzata's balcony.

11

Professor Jankowski folded and unfolded his arms. He circled the table where my sculpture sat. Poor Mother. I clenched my fists in a bid to stop myself from covering her with a sheet.

As he exhaled, he released a phlegmatic sound from the back of his throat. A throng of students hovered nearby, awaiting his verdict. Last week one of them had cried when he heard the professor's assessment of his piece: it was a terrible painting, the professor said, but it would be perfectly adequate as a design for a carpet.

Professor Jankowski traced the top of my sculpture, examining its elongated eyes and mouth. Someone in the room sneezed. He glanced at the offending sneezer and then removed his glasses and polished them on his shirt. 'It's good.'

A sense of pure joy washed over me. I bit back my smile but it was too late – he had seen.

'Don't get complacent Pani Skowrońska. You've got a long way to go. Keep at it and I'll tell you when you're getting close.'

I rested my hand on Mother's back. At last she was safe.

He moved on to the Picasso-esque painting of a woman in a bath and shook his head. 'I don't know where to begin with this.'

The boy whose painting it was blinked hard, and I regretted the harsh words I'd spoken to him.

The professor skewered a dry paintbrush in his hand and jabbed it at various parts of the canvas. 'No no no, no no.' The other students lowered their gaze or stared hard at their own work. 'Sometimes …' Professor Jankowski gave an exaggerated sigh. 'Sometimes I think this class has learned nothing at all.' His disappointment settled over us like smog. Even so, in my corner of the room I breathed easy.

Emboldened by my teacher's praise, I decided to do something I'd never done before: spend the night at Dominik's. I called him from the dormitory phone to give him the news and then said, half in jest, 'What will your cousin think? She's a married woman.'

Without hesitating, he replied, 'She'll think we're in love. And rightly so.' This offhand declaration sent a jolt of thrill through my chest. He cleared his throat and said, 'There you have it. I'm in love with you and I've been thinking it for the longest time and I've finally said it out loud.'

'See you soon.' I spat out a goodbye and hung up.

Love. If Dominik felt the way I did, it was time to tell Father. In my letters home I'd mentioned Dominik as casually as the written word would allow, referring to him as a friend and always evoking his name in tandem with Małgorzata's and Krzysio's.

I was overcome by the urge to speak to Father. If only he wasn't so stubborn and would pay the bribe for a telephone instead of languishing on the waitlist for years on end. At times it felt as though the village was in another country rather than two hours away by train.

When I knocked on the apartment door, Dominik's cousin Danuta opened it, a small girl in a blue dress balanced on one hip. 'Pani Skowrońska?' She smiled broadly. 'You're a good influence on that cousin of mine. Ever since he met you he's become an old romantic, talking about marriage all the time.'

Their kitchen had the welcoming smell of onions fried in butter. The linoleum floor was made to look like wood

53

panelling and there were saucepans stacked on the bench by the sink. A plastic doll peeped out of the top saucepan, her arms held high as though she were under arrest.

'I thought you might like these.' I handed Danuta the bag of apples I'd bought at the markets, tiny knobbled fruits that were nearly as sweet as the ones we grew at home.

Released from her mother's hold, the girl stumbled towards a miniature red pram, grabbed it, and then hurtled towards me. When Dominik appeared she let go of the pram and shrieked with glee.

'Here's my biggest fan.' Dominik scooped up the child and then kissed me on the cheek. 'So you two have met.' He surveyed Danuta and me.

'Yes, at last I get to see the famous Ania,' Danuta said. 'You've been hiding her away.'

'I didn't want to make this one jealous.' Dominik hoisted the child above his head and blew loudly on her belly. She grabbed fistfuls of his hair and laughed, revealing a smattering of uneven teeth.

His room was as cluttered as I imagined it to be, with clothes and balled-up pieces of paper colonising the floor. The walls were decorated with photocopied posters for concerts and a woven hanging of a ship at sea. I tossed Dominik one of the apples I'd bought and he caught it in one hand.

He took a bite and said, 'What did that professor of yours say about your sculpture?'

'Apparently he liked it.'

'I knew it!' Dominik tossed the apple on a chair. He picked me up and twirled me around. 'Well done, Aniusieńka. I'm glad he recognises genius when he sees it.' With a laugh, he set me back on the floor. I circled my arms around his neck and reached my face to his. Between kisses, he said, 'We're going to the Rura Club. Who cares about Hemingway's influence on Hłasko? We've got celebrating to do.'

I pulled away. 'Are you still working on that paper? When's it due?'

'Three weeks ago.' Dominik retrieved the apple and took another bite, finishing the core. 'Tomorrow's probably the last day they'll accept it but this is more important.'

'I'm not going to drag you away from your work.'

'I want you to.' He strode about the room. 'I need to get away from this damn typewriter.'

'But you love writing.'

'No I don't, I hate it! I only tolerate it when it's over. But my God, till then … It's excruciating sitting for hours in one place, typing, typing, typing.' He shook his hands, as though ridding himself of the burden. 'I'd rather be out in the world,' he gestured to the window, 'doing things.'

'If that's how you feel, perhaps you should be a factory worker instead.'

'Perhaps.' He gave me a dimpled grin. 'But I'm too lazy.'

In the next room, the child let out a high-pitched scream. Dominik retrieved a jacket from the floor. 'That's a sign we should leave.'

'No way.' I navigated him towards his desk and pushed him into the chair.

'Alright, alright.' He cracked his knuckles. There was a ratcheting sound as he loaded a sheet of paper in the type-writer, then the chitter of metal arms stamping letters on the page. I extracted a book by Mickiewicz from the shelf and flicked to a poem I'd learned at school.

Monsters merge and welter through the water's mounting
din. All hands, stand fast! A sailor sprints aloft,
hangs, swelling spider-like, among invisible nets …

The typing stopped. 'It's no use,' Dominik said. 'I can't stay still. A walk will sort it out.'

'You're hopeless.' I tossed the book down. 'The only way you're going to finish that essay is if I hold you cap-tive.' Struck by inspiration, I dug around his desk drawers until I came up with a ball of string. 'Sit.'

Dominik lowered himself to the chair. I crouched by his side and wound the string around his calf and the chair leg, securing the end with three knots.

'Are you serious?' He wriggled his imprisoned leg for effect. Nonetheless he didn't resist when I tied the other one. I stood up and leaned behind him, my chin close to his shoulder as I wound the string around his chest, fastening him to the back of the chair. 'Aniusieńka,' he whispered. He ran his hand down the length of my plait, releasing my hair so that it spilled around his shoulders.

'I'm not letting you go until the paper's done.' I tapped the machine lightly. A metal arm rose but didn't hit the page.

On his bed, I tried to read. It was only when a ball of paper landed on my face that I realised I'd been asleep.

'Untie me.'

It took me a moment to remember where I was. 'What time is it?'

'Four o'clock.' Dominik massaged his forehead.

There was a stack of pages on his desk. I took one, struggling to focus my bleary gaze. The writing was unfamiliar, a type of not-quite Polish, and I realised that the letters were missing the accents. Dominik grabbed the page and bent over his desk, adding an overdot to a 'z', and then a tail to an 'e'. He handed it back and I continued to read.

He gave me a tired smile. 'Is it okay?'

'I honestly don't know how you do it,' I said. 'This is so much more than a paper about Hłasko and Hemingway. You start with them and then you go deeper, until I feel like I'm learning, not just about a couple of dead writers, but about the very world around me. Does that make sense?'

'A couple of dead writers?' He shook his head and then laughed.

'You know what I mean. It's good.' The paper was brilliant, in fact. And he might not have produced it if I hadn't been here. I was buoyed by his talent and by my awareness that I had been the one to inspire – or force – him to work.

Dominik's hand slid under my jumper. He traced the ridge of my spine as I bent to retrieve the scissors. I rested my chin on his shoulder and then wedged the scissor blade between the string and his chest, and cut.

12

Clusters of bees clung to the sticky mouths of the hives. Insistently humming. Above them the apple trees were in blossom, shedding white flowers onto the cracked concrete path below.

A bee darted towards me, zipping so close I could make out its furred body, its translucent veined wings. I slowed down my movements. It hovered near my nose and then headed for Dominik, who let out a yelp. 'Damn it!' He swatted madly. At this commotion more bees darted his way.

'Remember what I said? If you're calm, they won't sting.'

'That's an interesting theory.'

I ran my thumb along Dominik's palm, hoping that Father was busy in the work shed, giving us time to compose ourselves. The other week I'd written to him and rather formally announced I had a boyfriend, a journalist who was clever and funny and kind. Could we come visit? He wrote back and said, of course. His letter gave no indication of what he thought of the news and I began to wonder if it wouldn't have been better to try to get Father to come to Wrocław. Dominik wasn't at his best in the country – there were too many bees and not enough bars.

'Come.' I pulled Dominik towards the house as Father opened the front door. He was wearing a shirt I hadn't seen before, red chequered, with no signs of granite dust. He'd lost weight since I saw him last and though it was spring, his complexion was pallid. Perhaps the business was too much for one person. I resolved to come home more often.

'*Tatuś.*' I dropped my satchel and rushed towards him. Breathed in his soap-clean skin.

He held me to his chest. 'She's back at last.' When he let go, he wiped his eyes.

Then he cleared his throat and turned his attention to Dominik. 'I hear you're a writer.'

'Not a very good one, I'm afraid.' Dominik stretched out his hand, which Father gripped before pulling him into an embrace. When Father let go Dominik seemed uncertain of what to do with his hand, resting it on his hip before letting it dangle by his side.

'Dominik writes a lot of important things,' I said. 'About politics and art.' I wondered if Father had read the clippings of Dominik's articles that I'd sent. Probably not. He always said that after carving all day, the letters of the alphabet were branded on his irises. He preferred to listen to the radio in the dark.

Father stooped to collect my bag.

'I'll get it,' Dominik said, reaching it first.

Father continued to stretch his arm out for the bag and then, seeming to think better of it, turned away and led us inside. Dominik took his shoes off and asked to use the toilet.

I should have told him.

'Out there,' Father said, pointing to the back garden.

'Oh.' Dominik put his shoes back on.

My cheeks flushed at how paltry our living arrangements were. 'I'll take you.' I lead Dominik outside. Chickens darted around our legs and pigeons cooed overhead.

'I'd forgotten what the rural parts of Poland were like,' Dominik said. 'It's like stepping back in time.' The warm day heightened the stink of the toilet and he took a deep breath before going in.

I waited on the other side of the closed door. Perhaps it was a mistake to bring him here. 'Why don't you get an earlier train back to Wrocław,' I said. 'After we eat, I can walk you to the station.'

'Are you crazy?' There was the sound of liquid hitting dirt. 'I'm not leaving early.' Dominik kicked open the toilet door and went to hug me before stopping. 'I need to wash my hands.'

The kitchen table was crammed with bread and butter and honey and, incredibly, a roast chicken. 'It's fresh,' Father said. 'I killed it today.'

'Chicken! My prayers have been answered.' Dominik clasped his hands in mock thanks. 'Just try to keep me away.'

I cast a glance at Father, who had his gaze fixed on the meat as he carved it. We fell silent as we heaped food on our plates. *Real* food at last. With each bite I was fortified. Our university meals of cabbage and potatoes didn't fill me up, even though I drank a glass of water first, lining my stomach the way they taught us at school.

Before I'd finished, Father sawed off more meat and gave it to me. He licked his fingers and then apportioned some chicken to Dominik. With his utensils, Father pushed around the food on his plate. Perhaps he was more apprehensive about this meeting than I had thought.

'So tell me what's been going on,' I said to Father. 'I'm sure you have lots of gossip – I mean *news* – for me.'

'Ha!' Father sucked the food off the prongs of his fork and then used it to whack me lightly on the back of my hand. 'Things are the same. Business is slow and people keep trying to pay me in ration cards. I tell them, what good are ration cards when the shops are empty?'

Dominik put down his cutlery. 'It's not much better in Wrocław,' he said. 'Although everyone's excited about this new union. Have many of the villagers joined?'

'Solidarność?' Father coughed and thumped his chest. 'Some, yes. Who knows if it will come to anything.'

'I wrote an article about it, actually. The movement's gaining a lot of support.' Dominik reached for the bread and grabbed a slice, then another. This talk of politics had a stabilising effect on him. 'Other countries are looking to our example. We give them hope.'

'That's the problem,' Father said. 'Do you think the Russians will stand for it? I, for one, can remember what animals they can be.' His breath made a cracking sound and he broke off before saying, 'You don't want to hear those old war stories.'

Dominik finished chewing and said, 'Yes I do.'

Father gave a pleased grunt. He got up and fetched a bottle of the peach liqueur he'd made last summer. When he sat down, he began the story the same way he always did, by clenching one fist in his other hand. 'What a sick joke, to be saved from the Germans by the Russians. They were still butchering people when so-called peace was declared. My mother and sister and I spent a month hiding in the forest. When the war ended we set ourselves up in an apartment block. There was no electricity or water, you understand, but it was a home of sorts. Another family moved in next door. They had a girl who was thirteen, a year older than me. One night she asked me to go hunting with her – that's we called it, you know, when we searched dead bodies for treasures that the soldiers had missed. We left at midnight. She went to an old factory and left me scrounging in the alleyways. That night I found a watch in a dead man's shoe. I hid it in a secret pocket in my pants and went to the factory for the girl. On the way I saw three Russians. They were drunk, singing one of their victory songs. As soon as I saw them I got a bad feeling. When they passed me, I started to run. I ran and when I got to the factory, the girl was on the floor. Her clothes were torn and her face was bloody. I rushed back out with my pocket knife but the soldiers were gone.'

Here, I had to look away from Father. I focused my attention on the last of the afternoon light. On the way it lit up the hairs on Dominik's arms.

Father cleared his throat. 'I went back to the girl and begged her forgiveness. "What can I do?" I said. The girl

61

asked me if I'd found any treasures. When I showed her the watch she said, "Let me have it." You know, that watch … It was a paltry thing, but it was all I had. She tucked it inside her skirt.'

Dominik spread his fingers on the table and I waited for him to speak. He opened his mouth. Shook his head. Then he leaned over to Father and embraced him.

13

The next day I woke with a battered skull, the result of too much peach liqueur. I tried to overcome the pain by occupying myself with housework; Father had let the place slip while I was away. Chicken stock bubbled on the stove as I stood on a chair, wiping dust from the kitchen shelves. The saucepan lid rattled and clanked and I hurried over to turn down the heat.

Father came inside with an empty scrap bucket in hand. 'Ania! Are you pretending to be one of those rich ladies sitting in a sauna?' He opened the window.

Despite my hangover I was buoyed by the success of yesterday's meeting. After hearing Father's war stories, Dominik had entertained us with anecdotes about the characters he met on jobs for the paper. He kept delaying his departure until twenty minutes to the last train. We rushed to the station, Father riding his bike, Dominik and I half-running, half-stumbling, behind him. We arrived just in time, panting and red. 'Oh my lord, I need to clear my lungs,' Father had said, reaching into his coat for his cigarettes. As Dominik was about to board, Father said, 'I read some of those articles of yours. They made a lot of sense. You have a way of putting things that makes a person want to read on.' Dominik's face had coloured and he ducked his head in thanks.

A breeze drifted into the kitchen, easing my headache. 'I'm so glad you like Dominik's writing,' I said to Father. 'I told you he was clever.'

'He's certainly that.' Father joined me by the stove, where bones and carrots bubbled in water. 'That chicken's gone a long way,' he said. 'You see, Aniusieńka, around here we don't waste a thing.'

'Who can afford to?'

'It's that abattoir again.' He sat down at the table with a groan. 'You won't believe what they're doing.' There was a bee clinging to his shoulder and he leaned towards the open window and set it outside. 'Pani Wedel actually admitted that they're pouring all these buckets of blood down the sink. *Every day.* I told her, "Surely you can put them to use?" She said I was welcome to take them off her hands. What do you think, Aniusieńka, fancy helping me make some blood sausages?'

I stirred the stock and then pointed the spoon his way. 'The rest of the village would love that. The gravedigger and his daughter carting buckets of blood home from the abattoir. Can you imagine?'

Father laughed so hard that he had trouble breathing. He wiped his eyes. 'We have to do it just to see their reaction.'

He started wheezing and I patted him on the back before getting him a glass of water. Sitting next to him at the table, I said, 'I'm happy you and Dominik got along so well.'

He took a sip of water. The bee was clinging to the outside of the window pane. He tapped it through the glass and it flew away. 'Like you say, he's clever.'

'But?'

'He's a bit ... what's the word? A bit sure of himself, isn't he?'

I got up and went to the oven. 'City people are like that. They're confident. That's good, isn't it?' I banged the spoon on the edge of the pot.

Behind me, Father sighed. 'Aniusieńka, I want you to be with someone who'll take care of you. Don't listen to me, what do I know about these things? If your mother were here it would be different.' He switched on the radio. It crackled before picking up the muffled voice of a newsreader:

> … world is in shock as John Paul II lies in hospital in a critical condition.

I dropped the wooden spoon on the stovetop. 'What?' Father shushed me and turned the radio up.

> Thousands of people are holding vigil at the Vatican, following the attempted assassination of the Pope. They have gathered to pray, bringing offerings of flowers, crucifixes and Polish flags. A Turkish terrorist has been apprehended for the crime. We now turn to our reporter at the Vatican for more details.

'A Turkish terrorist?' Father said. 'Those Russians must think we're fools. They're warning us to stay in our place. They couldn't stand it that a Pole has the top job. What did I tell you, Ania? Those bastards fear nothing, not even God.'

The crucifix on the wall behind him was drenched in condensation from the steam-filled room. Liquid slid down the thin face of Jesus, onto his torso and feet and dripped to the floor.

14

On the day I returned to the city, the Pope was released from hospital. I caught a train to Wrocław Główny and then went straight to Dominik's, laden with eggs and honey from Father. Dominik wrapped me in his arms and lifted me onto his desk to kiss me. 'I missed you, I missed you, I missed you,' he said. I told him I missed him too.

We lay together on his foldout bed, the bone-weight of his head against my chest. We talked. While I was gone, Dominik went to Kraków to cover the march that had taken place for the Pope. Thousands of people, all wearing white, had carried crucifixes and banners that read, *May our protest be peace and reflection*. The Turkish man was arrested for the attack.

'Father says the Russians put him up to it,' I said, losing my fingers in the mess of Dominik's hair.

'Who knows. The fact that people *believe* they put him up to it is enough to piss them off. No meat, no money, no dignity. And now this.'

He was right. Those bullets had struck, not just flesh, but the very idea that things in our country could change.

'What do you think will happen?' I asked.

Dominik kissed me, his lips brushing my eyelids. 'I think I'm going to spend the day in bed with my girlfriend, that's what.'

I laughed and kissed him back. 'Half the day. We're seeing a movie with Małgorzata, remember.'

Małgorzata had been commissioned by the State to design a poster for an American film called *Apocalypse*

Now. She'd invited us to attend a private screening with her and Janusz the Censor. It was the first time that Dominik and I were going to the cinema together.

He flopped his head back on the pillow. 'I'd rather be here with you.'

Małgorzata was waiting for us by Saint Elizabeth's Church. As we approached, she took another puff of her cigarette and stamped the butt underfoot. 'There's been a change of plan,' she said.

'No film?' I regretted pulling Dominik out of bed.

'Oh there's a film,' she said. 'But not the right one.' She marched ahead, her leather satchel swinging by her side. She spun around to face Dominik and me, walking backwards as she spoke. 'Do you know how long I've been wanting to do *Apocalypse Now*? It finally gets released here and they give it to some other artist ... Some *man*.'

She continued walking backwards, nearly pounding into an old woman who was lugging her groceries in string bags. The woman glared at me and I hurried towards Małgorzata and turned her the right way. We linked arms as we walked, Dominik a few steps behind us.

'Who is he, this other artist?' I asked.

'That's not important,' she said. 'What's important is that he has a penis and I don't. You know what they're giving me instead? *The Blue Lagoon*.'

'*The Blue Lagoon* ...' echoed Dominik.

'Apparently it's a *romance*.' The wind picked up Małgorzata's hair, flicking it in her face.

We made our way to the Ministry of Culture, a tall building with windows that glinted like silver eyes. Holding hands, Dominik and I followed Małgorzata to the screening room. It was decked out like a miniature cinema, with rows of plump maroon chairs, and free-standing ashtrays between the aisles.

'Janusz.' She threw her satchel to the floor.

I hadn't seen him since the night of Małgorzata's exhibition. Once again he looked stylish, wearing a suit of the palest blue. He greeted us and then said to Małgorzata, 'You're going to love this film.'

'Don't,' she said. 'I'm still angry with you.'

Janusz raised his hands in a gesture of powerlessness. 'You know what, darling, anyone can do a poster for *Apocalypse Now*. This film needs a woman's touch. It's sexy, so I immediately thought of you.' Cigarette in mouth, he sauntered to the back of the room and picked up a scroll of paper. Unrolled, it revealed the American poster for *The Blue Lagoon*; an image of a beautiful and startled-looking girl who was draped in scraps of brown fabric. The tagline, written in English, was *A story of natural love*.

'Natural love?' read Dominik. 'Sounds like Adam and Eve.'

Dominik and I sat near the front of the cinema, our shoulders pressed together. Janusz passed us glasses of beer. Lights off, he positioned himself a couple of rows behind, next to Małgorzata, who was resting her feet on the opposite chair. The opening credits were rolling when I heard a low moan. I turned around as Małgorzata and Janusz pulled away from a kiss. But that couldn't be right.

When the film started Dominik put his arm around me. 'As soon as this is over, let's go back home.' His fingers traced the back of my neck, making me shiver with pleasure.

The film was about two young cousins who survived a shipwreck to be castaway on an island. In time, they fell in love. One day the girl waded into a lake, where she discovered something was wrong between her legs. The boy was watching from a cliff. 'I'm bleeding,' she said to the boy. Alarmed, he told her he would come down and help. A look of horror and then comprehension crossed the girl's face. 'No!' she shouted. 'Go away!'

Małgorzata gave a loud snort. 'This isn't art. It's dishonest and manipulative. What do you want me to do with this junk?'

'Use your imagination,' Janusz said. 'That's why I hired you.'

A group of sparrows circled above our heads before settling on the tram wires in rows of two. Dominik and I walked underneath them, his arm around my shoulders, my arm around his waist. When we reached the other side of the road, he drew me to him and we kissed. As we pulled apart a tram rumbled towards the sparrows and they scattered in the sky. Two of them landed on a white-domed building that housed a swimming pool. According to Krzysio, the building had been a synagogue until ten years ago, when the city was 'cleaned up'. Krzysio had lots of stories like that. He said that, for hundreds of years, the city had been inventing and reinventing itself after wars and conquests and tragedies. For a while, Wrocław had become Breslau, before recovering its true name. The past lives of the city were all around us. Though if it wasn't for Krzysio, I would never have known it.

Dominik held my hand as we walked through Plac Solny. We were on our way to Małgorzata's studio, where she was going to reveal her poster design for *The Blue Lagoon*. Something had been bothering me since the day of the screening. 'I've probably got this wrong,' I said to Dominik. 'But when we were at the cinema, I thought I saw them kiss. Małgorzata and Janusz. Properly kiss, I mean.'

'Oh that,' he said. 'They're lovers.'

His flippancy startled me. 'Małgorzata's having an affair?'

'It's not an affair. Małgorzata and her husband have what she calls a civilised marriage.'

I gave him a quizzical look.

'Their partnership allows for a certain degree of freedom.' He punctuated the word 'freedom' by wriggling his fingers in the air – a surprisingly effeminate gesture that made me feel tender towards him.

Yet this tenderness gave way to a nervous squeeze in my stomach as I recalled the meaningful looks that he and Małgorzata sometimes exchanged, the easy manner between them. Until now, I had thought: *at least she's married.*

Małgorzata was kneeling on the studio floor, a paint-flecked scarf around her head. I pushed down my unease and gave her a quick smile.

'We're ready for the grand unveiling,' Dominik said, leaning against the table.

She rearranged some hair that had escaped from her scarf. 'The poster's in the bathroom. Wait here.'

'You think she's captured the tranquillity of a tropical island?' Dominik asked, an eyebrow raised.

'I'm not sure tranquillity is Małgorzata's aim in art,' I said. 'Or life.'

As he was laughing, she called out to us. 'Close your eyes until I say open.' I did, listening to the shuffling of feet and the rustling of paper, and then Małgorzata said, 'Now!'

Though I hadn't been expecting tranquillity, I wasn't prepared for this. A poster that seemed to have been painted not with a brush but a knife. Fierce blue in the background, cut with slashes of red and white, and in the centre, the distorted face of a young girl. Her eyes were distended with horror and her hands, hovering before her face, dripped with blood.

I struggled to find a link between this image and the film.

'I was inspired by the menstruation scene,' Małgorzata said.

Dominik took a step closer. 'It's beautiful and utterly deranged.'

After looking at it longer, I decided that he was right. In fact, the poster was clever precisely because of the way it coupled beauty and terror. The question was, what would Janusz the Censor think?

'Janusz wants me to come up with something creative so he gets to feel like an artist. He doesn't give a damn whether people actually see the film,' Małgorzata said. 'In fact, his bosses prefer that people steer clear of anything from the West. So as long as my poster doesn't step on politics – at least not directly – then it's fine.'

Dominik said, 'It may not say anything about politics, but it says a lot about life.'

'I'm glad you think so.' She spread the poster on the table and stood between Dominik and me. 'That's precisely what I was thinking when I made it. This is life: we bleed, we shit, we die. We're slaves to our bodies, all of us. It's just that women are more aware of it than men.'

15

As Małgorzata predicted, her poster got through the censorship office without difficulty. When she told me this, I thought back to the kiss at the screening. Was this the real reason why Janusz the Censor gave her so much leeway with her art? Along with so many well-paid commissions? Or was I simply being unkind? Without saying anything about the kiss, I jokingly asked Małgorzata what she'd done to convince Janusz to approve the poster. 'Nothing,' she said, narrowing her eyes. 'He loved it. I told you he wanted me to produce something radical.' I had left it at that.

Soon Małgorzata called on Dominik, Krzysio and me for our help with plastering copies of the poster around town. We had to work in the middle of the night, she said, so the posters had maximum impact. Apparently all the artists did it like this; they wanted people to wake up to a city that had been transformed into a gallery, bursts of colour amid the pigeon-coloured buildings. They wanted their posters to be the only thing people talked about that day.

The nights were getting warmer now. At midnight I left my coat behind in the dormitory and walked to the town centre to meet the others. Jazz music leaked from behind the closed doors of a nightclub. My footsteps fell into line with its beat. As I passed the market square, the music faded away. I met the others by the theatre, where Małgorzata allocated buckets of homemade glue to Dominik and Krzysio, and a trolley of posters to me.

Her job was to be the curator, she said. Standing in front of a concrete wall, her thumbs looped in the straps of her overalls, she delivered instructions. 'We've got a generous print run, so paste these things everywhere. I want them to outnumber all the other posters.' As she said this, she gestured to the middle of the wall, which displayed a poster for *Apocalypse Now*. By the lamplight, I could make out the disembodied head of a man, lying on its side. One half of his face exploded into the top of the poster. Although the poster was unsettling, Małgorzata's was more so.

'Hey,' said Dominik, swinging the handle of his glue bucket. 'Do you want to cover these things up?' He jerked his thumb towards a nearby pole which displayed a couple of posters for *Apocalypse Now*.

Małgorzata wagged a finger at him. 'I don't know how you writers do things but we artists have ethics. Sort of … Put my posters around the other ones, not over them.'

We quickly developed a routine. Being the smallest, it was my job to dip a broom into the bucket of glue and sweep the liquid onto the wall. Krzysio, with his long arms, spread the posters, while Dominik smoothed the air bubbles. Małgorzata darted about, making sure that the layout of the posters was to her liking. The street lights had been switched off and we worked in the dark, using torches to guide us. As the sun rose we rested by the plinth of Alexsander Fredro. The playwright twisted his trunk in his chair, straining to get a better look at our handiwork.

The rising light illuminated the posters, with their mad slashes of red and blue. They were incredible. I changed my mind about Małgorzata. Her success was surely her own doing. She had earned it.

I dozed for a while, my head against Dominik's shoulder, listening to the clunk and screech of the trams. When I woke up it was to the voices of a young couple who were standing in front of Małgorzata's poster. '*The Blue Lagoon*,' the girl read. 'It gives me nightmares just looking at it.'

The boy grinned and put his arm around her. 'A horror film! I might have to see this one without you.'

Małgorzata got up, her camera in hand. 'That's the reaction I wanted.' She put her eye to the viewfinder and took a shot of the wall. In the middle of all those screaming girls was a single, timid poster for *Apocalypse Now*.

A fish transformed into a bear by the shadow of a black sun. Nearby, a goblin wrenched weeds from the earth and a hunter watched from behind an oak, his arrow pulled back on his bow. Around them I painted flowers, their petals and stamens more ostentatious than any I'd seen in real life.

I stood up to examine the mural, grateful for this holiday from sculpture. The professor's praise of my last work, the Mother-sculpture, should have given me the drive to create another piece. But the initial euphoria had worn off and I was left with a sense of dread. The higher the professor's expectations, the more severe his reprisal if – when – I produced something mediocre. Though in reality, he wasn't the only thing holding me back. The one thing I dreaded more than disappointing the professor was disappointing myself.

Crouching down, I began to add another layer of paint to the sun. Silver would have been a nice touch if I could get hold of such a luxurious colour. I continued painting and when footsteps rapped across the studio floor, I looked up.

'You're here.' Dominik appeared before me, a canvas bag slung over his shoulder. 'I wanted to see you before I left for Gdańsk.'

'Gdańsk?' My brush was dripping paint. I dropped it into a jar of water. 'What's going on?'

'More strikes at the shipyards. The paper's asked me to cover them. I was sure they'd pick one of the older men – they always get the best jobs.' He shifted his bag to his other shoulder and paced around my mural.

'When are you leaving?'

'Now.'

'Oh.' I grabbed my satchel and checked to make sure I had everything.

Dominik eyed my movements. 'Stay here,' he said. 'I need to run if I'm going to make it.' He cracked his knuckles and then glanced at my mural. 'Looks good.' Taking a step closer, he said, 'It's like something out of a picture book, but for adults. No, actually, you know what it's like? It's like stumbling into a strange and wonderful dream.'

'Thanks,' I said. But the praise felt shallow. What good was a picture when people were suffering?

Dominik wrapped his arms around me, his feverish energy rubbing off on my skin. He kissed my forehead and told me he loved me. Then he rushed out.

I selected a tube of blue paint, rolled it in my palms and then put it back down. The mural looked wrong. Silly and self-conscious and over the top. Perhaps the best thing to do was to start again.

I arrived in the village with a wreath of toilet paper hanging around my neck. The rolls wouldn't fit in my bag so I strung them together and wore them. They bounced awkwardly against my chest as I got off the train and then hurried towards Father's house. It was a relief not only to be seeing him again but to be getting away from the city. Without sculpture – without Dominik – Wrocław didn't feel like home.

The gate dragged against the concrete path as I pushed it open, the noise setting off the chickens. Father appeared from the work shed and kissed me on both cheeks. 'My *słoneczko*'s back at last.'

It took me a moment to reconcile my image of Father as someone who was strong and capable, with the thin, slightly stooped, man before me. 'Have you eaten?' I asked. 'I'll make us *obiad*.'

He lifted the toilet rolls from my head and slung them on his arm. 'How soft these are. They'll make a change from *Trybuna Ludu*.'

The Party newspaper was only good for one thing, Father maintained: wiping your backside. We must have thrown hundreds, perhaps thousands, of them down the long-drop toilet, down where the rats scurried with the composting waste.

The Mother-sculpture was too heavy to transport to the village by train so I'd brought photos to show Father instead. I spread them on the work shed table, my heart quickening as I waited for his reaction. Perhaps he would think it wrong to use Mother in this way.

He directed the beam of the lamp towards the table and stroked his moustache as he examined the photos. Finally, he said, 'Can you bring her home? I'd like to have her here.'

'So you like it?'

He lifted a photo closer to the lamplight. 'It's funny, you've reminded me of that expression she used to get when she was reading a book or peeling potatoes at the sink. I thought I'd forgotten.' He cleared his throat. Wait till you see some of the rubbish I've been putting together.' He turned to me dramatically, shining the lamp on his face. 'Prepare yourself ...'

'Surely it can't be that bad,' I laughed, wrenching the lamp back down.

'It's a commission for Pani Wedel,' he said, giving me a meaningful look. 'Her father died and she wants me to put together something *befitting of his station*. Or rather, *her* station.' He handed me a design with an elaborately fussy text surrounded by curlicues.

'I think you've gone a bit overboard.' I selected another design, simple with elegant lettering. 'This one's nice.'

'It's the best,' Father said. 'Also the cheapest. So if she decides to throw her złoty at bad taste, who am I to object?' He slipped the designs in a folder.

Father and I walked arm in arm along the curved path by Kolejowa. Smoke unfurled from the brewery, infusing the air with hops and mashed barley. The abattoir was close by and its odour of death collided with the hops. Perhaps this was why, whenever I drank the beer from my village, I could detect an aftertaste of blood.

Even in reception the abattoir reeked. I inhaled, testing the smell in my nostrils.

'Is the boss around?' Father asked a woman who was wandering past. Her hair, pale and curly, was trapped in a clear plastic cap.

'What's Pan's business with Pani Wedel?' she asked.

'Excuse me, I'm Pan Skowroński.' Father took off his hat 'I'm the –'

'The gravedigger,' she said. 'Yes, I've heard of you. Wait here.'

As she disappeared behind a set of swinging doors, Father and I exchanged amused glances.

Pani Wedel appeared, her cheeks slashed with pink makeup. 'Come into my office.' She led us to a small, wood panelled room, which was adorned with health inspection certificates and a picture of three kittens sitting in a basket. We offered her condolences for the loss of her father and she offered us tea.

'Sugar?' she asked, holding up a crystal bowl. Pani Wedel clearly had good connections. Though we had ration cards for sugar, there was none in the shops.

'No, not me,' Father said. He had a sweet tooth and I could see him trying to disguise his eagerness.

'A man like you needs his energy, surely.' Pani Wedel pointed a teaspoon his way.

'Well ...'

With a gratified smile, she plunged the teaspoon into the sugar bowl and then Father's cup. She stirred quickly, without clinking the sides.

'I've got the designs,' Father said. 'For a man of your father's standing in the community I would suggest a headstone that's imposing, yet dignified.'

'Dignity is key.' Pani Wedel wiped a biscuit crumb from her lips.

'You might like this.' He passed her the design that was simple and elegant.

She examined it, her face as expressionless as the cow that was painted on the front of the abattoir. 'I see, yes.' She set it on the table. 'What else have you got to show me?'

Father handed over the rest. She flicked through them and when she came to the one that was ornate to the point of tackiness, she stopped. 'He would have liked this one.'

'Of course.' Father said. 'A fine choice.'

Quickly, I took a gulp of my sugary tea.

Pani Wedel nodded as she continued to examine the design. 'I'll consult my son. He works for me as a floor manager, you know. I'll find him now.'

'We could come with you.' I ignored Father's expression of disbelief. I'd never been all the way inside the abattoir and I was curious to see it for myself. 'You could give us a tour.'

'So you're interested in working here after all?' she said. 'Your father would like that, I'm sure.'

From a steel cupboard, she retrieved protective caps and gowns. We put them on and she led us into the body of the abattoir.

The workers, all women, glanced at us as we entered. They stopped talking and concentrated on hacking slabs of meat. Their white coats were streaked with blood around their waists from where they'd leant against the benches. They looked as though a magician had tried to saw them in half.

At the back of the room, cow carcasses hung from ceiling hooks. The smell, which had been intriguing in the reception area, was now revolting. A churning sensation passed through my stomach and I prayed I wouldn't gag. Yet, despite the stench, I was struck by the vivid colours of the bodies. Rose hues, mottled with streaks of white. They reminded me of Małgorzata's poster for *The Blue Lagoon*, in which beauty coalesced with horror.

'This is where we cut the product,' Pani Wedel said. The workers cleaved the meat while she spoke about what she called 'the mechanics of the operations'. Then she took us to a smaller room out the back. Here, lined on a silver bench, was a row of plastic buckets filled with dark liquid. 'This is where we drain the by-product,' she said, pointing to the sink.

'Can I?' I hovered a gloved finger over a bucket.

'It's not used for anything,' she said. 'So yes, go ahead.'

'Seems an awful waste,' Father said, returning to that bugbear of his. 'Especially when we could turn it into sausage.'

Pani Wedel sighed. 'We can't waste staff time when we've got quotas to fill. All we can do is dispose of the by-product quickly and efficiently.'

I peered into the bucket and then lowered my gloved finger inside. When I took it out, it was crimson.

A small woman approached, limping under the weight of a full bucket. She cast a dubious glance in our direction and then, with a heaving motion, tipped the blood into the sink. She placed the empty bucket on the bench and then started on the others. Red whorls sucked down the mouth of the drain.

17

Inside the Sopota Club, jazz music played from overhead speakers. The flat, slow rhythms gathered intensity and then burst into the elevated solo of a trumpet or perhaps a trombone. We spotted Krzysio at a table by the low, wood-panelled stage. He was toying with the white table-cloth, rolling the fabric around his hand like a bandage. When he saw us, he let go of the fabric and smiled. He enfolded me and then Dominik in a hug.

'You look too good for a man who's been working day and night,' Krzysio said.

'Who needs a health resort when you've got all these strikes to cover?' I said. Dominik was tanned and energised by his assignment in Gdańsk. *The Ship-Strike Holiday* was how I referred to his time away.

Dominik pulled out a chair for me. 'This is what I need for my health.' Seated, he lifted his glass of vodka and took a gulp. Then he said, 'Meanwhile, Ania here has returned to Wrocław with blood on her hands.'

I knocked my glass against his. 'That's terrible. You're a writer, can't you do better than that?'

'Afraid not. I told you I was shoddy.'

'Even so, I'm intrigued,' Krzysio said.

There was a lamp on the cabinet beside us and its bulb sizzled, the light disappearing before coming back on. I glanced at it and then said, 'I had the pleasure of touring the local abattoir.'

'All in the name of art,' Dominik said.

Krzysio gave a low laugh. 'What have you got planned?'

'I don't know yet.' I swirled the clear liquid in my glass. 'Maybe nothing.' The colours and smells of the abattoir had stayed with me and I knew I wanted to make something that recalled the experience, but I didn't know what. 'Anyway,' I patted Dominik's arm. 'Krzysio will want to hear your stories about the strikes.'

Dominik traced the circumference of his glass with his forefinger. 'You know how *Trybuna Ludu* is saying that one hundred workers are on strike? Well, they underestimated the numbers by a *few thousand*. I've never seen anything like it. I got the feeling, out there, that we're on the brink of something. Something big.'

'See what happens when you mess with a man's meat?' Krzysio stretched out his arms and then, as though embarrassed by their length, folded them over his chest.

'That's only part of the story,' Dominik said. 'These workers, they want more than pork chops. *Dignity*. That's what they kept saying, "We want our dignity." Women brought flowers and sweets to the shipyard gates, like they were visiting the Pope. It was almost enough to move an old cynic like me.'

Dominik's sleeves were rolled up. I traced the line of muscle along his arm and said, 'Tell Krzysio about the poet.'

'Oh yeah.' Dominik took another swig from his glass. 'Day and night, the voice of the strike poet boomed across the shipyard, reciting Mickiewicz, or saying things like, "Let all Polish drunkards start decent work."' He grimaced. 'God, I hope he didn't mean me.'

'What about Wałęsa?' Krzysio asked. 'Was he there?'

At university there was a lot of talk about this Lech Wałęsa, an electrician who'd become leader of the Solidarność union. My roommate Basia thought him handsome and lamented the fact he was married.

'Wałęsa.' Dominik shook his head. 'He was there alright. Centre-stage, every day. I'll tell you this, the man loves the sound of his own voice.'

Krzysio rested his hands, palms up, on the table. 'He's charismatic. That's what the movement needs.'

Dominik inspected his empty glass as though he wasn't sure where the vodka went. I tipped some of my drink into it and he leaned over to kiss me, his lips soft against my cheek. 'The people love Wałęsa,' he said. 'He's a working man so he knows how to speak on their level. But half of what he says doesn't make sense. How am I supposed to quote a load of gibberish?'

'So you've started the article?' I asked. Since Dominik had returned from Gdańsk he'd done a lot of talking about the strikes but, from what I could see, not much writing.

'Not yet.'

Leaning in, I said, 'Am I going to have to tie you up again?'

His fingers stroked my wrist. 'In that case, I'm *definitely* not going to start it.'

'Enough of that,' Krzysio said with a grimace. 'I want to hear about Wałęsa.'

'The thing about Wałęsa,' Dominik said, 'is that he knows how to inspire people. But there's not much going on up here.' He tapped his head.

'That's not quite true,' said Krzysio. 'What he's good at is –' He stopped talking and a grin spread on his face. 'Where does she find them?'

I turned to see Małgorzata coming our way, her arm linked with a blonde boy who had the clean good looks of the people in the Soviet posters that were pinned to our walls at school. Małgorzata kissed us and introduced her companion as Jakub. She sent him off to fetch extra chairs.

'Very nice.' Krzysio nodded in Jakub's direction.

'I thought you'd approve,' she said.

Jakub returned, dragging two chairs behind him. He took a place at the table and then made a show of looking around. 'I heard this place was pretty crazy …'

'Just wait,' Małgorzata said.

'I was telling everyone about Gdańsk,' Dominik said.

'Ooh.' Małgorzata leaned towards him. 'Did you see Wałęsa? He's gorgeous.'

Dominik shook his head with a laugh. 'Not you too.'

A spotlight shone on the stage and the jazz music stopped playing. We rearranged our chairs. Dominik put his arm around me. Next to us, Małgorzata sat close to Jakub, stroking his leg.

A woman strode onstage in a white lab coat. She regarded us silently.

'Put the music back on!' Someone yelled.

Ignoring them, the woman stood at the centre of the stage, completely still, before slipping off her coat. Underneath she was naked. She looked towards the ceiling and stretched up her arms, lifting her small breasts. Her ribs protruded as she reached for a rope that was being lowered towards her by way of a pulley system. When it dangled in front of her chest, she tied the end into a loop and slipped her head through. The rope dangled slack from the ceiling, but then got tauter, pulling her up as she grasped the noose around her neck. Soon she was on tiptoes, swinging. I reached a hand to my own throat. The performance, so strange and macabre, brought to mind images of carcasses hanging from steel hooks.

It dawned on me that this was what I wanted to capture in my next piece; the idea of mortality, of bodies altering from one state to another. To do this, I needed to move away from the solidity of clay and try a material that was less permanent. It was an outlandish concept for a sculpture but perhaps Father could use his charm on Pani Wedel and arrange it.

Onstage, the noose got tighter. It was excruciating but I couldn't look away. When I felt the squeeze of rope around my own neck, the woman made a strangled sound. The noose slackened. She fell to her hands and knees, panting.

'She's a friend of mine,' Małgorzata announced in a loud whisper.

People in the audience began to clap, slowly at first, and then faster. Everyone except a girl who was sitting at a table next to us. She rested her chin on one fist and stretched her mouth into a yawn.

18

White hollow bodies, each the size of a child, lay on the work shed floor or stood erect next to the headstones. There were five moulds in total; abstract human forms that I'd fashioned from plaster and bandages, and braced with thin lengths of wood. Each mould had been cut in half and was ready to paint with pig fat, which, according to Professor Jankowski, was an excellent release agent. I stirred the lumpy yellow liquid, mixing it with kerosene to soften it.

The release agent smelt like pork gone bad. Despite this, Father grinned when he bent over to sniff it, 'See, what did I tell you?'

I lowered my voice to imitate his, 'Around here we waste nothing.'

When Father laughed, his whole body shuddered. He held onto the table to steady himself.

Stroking his back, I said, 'You've got to take a break from those cigarettes.'

'Too late.' He thumped his chest. 'I've been smoking since I was twelve.' Retrieving a cigarette from the table, he lit it, the match releasing the smell of sulphur in the room.

'You're as bad as Dominik.' I waved the fumes away from my face. 'How did you convince Pani Wedel to let us do this, anyway? I was sure she'd say no.'

He shook his head and chuckled a gust of smoke. 'She was so pleased with that eyesore I created for her father that it didn't take much to sweet-talk her into your scheme.

As I said, she'll let us use the abattoir so long as it's after hours and we wear protective gear at all times.'

'That's it?'

'As far as you're concerned, yes. For my part I'm giving her eggs and honey, and,' he raised his eyebrows, 'going to her house for dinner.'

The image of Father suffering through an intimate dinner with Pani Wedel made me laugh. I picked up a plaster mould, positioning one hand on its shoulder and the other on its back, twirling it around in a mock romantic dance. 'Before you know it, she'll be calling herself Pani Skowrońska,' I called in a sing-song voice.

As I whirled past, Father raised his hand as though to cuff me around the head. 'What nonsense.'

Pani Wedel was waiting in front of the abattoir. As she hurried us through, she said, 'I don't pretend to understand art, but it's good that you're home, Ania. For your father's sake.'

I cast a questioning look at him but he kept his gaze fixed on Pani Wedel. 'How's business?' he asked.

'Well,' she said, 'our quotas are up ten per cent, which means that ...' I blocked out her chatter as Father and I pulled the trolleys loaded with moulds into reception. There, we dressed in bloodied coats, plastic caps and surgical masks, and then followed Pani Wedel.

The smell of the abattoir was much worse this time. It made me gag, bringing up bile in my throat. Father was unperturbed. He lifted his mask to ask Pani Wedel about her sons.

In the meat cutting area, I gazed at the dismembered bodies of cows hanging from the ceiling. A white ribcage spread like wings, strips of red flesh between the bones. A stump of a leg pointed towards the tiled floor in a plaintive, elegant gesture. Another carcass opened like a bat ready to take flight. They were all sculptures in their own way: strange and beautiful and terrifying. Most artists could only dream of coming up with such powerful works. This gave me the notion for a back-up plan. If my own sculptures failed (there was so much that could go wrong with this piece), I would bring the professor and the others to the abattoir and present it as my art project. The concept was so bold that it was bound to do spectacularly well. Either that or earn me a fail.

Ahead of me, Father talked to Pani Wedel as he wheeled the trolley of moulds into the steel and tiled room.

'The by-product is over there.' She pointed to the buckets that gleamed with dark liquid. 'And the freezers are next door. It's not very convenient for us to store your things. We don't have much space, you know.'

I pulled down my mask and said, 'They won't be here long.'

'No.' She clasped her hands in front. 'Well, as I said, I don't pretend to understand art ...'

On a whim, I asked her if she'd like to come to the exhibition. 'Of course, it might be a bit strange.'

'I would be happy to attend,' she said. 'When you're done in here, come to my office so I can lock up.' Her heels clicked on the floor as she departed.

I took a shallow breath, wishing I could rid my nostrils of the stink. Father must have noticed I was feeling unwell as he gave me an encouraging nod and then set about unpacking the moulds.

'We'll fill them in the freezer,' he said. 'Otherwise they'll be too heavy to move.'

I followed him, carting a bucket of blood, the metal handle digging into my palms. Father pulled back the freezer door and we stepped inside. He instructed me to turn a mould upside-down and lean it at an angle against the wall. After I did so, he placed a funnel in its open feet and poured the blood inside. Some of it seeped over the edges, staining the white plaster. He held the mould in place while I fetched more blood, and when the mould was full, we wedged it in a corner of the freezer, reinforcing it with piles of frozen meat. It was good to be working with Father again – this time on one of my projects. He had an aptitude for the logistics of the task, for calculating volume, freeze-time and weight. I wondered how his life might have turned out if he'd had the chance to go to university like me.

When we finished I closed the freezer door and fled through the abattoir, holding my nose. Behind me, Father laughed. He took a deep breath and gave an exaggeratedly happy sigh. 'I think it smells delicious,' he said, enjoying my disgust.

19

At the end of the week, my friends tore into the village in Małgorzata's green Trabant, the car pulling up on the kerb near Father's house before shuddering to a stop. Małgorzata emerged from the driver's seat, letting Dominik and Krzysio out after her. All of them had dressed in black the way I'd asked.

Małgorzata leaned against the car in a floor-length dress. It had long sleeves, like wings. She whirled the car keys around her finger and said, 'So this where you come from.'

'This is it.' I looked at the tiny house I grew up in, at the holes in the roof patched with offcuts of wood. The late autumn garden looked bereft. Across from our place was the orphanage, a green slab of a building with a lone swing out the front. I had never seen anyone play on it.

'This is perfect for the exhibition,' Małgorzata said. 'I'm envious.'

Krzysio circled his arms, stretching them after the drive. He said, 'I feel like I'm in one of my mother's poems. She grew up somewhere like this, in a small village where they believe in witchcraft and God.'

'No wonder you're an artist,' Dominik said. His dark trousers and jacket lent him a handsome formality, as though he were going to the opera, not the abattoir. He enfolded me in a hug and kissed me deeply. I pulled away when I heard Father coming, his cough announcing his arrival.

We walked along the stretch of road by the forest. Father, Dominik and Krzysio took turns dragging the steel trolleys behind them. Father was slower than they were, but still insisted on pulling a trolley. When I offered to help he wouldn't let me. I didn't like seeing him in this light and I was relieved when we reached the abattoir.

We sheathed ourselves in protective clothing. Of all my friends, Krzysio seemed the least perturbed by the blood-flecked coats and greasy plastic caps, pulling them on without complaint. Dominik acted the joker, the way he did when he first met Father. Małgorzata shuddered as she inched her way into her coat, the stained garment contrasting with her glamorous attire. I handed her a cap which she refused. As we walked through the abattoir, she lifted the hem of her dress so it wouldn't drag on the floor. When we came to the women cutting meat at steel benches, she let go of her dress and fiddled with the camera around her neck. The women ignored her while she took photos.

'Come on,' I hissed, mindful of what Pani Wedel would say.

'Oh my God, this place is disgusting.' Małgorzata made a gagging sound. 'Worth it though, I think I got some great shots.'

Father and I wrenched open the freezer door. The moulds were still in place, leaning against the walls. Małgorzata peered through the eye of the camera and snapped. I inspected a mould, my knuckles thumping its white body.

'What do you think?' I asked Father.

He knocked on it and said, 'Should be frozen.'

Filled with ice, the moulds were heavier than a same-sized person would be. The men and I handled the moulds, stacking them on the trolleys and securing them with rope while Małgorzata documented the process. When all five were secured, we dragged the trolleys back through the meat packing area and, after removing our coats and masks, went outside.

Małgorzata took a photo of me wheeling a trolley past the roadside Madonna. The ice sculptures bumped against each other with a heavy thud. 'So tell me,' she said, 'when you came up with this project were you inspired by my poster for *The Blue Lagoon*?'

'Oh ...' I thought of the girl with menstrual blood dripping from her hands. Małgorzata was right: she was my influence for this piece. I certainly would never have been bold enough to execute it if I hadn't seen the lengths she went to for her own art. 'Yes,' I admitted. 'This wouldn't have happened without you.'

With a sudden movement, she lurched over and gave me an awkward kiss, her lips grazing the space between my cheek and my ear. Still dragging the trolley behind me, I gave her a grateful smile. Whatever had taken place between her and Dominik was in the past. I liked Małgorzata. She was, I realised, my first female friend.

In the forest, we unloaded the moulds onto the moss-covered ground. Timing was critical with this piece. 'What if the others get here too early, while we're still setting up?' I asked. 'Or if they're too late and the sculptures melt?' Although it was a cold afternoon I wasn't sure how long the blood would stay frozen.

Father exhaled cigarette smoke into the canopy of pines. 'Don't worry, *słoneczko*. All of us are here to help.'

'Tell us what to do,' Dominik said. A pair of pliers dangled in his hand.

I took the pliers. 'First we'll break them open.'

After I removed the wooden bracing from a mould, Father helped me peel back the plaster. To my relief, the pig fat worked well as a release agent and the mould came away easily. Dominika and Krzysio stepped in to help, cutting off the plaster to free the body inside. With a staggering motion, they pushed the sculpture upright, holding it in place while I contemplated it.

The shape of the figure was, disappointingly, not quite what I'd imagined. The intricacies of the mould – the ears, nose and eyes – were blunted when cast in ice. I removed my glove and placed my hand against the cheek of the sculpture, stinging my palm. The lack of distinct facial features gave the sculpture a certain anonymity which, upon reflection, I didn't mind. Neither man nor woman, it was a squat figure with a shrunken head, arms that pressed close to its sides and a ridge down the lower half of its body to signify two legs. It was wider at the bottom to allow it to stand. When putting it together, I'd spent most of my time thinking about logistics such as volume and weight. However, now that it was finished (or halfway finished, rather, for there was more to come), it turned out that my favourite thing about it was the colour. The blood, which had been so dark when it was liquid, had turned a luminous shade of raspberry. Some of it had clotted, leaving streaks of black.

Dominik came and put his arm around me. 'I love it. It's powerful. Eerie. You've managed to evoke what it is to be human, the frailness of us all. Everything comes to an end so enjoy it while it lasts, right?'

I was gratified that he understood my work so well. He wiped a trace of blood from his hands and then stroked my hair.

'I have to get back to the house,' Father said. Professor Jankowski and the others were meeting him there. He kissed my cheek, his moustache scratching my skin. 'It was the right thing for you, going to Wrocław.' As he walked away, the autumn leaves made a swishing sound beneath his gumboots.

Małgorzata stopped taking photos and lowered her camera. 'Didn't I tell you that you could make something different to anything I'd seen before?' She checked her watch. 'Now hurry up with the rest.'

Though the sculptures were made to stand on their own, I wanted them to have additional support. Dominik and Krzysio and I dug shallow holes for the sculptures to stand in. We arranged them in two rows of two, and then placed the short sculpture, made from the leftover blood, at the front. We drove bundles of twigs into the earth, their tips soaked in kerosene.

As we finished, there was a shout behind us. A couple of young men in black turtlenecks arrived, violin cases in tow. These were the musicians that Krzysio had arranged. Dominik spoke to one of them while the other one approached Krzysio and me. His black hair glistened with brilliantine. There was a hint of moustache on his upper lip and he had shadows under his eyes. His face erupted into a smile when he neared Krzysio. The two of them kissed full on the lips, the boy's violin pressed between them.

Krzysio said, 'This is Dariusz.'

It struck me, then, how little I knew about Krzysio. How little I knew about these types of relationships. In a bid to cover my surprise, I quickly leaned in to kiss Dariusz on the cheeks and thanked him for coming.

He lowered his violin case to the ground, resting it between his legs. 'How could I say no to Krzysio? Besides, I was told it would be an unforgettable experience.'

As Krzysio gave Dariusz instructions for the performance, I moved away to check the arrangement of the sculptures. I was considering asking the others to help me shift one of the sculptures further back, when loud voices pierced the calm of the forest. The audience had arrived: Professor Jankowski and a couple of other teachers, a few students from the Academy, Father and, surprisingly, Pani Wedel, who picked her way through the forest in high-heeled shoes. They stopped in front of the scene we'd created, five abstract human forms, cast from blood, standing in the damp earth. A last ray of sun pierced through the pine trees and fell on the sculptures.

Except for the screech of a crow circling above our heads, it was quiet. My skin changed as I soaked in the movement and stillness, the atmosphere of growth and decay. I had been coming to this forest ever since I was a little girl and it was home to me. By bringing people here I was exposing myself – not just my outer shell, but my inner self as well. Perhaps they wouldn't like it. But in this moment, it felt good.

I stood in front of the sculptures. 'This piece is called *Burning*.' I nodded to Krzysio. It was time for the performance to begin.

He and Dominik led the musicians, who were blindfolded, towards the sculptures. Dariusz propped his violin under his chin and began to play. Krzysio and Dominik retreated as the other musician took up his instrument. Slowly, exquisitely, the two musicians drew out a mournful song on their violins. The crow, which had settled on the branch of a pine, was silenced.

Małgorzata strode towards the sculptures, a white cape draped over her black dress. She lit a match and held it to the bundles of twigs. Flames crackled between the sculptures. She stepped back.

The fire was an integral part of this piece. It set the colours ablaze, bringing the sculptures to life at the same time as it brought them closer to death. Dark pools of blood collected around the feet of the sculptures and soaked into the earth. The sky darkened above us as the fires burned next to the ice, melting it, the flames crackling and spitting as the violins reached their crescendo.

The fires worked quickly. Whittling the sculptures to half their size, licking away their human forms until they became stalactites.

Professor Jankowski stood next to a female teacher, whose beehived hair glistened by the firelight. His arms were crossed and he rocked from side to side, like a pendulum. He stopped and leaned over to whisper to her. She nodded. Neither of them smiled.

To my left, Father stood near Pani Wedel. She looked agitated, chopping her hands through the air as she spoke. She turned from the sculptures and strode away.

I moved closer to Father. 'What happened?' I asked, keeping my voice low. 'Is she angry?' I thought back to today's visit to the abattoir – perhaps she'd found out that

Małgorzata had taken photos. I didn't want her to make life difficult for Father. 'What is it?' I prodded him.

'This is your big night.' He looked intently at the sculptures.

'Did I do something wrong? I'll go and apologise.' I was about to hurry after Pani Wedel when Father grabbed my arm.

'It's not that.' He shifted closer. 'I was going to tell you later … I was talking to her on the way here, you know she has contacts all over the place.' He rubbed the inner corners of his eyes. 'It seems the Russians are getting ready to invade the country. Put an end to this Solidarność business. Or as they call it, "the Polish crisis".'

'We're going to war?'

Father enclosed my hand in his. I remembered the stories he'd told me about the Russian soldiers. Of what they did to our country and people. Of what they did to women. I buried my face in the sleeve of Father's jacket and he said, 'I shouldn't have told you. Not tonight.'

He let go of my hand.

The burning of the flames, the melting of the blood and the kerosene fumes in the air. An image of Russian troops advancing towards Poland. The way they had before.

Professor Jankowski caught my gaze and gave me a single nod. He turned back to the sculptures, his face bright by the light of the fire.

Steel

1

Poland, December 1981

The carp regarded me dolefully from its enamel tank. Though its tail fluttered from side to side, it gained no traction, remaining at the tap-end of the bath. I lowered my head to the sink and drank the cool water. Then I wiped my mouth and moved into the kitchen, joining the others.

Paranoia clung to us as we waited for the knock on the door. Dominik sat next to me at the table. He tapped a pen against a cup while I clutched the seat of my chair, my throat parched again.

Tap, tap, tap.

I wrenched the pen from Dominik and set it out of reach. He extended his hand towards it, glanced my way, and then cracked his knuckles.

The walls were thin enough that we could hear the militiamen search the apartment next door. There was shouting, questions about a disturbance. Silence.

When the frenzied banging of fists hit Małgorzata's front door, it was a relief. She patted her cheeks and smoothed her hair before she got up to answer it. Her voice carried into the kitchen. 'A disturbance? Come in, then.'

My nerves got to me and for an awful moment I thought I would laugh. I clamped my hand over my mouth, remembering how we'd gathered here on May Day when the militiamen had come. I remembered how the older one seemed amused by our student antics. But that was *before*. General Jaruzelski's announcement made it clear that things were different now.

Two men in green uniforms, hot with adrenaline, stomped into the apartment. Their boots trampled the books on the living room floor. Anxiety surged through me and the beginning of a laugh caught in my throat.

Krzysio, seeing me on the verge of hysteria, leaned across the table and gripped my shoulders. 'Ania!' The hiss of his voice was enough to sober me.

The men were in the kitchen. One stood under the light with his cap pulled low, a shadow cast over his brow. The longer I looked at his face the stranger it became. His eyes, nose and mouth were crammed in the centre, leaving too much space around them. I couldn't turn away. Why did I smoke that hashish?

'Get up.' His rifle was slung across his shoulder. He nudged it, tilting the barrel-end our way. I leapt from the table, Dominik and Krzysio standing after me. 'We're seeking information about a disturbance to the peace,' the man said.

A disturbance to the peace. That's what they said last time. Were all their words – their thoughts – sanctioned by the State? Disdain took the edge off my fear and I stood straighter. Dominik gave me a nod.

Krzysio tugged at the sleeve of his jumper. 'A disturbance to the peace?'

'The broken television,' the man said.

Małgorzata had a smile that she reserved for men when she wanted them to do something, a smile that was both complicit and demure. She used it now. 'As you can see, our television is still intact.' She edged further into the kitchen, clamping a sneakered foot on the corner of the lino where the hashish was concealed. 'We watch a lot of television on account of my husband being in the business. He's a director. Ryszard Wiater. You might have heard of him?'

'No.'

'Oh.' Małgorzata crossed her arms. 'Well, as you can see, everything is in order here.'

The other militiaman, who had disappeared to search the rest of the apartment, now clomped into the kitchen. He was a boy about my age, with high cheekbones and clean-shaven skin. 'Found this,' he said. 'Pani is in possession of forbidden reading materials.' He held up a copy of *Tygodnik Solidarność*, which had been banned with the introduction of martial law. He tore the paper. The pieces snowed to the kitchen floor.

The other man watched. When the paper was destroyed he nodded towards the window. 'Better close it,' he said, 'don't want to freeze to death.' As Dominik pulled the window shut, the man added, 'Your names are going on a list. We'll be keeping an eye on you.'

The door slammed behind them.

I opened the window, gulping the cold air.

'Going on a list ...' Dominik squatted to retrieve the hashish from under the lino.

I heard the militiamen pounding on the door of the neighbours, shouting again about a *disturbance to the peace.*

'Why do you think they let us go?' I asked.

Krzysio was leaning against the kitchen bench, balancing on one foot, then the other. He kicked aside a piece of *Tygodnik Solidarność*. 'Every person in Poland owns copies of this paper. They can't arrest us all.'

2

Overnight, the city transformed into an army camp. Tanks loomed outside the cinemas, the churches and shops. The government said we were living in a *state of war*. What they didn't say was that the enemy was us, the Polish people. All this time we thought it would be the Russians who put guns to our heads. Instead, our own leaders did it for them. Better than waiting for an invasion, they said.

Sunlight glared off the morning snow as Dominik and I walked past the markets on our way to university. Despite everything, the preparations for Christmas were going ahead. Stall holders were selling pine trees, poppy seeds and tinsel. There were makeshift tanks for the carp; the fish scales were glinting lights against the black tarpaulin. An old *babcia* in a floral headscarf presided over one of them with the sort of pride normally reserved for grandchildren. 'Pretty fish, pretty fish,' she called as we passed. 'The prettiest you'll see.'

A couple of weeks ago, before this all happened, Father bought our carp. It was big enough for Christmas Eve dinner plus leftovers, he said. Soon after, we learned that travel was banned unless you had a permit issued by the State. When I applied for one I was told it would take months to process the request. Even so, I refused to believe it. I had to go home. It was *Christmas*.

There was a skin of ice on the surface of the Odra. A soldier perched on a log near Grunwald Bridge, his olive cap askew on his adolescent head. As Dominik and I stepped onto the bridge, a middle-aged woman approached the soldier, two children by her side. She passed him a couple of bread rolls and a plastic bag of milk. She leaned in to kiss him before wiping the lipstick from his cheek.

A yellow peace sign, paint dribbling down the edges, adorned a banner that hung from the university entrance. Black letters at the bottom declared, *Make love not war.*

Dominik and I went to the basement, where about forty people had convened. It was as cold in here as it was outside. Some people had spent the night in the basement and their sleeping bags were arranged in neat rows on the floor. A girl with an orange blanket draped over her shoulders was brushing her teeth by the window. She pushed the pane up a fraction, lowered her head to the gap and spat outside.

Krzysio darted over to us. He must have got dressed in a hurry because his shoes were mismatched; one was brown with muddy laces and the other was maroon with velcro straps. He wore a red and white armband around the sleeve of his jumper, a sign of solidarity with the teachers and students who'd been interned. The university had called a strike in their support. 'All our classes are cancelled,' Krzysio said. He cupped his hands and breathed on them for warmth.

'At least something good's come out of this,' Dominik said. 'I've got an essay due tomorrow. Guess I won't have to worry about that.'

Krzysio shook his head in mock dismay and then punched Dominik on the arm. 'Always look on the bright side, hey?'

We joined a group of people sitting on the floor. Everyone was scrambling to find out what martial law meant. A student with a sleeping bag pulled up around his waist was consulting an encyclopaedia, but that only told us what we already knew: that the country was under military dictatorship. 'Useless,' he said, throwing the book to the floor. Someone said there was a curfew, that if we stayed out past ten at night we could be arrested. Another person claimed that the nightclubs and art galleries had been shut down.

'Can they do that?' I asked.

'Apparently,' Krzysio said. 'I heard that all public gatherings have been outlawed. You know what they count as a public gathering? Three or more people together on the street.'

'That's ridiculous.' I thought of the woman we had passed near the bridge, two small children by her side. Could they get arrested for holding a public gathering? Unlikely, given she had a soldier in the family. Things were different for us. I remembered what the militiaman had said, *Your names are going on a list.* But then, half the people in the country probably had their name on a list. Either that or they were in prison.

My skin tingled with cold and I tucked my hands into the pits of my arms. Around me, people talked agitatedly. Debating what we should do. 'This is useless,' I said.

Dominik said, 'Let's go to the paper. They'll have more idea what's going on.'

'I'm coming too,' Krzysio said. He pulled on a beanie. It plastered down his hair and he tucked the tendrils behind his ears. White reindeers leaped around his forehead, their hooves tucked to their bodies.

Outside, the snow burned my cheeks. We huddled together before Krzysio touched my elbow. 'Three people, remember?'

'What a load of crap,' Dominik said. Nonetheless, he and I waited while Krzysio walked ahead. The wind beat my face as I kept my gaze on Krzysio's languorous gait, his mismatched shoes clearing a path in the snow.

'Who's going to kill it?' Małgorzata sat on the edge of the bath and trailed her fingers in the yellowed water. The carp floated listlessly at the tap-end, too tired or too defeated to swim.

'It's your fish.' I knelt on the floor, the cracked tile digging into my knee. I smiled at the memory of how Dominik and I had broken it.

'Ryszard usually takes care of it,' Małgorzata said. Her husband was stuck in Lublin where he'd been working on a film. Even Ryszard, with his connections, couldn't get a travel permit. It was no wonder I couldn't get home to see Father. The one consolation of this lock-down was that Dominik and I were spending Christmas together.

I called out to him now. 'We need you in here.'

The sweet smell of hashish announced his arrival. He leaned against the open door, a joint in his mouth.

'Can you take care of it?' I pointed to the fish.

He passed me the joint and then picked a bit of hashish off his tongue. 'I guess I'm the man around here.' Krzysio was joining us later, though I wasn't sure if he'd be any better at killing the fish. 'One more puff for good luck,' Dominik gestured to the roll-up in my hand.

I took a drag and then stepped towards Dominik and positioned the joint in his mouth. He breathed in, his lips pressed against the pads of my fingers.

'I'll get started on the potatoes.' With a swift movement, Małgorzata filched the joint.

At home, Father always killed our carp in the back

garden while I stayed inside. This time I wanted to see it. Dominik rolled up his sleeves and knelt by the bath. His broad shoulders cast a shadow over the fish. His hand hovered by the water and then withdrew.

'Are you sure you can do this?' I asked.

Without saying anything, he plunged both hands in the bathtub. The fish came to life, darting away from his grasp. He continued to chase it back and forth, but the fish was too fast for him, too slippery.

'That's not going to work. Why don't you empty the bath?' I said. 'It's not like it needs the water.'

He gave me a dark look. 'You want to kill it instead?' Nonetheless, he pulled the plug. Water gurgled down the drain, sucking the fish back, and Dominik managed to catch it. The carp tried to wriggle away as Dominik repositioned his hands, grabbing the fish by the tail. His mouth twisted as he pulled the fish out of the bath, swung it over his shoulder and then slammed it on the edge of the tub with a bone-crunching *thwack*. The fish's head shot up from the force of the motion. I thought that surely it must be dead but it kept moving – twitching and spasming and trying to get free. Dominik struggled with the fish and, with a low moan, he threw it in the empty tub. The fish writhed about, gasping for water. I closed my eyes.

When I opened them Dominik was sitting with his back against the bath, panting. Perspiration trickled down his forehead. He wiped it with the back of his arm and then reached into the tub for the fish.

The carp dangling by his side, he went to the kitchen. I followed. He slapped the fish onto the counter, where Małgorzata was cutting beetroot. Without stopping to wash his hands, he took the joint from Małgorzata's lips and slipped it between his own.

When the first star came out, signalling the birth of Jesus, we sat down to eat. Krzysio had ducked away from his family celebrations to be with us for a while. He brought Dariusz, who was looking as refined as he had that night of the blood sculptures, again wearing black. As though inspired by Dariusz, Krzysio had also dressed up for the occasion in a maroon corduroy suit. When Krzysio recounted his family Christmas, he kept glancing at Dariusz, touching the sleeve of his boyfriend's shirt. Delicately, as though he didn't want to get it dirty.

Dominik had showered after his exertions with the carp. His hair was soft and his skin smelt of tobacco and soap. Under the table, our thighs touched. I was grateful to him for killing the fish. If he hadn't done it, the responsibility would likely have fallen on me, the girl from the country. I watched him take a swig of liqueur and squeezed his leg.

Małgorzata struck a match, lighting a candle in the centre of the table. The gamey smell of carp hung over our Christmas blessings. Dominik went first. He tore his *opłatek* into sections and offered me a piece that was embossed with the head of a wise man. Our fingers touched as we held the wafer and he said, 'Aniusieńka, you have my heart already. My wish for you – for us – is that we live big lives. Together. That we have at least four children –'

'Maybe three.' My cheek grew red and I concentrated on Dominik's eyes, trying to pretend the others weren't there.

'Okay, however many children,' Dominik said. 'And that we always, always remember how lucky we are to have found each other.' He kissed me full on the lips and then we broke the wafer in two, each of us eating our half to seal the blessing.

'Can you beat that?' Małgorzata asked Krzysio.

He offered her a piece of wafer. 'Let me see … How about I wish you a string of pretty boys for the new year?'

'That'll do,' Małgorzata said.

Krzysio laughed and stuffed his half of the wafer in his mouth. His movements were more animated tonight. It was as though Dariusz's presence drew Krzysio out of himself.

Krzysio had told me that, as well as being a virtuoso violinist, Dariusz could play several other instruments. Across from me, Dariusz sat very straight, his fingers fluttering across the table as though seeking the keys of a piano.

Krzysio tore his wafer and held out a piece to Dariusz, who accepted it. Dariusz said, 'A string of pretty boys, hey? You'll need to be a little more romantic with my wish.'

'Well ...' Krzysio looked around at our expectant faces. Then, embarrassed, he leaned towards Dariusz and whispered something to him. Dariusz breathed in quickly, his nostrils flaring a little. He nodded.

'Come on, there are no secrets around here,' Małgorzata said.

Dariusz and Krzysio exchanged glances, refusing to say anything further. I was happy for them – happy for me and Dominik. I wished Małgorzata could have Ryszard here too. As though sensing this, she gave me a tight smile. Amid the dying laughter she reached to the middle of the table for a knife. The blade gleamed silver in her hand. She dissected the carp, giving me the tail-end. I scraped off the scales and put them aside for good luck.

As I prodded the fish, I tried not to think about the dreadful sound of life leaving its body. I took a bite. The tang of dill gave way to the richness of melted butter. Underneath that was the meatiness of the carp, with its aftertaste of stale water and dirt.

4

In the new year the university declared an end to the strikes, stating that now, more than ever, we needed education. My excitement about returning to the studio was soon tinged with dread: Professor Jankowski had summoned me to a meeting in his office. I had heard of other students being called there to be told they didn't have what it took to be an artist. He wasn't going to boot them out of his class, he said, but his *gentle suggestion* was that they should choose to leave. Even students with half-decent marks had suffered this fate. It was as though there were two examination systems running in tandem: the formal academic one, and the capricious one laid down by the professor, who could grade you an A one day and then drive you out of the Academy the next.

As I waited outside his office, I fidgeted with the hem of my woollen skirt. The professor was late. I kept returning to the memory of the carp. To me, the image of the fish had become inseparable from everything that was happening in Poland. The snow-encrusted tanks on the streets. The thousands of people who'd been interned. The protests in which the Zomo riot police attacked people with truncheons or pummelled them with cannons of water, the liquid taking on the force of concrete.

I smoothed my skirt and folded my hands in my lap.

At last Professor Jankowski blustered down the hallway, a folder in one hand and a set of keys in the other. 'Pani Skowrońska!' he said. 'Did you enjoy your holiday?'

I detected no sarcasm in his question, no allusion to the university strike or to martial law.

'My holiday?' Standing up, I slid my bag on my shoulder. 'It was okay.'

'Good, good.' He guided me inside his office, where we sat across from each other at a desk the size of a ship. He removed his glasses. They left ridges along his forehead and under his eyes, making him look like he had just woken up. 'I enjoyed your exhibition,' he said. 'Remind me what it was called. *Fire*? No, *Burning*, that's it. Thank God you didn't drag us to the country for nothing. And your Father makes a decent batch of honey wine, which helps.'

I released my fists from the arms of the plastic chair. He put his glasses on, and the sight of them back in place caused me to clench up once more.

'I have an opportunity for you,' he said. 'There's an exhibition taking place in Paris. *The Ones to Watch*. It'll showcase upcoming young Polish artists. Mostly Warsaw kids, but I've been given a few spots for my students and I've picked you to go. The whole thing is State funded so your expenses are covered.' He picked up a pen and then dropped it back on the desk. 'This is it, Pani Skowrońska. You're on your way.'

'Paris?'

I was an insignificant girl from the country. The idea that I could exhibit abroad was incredible. *Paris*. I let the name settle over me as I thought of the famous artists who'd lived there, Picasso and Matisse and our own Tamara de Lempicka. My nerves gave way to elation.

But there were things about this offer I didn't understand. How was it that the exhibition was happening now, when no one was allowed to leave the country?

'What about visas?' I asked. 'I can't even get clearance to go back to the village to see my father.'

'There's an exception to every rule, of course,' the professor said. 'In this case, the government wants to keep up the appearance of normality. At least as far as the international community is concerned.'

'Normality … That doesn't exist anymore.'

Professor Jankowski seemed unperturbed by my directness. He flourished a handkerchief from the pocket of his trousers and blew his nose. 'Listen, you're an artist. Your work should rise above all that politics business. The important thing is that you're getting funded to go to Paris. You'll find that they're very interested in what they call "art from behind the Iron Curtain". My advice is to make that work to your advantage. An exhibition like this can establish your career.' He retrieved his handkerchief and dabbed his nose again. 'All you need to do now is think of an impressive sculpture to exhibit. Preferably one that doesn't melt blood all over the gallery floor.'

On that note I was dismissed.

5

With everything that was going on in Poland, Dominik was busier than ever. He had spent the last few weeks working on an article that revealed the names of famous activists and writers who'd been interned under martial law.

Wałęsa, Michnik, Kuroń.

Anderman, Nowak, Walentynowicz.

Thousands of people, famous and unknown, had been rounded up in prisons without formal charges or trial. Apparently the government could now lock us up *before* we'd done anything wrong. This was for the greater good, they said. *Trybuna Ludu*, the Party newspaper, was full of success stories about martial law: how the economy was stronger than ever, how the country had been returned to law and order. In one article they claimed that rape had been eradicated and the streets were now safe for women at night. To this, Małgorzata had scoffed, 'But we're not allowed out at night!'

I longed to go home to Father. My travel permit still hadn't been approved and I wished I could afford to buy the clerk an expensive gift to move things along. At least the phone lines had been reinstated. Father and I arranged a time to speak, and I used the dormitory phone to call him at the post office.

'Aniusieńka, my *słoneczko* –' Father's voice, clogged with tears, was cut off by a recorded message, *This call is being monitored. This call is being monitored.* 'For God's–' Father stopped himself from cursing and I could hear his raspy breath as he calmed himself.

Aware of the censor listening to our call, I asked him if it was very cold in the village.

'It's colder than a nun's backside,' he said.

In the dormitory hallway a girl coughed loudly, signalling she needed the phone. I pressed the receiver to my ear and turned away.

'How are your studies?' Father asked.

'Good. Actually, I have some news. Professor Jankowski says he likes my work. He wants me to go to Paris. To exhibit.'

Again, the recorded message punctured our conversation, *This call is being monitored.* Then Father said, 'Paris! That sounds wonderful. How much will it cost? Can we afford it?'

'Everything's paid for,' I said. 'By the State. I don't know ...'

There was a long exhale at Father's end. In the background, a woman in the post office said to him, 'Five more minutes, Pan Skowroński.'

'Listen Ania, I haven't done much with my life, but my feeling is that you have to take these chances when they come your way. I've seen what you're capable of doing with your art. The rest of the world should see it too.'

The woman at the post office interrupted him again. 'Sorry Pan, other people need the phone.' The call was ended and my goodbye died on my lips.

That night, I waited for Dominik at the *bar mleczny* near the university. The diner was filled with steam from the bain-maries, thawing my frozen hands. The smell of warm food set off a loud grumble in my stomach. I sat by the window, pressing the prongs of my fork into the greasy plastic tablecloth. They left a trail of bitemarks behind.

A metal bell tinkled as the door opened and Dominik rushed in, his shoulders dusted with snow. When he saw me his harried expression gave way to a broad smile. 'Darling.' His lips were cold against mine and his nose was damp. I clasped his cheeks to bring the life back to his skin. He shrugged off his coat, hanging it on the back of a chair. 'It's been torture being away from you,' he said.

'Make it up to me, then.' I rearranged the collar of his shirt. 'Tonight.'

Dominik groaned. 'Can't. I have to go back to the newsroom after this.' He reached over to his coat and pulled out a flask. 'I'm helping one of the older journalists with a breaking piece about a student who got killed in the protests. It's going to be on the front page.' He took a swig.

I sighed. 'So how long have we got?'

'Half an hour ... They only let me out because I promised to bring back more cigarettes.'

We served ourselves *gołąbki* and bowls of tomato soup and then sat back down. Dominik pierced one of the cabbage parcels, revealing the white filling inside. 'Nothing but rice,' he said. 'Meat has been rationed to non-existence.'

'Not according to *Trybuna Ludu*,' I reminded him.

'Of course not.'

As Dominik ate, I said, 'I have some news, actually. My professor's asked me to go to Paris to exhibit my work. All expenses paid.'

Dominik picked something out of his teeth. 'Paid by ...'

'The State.' I reached for his flask and took a sip, the liquid heating my chest.

'So you said no?'

Dismay lodged in my stomach, gluggy as the overboiled rice I'd eaten. 'I said I'd think about it.'

'Ania, you really need to think about it? This is damage control. They want to convince the rest of the world that this military dictatorship of theirs is working just fine.'

'It's not *just* propaganda.' My voice was getting louder. 'It's a real exhibition, in a real gallery. It has nothing to do with politics,' I said, echoing Professor Jankowski.

'Everything has something to do with politics.' Dominik leaned back in his chair. He raised his hands and shrugged. 'That's just the way it is.'

'You could at least be happy for me. The professor thinks I'm good at what I do.'

'Of course you're good. You're amazing. That's why you don't need to make these sorts of compromises. You deserve better than this.' Dominik shoved his flask in the pocket of his coat. 'I've got to go.' He leaned in to kiss me and I moved away. He looked as though he was going to say something else, but he just shook his head.

He strode towards the door, pulling on his coat as he left. I watched him through the window. The lace curtains cast a net between us. He hurried along the cobblestones, his head bent low against the wind.

6

Małgorzata, undeterred by the fact that the galleries had been shut down under the new rules, was holding a photography exhibition in her apartment. It would be for one night only. Any longer would be too great a risk.

After a morning spent hammering nails into the flimsy apartment walls, we sat at the kitchen table to examine the photographs of the May Day performance, which she'd called *Molly's Coda*. To my surprise she had credited me as co-artist. 'You did take them, after all,' she said.

She passed me a framed photo. In it, she was sitting on the balcony, pleasuring herself while she read a book. The photo was so provocative that I had to look away. I took a breath and then tried to examine it with a cool eye. The lines of Małgorzata's body directed my gaze to the top right corner of the shot and then down to the bottom left. The black and white print emphasised the shadows cast by her limbs, the play of light on her face. I liked it. It was a well-composed photograph and, in some ways, more discreet than the paintings of naked women in my art history textbooks. I was pleased for people to know I had taken it.

Małgorzata said, 'Let's hang it near the balcony.'

This struck me as being too obvious. 'It might be more interesting to have it in the bathroom,' I suggested, 'above the tub.'

'I'll check what it looks like.' The photo in hand, Małgorzata went to the bathroom. She hung the photograph on the wall, standing in the tub to straighten it.

Then she hopped out of the bath and slammed the door. I heard the toilet flush and Małgorzata re-emerged, carrying the photo. It clattered as she tossed it on the table. 'Shit.' She sat down and her whole frame collapsed. 'Shit, shit, shit.' She pressed her finger to her nose and then dragged her palm across each eye. 'I really thought it would happen this time.'

I knelt by her chair.

She took a deep breath and said. 'I'm trying to get pregnant.'

'To Ryszard?' I asked, thinking of her various lovers.

'Of course to Ryszard.' She shifted away from my embrace. 'He's my husband.'

Embarrassed, I returned to my chair.

Małgorzata wiped her nose again and then picked up the photo of herself. She said, 'I *was* pregnant a little while ago. And then something happened. I had to sit on that toilet and wait for the baby to bleed out of me.'

My stomach clenched. I thought back to Małgorzata's poster of the screaming girl. *We're all slaves to our bodies,* she'd said, *it's just that women are more aware of it than men.* At the time I thought she was being provocative. I felt stupid for not understanding that she was going through all this.

I had no words of advice. A miscarriage seemed like a very foreign, very adult problem to have. The girls in my dormitory sometimes talked about pregnancy scares, but never about this.

Remembering something, I scooped up my satchel and dug around for my purse, extracting a piece of paper that was folded to the size of a postage stamp. I gave it to Małgorzata. 'This might bring you luck.'

She unfolded it and prodded the contents. 'What is it?'

'Fish scales. From the carp, remember?'

Małgorzata hid her face with both hands and shuddered. When she released them I saw she was laughing. 'God, that's so weird,' she said. 'But I'll try it.' She pressed her finger to the fish scales and then scraped them off with her nail. 'Sounds like a lot of people are coming to the exhibition. Most of them just want a party, but you never know, we might sell some photos too.'

'I didn't tell you,' I said, 'but my professor wants me to take part in an exhibition. In Paris.' A *real* exhibition, I wanted to say. I told her about Professor Jankowski's offer and the fight I'd had with Dominik. 'I haven't spoken to him since that night at the *bar mleczny*,' I said. 'He's so uncompromising.'

'He can be …' Małgorzata said. 'But he's also got a point. It's a trade-off. They help you with your art and you help them look good to the rest of the world. You'll have to toe the Party line. That might be okay now, but later on will you regret it?'

I began to wonder why Professor Jankowski had picked me to go to Paris. Maybe it wasn't because of my art. Maybe he was looking for someone who seemed pliable, someone who would go abroad and pretend that, back in Poland, we weren't living under lock and key.

'Would you go?' I asked Małgorzata. 'If you'd never exhibited abroad and this was your big chance.'

'You'll get other chances.'

'Would you?'

Małgorzata exhaled, blowing out her cheeks. 'I'd like to say no, but …' She shook her head. 'Probably. I probably would.' She nudged the fish scales with the tip of her finger. They had faded since Christmas and were now a dull shade of orange, streaked with lead.

People arrived at the exhibition at the appointed time of six o'clock. Given the curfew, being fashionably late was a thing of the past. There were about fifty people crammed shoulder-to-shoulder in Małgorzata's apartment. Some perched on the kitchen table and benches, holding onto each other so they wouldn't topple off. Others crammed in the bathtub, their knees pressed to their chins as they shared a bottle of homemade liquor. The photo of Małgorzata hung on the wall behind them.

I leaned against the bathroom doorframe, looking in at Krzysio and Dariusz, who were sitting cross-legged on the floor. 'I can barely breathe in here,' Krzysio said, fanning his face.

'Take off the jumper,' Dariusz said. He held Krzysio's t-shirt down to help him. Krzysio tugged the jumper over his head, leaving his hair static. Dariusz leaned in to smooth it. 'That's better,' Dariusz said.

'Ania,' Krzysio said, 'come join us.'

'Later,' I said, moving on. It was too crowded in the apartment and the lack of oxygen was making me feel faint.

In the living room, people shed their overclothes, leaving scarves and coats and shirts piled on the floor. Their skin released an earthy, pungent smell that reminded me of being on a farm. Most of them didn't pay attention to the photographs. Instead they drank and laughed and shouted to each other, the conversations reaching fever pitch until a young man with white-bleached hair and dark eyebrows stuck two fingers in his mouth and whistled. 'Keep it down! Unless you want the neighbours to report us for holding a public gathering.'

'This isn't a public gathering,' someone called back. 'It's a private get-together between friends. Nothing illegal about that.'

The man with bleached hair raised his hands in defeat. 'Even so, people have been arrested for less.'

This quietened everyone. Until a girl said, 'This could be my last party. I'm going to enjoy it.' The noise started again.

People said that a lot these days. *This could be my last drink. My last cigarette. My last screw.* No one believed in the future anymore.

I felt a sharp need to be close to someone. Dominik was at the paper again and we still hadn't made up. I squeezed into the hallway, where Małgorzata was clinging onto an older man. She grabbed my arm.

'This is Ryszard.' Her face flushed with pride.

Though Ryszard was at least twice our age, he was attractive. His short sleeves revealed strong arms flecked with dark hair. He had an intense demeanour. When he looked my way, I felt as though his whole body was focused on me, not just his eyes. He said, 'I heard all about *Burning*.' He stepped closer as someone else pushed past. 'I wish I could have been there but these photos are the next best thing.'

Ryszard's attentions caused me to blush. To avoid his gaze, I looked around the apartment and was surprised to catch sight of Jakub, Małgorzata's lover. Despite the chaos of bodies around him, he looked as clean-cut as he had that night at the Sopota Club. Jakup waved and made a beeline for us. He quickly greeted Małgorzata and then thrust his hand at Ryszard. 'Pan Wiater, it's an honour to meet you,' he said, shaking Ryszard's hand. 'I'm a huge admirer of your work.'

Małgorzata rolled her eyes. I laughed and made my exit, going further down the hall where the photographs from *Burning* were displayed. Małgorzata usually printed her photos in black and white, but these were in colour. Near the umbrella stand was a picture of Father and Krzysio pulling trolleys towards the abattoir. Above, was a photo of carcasses hanging from steel hooks, their bodies glistening red and white. Next to this was a photo of Dominik and me in the forest. We were peeling back the plaster mould from a sculpture, our heads bent together. I traced his profile, his decisive nose and the mound of his chin. Then there was a photo of the performance, in which the sculptures flared crimson by the light of the fires. A close-up of Dariusz, his black hair glistening, a blindfold over his eyes. In the din of the crowded apartment, I heard the song of the violin, the way it had moved us to silence.

Looking at the photographs gave me a strange sensation, as though I were inside and outside the exhibition at the same time. I began to see the sculptures as others might. A shiver coursed up my spine as I realised that Professor Jankowski wasn't lying: they were good.

'Ania.' A hand brushed my back and I turned around to Dominik. There was no space in the hallway and we were pushed together, his chest close to mine.

'I thought you were working tonight.'

He shook his head. 'I'm sorry. I hate fighting with you.'

'My professor thinks I can be a real artist,' I said. 'Someone who shows their work abroad.'

Dominik craned to see the photographs on the wall behind me. Then he said, 'I don't think this is the best way of bringing your work to the world. But let's face it, nothing is ideal at the moment. You should go to Paris.'

My arms were folded in front of me and Dominik gently pulled them aside. '*Kocham cię*, Aniusieńka.'

He was so familiar to me, so contrite. After a moment I pulled his coat, bringing him closer. 'I love you too.'

He rested an arm against the wall as he leaned towards me. Vodka lingered on his tongue and his lips were full and warm. We pressed together as we kissed, and behind me a photograph frame scraped against my neck.

The sky was a sealskin, sleek and wet. As I hurried down the street towards Dominik's, I tucked my chin into my chest. Pellets of sleet flicked against my face. Across from the library, a soldier was standing in the manhole of a tank. 'Come warm yourself on this,' he called to me, gyrating his hips. The gesture should have been obscene but the confines of the manhole made it awkward, ridiculous. I turned up the collar of my coat and walked faster.

The high-rise apartments looked particularly shabby today. Their ashen faces were lined with dirty snow. The only eruption of colour was the new graffiti on a brick wall in the centre of town. In red paint someone had scrawled, *Time to throw over Stalin's saddle.* And in yellow, *Winter is theirs, Spring will be ours.*

Every time the militiamen painted over the graffiti, it appeared again the next day. With new slogans, bigger writing. It was an ongoing battle between us and them: *slogan, silence, slogan.*

When I reached Dominik's apartment he hurried me in. He said, 'My love, you're freezing.'

I sat on his bedroom floor and he wrapped me in a blanket before giving me a steaming glass of cherry compote. My hands were so cold that when I pressed them to the glass I couldn't feel its heat. In the next room, the television was playing and his cousin Danuta was arguing with her husband about the baby. If I went to Paris I would have my own hotel room, a double bed and maybe even a balcony with a view of the city.

I put the compote down. 'Next week I'm seeing Professor Jankowski. I think I'm going to tell him, yes. I'm going.'

'That's good. I'm happy for you, really I am. ' Dominik lifted the blanket on my lap and shifted next to me, his leg pressed against mine. He brought his fingers to my cheek. 'You're still cold.'

When he rearranged the blanket around me, I noticed there was a copy of *Czerwony i Biały* on the floor. 'Does this have your new article?' I asked.

'Look where it is.' He flicked through the paper. 'Page ten. Next to the comics!'

"Political Crisis Worsens", announced the headline. And underneath, his by-line: "Written by Dominik Duwak".

'You're still using your real name?' I said. 'You know how many people have been interned.'

'If you're going to bother writing something, you should put your name to it. Only cowards use pseudonyms. Cowards and shoddy writers.'

I fished out a piece of cherry from the compote. Its boiled flesh had turned slippery and limp. 'You can be brave without being stupid.'

He flicked back to the second page of the paper. 'You see this guy.'

'"A political dissident's view on the state of war",' I read.

'He's younger than me. Got himself arrested at a protest and now he's in Białystok, publishing more than ever.' He tossed the paper to the floor. 'All the good writers are in prison.'

'You're not.'

Dominik gave me a dark look. 'Precisely.' He knocked the back of his hand against the floor. 'Writers need to engage with their times. These are our times.' He picked up the paper and shook it. 'And what am I doing? Sitting in my bedroom drinking compote.'

'If you've got better things to do …' I tugged the blanket off, ready to leave.

'Ania, I'm sorry.' He rubbed his brow. 'I've been at the paper all night. I'm tired.' He leaned in to kiss me but then drew away. 'What's this?' He stroked the edge of my mouth. To his touch, it felt tender and raw.

I went over to the small mirror he kept on his desk. The sleet had cracked open my lips.

The next day we went to Krzysio's place. His parents were out and we had the apartment to ourselves. The television was on with the sound turned low, playing a cartoon of *Maya the Bee*. Krzysio lay on the sofa, his head on Dariusz's lap, while Dominik and I sat on the floor. Dominik lit a cigarette as Krzysio told us about an American student he'd met who'd recently arrived in Poland. Officially she was here to learn the language. In fact she was going to study us.

'Her thesis is called *A Country Under Siege*,' Krzysio said. 'She's looking for people to tell her how *terrible* our lives are. Well, when Małgorzata heard about that, she immediately had an idea for an art project. She wants to turn things around and study the American right back –'

'Hey!' Dominik interrupted. 'I know that man.' He gestured to the television. The cartoon had finished and a blonde man in civilian dress, a brown suit with flared trousers, was sitting in a studio. Dominik turned up the volume. 'That's Aleksander Kapowski,' he said.

The name was familiar but I didn't know why.

'He's a writer,' said Dominik. 'You must have read him?'

'No,' I admitted.

'Me neither.' Dariusz took the cigarette from Krzysio.

'Oh you must,' Krzysio said. He shifted to seating position. '*A City of Winter* is so dark and intense. You'd love it.'

'Okay.' Dariusz lowered his chin to Krzysio's shoulder. The gesture, full of tenderness and respect, recalled the way he rested his chin to his violin the moment before he began to play.

'What the hell is he doing on television?' Dominik crawled closer to the set.

Onscreen, Aleksander Kapowski uncrossed his legs and rested his hands in his lap. The camera zoomed in on his face and, ever so slightly, he flinched. There were streaks of beige makeup under his eyes. He cleared his throat and said, 'The temporary restrictions on our rights are a minor inconvenience when we look at the bigger picture. What's at stake here is the good of the People's Republic. We can't be selfish at a time like this. Poland must come first. We must observe the new rules to ensure the continued safety and security of our country. That is, quite simply, our duty as citizens.' At the end of this speech, he straightened and glanced to his right, as though conferring with someone off-screen.

Dominik gave a snort. 'What a prick.'

'How much did they pay him to say that?' Krzysio asked.

'The man's finished,' Dominik said. 'Everything he's done is tainted.'

Dominik used Krzysio's phone to call his editor. They had a veiled conversation about Aleksander Kapowski, referring to him as 'the man in the brown suit.' At the end of the conversation, Dominik said, 'So it's settled.' He marched to Krzysio's bookshelf, searched it and pulled down a thin paperback. '*A City of Winter*,' he said to Krzysio. 'I knew your mother would have a copy.'

'I doubt she'll want it now,' Krzysio said.

'Of course not.' Dominik told us about the conversation with his editor, who had said that everyone was outraged and a plan was being put in place.

By the next morning, hundreds of copies of *A City of Winter* had been dumped outside the bookstores of Wrocław. The booksellers wouldn't take them back – in fact, they tossed their own copies to the street. The books stayed there, littering the city, until the militiamen turned up in their blue vans and hauled them away.

The image of the books stayed with me. Useless stacks of paper that people kicked aside as they hurried through the town square.

It wasn't just the books I couldn't stop thinking about. It was Aleksander Kapowski. The way his face had become drawn when he launched into his speech. The way he was wearing too much makeup under his eyes and the way that, as soon as he stopped talking, he checked his performance with someone off-screen. The expression on his face, asking, *Did I say the right things?*

Damn him.

This man whom I'd never met, whose book I'd never even read, had ruined things for me. I couldn't go to Paris. Not because of the likelihood of public shaming, galling as it was. Not even, strictly speaking, because of the politics. The problem, I saw now, was that this type of compromise – this collaboration – diminished a person. It diminished their courage. And without courage it was impossible to make art.

8

Not long after I made my decision about Paris, someone spray-painted the word 'Traitor' on Professor Jankowski's office door. It was quickly covered up with a black and white chessboard pattern to discourage further graffiti. The job was sloppy and the squares bled into each other. I could still smell the paint as I waited for the professor. When he appeared, he said, 'Isn't it ridiculous. The cleaners did it one night after I left. I'm half tempted to graffiti over it myself.'

He sat me down at his desk and talked about how cold it was but I wasn't listening properly. As I rehearsed what I was going to say, my gaze rested on a bowl of oranges on his desk. I hadn't had an orange since the last Christmas I had spent with Father. He'd given me one as a gift. It was wrapped in wax paper with palm trees printed on it.

Professor Jankowski followed my line of vision. 'A gift from a rich student who wanted to take my course. The truth is, I don't even like oranges.' He tossed one my way. I cupped it in my hands and breathed in the tang of its skin.

'Take more if you like,' he said. 'They're useless sitting there as decorations.' He pushed the bowl towards me. 'How's your sculpture coming along? A lot of artists get very anxious before their first big show. But let me tell you this: the art in Paris isn't as cutting edge as they'd like you to believe. It used to be good but then the whole scene became self-satisfied. An injection of new blood is precisely what they need.'

'I can't go. Not with the way things are in Poland. I'm sorry.'

He sighed and rested his hands on the back of his head. The bulge of the orange sat awkwardly on my lap and I cupped my palm over it. At last the professor said, 'Okay, Pani Skowrońska.' His tone as casual as if we were still discussing the weather. 'You want to take the moral high-ground – take it. The only thing you'll achieve is damage to your career.'

'Well I hope that –'

He raised a hand to silence me. 'The truth is I've been around for a long time and I've learned that you have to find a way to work the system. That's what we did when all this socialist realism nonsense was the order of the day. Sure, we made the art that the Party commissioned, but we found ways to inject life into it. The challenge was good for us. It pushed us to be more creative.' He picked up a book from his desk and flicked through it before glancing at me and saying, 'The worst thing an artist can have is too much freedom.'

A week later, Małgorzata called upon Dominik, Krzysio and me to attend her apartment. She wouldn't tell us why. 'Maybe she's doing a companion piece to the May Day performance,' Dominik teased as we walked through the park. 'As it turns out, you're pretty good at taking erotic photos.'

'I'm not planning on making a career out of it.' The mention of my *career* left an acidic taste in my mouth. Professor Jankowski had been cool towards me ever since my visit to his office.

We passed a small pond. Ducks glided through the water, clearing trails in the algae. Winter had at last given way to *przedwiośnie*. Pre-spring was an erratic season, but at least the snow had melted and the first shoots of plants had started to emerge. In the village we marked the beginning of the season by setting fire to a Marzanna doll and drowning her in the lake. I hadn't seen it done here.

I said to Dominik, 'I told my professor I couldn't go to Paris. I told him it wouldn't feel right.'

'Oh, Ania.' He stopped walking and faced me square on, clutching me around the waist. 'I'm sorry.'

'Me too.' Even though it was right thing to do, I felt deflated.

In the pond, one of the ducks raised itself and flapped its wings. Drops of water landed on the emerald plumes of its head.

There was a feast waiting for us at Małgorzata's apartment. The table was laid with plates of salted herring and boiled eggs. Sausages that strained in their casings. It was like Christmas except that Ryszard was here too. He carved a loaf of rye bread and set it down next to the herring. 'Eat, eat.' He wiped his hands on a floral tea-towel and then flung it over his shoulder.

The sight of all this food set my stomach rumbling and I placed a hand over it, trying to quell the sound. Ryszard must have heard because he gave me a kindly look and scraped an extra sausage onto my plate. 'I'm not very hungry,' he said.

I pierced the sausage with my fork and brought it to my nose, inhaling its delicate spice scent. Before I'd taken a bite, Małgorzata took Ryszard's hand and without preamble said, 'We're having a baby.'

'A baby!' Krzysio kissed her, and then Ryszard, on the cheeks. 'Does that make me an uncle?'

'How about godfather?' Ryszard said.

'Godfather ...' Krzysio raised his glass to them both.

When I hugged Małgorzata, she laughed and said, 'Ania, those smelly fish scales of yours actually worked.'

'We're so happy for you.' Dominik reached over to shake Ryszard's hand and then hugged Małgorzata. 'It's wonderful news – just wonderful.' Dominik sat back down and said, 'I have to admit, part of me thinks you're brave, bringing a child into this.'

At first I thought he was referring to Małgorzata's and

Ryszard's marriage, but then I realised that he was talking about what was going on in Poland.

'Might as well do it now,' Ryszard said. 'When I've got too much time on my hands.'

'Are you between projects?' Krzysio asked.

'That's putting it nicely,' Ryszard said. He flicked his tongue over his front teeth. 'It seems I've fallen out of favour.' He said that his latest project, about a steel factory worker who lost his job following a conflict with the boss, had been deemed "contrary to the interests of national welfare". The Party had banned the film in Poland and pulled the funding for his next project. 'There's nothing left for me here,' he said.

Małgorzata elbowed him. 'Excuse me, what about your wife and baby? And all this.' She gestured around the apartment.

'You know what I mean.' Ryszard lowered his voice. 'A man has to work, has to support his family. Otherwise what use is he?'

'If you want to be useful, pour me a nip.' Małgorzata held up her glass. 'Half a nip. It helps with the nausea believe it or not.' She patted her belly, its flatness belying the life that had sparked within.

I was in awe of her. Over these next months, she would double herself. She would make a pair of hands and feet, a mouth and neck and spine. There would be two hearts pulsing inside her body.

'Are you sure this is still Wrocław?' I asked Krzysio as we got off the tram at Fabryczna. Dariusz hopped off behind us. Stray weeds skidded along the tram tracks. A young boy came our way, pushing a wheelbarrow loaded with bricks. A girl in a tatty green dress was perched by the bricks, her bare legs dangling over the side of the wheelbarrow.

Krzysio waited for them to pass us before stepping over the tram tracks. 'This is why they call it the Wild West.'

For me, Wrocław was the epitome of sophistication, so I'd never understood the term. However, out here things were different. The buildings by the tram tracks were crumbling, their windows boarded up. They were flanked by mountains of rubbish: wedges of concrete and planks sieved with dust. This was a place the rest of the city wanted to forget.

Dariusz kicked a broken bottle out of his way. 'Next time I'm choosing where we go on a date.'

'Come on,' Krzysio said. 'This will be educational.'

Like me, Dariusz was from a small town. When Krzysio found out that neither of us had been far beyond the city square, he decided we needed to see the 'real Wrocław'. I wasn't convinced it was worth the trip. We had to catch a bus and two trams to get here. Before we reached Fabryczna, a couple of militiamen had approached us on the tram, demanding that Krzysio remove his badge of a peace sign. 'I didn't know it was illegal,' Krzysio said. His fingernail made a flicking sound against the plastic badge. The militiamen barricaded us from the other passengers, their legs spread ostentatiously. Dariusz made a point of meeting their gaze. The militiamen exchanged glances before one of them smirked and tilted his gun at the badge. 'It's a bit fruity for men to wear jewellery, isn't it?'

Now, as we made our way along the rubble path by the tram tracks, Krzysio dug the badge out of his pocket and pinned it back on.

He and Dariusz walked side by side, Dariusz stopping to flick a bit of dirt off his shoe. In many ways he and Krzysio were a mismatched couple. Yet when they held hands, their differences seemed right together.

'I'm sorry,' I said. 'About what happened on the tram. I should have done something.'

'It's not worth getting arrested over a badge.' Krzysio bent to scratch behind the ears of a skinny dog that was trailing at his heels.

'It wasn't just the badge,' I said.

'I know,' Krzysio said. 'But men like that are always going to be scared of guys like us.'

Dariusz said, 'You know what I was tempted to do? Fix the badge to one of *their* jackets. It would look good against green, wouldn't it?'

'I would've loved to have seen that,' Krzysio said with a laugh.

Krzysio's grandmother had lived in Fabryczna before she died, so he knew the area well. As we walked, he pointed out a pile of rubble where a church had been bombed during the war. A couple of slashed tyres lay on top of the debris.

'We should have brought Małgorzata along,' I said. 'I can see her taking photos of all this. '*The Wild West* – not a bad name for an exhibition.'

'You're starting to think like her,' Krzysio said. 'Who knows where that will lead ...'

The dog, which had stopped to inspect the grass, now ran over to us. It bounded onto the tyres before losing interest and jumping back down. The dog scurried over to a ditch at the side of the road. It sniffed around the edge and then slid out of sight.

'If he got in, he should be able to get out.' Krzysio kicked of pebble towards the ditch.

'Even so ...' Dariusz said.

We followed Dariusz towards the ditch and peered over. The dog looked content, prodding a pile of metal scraps with its nose. When it caught sight of us it scrambled out.

'You see, he's fine,' Krzysio said.

As the boys talked, I crouched by the ditch, my sights set on the metal. I took off my coat and folded it, arranging it on a patch of grass. 'Give me a hand,' I said.

They gripped my wrists, lowering me down a muddy bank the height of my chest. Mud sucked at my shoes as I examined the metal pieces. They were all the same shape: a circle studded with holes around the perimeter and set with a hexagon in the middle. I held up a piece of metal to the others. 'Take it.'

'Really?' Dariusz said. 'It's filthy.'

I passed the metal to Krzysio, then another, and then Dariusz caved in and helped, periodically stopping to wipe his hands on the grass. They pulled me out of the ditch, the dirt scraping against my chest and legs.

'You look a sight,' Dariusz said with a laugh. 'Let's hope we don't bump into any more militiamen on the way home. We won't exactly blend in – two queers and a woman covered in mud.'

Krzysio was squatting by the collection of metal I'd passed up. 'You know what,' he said, 'these are car parts. Clutch discs by the look of it. I don't understand why someone would dump them like this.'

'They're incredible shapes,' I said, joining him. 'You know, I could use them in a sculpture.'

'Sure,' he said. 'You could do that. How about you use some for your art and we'll sell the rest. Help our friends in prison.'

It was a selfish impulse, wanting to keep the car parts for myself. I tried to put aside my regret that I wouldn't be able to work with metal after all. 'Your idea is better,' I said.

We decided to return in a car to collect the metal and keep our fingers crossed that no one else got to it first. Even though I couldn't use the discs for my art, I was still entranced by them. Identical objects, but for the markings of water and rust. Each one a sculpture in its own right.

10

'Where did they come from?' Dominik asked. We were in Krzysio's bedroom and he was inspecting a photograph that Małgorzata had taken of the car parts.

'We know as much as you do,' Krzysio said. 'It's strange.'

'It's a story, that's what it is,' Dominik said.

'We can all rest easy now that Dominik's on the case.' Małgorzata rearranged herself on the floor. She placed her hand on her small belly, the way she did these days.

Krzysio's plans to sell the parts had come to nothing. Małgorzata had spoken to a mechanic who'd told her they weren't worth much. Clutch discs were just about the only car part available in the shops. They usually lasted for years anyway, so there wasn't a need for them on the black market.

I couldn't help but be excited. Ever since I'd seen the discs, I'd been thinking about the possibilities they offered. I didn't know if I had the technical skills to work with metal but I wanted to try.

Dominik slipped the photos in his satchel and then wriggled up behind me, looping his arms around my waist. The press of him sent a heat through my body and I strained to concentrate on the music that Krzysio wanted us to listen to. A friend of Dariusz's had gone to a concert in Berlin and recorded it on a tape deck. It was an English punk band and Dariusz said that once we heard their music we would never be able to forget it. The recording was muffled, as though we were listening to it over a bad phoneline. It was layered with the sounds of the audience: the low buzz of voices and a girl's incessant laughter. I strained to hear the lyrics. *Isolation … Isolation.*

'What does that mean?' Krzysio asked. Unlike Dominik and me, he had learned German at school, rather than English.

'It's about being alone,' I told him. 'Where no one can reach you.'

'Goes to show that Poles don't have a monopoly on suffering after all,' Małgorzata said. She straightened up and said, 'I might as well tell you our news.'

Krzysio patted the small mound of her stomach. 'Don't tell me you've got more than one baby in there … Now that you're showing, does it mean you get to push to the front of queues?'

Dominik grazed my earlobe with his lips before he spoke. 'Maybe after the baby's born you can go shopping with a pillow stuffed under your dress so you don't have to wait in line.'

'That won't be necessary.' Małgorzata spread her legs and shifted position on the floor. 'There are no queues in Paris. You walk straight into a shop and buy whatever you want. Easy as that.'

The tape crackled, and in the pause between songs, a male voice from the crowd said in English, *Fuck I need a beer.*

Krzysio turned it down. 'What?'

Małgorzata's cheeks flushed. It was the first time I had seen her look self-conscious.

'It's Ryszard,' she said. 'You know he can't get work anymore. And when he's not working he gets depressed. He puts on a good show when other people are around, but when we're alone all he does is lie on the sofa and stare at the ceiling like he's a man who's sentenced to be hanged. I can't have him bothering me all day long. I need my space. I want him to go back to being the man I married. Someone who's busy. Someone who's excited by life.'

There was an exhale of breath, hot against my neck. 'You're moving there for good?' Dominik asked.

'We've got visas to leave the country for three months. If we stay longer, we won't be allowed back.'

There had been times, in the past, when I entertained the notion of Małgorzata going away. Leaving me here with Dominik. Now that it was happening, a different type of jealousy pricked at my chest. I had missed out on going to Paris because of everything that was happening in our country. And now Małgorzata was moving there. Why was it that for her, everything was simple?

'Paris,' I said. 'I've never been. You'll have to write to us, tell us what it's like.'

My disappointment must have been clear because Dominik squeezed my hand. In a low voice, he said, 'Sorry.'

Without a word, Krzysio walked out of the bedroom. Małgorzata picked at a cuticle with her teeth while Dominik examined the tapes in Krzysio's collection.

Krzysio returned, a bottle of Krupnik in hand. 'We should celebrate.' He gave us each a glass and poured us nips.

Dominik pointed his drink in the direction of Małgorzata. 'Na zdrowie to the little Parisian.'

'Actually,' she said, 'I'm going to make sure he knows he's a Pole.'

The Krupnik warmed my lips with its cinnamon and honey. I wasn't being fair on Małgorzata. This was the best thing for her and her family. Besides, I had no reason to be jealous – she was giving up her home. Though I would have loved to visit Paris, I couldn't bear the thought of losing my country as a result.

I took another sip of Krupnik before asking Małgorzata, 'You're counting on a boy?'

'It better be. Girls are too much trouble. And they have all these weird hang-ups about their mothers.' She tapped me lightly on the leg. 'You know how it is.'

'My mother's dead.' I gave her a tight smile.

'Oh God, sorry, I forgot.' Małgorzata clapped her hand over her mouth.

There was an uncomfortable silence. Dominik stroked some hair away from my cheek.

Krzysio glanced at me apologetically and then said, 'Małgorzata's right about one thing, this baby's going to know its roots. We'll feed them the best of Polish punk.' He pushed himself up from the floor and inserted a tape by Deadlock into the mouth of the deck.

'More booze while you're at it,' Dominik held up his glass.

Krzysio poured us each a shot of the tea-coloured liquid. I drank mine while Dominik looked on, his glass already empty.

11

Now that the weather was warmer, the other students were spending more time in the studio. I missed the days when I worked here alone, wrapped in two jumpers and a pair of fingerless gloves, trying to order my thoughts in the cold.

With the help of Krzysio, I'd transported the car parts to the studio. I'd spent the morning arranging them in different patterns, trying to see what looked right. I was laying out the discs concentrically when Professor Jankowski appeared. He headed straight for the girl who was going to Paris in my place. From my corner of the room, I had been keeping an eye on her progress. She had chosen an unconventional material for her sculpture: nettles. There was a huge pile of them on the floor; they had long stems and ridged leaves and the other students took a wide berth of them when they walked past. As the professor approached, the girl pulled off her pink rubber gloves and explained the piece to him. She said that she was weaving the nettles into a long dress which would hang from gallery ceiling. The sculpture was called, *A Walk Through the Polish Fields*.

Professor Jankowski pressed his fist to his lips before saying, 'It's not your most original piece.'

'I can change it,' she said quickly.

'No need. It will go down well in Paris. Especially with that title – it'll give the critics something to write about.' The professor bent over and picked up a nettle stem in his ungloved hand. He shuddered and held it a moment longer before letting it fall to the ground. 'Nettles remind me of my childhood. My grandmother had a garden full of them. Even though I knew they would sting, I couldn't stop myself from touching them. What do you make of that?'

The girl looked at the ceiling as though it would give her the answer. 'Well, Jung would say that ...'

'Jung.' He exhaled loudly. 'Jung didn't drink enough, that was his problem.' He inspected his hand and then said, 'The sting's gone now.'

The girl watched the professor walk away. She stroked a nettle leaf against the back of her hand and winced.

I tried not to think about Paris and went back to rolling a clutch disc along the floor, listening to the scrape of metal against wood.

'I see you're taking my advice about making a sculpture that won't melt,' the professor said, giving me a start. He was always so quiet when he walked around the studio, deciding who to pounce on. I wondered if he was still annoyed with me for turning down Paris.

'Metal is an unforgiving material,' he went on. 'Very masculine. Do you know how to work with it?'

I shook my head. I had no idea how to tame metal and that was part of the attraction.

He said, 'I'll show you how to weld. My friend has a workspace we can use. We'll go next week.' He got up and strode over to a girl who was standing at the table, sketching.

The professor was right. Metal was a masculine material, the stuff of guns and tanks. If I was going to work with it I had to find a way to use it slyly, with a wink in the other direction. Take the notion of hardness and turn it on its head.

That afternoon, Dominik and I met for *obiad* at the *bar mleczny* near the Academy. We sat at a table in a back corner of the room and while he excavated a boiled potato I told him about my day in the studio.

140

'I can't wait to see what you come up with next,' he said. He screwed the lid off a shaker and used his finger to scrape salt into the potato.

'You're worse than Father. Do you want a heart attack?'

Dominik forked some potato into his mouth and gave a happy sigh. 'What's the point of living a long life if you don't get to enjoy your food?' He took another bite. 'I'm looking forward to seeing him again. To tell you the truth, I was a bit out of sorts last time. It's a big deal, meeting the father of the woman you want to marry.'

When he said this, the diner got smaller, enclosing just the two of us, enclosing me in the warmth of his smile. 'You did fine.' I reached for his hand, feeling the ridges of skin in the middle of his fingers and the bones underneath. 'Father loved you.'

My travel permit had finally been approved. I was going back to the village as soon as the university term ended. Dominik had also applied for a permit and we hoped he would be able to join me. The other day I had called Father at the post office to tell him I was coming home soon. 'What about Paris?' he had asked. 'I can't go,' I said. 'It wouldn't feel right.' When he didn't say anything, I added, 'You didn't raise me that way.' Father had sighed and said, 'Don't follow my example or you'll end up a poor gravedigger.' His breath sounded raspy and I asked him what the doctor had said about it. 'Just a cold,' he said. 'Everyone in the village has had it.'

Dominik speared some boiled carrot from my plate and brought it to his mouth. 'When I finish this story we'll have earned ourselves a holiday in the country. The editor thinks it's going to be big news. She's talking about putting it on page two.'

For the last few weeks, Dominik had been investigating the engine parts we'd found in Fabryczna. I didn't see why they warranted so much of his time, especially given everything else that was going on in Poland. 'Are dumped car parts really such a big deal?' I asked.

'Not on their own they're not. But they're symbolic.'

'Of what?'

'Waste.' He punctuated the word with his fork. 'Corruption. A massive economic crisis. You know how much debt our country is in? Twenty *billion* American dollars. The government is borrowing and borrowing and spending and spending without actually planning what we need. That's why the clutch discs are important, because they're part of a bigger problem. It turns out that the same thing has happened with other goods. Televisions, saucepans and even, it pains me to say, cigarettes. Can you believe it? When some bureaucrat orders too much of a certain product they dump it somewhere to cover up their mistake.' He leaned forward and cupped my chin. 'It's a big story, Aniusieńka. And I've got you to thank for it.'

'It's worked out well for both of us,' I said. 'You get a nice bit of political corruption for your story and I get some metal for my art.'

Dominik laughed. 'You've changed.'

'What do you mean?'

'You're not that innocent girl from the country anymore.'

'Ha,' I said. 'Must be your influence.'

I was carving into my egg cutlet when a girl in a miniskirt sidled up to us. 'Dominik!' she said, grabbing onto him with her smile. 'I loved your article about the strikes. You know, when I read it I felt like I was right there with you.' She glanced at me and said, 'He's a great writer, isn't he.'

'Where are my manners?' Dominik said. 'Ania, this is Mischa. And Mischa, this is my girlfriend – soon to be fiancée – Ania.' As Mischa rearranged her tray in her hands, Dominik told me she was an economist. 'Precisely what our country needs right now,' he said.

'Not that anyone listens to our advice,' she said. 'Look at the mess we're in.'

'We were just talking about that,' Dominik said. 'Come to think of it, I could do with your help with an article I'm writing. Shall we meet up sometime, maybe next week?'

142

'I'd love to.' She glanced at me – triumphantly, I thought – and then said goodbye, her long legs striding away.

I picked at my cutlet. 'How do you know her?'

'Oh, from around.' Dominik pushed back his chair, the legs scraping against the tiled floor. 'Actually we used to go out. Nothing serious, you understand. Just fun.'

'Just fun … And Małgorzata? What about her?' I knew I sounded petulant but I wanted things to be out in the open.

'Małgorzata?' Dominik's eyes widened and then he caved in and gave a shrug. 'You know she likes to have fun too. We did, for a while. Again, nothing serious. She's a woman of the world. Ask Krzysio.'

'Krzysio? That's not possible. Is it?'

Dominik gave me an amused smile. 'What? He's not allowed to experiment?' He reached out and took my hand in his. 'All that stuff with Małgorzata and the other girls is behind us, Aniusieńka. You're the one I want.'

12

The welding torch crackled as I switched it on, releasing its electric charge. It zapped against the metal, shooting tiny bolts of light. Heat flared next to my gloved hands. Perspiration streaked the lenses of my welding helmet. I waited for the torch to fuse the disc to the end of the rod, watching as the metal glowed red. When the two pieces had joined I switched off the torch. The metal hardened once more.

Next to me was a hollow face, nearly my size, made of bronze. The sculpture regarded me with holes-for-eyes as I pushed my helmet onto my head. I was in the workshop of a well-known sculptor who was a friend of the professor's. The sculptor had allowed me access to the place after hours, saying that he liked to encourage Professor Jankowski's *protégés*. On my first day in the workshop he and the professor had given me a lesson in welding. I was armoured with a helmet and long gloves so that the torch wouldn't burn the hair off my arms. I was relieved to find that welding wasn't difficult. The professor's friend had said, 'You've got a steady hand. You say you've never done this before?' Never, I told him. 'But my father's a headstone carver,' I said, 'so I know my way around tools.' Looking relieved, he had told me that in that case, I wouldn't require babysitting from him.

The car parts were scattered on the workshop floor. As entranced as I'd been with their shapes, I had decided to change them, using an electric saw to remove the inner hexagon so that I was left with the outer ring. For all the talk of me being a natural with the tools, I'd ruined the first few discs that I tried to dissect and was glad that neither the professor nor his friend were there to see it. My later attempts were better, leaving me with five rings that I joined together with short metal rods, stacking them on top of each other in the manner of a totem pole.

I switched the torch back on and fused the bottom ring to a metal base so that the sculpture stood upright. This done, I took some photos for Dominik. He was going to include a picture of the sculpture with his article. Though the sculpture wasn't yet finished, he wanted a picture of it in this form, before I'd covered it with feathers. It would be more impactful if people could view the metal clearly, he said. I would have preferred that people see my sculpture in its finished state, but it was Dominik's article. He knew what would work best.

After taking the photos, I untied one of the hessian sacks that Father had arranged to be transported to Wrocław. There were three sacks in all. The two larger ones contained feathers from pigeons and chickens. The third, smaller sack, held the feathers of crows. Along with the sacks, Father had sent me two jars of honey and a letter in which he described the goings-on of the village.

I sank my hand into a sack of feathers, stroking their down and the hard lines of their quills. As I inhaled the tang of bird droppings and dirt, I pictured Father throwing kitchen scraps to the chickens, shooing away the bossier ones so the others could eat. Father and I had been collecting the feathers for as long as I could remember. 'You just happened to have these lying around the house?' Dominik had asked when he saw them. 'Yes,' I told him, 'what's wrong with that?' 'Nothing, but you're going to have to curb this hoarding of yours if we're going to live together in a one-room apartment,' he'd said. 'Otherwise there won't be room for us, let alone our tribe of children.'

I picked up a crow feather and held it against the metal sculpture. The feather's purple-black sheen was luxurious but too dark for this piece, I decided. The pigeon feathers and the paler chicken feathers would be perfect. I assessed my sculpture, making up my mind to leave the bottom disc as it was. The second one would be covered with a smattering of feathers the colours of ivory and ash. Gradually the feathers would consume the discs, so that the metal of the top disc was hidden entirely.

Feathers drifted to the workbench as I separated the dark ones from the light. When I had a good selection I cut them in half and put aside the quilled ends. Then I started to glue the tips onto the discs, carefully arranging them side by side. Having completed a row of feathers on the inner rim of a disc, I started on the next row, overlapping them like scales. In time, the feathers transformed the metal into something eerie and delicate and soft to touch. This piece was called *Flight*.

There was a meditative quality to this part of the job, the gluing, the arranging and smoothing of feathers. One feather was the white-peach of a baby's skin. Another was charcoal and blonde. The task was so absorbing that I forgot where I was – even who I was. Past and future disappeared, erasing me, so that nothing was left but the work.

I jumped when I realised someone was calling my name. Professor Jankowski's friend was standing at the door. 'You scared me,' I said.

Without smiling, he said, 'There's a man on the phone for you.' He gestured for me to follow.

I was taken aback by his curt manner, and checking my watch, noted it was time for *obiad*. The phone call had probably interrupted his meal. He led me into a house that gleamed with wooden furniture and pointed me to the telephone in the living room. I took the receiver. My hands were dirty and I pried my fingers away, trying to minimise contact with the phone.

'Hello,' I said, as he moved to another room.

'Ania.' It was Dominik. The waver of his voice made my heart skip a beat.

'Are you alright?' I pressed the receiver harder against my ear. 'Dominik?'

'I'm at the hospital.'

My knuckles strained as I clutched the phone. 'You're hurt.'

'No. It's Krzysio.'

13

Dominik and I sat in his room, my fingers picking at the tasselled rug as I tried to understand how this could have happened. All I could think about was Krzysio lying on the hospital bed, his face lurid with bruises. One was a purple rod against his cheek. Another swelled blue around his eye. A section of his forehead was bandaged. The shock of it had made me want to flee the room. I didn't know how his mother could bear it. She sat by his side, stroking his hand. 'Your friends are here,' she had said, leaning close to her son. His chest rose and fell underneath the white sheet. Dominik had put his arm around Krzysio's mother and taken her into the corridor for a cigarette. I watched as she leaned her head against him and cried.

Dominik stilled my hand to stop me from picking at the rug. He kissed my eyelids, my brow.

Last night, Krzysio and Dariusz had been walking past the botanical gardens when they were beaten up by two militiamen. There was a witness to the event, an old man who lived in an apartment block close by. The old man had taken his dog outside to urinate when he saw the militiamen attack. He said that Krzysio and Dariusz lay on the ground as the militiamen kicked them with their boots and pummelled them with truncheons. According to the old man, it was only five minutes after curfew.

I wiped my nose with the back of my arm. 'Five minutes …'

It was Dominik's turn to pick at the rug. 'The old man said they were holding hands.'

'So the curfew was just an excuse?'

'I guess,' he said. 'That's what happens when thugs get high on power.'

Dariusz was in a special care unit and wasn't allowed visitors. The militiamen had beaten him so hard that they'd broken three of his ribs. He was bleeding inside his body. Apparently the hospital had called his parents to tell them they needed to come to Wrocław straightaway. I thought of Father getting a phone call like that and wrapped my arms around my stomach.

'There's really nothing we can do?' I said.

Dominik tipped his head back, releasing the bulge of his Adam's apple. 'There's not much point in reporting a crime to the same people who committed it.'

'So we do nothing.'

'They'll want to keep this hidden. Our job is to get it out in the open.'

A shrine marked the spot where Krzysio and Dariusz had been beaten. Dominik took me there on the way to his place. Candles were wedged in the earth around the base of a birch tree. A handwritten placard was nailed to the trunk. It informed people that, "On this spot, two students were attacked by militiamen." It stated that the students had done nothing to provoke the attack and were now both in hospital. Beneath the placard, a bunch of carnations was tied to the tree. Dominik told me that more shrines like this had cropped up around the country. 'For other people who've been assaulted?' I had asked. 'Assaulted, yeah,' he said. 'Or worse.'

Dominik pressed his fingers to his eyes. 'I'm exhausted. Tell me about something good. Tell me about your sculpture.'

That all seemed like a long time ago. Without any real enthusiasm, I told him about my piece. I retrieved the camera. 'Here you go. There are some shots of the dumped metal as well as the sculpture. Without the feathers, like you asked. And who knows what else Małgorzata has got on the film.'

'I've been thinking about my article.' Dominik jiggled the film cartridge in his palm. 'Your sculpture's given me an idea about how to end it on a more lyrical note. After all that stuff about political corruption and waste, I'm going to write about how resourceful our artists are. About how that symbolises the Polish people in general, that we can make something out of nothing.' He placed the cartridge on the floor. 'Anyway, that's the gist of it. I still have to figure out how to put it eloquently. And we'll have to choose a pseudonym for you, to go with the picture of your sculpture. What about 'The Sparrow'? That's a nice play on Skowrońska.'

I took the film from him. It weighed almost nothing. I thought back to Krzysio lying on the hospital bed with his battered body. And Dariusz, who was so badly hurt that we weren't allowed to see him.

My thumb and forefinger gripped the cartridge. 'I don't want a pseudonym,' I said. 'I want you to use my name.'

14

After what happened to my friends, I lost the impetus to work. What good was sculpture at a time like this? Unlike Dominik's writing, it couldn't change the world. For the next couple of weeks, I stopped going to the workshop and skipped many of my classes. It was Małgorzata who pulled me into line. She visited me at the dormitory one afternoon, the small mound of her belly showing under her geometric-print dress. I was still in my nightgown. Małgorzata said, 'You look like you've swallowed a cup of vinegar. Stop moping about – that's not going to do anyone any good.' Sitting next to me on the bed, she told me a story. She said that Ryszard remembered going to the theatre a few years after the war had ended. There'd been a blackout and everyone, including the children, waited in the dark for two hours, without complaint, until the lights came back on. When the play started they all stood up and clapped. The point was, Małgorzata said, that people needed art. 'Maybe you're right,' I had told her. 'Of course I'm right!' she said. 'When have I ever been wrong?'

I returned to the workshop to complete my sculpture. What Małgorzata said was true, but I still wanted to feel that my work was useful in some way, that it wasn't an indulgence. As I glued the remaining feathers onto my sculpture I had an inspiration. Perhaps Małgorzata and I could curate an exhibition of artworks that responded to martial law. A lot of students at the Academy were making this sort of work, why didn't we show it? Małgorzata liked the idea but said we couldn't use her apartment.

'Last time my neighbour complained about the noise. If we keep her little darlings awake again, she might report us.' However, Małgorzata knew of someone who might be able to help.

We went to see the priest at the Church of Three Saints, who was a well-known Solidarność activist. His church was a gothic building made of stone, with ash trees in the garden. There was a single white crucifix by the entrance. Małgorzata and I made our way inside and came upon the priest in a back office. A handful of women in floral house dresses were with him, organising food parcels for people in prison. The priest gave us a crooked-toothed smile and told us that he would host our exhibition, provided we made sure everyone cleared out well before curfew. As we left, he held the door open for us and said, 'If you'd like to collect donations for the church, these would be *most* welcome.'

The exhibition opened in late spring, on a Tuesday afternoon. People filed in quietly, stopping to dip their fingers in holy water and cross themselves, shoulder to shoulder, forehead to chest. Inside, the church smelt of old prayers. Stained-glass windows threw fragments of colour onto the stone floor.

Though Małgorzata had been the one to secure the church as an exhibition space, I took the lead role in curating the show. I had anticipated that the bulk of my time would be spent selecting the artworks for the exhibition. Very quickly, I learned that the key part of my job was to delicately manage the artists' egos and insecurities. I sympathised with them. To be an artist, you needed to let yourself be so vulnerable and porous that you could feel – very acutely – the joy and pain of the world. Yet, at the same time, you had to remain tough in the face of obstacles and criticism. It was a tremendous risk, putting your dreams and fears on display for everyone to judge. I could see how it made people crazy with anxiety. I sensed that, like me, some of the artists felt like frauds.

For my part, I had been so busy orchestrating the show that any insecurities regarding my own sculpture had all but disappeared. My focus was consumed by the need to bring to life a collective vision. It was rewarding – and precisely what I needed at this point in time – to be part of something bigger than myself. I had overcome my fear that art was an indulgence. I understood that this show was important.

Looking around the exhibition, I took immense satisfaction in how it had come together. After clearing the pews, we had stacked wooden crates in the nave of the church. The photographs and smaller sculptures were displayed on top of the crates. The larger sculptures, and the installation piece, were freestanding. The priest hadn't wanted us to remove the holy pictures hanging from the walls. For this reason we positioned the larger paintings on the floor, leaning them against the slate walls.

For the exhibition, Małgorzata had created a series of photographs about the people who were missing from our lives because of martial law. People who had been interned or, as in a couple of cases, had simply disappeared. She had approached their families and asked them to choose an object that represented the person they'd lost. Among the items she'd photographed were a pair of brown shoes, their laces worn at the ends; a mug adorned with a photo of the Pope; and a cushion embroidered with folk-style flowers and trees. Simple, everyday items that any of us could own. *Objects of the Missing* was, in my opinion, her most affecting piece of work.

One of the students from the Academy had created a huge painting on hessian, called *History Repeats*, which displayed a shadowy figure lying face-down on a forest floor. This was a clear reference to the Stalinist massacre in Katyń and the work was more politically charged than aesthetically interesting. However, the artist had been so passionate about our exhibition, and had spoken so clearly about the links between Stalinism and martial law, that I told him we would display his piece. A more interesting painting was *Parts Between Us*. Composed entirely of shades of blue and green, it showed a man sitting on a wicker chair in a room without windows, his head in his hands. The painting made me feel lonely without being able to pinpoint why.

But the work that I kept returning to was a performance piece, *For Those We Mourn*. The artist lay on a bed at the front of the church where the choir would normally sing. She was shrouded in a white sheet, her dark hair spilling out the sides. The artist was going to lie there for the duration of the eight-hour exhibition without eating or going to the toilet, only moving the bare minimum required to breathe. Her performance, so simple, made my throat catch.

Though Krzysio had been released home, Dariusz was still in intensive care. I hadn't seen him since the attack. He was only allowed visits from family, which meant that not even Krzysio was allowed in the room. I wondered how Dariusz was looking, whether he was covered in bruises, or whether the worst damage had been done on the inside.

I walked up three stairs to the apse of the church, where my piece was displayed. The sculpture, set on a crate, towered above me. The circles of metal morphing into feathers, into flight. They were illuminated by light streaming in from the stained-glass windows. Specks of red and yellow danced on the feathers. On a placard next to the sculpture was Dominik's article about State corruption. It contained a photograph of my sculpture without its feathers. Dominik had attributed the sculpture to me, using my full name, Anna Izabela Skowrońska. It was the first time I had seen my name in print. Though I had expected to feel a thrill of recognition, I felt oddly divorced from it, as though my name belonged to someone else.

As I stood back from my sculpture, Dominik climbed the stairs to join me. He circled his arm around my waist as he examined my piece.

'You were right,' he said. 'It's better with the feathers. When you told me what you were going to do, I couldn't

154

picture it. I don't have the imagination you do. You've made something strange and fantastic. Something that makes me feel lighter when I look at it.' He drew me in for a kiss before quickly pulling away, mindful that the priest was standing not far from us, his hands smoothing the skirt of his black cassock.

Dominik's praise elevated me. Arm-in-arm, we made our way to the nave of the church and lined up to see Małgorzata's work. In front of us, a man in a tweed suit was looking at a photo of an empty vase. As Dominik and I contemplated an image of a dressing gown hanging on a door, I asked, 'What object would you choose for me? If I was gone?'

He squeezed my hand. 'Nothing's going to happen to you.'

'But if it did?'

'This,' he said, stroking the woollen neck of my jumper. 'Who else would knit a jumper from hundreds of different offcuts of wool?' We moved on to examine another photo and then he asked, 'What would you pick for me?'

'Probably your typewriter.'

'Not these?' He retrieved a pack of cigarettes from the pocket of his sheepskin jacket, slipped one in his mouth and affected a crinkled forehead.

I grabbed the cigarette and put it back in the pack. 'Definitely not those.'

'Actually I was wrong,' Dominik said. 'I don't think I'd pick your jumper after all. I think I might pick this.' He pulled out a small box, which he opened to reveal a ring. There was a quiver in his lips and he gave his head a quick shake. He bent down on one knee. 'Ania, I love you. I can't imagine who I would be without you. Sometimes I feel like I only exist because you're around. You're my life. You're so much better than me, my darling. In spite of that, will you marry me?'

Though we'd talked about marriage for some time, I always thought it was half in jest. I wasn't expecting Dominik to actually propose – not yet, anyway. I looked around the church, reminding myself that all this was real. Before I came to Wrocław I'd never even attended an art exhibition and now I had *curated* one. Before this, my one clumsy attempt at lovemaking involved hurting a man before he could hurt me.

I was no longer afraid. I had fallen in love with a man who was talented and funny and charismatic and – incredibly – he wanted to marry me.

Through my tears I nodded, *yes, yes*, and pulled Dominik up from the ground. He laughed with relief and wiped his eyes. Then he slipped the ring on my finger. I held out my hand to a nearby candle to better see it. Set with a pink ruby and raised on a filigree of gold, it was a beautiful old-fashioned design. As I examined it, the band started to slip off, too large for my finger.

'Don't worry, we can fix it.' Dominik slid the ring back in place. 'We'll do everything, my love. We'll go to Paris and you'll show your art. We'll go everywhere you want.'

'How about Fabryczna?' I said with a laugh.

'What?' Dominik said with a bemused smile. He wasn't there with us on that trip. The thought of Krzysio and Dariusz sobered me, but then a wave of joy took over.

Father would be happy for me. He didn't have to worry about me anymore because Dominik and I were family. The ring on my finger would tell everyone that. It would tell everyone that this was love, this was love, this was love.

15

Krzysio's mother opened their apartment door. Her mulberry lipstick was oddly dark against her pale skin. 'It's so good to see you,' she said. 'So good.' She blinked fast and then turned away from us. 'Sorry.' She shook her head. Dominik stepped over to hug her and she pressed her face to him for a long time. Małgorzata and I hugged her next.

Krzysio was in bed, his pyjama-clad legs stretched on the covers. As we walked in, he turned down the romantic strains of the violin that was playing from the tape-deck. 'Chopin's *Nocturne Number Two*,' he said. 'See, I have learned something from Dariusz.' He gave a short laugh and then winced, testing his face with his fingers. The bruises were faded now, yellow-grey shadows on his cheeks. The bandage on his forehead had been removed, revealing a deep gash.

I perched on the bed and lightly grazed my lips against Krzysio's cheek. 'We brought you these.' I gave him a jar of Father's honey and a copy of *Biały i Czerwony*, with Dominik's latest article in it.

As I passed him the newspaper he grabbed my hand. 'You did it,' he said, running his thumb along the ring.

'I told you I'd marry her.' Dominik was sitting on the floor, tapping a pen against his shoe.

'And rightly so,' Małgorzata said. 'You're a better man when Ania's around.' As she and Dominik looked at each other, something passed between them.

Dominik reached over and cupped my ankle. 'Now, we have to hurry up and do it before you change your mind.'

I twisted the ring on my finger, letting myself enjoy the feeling that I belonged in Dominik's life. I held out my hand to Krzysio so he could look at it once more.

'What's that?' He peered at the line in the band.

'I cut it,' I said. 'To make it fit.'

I'd returned to the workshop owned by Jankowski's friend and, with his help, sliced through the ring and then soldered it back together. Though I'd filed the ring, there was a very faint line where it had been cut. Perhaps a jeweller would have done a better job but Dominik and I were saving money for our new life. Father was going to help us, he said. When I had called him at the post office to give him the news, he said, 'If this makes you happy *słoneczko*, then it makes me happy too. You're all grown up now and it's time to let you go.' Though I'd wanted his congratulations, a sense of unease came over me. 'You don't have to let me go just yet,' I said.

Standing up, Małgorzata swayed from side to side, rocking the baby inside her. She was as slim as ever but her stomach protruded; it looked the size of two fists. Turning to Krzysio, she said, 'Your mother tells me you haven't left the house in days.'

'So?' He bunched up some sheet in his hand and then smoothed it out. 'What's your point?'

'Just that ...' Małgorzata stopped swaying. 'Just that the longer you stay in here, the harder it's going to be. Don't you want to see Dariusz?'

'They won't let me,' he said. 'I'm not family.'

'Well if those are the rules I guess there's nothing we can do.' She gave him a pointed look.

'Dariusz needs you,' I said to Krzysio. 'And Małgorzata can arrange this. She has a way of getting what she wants.'

He smiled ruefully and then shook his head. 'It's asking for trouble.'

'You won't be alone,' Dominik said. 'We'll come.'

Krzysio closed his eyes. Then he got up and padded his way over to the tape deck and unplugged it from the wall. 'He'll be missing his music.'

The hallway of the hospital smelt of antiseptic and cigarette smoke. A couple of nurses strode by, their heels rapping the concrete floor as they chatted about a television program that Father and I used to watch, *All the Sundays*. They stopped to briefly examine a man who was lying on a wheeled bed in the narrow hall. His eyelids fluttered, and he clasped his stomach and groaned. 'The doctor will see you tomorrow,' said one of the nurses, giving him a pat on the shoulder.

'Intensive care is at the far end of the building, to the left.' Małgorzata joined the rest of us in the hallway. She led the way. A passing doctor directed a kindly smile at her belly. When we reached intensive care, Małgorzata strode up to reception, announcing that Krzysio was Dariusz's cousin and had travelled a long way to see him. She drummed her fingernails on the counter. 'We'll wait here while he goes in.'

The nurse, a middle-aged woman with doughy cheeks, shook her head. 'Room twenty-three? His parents didn't say anything about a cousin.' She opened the drawer of a nearby filing cabinet, retrieved a manila folder and inspected the contents. 'Nothing,' she said. 'Nothing in here about family, other than the parents.' The filing cabinet clattered as she pushed the drawer shut. 'Please move away from the desk,' she said to Małgorzata. 'You're holding up the queue.'

Małgorzata surveyed the room. It was empty except for the four of us and the nurse. Reaching to her throat, she undid the clasp of her necklace. She dangled the gold chain before depositing it on the counter. 'Dariusz's cousin would like to see him now.'

The nurse glanced behind her and with one swift motion swept the necklace into her palm.

159

'Which room was it, Pani?' Małgorzata asked.

'I've only just started my shift. I'll make sure he's ready for visitors.' The nurse bustled off.

We waited quietly in the room, exchanging glances but not saying anything. Krzysio put down the tape deck and tucked his shirt into his pants. Then, looking at his reflection in the glass door, he arranged some hair over the gash on his forehead. He picked up the tape deck and swung it back and forth in his fist.

The nurse reappeared. She licked her lips and then said, 'Państwo, there's been a misunderstanding. Unfortunately we don't have him. As I told you, I just started my shift. I wasn't aware.'

'He's been discharged!' Krzysio said. He hugged the tape deck to his chest and I kissed him, stress unravelling in my stomach. Thank God.

A grin spread on Dominik's face and he grabbed Krzysio and pulled him into a hug. 'I told you he'd be okay,' Dominik said. Krzysio was shaking his head with relief.

'That's wonderful,' I said.

Everyone started talking at the same time. 'In that case we can go see him at home.' 'A gift. We'll get him a gift.' 'Didn't I tell you?'

'No.' The nurse had to raise her voice. 'The patient wasn't discharged. He died. There was internal bleeding around the heart, poor boy. I just started my shift.'

Krzysio inhaled sharply and slumped towards the counter. The tape deck dropped to the floor. Dominik swooped in to support him. 'It's okay, it's okay.'

There was a plunging sensation in my chest. The hospital floor was treacherous under my feet.

'This is confidential information.' The nurse's eyes darted between us. 'I'm only telling you because you're family.'

16

Every time I saw a militiaman on the street, my ribs squeezed against my chest, forcing the air out of my body. Blood rushed to my temples and I wanted to shout at them, punish them for what they'd done. My anger and my impotence left me short of breath. I wished Dominik was here. He and Krzysio had gone to the country for Dariusz's funeral. They would be away for four days. Upon Krzysio's insistence, I had stayed put in Wrocław. He said that Dariusz never told his family how things were between them so his attendance at the funeral had to be low key. As far as Dariusz's family was concerned, he was there as a friend.

With Dominik gone, I had no reason to leave the dormitory. I stayed in bed, falling in and out of consciousness. I kept seeing the boy from my school who walked to the middle of a frozen lake and then fell in and drowned. Instead of a school satchel, he was carrying a violin.

My roommate Basia was bent over my bed, shaking me. 'You've got a phone call.'

In the dormitory hall, I picked up the telephone receiver. 'I'm listening.'

'Aniusieńka.'

As soon as I heard Father's voice I started to cry, tears sifting through my eyelashes and wetting my cheeks. I wiped them away.

'What is it, *słoneczko*?' he said.

I thought of telling him about Dariusz but didn't trust myself to do so without breaking down completely. I needed to tell him in person, not when there was a censor listening to our call. 'I miss you,' I said. 'I can't wait to come home.'

He clicked his tongue. 'Stay where you are. You need to concentrate on your studies.'

'What? I need to see you. It's been too long.'

'Now isn't a good time.'

At that moment we were interrupted, *This call is being monitored. This call is being monitored.* When the message stopped, I said, 'Do you have a girlfriend? Because I'm happy for you to have someone … Pani Wedel has a lot of good qualities.'

Father laughed straight from his chest. 'Pani Wedel? The stories you come up with, Ania.' He coughed and said, 'I'm busy right now.'

'Doing what?'

He sighed and said, 'The doctor wants me to attend these stupid appointments. It's nothing.'

A cold feeling crawled over my scalp. 'I'll get on the next –'

'You'll do no such thing. Dear Lord, what a drama. You know why this is? We have a new lady doctor in the village and she's so eager to show off her learning that she invents illnesses where there are none.'

'What does she say is wrong with you?'

The recorded message interrupted us once more and when it was finished, Father said, 'Nothing, nothing's wrong. Tell me about that exhibition of yours, that's why I called. Tell me everything. Quickly, before the clerk snatches the phone off me.'

I told him about the exhibition at the Church of Three Saints and then said I would come home at the end of term, which was only a few weeks away.

'I can't find them anywhere,' Małgorzata said.

Dominik and I helped her rummage through the mess of papers on the kitchen table, looking for the documents. The restrictions on travel had been eased and she and

Ryszard had been granted visas to go to Paris for three months. If they didn't return within that time, their Polish passports would be cancelled.

Małgorzata upended her handbag on the table, spilling out a notebook, a couple of rolls of film and some scraps of tobacco. Dominik scraped the tobacco into his palm, adding his own to make a cigarette. He offered it around. 'One puff,' Małgorzata said. 'I'm past the danger zone.' She drew on the cigarette and then quickly returned it to Dominik as Ryszard appeared in the kitchen. 'The travel documents are gone.' Małgorzata wove the remaining smoke from her mouth.

'I told you I had them. They're right here.' Ryszard reached into the inner pocket of his jacket.

'Oh. I thought they were missing.' She gazed around the kitchen and then picked up a photography book from the table. 'I don't have room for this.'

'We'll get new things,' he said.

They were each taking two bags of belongings to Paris. Any more would arouse suspicion. For the same reason, they had left things in the apartment much as they were. 'Besides,' Małgorzata had said to me, 'it might be a holiday after all. You never know.' The rent was paid on the apartment for the duration of their travel visa. Dominik and I would live there while they were gone.

'I forgot to show you something.' Małgorzata dragged me to the bathroom and wriggled the taps, directing the shower-hose into the bath. 'There's a trick to it. Otherwise you end up with scalding water.'

'I know,' I said. 'Dominik and I stayed here once.'

'That's right.' She lowered herself to the edge of the bathtub.

I sat beside her. 'Remember the Christmas we all had together?'

'I remember.' She put her arm around me, then withdrew it to check her watch. 'Krzysio's not coming.'

I didn't think he would. Dominik said that their attendance at the funeral had been a disaster. Dariusz's father had approached them and accused them of leading his son astray. He said that they were a bad influence, that what happened was their fault. Apparently Krzysio had tried to pull Dominik away, saying they shouldn't have come. In the end, they sat in the back pew and hurried out before the service had ended. Since returning to Wrocław, Krzysio hadn't left the apartment. His studies were put on hold.

Małgorzata rested her head on my shoulder. I stroked her hair before she pushed herself up and said, 'I'll show you where we keep our sheets. Although, I guess they're yours now.'

She was digging in the hallway cupboard when Ryszard approached. 'We're going to be late.'

A silence descended as Małgorzata and Ryszard pulled on their coats and collected their bags. They didn't want us to see them off. The best thing to do was to get on the train as casually as possible: they were simply going on a holiday, like their travel documents said.

'Right.' Małgorzata scanned the living room. 'I guess that's everything.'

I hugged her, the hard mound of her belly pressing into mine.

With her mouth close to my ear, she said, 'You and Dominik could come, you know. Ryszard could arrange it.' She pulled away to look at me.

I gave her a smile.

She nodded. I had already told her that I would never leave Poland for good.

There were promises to write, and more kisses, until Ryszard took Małgorzata by the shoulder and gently pulled her away. 'You don't want us to miss the train.'

She shook her head quickly. They walked out of the apartment and I closed the door.

The apartment normally had a chaotic appearance, littered with books and photos and ashtrays, but Małgorzata had cleaned it for us. The order was disturbed only by a crate-like structure in one corner of the living room, off-cuts of wood piled by its side.

'What's that?' I asked.

'Oh that,' said Dominik. 'It's the cot.'

I remembered that he and Ryszard had started making it on the day that Małgorzata had announced her pregnancy. While the rest of us sat in the kitchen and talked, they had retreated to the living room and banged away with much swearing and carrying on. Looking at the cot, I thought that I could have done a better job. The planks of wood were sawed unevenly, their edges unfinished. I felt inside and something jabbed my palm. I withdrew my hand. It had been pricked by the sharp-end of a nail.

'You really thought a baby could sleep in this?' I asked Dominik.

'No.' He settled onto the sofa and put his feet on the coffee table. 'As it turns out, I was right.'

17

Małgorzata's apartment, which used to be an eruption of activity, was now a mausoleum. More and more often, Dominik worked at the underground paper until late. I filled my time by drawing and painting. I hadn't worked on another sculpture since *Flight*. After the exhibition, I'd transported my sculpture to the Academy. When Professor Jankowski returned from Paris he told me he was pleased with the piece. He said I should take my time with the next one. Keep exploring new materials, new trains of thought. If he had heard that a picture of my sculpture had appeared with Dominik's article about State corruption, he didn't say anything about it.

Professor Jankowski had told me that the exhibition in Paris was a success. The nettle dress, in particular, had been a hit. 'Your replacement isn't half the sculptor you are and she got herself a fellowship in Barcelona,' the professor said. She would be leaving at the end of term. I pictured her sitting in the sun eating oranges, surrounded by all the Gaudís. I would have loved to have seen them.

I spread a large sheet of paper on the floor and weighed down the corners. Next I wedged open a tin of blue paint and dipped in a brush, thinking of the fantastic creations Gaudí brought to life. Working quickly, I painted two interfacing cliffs with tangles of flowers and weeds sprouting from their tops. Then, using black, I painted a glass house perched between the cliffs. I imagined standing on its glass floor, peering down at the cavernous space beneath.

When Dominik came home my painting was pinned to the living room wall and I was in the kitchen, making *bigos*. 'I was hoping we'd have cabbage tonight and here it is!' Dominik joked.

'Ha.' For the last couple of weeks, we'd eaten cabbage nearly every night – there was still no meat in the shops. 'I wasn't expecting you home for another couple of hours.'

'My editor gave me an early mark.' With a fork, Dominik scooped a bit of *bigos* from the saucepan and tasted it. 'She had some first-years coming in to do the night shift. She wants me to get my sleep, apparently. I've been getting special treatment since that corruption piece.' He forked some more food into his mouth. 'Actually, this *bigos* is delicious.'

Since that article, Dominik had become a talking point at university. By association, so had I. People now called me, 'the girlfriend of the handsome young journalist'. An irritating title that wasn't even correct. I was his fiancée.

'How long until dinner?' Dominik's hand moved down my back, making me lightheaded.

'This can wait.' I turned off the stove.

He led me into the living room. 'Nice painting,' he said, glancing at the wall. Then he kissed my neck. 'I was thinking about you all day. I couldn't wait to get home.' He slid his hands under my dress. 'You see, this is what it will be like when we're married.'

I unbuttoned his shirt. 'We could honeymoon in Paris. Or even somewhere more exotic, like Spain.'

'Spain.' He knelt on the floor and lifted my dress, kissing my stomach. 'I like that.' The rest of his words were muffled by my skin.

A heart thumped steadily against my cheek. We had fallen asleep on the living room floor, among my sketches and painting materials, the side of my face pressed to Dominik's chest. The sound of his heart reminded me of holding a seashell to my ear to listen to its inner roar. When I was young, Father took me to the beach at Sopot.

We ate boiled eggs and pickle sandwiches and he told me that Mother loved to swim but that he didn't know how. We walked hand in hand to the edge of the sea. Salt water lapped at my ankles. I wanted to go further out, but Father said no, 'Stay here with me.' I sat on the wet sand, splashing icy water onto my legs. Father wrote my name in the sand, *Ania*, with a heart around the letters. I turned my face to the sun, daring myself to look straight at it. At the last moment I scrunched my eyes. How could I help Father with the stone carving if I was blind?

The thumping was louder now. It travelled from my eardrums, into my throat. 'Dominik,' I mumbled.

The thumping kept coming and then there was shouting too: 'Open the door! You're under strict orders to open the door immediately.'

Fear iced through my veins. I fumbled on the floor for my dress and pushed my arms into it, hastily doing up a button, then another. 'Dominik.' I shook him. 'Someone's at the door.'

He rolled over. 'Tell them to go away.' A loud sigh escaped from his mouth and then he sat up. 'Someone's here?'

I turned on the light in the living room while Dominik made his way to the door. He opened it a crack. 'Can I help –'

Two militiamen stormed inside, truncheons in their fists. One of them aimed his weapon at Dominik and said, 'Put your shirt on.' His double chin wobbled as he turned to face the mural pinned to the wall.

'What's this about?' I asked. My dress was too short and I tugged at the hem.

The man smirked at my efforts at modesty. Then he said to Dominik, 'Pan Duwak, get dressed. You're going on a holiday.'

'I didn't ask for one.' Dominik ran a hand through his hair.

This seemed to throw the man. He regained himself by kicking a tin of paint. 'Well you're getting one anyway.'

The lid from the tin cracked open and I crouched down to secure it back on.

'Come on, get dressed.' The man was shouting now. 'Don't keep us waiting. You're coming too, Pani Skowrońska.'

I concentrated on practicalities. I had trousers and a shirt in the bathroom and I went there to change in privacy. 'Where are you going?' shouted the other man. He was younger-looking, and his military garb contrasted oddly with his pretty face, his pink lips and delicate nose.

'I'm getting dressed.'

The double chinned one said, 'Follow her. I'll stay here.'

In the bathroom, I shut the door behind me. There was a tightness in my bladder, as though my insides had been wrung like a wet cloth. I located my change of clothes as the door flung open and the nose of a gun pointed in. It was the militiaman with the pretty face. He prodded the bathroom window, as though it posed an escape route.

'We're on the seventh floor,' I reminded him. Hoping I sounded more confident than I felt. I replayed images of Krzysio, lying in the hospital bed. I didn't let myself think of Dariusz.

'You've got one minute.'

Through the closed door, I heard Dominik talking to the other one. 'I can understand you've got a job to do but we're entitled to hear the charges against us.'

'We'll get to that later,' the man said.

The toilet seat was cold against my thighs. I let my bladder go, feeling the warmth trickle from my body into the porcelain bowl. The bathtub was flecked with mould and I had a sudden desire to clean it. I wiped myself with toilet paper and then wound some around my fingers and stuffed it in the pocket of my trousers. A knock on the door. 'Pani, let's go.'

I quickly gathered a few things: my satchel and notebook, a jumper, a coat and boiled eggs. I gave a couple of eggs to Dominik and he slipped them in the pocket of his jacket.

The lift was broken and the men marched us downstairs. Outside, the sky was so black it dragged at the edges of the moon. One of the men shoved Dominik, and then me, into a van, banging my head against the ceiling.

'Watch it!' Dominik said.

There was a woman in the back of the van. Dressed in a beige dressing gown, she leaned her head against the wall. When she saw us she buried her chin in the folds of her gown and looked the other way.

18

All this time I had been living in a dream. Even after what had happened to our friends, I never thought I'd end up in prison. In hindsight my naiveté was astounding. I had, willingly or blindly, placed myself in the way of danger.

And yet, so had all the women in my cell.

There were eight of us here, living and sleeping in a small brick room with a single barred window by the ceiling. I was the new girl. I'd been here for five days, though it felt like months.

On the night they dragged Dominik and me away, the militiamen refused to tell us what we'd done wrong. They kept repeating the same thing: 'We have information that you've been engaging in anti-state activities.' *Anti-state activities.* Did they mean the exhibitions we held? Dominik's article and my photo? Or was it something else? I remembered the night they came to Małgorzata's apartment after martial law had been declared. *Your names are going on a list.* Had they been watching us all along?

Elżbieta, the dentist who slept in the bunk below mine, said that the oldest woman to get interned was eighty-one.

'What did she do?' I asked, trying to picture this revolutionary grandmother.

Elżbieta admonished me. 'You'll soon learn that's a useless question – *why*. It assumes there's some logic to this system. But since you asked, the old woman was talking to her grandson on the telephone, fretting about her sick canary. *The canary stopped singing*, she said. The telephone operator was listening and decided the old woman was speaking code. They pulled her in. Wanted to know who the 'singing canary' was. When she insisted the canary was a bird, they threw her in prison.'

'Is she still here?' The springs of my bunk bed creaked as I shifted.

'They only held her for two days,' said another cellmate. 'Then one of those foreign, what do they call themselves, "international human rights organisations", got word of it and threatened to start a campaign on her behalf. It doesn't look good, locking up an old *babcia*.'

'The important question is, how was the canary when she got home?' another woman asked. Everyone laughed.

Elżbieta said that this was the way of it now: they could lock us up without pressing charges. Half the time they threw people in prison to stop them from possibly doing something wrong in the future. None of us knew what we'd done or how long we would be kept here. 'We get treated better than the criminals at least,' Elżbieta said. 'Take my advice, stick to a routine and wait it out. You'll be okay.'

Although I had nodded, I couldn't let go of the conviction that this was a mistake and that someone, *someone*, had to be able to fix it. Maybe Dominik, who they'd carted off to the men's prison. Maybe a guardian angel or God.

Every time a guard strode past the cell, I waited for him to rush in and say, 'We got it all wrong. We're sorry. You're free to go home.'

The dining room, with its liverish walls and cold concrete floor, was packed for dinner. I sat on a bench at a steel-legged table with three of my cellmates. Across from me, an alpine scene hung on the wall. Next to it was a small wooden crucifix. The women were talking about the next edition of the prison newspaper, *Our Bars*. They wanted to write an article about how terrible the meals were here. If it wasn't for food parcels from relatives and the Red Cross, they said, we wouldn't survive.

I took a spoonful of the dirty liquid that posed as soup, swallowing quickly. It tasted like toilet water but at least it was hot. Sleeping in a cold cell was starting to make me sick. Though it was summer, our cells were impermeable to the warmth. As much as I hated sharing a bed with a stranger (a cleaner from Legnica whose knees and elbows dug into my back at night) at least her bulk helped keep me warm.

As I swallowed more soup, a middle-aged woman in a green housedress strode up to the table, carrying an aluminium cup. 'Pani Skowrońska?'

'That's me.'

She wedged herself onto the end of the bench. 'I was told to look out for a plait,' she said, gesturing to my hair. She placed a piece of paper by my bowl of soup. 'From Dominik. He also arranged for you to get this.' She reached into her pocket and then handed over an orange and purple package. It was milk chocolate flavoured with fruit. I thanked her and made an exit. Was the note really from him?

In my cell, I climbed onto my bunk and unfolded the paper. It was undeniably Dominik's handwriting; I recognised the narrow letters, the way they leaned forwards, each one in a hurry to see what came next.

Aniusieńka.

My darling, I trust you are keeping strong. I'm in Barczewo and who do you suppose is in the cell next to mine? None other than Adam Michnik! I have seen him in passing and am planning on asking him to have a look at an article of mine. Why not pick the brain of one of the finest writers in the country if you have the chance?

There is plenty to keep me busy here. While I allow myself short breaks for meals and twenty minutes of exercise each day, I spend the rest of my time writing. It turns out that I'm very productive when I don't have parties or women – that is, one woman in particular – to distract me. (I'm joking of course, my sparrow.)

People say the women's cells aren't too bad and I hope this is true. Every night and every day I miss you more. This missing is a

physical thing that makes my bones and my throat ache. When I
see you again I'm going to wrap you in my arms and marry you on
the spot. You are my life, little one.

All my love, D.

I had been holding my breath as I was reading and now
that I'd reached the end, I exhaled.

The way to survive this was to follow Dominik's example and keep myself occupied. I took out my notebook
and started a sketch that my cellmate had requested for
the prison newspaper. I drew our crowded cell with its
bunks and small barred window and its squat toilet next
to the sink. And then a girl with a long plait who was sitting on a bed, drawing. My cellmate had said that the
prison newspaper was smuggled outside once a fortnight.
Perhaps it would get to Barczewo.

19

The Colonel's office was stale with the brown smell of cigar smoke. A guard slouched near a bookshelf, blinking hard, as though trying to keep himself awake.

I sat at a desk, readying myself for the interview. My skin gave off an unpleasant odour – I hadn't bathed since Małgorzata's apartment. Adrenaline surged through me. I gripped my hands in my lap.

The guard yawned and then stood to attention as a tall man in military uniform entered the room. I understood, without it being said, that this was the Colonel.

The Colonel didn't lift his feet when he walked, he just slid across the carpet. 'Thank you for waiting.' He towered before me and when I stood up to meet his gaze, he motioned for me to sit. 'What a day.' He settled into his chair. 'All this paperwork ...' He picked up a manila folder from his desk and then tossed it back down. 'Well, it gets in the way of the real job, don't you think?'

I nodded and then stopped myself mid-way: I couldn't get into the habit of agreeing with this man.

He opened the manila folder and peered in it, 'Pani Skowrońska,' he said under his breath. 'Student, artist ...' Then he tutted and said, 'Dissident.' He sighed and looked directly at me. The edges of his eyes were pink and wet, like one of Father's rabbits when it had an infection. I shifted my gaze away but he had already caught me staring. He opened his drawer and retrieved a small glass vial and untwisted the lid. Then he tipped his head back and dropped liquid into his eyes. 'I have a daughter at university.' He sat straight again, blinking. Liquid dribbled down his cheek and he wiped it away. 'Same age as you or thereabouts. I worry about her, as no doubt your father worries about you.'

At the mention of Father, my lips went dry.

He breathed in loudly and then said, 'Of course, I taught her all I could. From a young age, she understood the aims of the People's Republic, understood what we're working towards. Not everyone is privileged to have that type of upbringing. The schools teach what they can but it's not the same as having a strong moral example in the home, wouldn't you agree?'

Don't nod.

There was a shuffling sound at the back of the room. I glanced behind at the guard, who sighed. How many of these interviews had he witnessed? And were they all as one-sided as this?

'A lot of people thought I would be disappointed when my first-born was a daughter,' the Colonel said, 'but I was overjoyed. Such beauty! And women can make a unique contribution to our country, don't you think? Without our wives, our sisters, our daughters, where would we be?' He smiled with pleasure at this little speech. 'Would you like a coffee? I know I would.' He beckoned to the guard. 'Two coffees. Oh, and a couple of biscuits.'

The rich smell was enough to weaken my knees. The last time I'd had coffee was at home with Father.

The guard placed a blue ceramic pot on the table and then sloshed coffee into our glasses. He stood by as the Colonel lifted his steaming glass and took a sip.

'Go on,' the Colonel said, nodding my way. 'It won't kill you.' His lips twitched with amusement.

I took a sip. It unravelled my insides, as though I were sinking into a hot bath.

The Colonel wiped his eyes. 'I'm sorry about your father.'

'Father?' This was the first thing I had said during the interview.

With a look of satisfaction, he said, 'Nasty thing, lung disease. All the worse that he's on his own in that dilapidated cottage in the middle of nowhere. No one to take care of him as he reaches the end. This is precisely the time when he needs his daughter by his side, wouldn't you say?'

My glass clinked as I placed it on the table. 'Father's perfectly healthy.'

The Colonel's interview methods were so transparent they were almost laughable. It was as though he had copied all his questions, all his mannerisms, from a bad film. I had heard that the Colonel was a pompous man, impossible to take seriously, and I looked forward to returning to my cell where I could scoff with the others about his pink eyes, his small fleshy hands.

He sorted through some pages before selecting one. 'Doctor's report.'

It was a letter stamped with the insignia of our local hospital. And there was Father's name, written at the top. My hand shook as I scanned the page and read the words: *Advanced lung disease, prognosis fatal.*

There was a taste of metal in my mouth. I swallowed it back – of course he was lying. 'Father's perfectly healthy,' I said once more. Not daring to stray from the script.

The Colonel flicked his tongue over his lips and smiled. 'You'll want to be getting home, what daughter wouldn't?' He took another paper from the folder and slid it my way. This one had my name written at the top.

I, Anna Izabela Skowrońska, confess to undertaking criminal activities contrary to the interests of my country. I declare that I hereforth renounce all activity detrimental to the State and commit myself to abiding by the legal order. I herein renounce my associations with known or suspected criminals and pledge my loyalty to the Polish People's Republic. I pledge to co-operate with the personnel representing the People's Republic, alerting them to any criminal or suspicious activities undertaken by people of my acquaintance.

A dotted line in the place where I was to sign my name. Elżbieta from my cell had told me about these loyalty documents. She said that only traitors signed them. I handed it back.

The Colonel gestured to the ceramic pot. 'Would you like some more coffee?' With the crook of his index finger he beckoned the guard to come closer. The guard skulked over and filled our glasses with fresh coffee. Then the Colonel nodded to the guard, who lifted my glass and with a sudden flick of his wrist, threw the contents at my face.

I gasped and leapt from the chair, my face doused with hot liquid. A spluttering sound came from my mouth and my eyes dripped with coffee and tears. I wiped my face and blinked. The pain was a throbbing thing that took on a life of its own, so I was nothing more than a body in this brown and airless room. I gasped again, waiting for the sting to pass.

As the shock subsided, anger overtook my fear. I wiped my eyes. The Colonel was a pathetic rabbit of a man. I wouldn't let him see how much he'd hurt me.

'Dear me, what a mess you've made,' the Colonel clucked before picking up a page from the manila folder. 'Take this with you.' He handed me the so-called doctor's report and then reached for his glass of coffee as the guard escorted me out.

As I wobbled away from the Colonel's office, I hid my face from the guard. He deposited me at the cellblock and then left. Elżbieta took in my enflamed face, my tears, and told me to wait. She returned to the cell with a wet handkerchief, which she pressed against my cheek.

'It's a shock, isn't it.' She stroked my hair. 'I take it you didn't sign, did you? That's good. They'll leave you alone now.'

Rocking back and forth, I told her that the Colonel had claimed Father was ill. That he was dying. 'There was a doctor's report.'

Elżbieta gave a sniff. 'Easy to forge. You know what they told me? That my mother was starving, living on the streets. I was mad with worry until I found out she was safe with my sister. This is what I'm saying – you can't believe their lies.' She lifted the handkerchief and said, 'It's looking better already.' She pressed it back in place. 'Call your father. If you don't have anything for the guards I'll give you a loan.'

The handkerchief had started to feel clammy and I peeled it off my skin. 'He'll be so disappointed in me.' I never imagined I'd be in this situation, calling my father to say that I was in *prison*. My fear was that he would blame Dominik.

'If he's half the man you say he is, he'll be proud,' Elżbieta said. 'Anyone who's done the right thing has ended up here.'

'You sound like Dominik,' I told her.

Elżbieta gave a laugh – she'd never met Dominik in person but was familiar with his writing. She tapped a foot against the floor. Her stockings, the colour of moth wings, were bunched around her ankles. She took the handkerchief from me and said, 'I know people. I can arrange for you to send word to Dominik. It will help you keep your spirits up. If you start getting depressed it'll be easier for them to break you. I've seen it happen before.'

Then Elżbieta got up from the bunk and said she had to leave. One of the inmates, a nun from Rawicz, was holding a sermon in the prison courtyard. I was welcome to attend.

After agonising about the phone call to Father for a couple more days, I decided I couldn't avoid it any longer. I approached a guard who was sitting in the dining room, his legs splayed on a plastic chair, a newspaper in his lap. I asked if I could make a call. 'Telephone's out of order.' He lifted his newspaper and turned the page.

'I have this.' I passed him the chocolate bar from Dominik.

He inspected the wrapper. 'Fruit … I prefer plain.' He slipped it into his pocket. 'The other phone might be working.' I followed him to the phone near the kitchen, which was being used by an older woman, smartly dressed in a cream jacket and skirt. When she finished speaking the guard handed me the phone. 'You've got two minutes.'

The guard hulked nearby as I flicked through the telephone book. I ran my finger down the list of names until I found it the details for the village abattoir. I wished there was someone else I could call – Pani Wedel wasn't the sort of person I wanted to reveal my problems to. But Father and I had always lived a cloistered life. Unfortunately, there was no one else.

I dialled. The phone rang once before someone picked it up. 'I'm listening,' announced a crisp woman's voice.

'Pani Wedel?'

'She's busy.'

I cupped my hand around the mouthpiece. 'Please,' I said, 'it's Pani Skowrońska. I need to speak to Pani Wedel.'

'Call back tomorrow. She's in meetings all day.'

'Please.' I clenched the receiver. 'It's a family matter. Very urgent. *Please*.'

A sigh on the other end of the phone. 'Just wait.'

Next to me, the guard tapped his watch. When Pani Wedel picked up the phone, I talked fast, telling her that I'd been interned and needed to get a message to Father.

'Oh Ania.' In the background, I heard her dismiss the other person. 'Your father tried to phone you at university. They said you hadn't been there in weeks.'

'I'm in a tricky situation …'

'Your father's sick,' she said. 'It's his lungs. You need to come home.'

The guard rapped the telephone with his knuckles. 'Wind it up.'

I turned away from him, shielding my face. 'How long has Father … How long has he had this problem?'

'The doctors say it's been years,' she said. 'Though it wasn't detected until last summer.'

Last summer … Had he really kept it to himself all this time? Surely I would have seen that he was ill. I thought back to when we'd spoken about his doctor's appointments. *Just a cold*, he had said.

'Ania, I don't know what what's going on with you, but your father needs you right now.'

I started to ask Pani Wedel what else she knew, but the guard reached over and with his thick fingers, hung up the phone.

21

That night I lay on my bunk listening to the sounds of my cell: the coughing and muttering of women and the creaking of springs on beds. The woman next to me was lying belly-up and her mouth made long gasping sounds, like she was being pulled out of water. I pressed myself against the wall, seeking the cool concrete. What did Elżbieta say, that in here we were fed nothing but lies? Perhaps Pani Wedel was in on it. She wasn't a bad person. She had a soft spot for Father, that was certain. Nonetheless she had a grasping nature, an inclination to want to please people in power. Surely that was how she'd held onto that prestigious job of hers.

If only I'd gone home sooner. The thought of Father being ill made my heart tumble in my chest. *His lungs*, Pani Wedel had said. And there was the doctor's report. *Prognosis fatal.*

When the too-fast beating of my heart steadied to a tolerable pace, I sat up. It was impossible to sleep. I wriggled to the end of the mattress and climbed down from the bunk.

I stood beneath the small, barred window and lit a cigarette. When the embers scorched my lips I threw it to the toilet bowl. Too alert to sleep, I stretched out on the concrete floor and, glad of the discomfort, waited for morning.

This time the Colonel didn't leave me waiting.

I, Anna Izabela Skowrońska, confess to undertaking criminal activities contrary to the interests of my country.

The dotted line awaited my signature.

'It's all very simple,' the Colonel said. 'Your travel papers are in here.' He pushed an envelope my way. 'If you get the afternoon train,' he glanced at the clock on his wall, 'you'll be home well before curfew.'

There was a coffee pot on the table and, instinctively, I held my hand to my face.

I herein renounce my associations with known or suspected criminals and pledge my loyalty to the Polish People's Republic.

It was the tone of Pani Wedel's voice that did it. The urgency when she told me I had to come home. And yet, even now I wondered: was she lying?

The Colonel informed me that my scholarship had been revoked and I'd been expelled from university. I wondered if the same thing had happened to Dominik. A heavy feeling bloomed in my chest. How could I tell him what I'd done?

I pledge to cooperate with the personnel representing the People's Republic, alerting them to any criminal or suspicious activities undertaken by people of my acquaintance.

My name appeared reluctantly on the dotted line. *Anna Izabela.* There was a rush of heat through my body and then I started to shiver. The Colonel, sitting behind his desk, loomed in and out of focus. I dug my fingernails into my palm and then readjusted the pen in my hand. *Skowrońska.*

The Colonel inspected the document. 'Go over it again,' he said. 'The writing's too faint. We need your name nice and clear so it'll show up in the copies.' I gave him a questioning look. 'A copy for each of your files,' he said.

I retraced the letters of my name. It didn't look like my usual handwriting, which was evenly sized and spaced. This writing was crooked and uncertain, like the first carving I had done as a child.

'You've got ten minutes to collect your belongings,' a guard said.

'I don't need anything.' I couldn't face my cellmates. I already had my engagement ring, the note from Dominik and the hospital report about Father. Everything else could be left behind.

As the guard escorted me out, I kept my head down, moving quickly behind him. He led me towards the dining room. It was filling up for breakfast.

'We can go the other way.' I pointed to the nearby hall, where there would be fewer people.

The guard gave me a scornful look. 'No we can't.' He marched me through the dining room, where the enquiring looks of the other women burned my cheeks. Elżbieta was there. She locked eyes with me and, as she realised, a look of disgust came over her face. She shook her head.

I'm sorry, I wanted to say. And also, *You would have done the same.*

22

Our house was bigger than I remembered. In my imagination I could fit it in the palm of my hand and take it with me to Wrocław, to prison. Yet here it was, stoutly holding its place between the field of globeflowers on one side and the dilapidated factory on the other.

The gate creaked open. I walked down the garden path. Father would be in the work shed, chipping away at stone. He would tell me that it wasn't as bad as I'd thought. Pani Wedel had got it wrong or perhaps she had lied.

I looked through the windows of the shed. The lights were off so I guessed that he must be in the house, eating dinner. The front door was unlocked and I pushed it open and called over the sound of the television. 'Father!'

'Ania?' His voice sounded thick in his throat.

He was in his room. When he heaved himself up from the bed I saw that he'd lost more weight. Despite this, the skin on his face had a bloated appearance. There were patches of skin on his skull where there used to be hair. The shock of it dragged at my temples and I thought: he's dying.

I stretched my mouth into a smile. 'It's so good to see you.'

'Aniusieńka.' When Father hugged me I could feel the bones in his back. He gripped me to his chest, his moustache tickling my cheek. I pulled out of the hug and he wiped his eyes and lowered himself to the bed. His breath made a cracking sound.

I fought to steady my voice. 'Tomorrow we'll go to the markets, buy some vegetables. I'll make you soup.'

He took a raspy breath and shook his head. 'Nothing tastes good anymore, *słoneczko*.' He beat his chest with his fist. 'These stupid lungs.' He cast me a sideways glance. 'And before you say it's the cigarettes, it's not. It's my time in the army that did it. The doctor says that's probably where they had the asbestos. Cheap materials and cheap labour to go with it, hey? That's the way of the world, Ania, people are disposable.'

'We'll see the doctor tomorrow,' I said. 'What about a health resort? We could go to the mountains, get some fresh air.'

Father put his hand on my knee. 'They're giving me these treatments. Not that they're doing any good.' He lit a cigarette and blew the smoke towards the ceiling.

I snatched it from him and stubbed it in an ashtray by the bed. 'You're going to be fine.'

Usually Father was up at five to feed the chickens, drink tea and listen to the radio. He said it was the best time of day, that dark hour when no one else was around. By the time I got up, around seven or eight, I would find sliced bread and honey on the table. As the sun brightened the sky, I would eat breakfast and then join Father in the work shed.

For the first time that I could remember, Father was still in bed when I rose. In the daylight I saw that there were plastic bottles of pills on the kitchen windowsill. Each one with his name on it.

It was ten o'clock when he got up. As he shuffled out of his bedroom, he clicked his suspenders onto the waistband of his trousers. I tried to adjust to this new Father, who was hollowed-out and pale. Soup was what he needed. Or maybe I could convince him to go to a doctor in the city, get a second opinion.

He sat at the table and turned on the radio. Classical music swelled into the room. He prodded his glass of tea. 'I've told you about my troubles, now what about yours?'

I inspected the cupboard. 'We're nearly out of margarine. I'll go to the markets today, see what they have.'

Father rubbed his eyes and then, with some difficulty, gulped his tea. I sat down with him and looked out the window at the chickens scratching in the yard.

He said, 'You turn up wearing those old rags. You don't have any luggage ... And those papers on your desk, they look very official.'

'Father! You went through my things.'

He scratched his cheek. 'They gave you my doctor's report so you know everything. Now tell me what happened to you.'

I dug the heels of my hands into my eyes. Without looking at him, I told him about the exhibition, the article, and prison. About the papers I'd signed.

When I finished talking, Father sighed. 'It goes to show what a rotten country we live in, when a good girl like you can get into trouble like that. There's no future here.' He pushed himself up from his chair. Steadying himself by holding onto the wall, he went to the adjoining bedroom. He returned with a small velvet pouch and tossed it my way. I untied the slippery rope around its neck and peered inside, at the chains and rings of gold.

Father said, 'You remember that Wiśniewski boy? He was a year above you at school. He's gone to Canada. His mother was telling me stories about his life over there. Aniusieńka, he lives in a house big enough for three families. He's got a job, money, everything he needs.'

I carved a slice of bread. 'What I need is to stay here and take care of you. And Dominik, when he gets out.'

Father muttered something that I didn't catch.

I dropped the piece of bread on his plate and said, 'I'm getting *married*, remember.'

23

It didn't take me long to understand that news of Father's illness was widespread. Every time I made a trip to the markets, people asked after his health. My response was to say he was doing well. At this, they looked vaguely disappointed and murmured, 'That's good to hear.' In these parts, there was nothing so invigorating as a tragic piece of gossip.

After another gruelling excursion, during which I'd had to ward off the collective pity of the village, I was relieved to be home. Father was in his room, sleeping. He'd had another blood transfusion yesterday and instead of making him feel better, it had left him weak. We'd had an argument after he said that he didn't want to go to the hospital anymore.

I packed away the groceries and then sat down at the kitchen table with the latest copy of *Bialy i Czerwony*, which one of the shop clerks was selling on the sly. As Father snored, I ran my fingers over the headline on the front page; "Economic Crisis Worsens". The pads of my fingers came away black. I lifted them to my nose and inhaled their inky scent.

Inside was an article about protests in Warsaw in which students had been beaten up by the Zomo riot police. I couldn't read it – it was too distressing. I quickly turned the page, where a headline caught my eye: "Notes from Prison". My heart quickened as I read the by-line: "Written by Dominik Duwak". Not only had he smuggled his article out of prison but he had, once again, published under his real name. His boldness shocked me. But maybe this was the very thing that would protect him. I had heard that foreigners kept an eye on people like Dominik. *Political prisoners*, they called them. Perhaps the safest place for Dominik was the spotlight.

Dominik's article was two pages long; he would have been pleased with the space dedicated to it. He wrote about the dismal conditions in prison, "Our two meals a day, of thin soup and hard bread, are supplemented by the black-market trade in cigarettes and homemade vodka." He went on to write about the people who were in prison with him:

> Among these 'criminals', you will find honest work-
> ing men who have been betrayed by the very sys-
> tem that is supposed to support them, together with
> some of the brightest minds in the country. For each
> of us here, it is an honour to be interned, for our con-
> dition signals to the world that we stand on the side
> of truth. We refuse to compromise our values, just
> as we refuse to be silenced. With the whole world
> watching us, with justice on our side, the spring *will*
> be ours.

Reading the article was like hearing Dominik's voice again. Not the private voice he used with me, but the one he shared with other people. Going slowly, so that the pleasure would last, I finished the page and then turned to the next:

> Some people are easily broken. I have seen men
> inside – good men – betray their fellow Poles by
> signing a dirty piece of paper to get out. What does
> this paper demand? It demands that they swear total
> allegiance to the State and renounce everything they
> stand for, everything that gives them dignity. I have
> seen this weakness surface in men I considered my
> friends. I have, tragically, seen this weakness surface
> in a woman I considered my wife.

The inside of my body went still. It was as though all my organs and muscles stopped working. When they started again, it was at twice the pace.

They think they are gaining freedom but the prison that encloses them in the outside world is far more insidious than the one in here. Give me steel bars over invisible ones any day.

Blood rushed through me. The back of my eyes pulsed. *How could he?* How could Dominik write such a thing? Especially when he knew nothing about it. There were ways to get messages out of prison and if he'd bothered to contact me, I could have told him about Father's illness. I had to be here. The pounding in my head escalated as I snatched the newspaper and stuffed it into the gut of the stove. With the stroke of a match, I set it alight. The fire ate Dominik's words. The edges of the paper blackened and turn to soot.

I concentrated on making Father better. Trying to tempt him with chicken soup and his favourite cake, *sernik*. He barely ate a thing. I couldn't eat either. The shame of Dominik's article sat heavy inside me. Who else had read it? There was no doubt Krzysio would have – he kept up with all the news in the underground press. After what happened to Dariusz, he would despise me. Had he told Małgorzata in Paris? What about everyone else at university, did they know? I was a leper now. No one would ever trust me again. And they were right not to. The only reason I'd been released from prison was because I had agreed, at least on paper, to cooperate with the State. Who knew when they would come to collect their dues.

The sight of Father shuffling out of his room returned me to the present. I *had* to be here. 'How are you feeling?' I asked.

'I want to show you something in the work shed.'

As we walked out, I steadied him by the crook of his arm. His breath was wheezy and light. I opened the door to the shed and gestured for him to go in. 'After you,' he insisted.

Inside, Father touched the faces of the headstones as if blessing them. 'There's four left,' he said. 'One for your old *tatuś*. The rest you can sell.'

'Stop it. You're being dramatic.'

I helped Father settle on a stool at the workbench. His limbs were insubstantial, as though they belonged to a doll. I bit my lips.

He prodded a chisel on the bench and then rolled it back and forth under his palm. He said, 'Have you thought about going to Canada? Or what about America? That Reagan's doing good things, I hear.'

'I'm not going anywhere.' I snatched the chisel and wriggled it into place in a canvas pouch.

'I won't have you stuck in this village carving headstones,' he said. 'You have to go to a real country. A rich country where people will buy your art.'

'Why don't we go outside? Enjoy the sun.' I couldn't stand being in the work shed now that Father was too weak to carve.

We walked to the garden and sat down on a wooden bench. Next to us, a couple of pigeons scratched on the roof of the rabbit hutch. The afternoon was filled with the discord of their cooing and the sweet rot of their droppings.

Father raised his face to the afternoon light. 'The rabbits should fetch a good price. For the meat and skin. And then there's the chickens,' he counted the items on his fingers, 'and the jewellery. You should go somewhere warm. Write and tell me all about it.'

The smell of wet lindens hung in the air and the sky was alight with violet. 'Look,' I said, gesturing around us. 'Isn't it a nice evening?' Father didn't answer. Though I tried to find a light topic of conversation that would engage him, I couldn't stop thinking about Dominik's article. I didn't want the article to ruin my time with Father. But if I couldn't talk to Father, who could I talk to? Keeping my gaze on the rabbit hutch, I told him what Dominik had done.

He picked up a feather from the bench, scraped off the muck from its quill and then stroked its down. 'You know,' he said, 'the day we brought you home from hospital you screamed until you turned purple, shaking your fists like an angry little elf, making us laugh. I didn't want a child, that was your mother's idea. But as soon as I saw you I knew the world had turned on its head because you were alive and for this shortest of time, you were mine. Your mother was always beautiful you know, so that made sense. But you came from me, too. Even though you came from an old fool like me, you were perfect. You still are, *słoneczko*. Nothing can change that.'

24

Father lay on his bed, his arms by his sides. I reached out and stroked his cheek. His skin was cool and soft and smelt of lavender and birch. A woman had come to clean him yesterday, after he died. She bathed his body in scented water and dressed him in his best church clothes, a stiff-collared shirt and black pants. He didn't look right. After she left I changed his shirt for the old one he wore when carving. I tucked its loose folds into his belt, straightened the cuffs on his wrists. 'There,' I said, 'you look nice.' A light kiss on his brow. The black cloth, which I'd draped over the mirror in his room, had started to slip. I got up and rearranged it, taking care not to meet my reflection.

Pani Wedel was helping with what she called 'the arrangements'. She was in the kitchen now, serving cake to the other ladies from the village. People I hadn't spoken to in years suddenly appeared at the cottage. They knelt by Father's bed and wailed.

I wanted us to be left alone, the way we always had been. I was tempted to tell them to leave. But his voice echoed in my head, *Be kind,* słoneczko. So I let them stay. The village women kept the candles lit day and night, and Father's room smelt of melting wax, like a church. I picked up his hand and kissed his fingers before resting them once more on the bed. There was a presence in the room, as intangible and real as the crackling of electricity. It buzzed around my head and heart.

Yesterday, while the village women were genuflecting by Father's side, I carved his name on a headstone.

Following the inscription he'd left, I wrote, *Here lies Henryk Skowroński, Husband, Father, Stonemason.* It was a paltry way to sum up his life, so I added, *He is loved and missed to this day.*

Pani Wedel crept into the room, a plate and dishcloth in hand. 'Why don't you get some fresh air? I'll keep watch,' she said. I shook my head but she prodded me with a manicured hand. 'It will do you good.'

The work shed was lonely without Father but at least it gave me a break from the mourners. I touched the head-stones and then caught sight of something behind them. It was the triskele I had carved in the forest all that time ago, before I left for university. It was supposed to keep Father safe. The wood made a clunking sound as I threw it against the wall.

The funeral was 'well attended', Pani Wedel kept saying. Her hair was permed for the occasion. At the cemetery she gripped my elbow, accepting people's condolences on my behalf. She kept whispering, 'Look how much people cared about your father. He was a good man.' If I'd been able to speak I would have said, 'He was better than any-one else and the tragedy is that he never knew it.'

Even though the funeral had only been yesterday, I couldn't fit it together in my mind. I remembered it in pieces that were as hard and sharp as a broken mirror. I remembered the mourners dabbing their eyes while I watched. I remembered how the post office clerk had removed his hat and then, noting he was the only one, slipped it back on. I remembered the way the priest kept tugging at his earlobe throughout the sermon.

Afterwards, people crammed into our cottage. They bustled about, singing mourning songs and drinking Father's honey wine. I left them in the kitchen and went to Father's room and sat on his bed. *Come back, come back.* But the electric charge in the room, or whatever it was that I'd felt, was gone.

25

For the first couple of weeks after the funeral, the village women came over to cook, bringing their husbands to take care of the outside jobs, the patching of the roof and the weeding of the garden. Then they stopped coming. Though this was the moment I'd been waiting for, being alone did me no good. Without other people I was as insubstantial as a leaf. My hands shook when I tried to perform the simplest task like making a cup of tea. I couldn't sleep at night because my bones were too hot. There was something molten inside me.

When Pani Wedel came to visit, I was relieved. She made us *obiad*. 'Do you want to change out of your nightgown before we eat?' she asked.

I took a section of the cotton fabric between my fingers, unsure of how long I'd been wearing it. After dressing in day clothes, I joined Pani Wedel in the kitchen. I tried to swallow some rye bread as she talked about a couple of workers at the abattoir who she said were as lazy as cats. 'All they want to do is gossip and take cigarette breaks,' she said. 'Well, I told them –'

I looked out the window. As soon as she left I would go to Father's work shed and sit with all the things he'd loved and touched.

'If you weren't going away, I'd invite you to work for me,' she said. 'But as it is, you won't be with us long.'

'Away?' I wasn't going back to Wrocław. Everyone at university would have heard about Dominik's article. They all knew what signing the loyalty papers meant: that

I had crossed the line from *us* to *them.* That I had sided with the people who killed Dariusz. The bread stuck in my throat and I swallowed some water to wash it down. 'I'm staying here,' I said.

Pani Wedel finished her cake and then retrieved a handkerchief from her bag and patted her mouth. 'Now, Ania. This is no life for a young girl, living among the dead. There's nothing here for you. Don't you want to go abroad?'

'There's Father's business. I'll keep it going.'

'Your father made me promise that I'd help you get out. I know people. I can arrange the papers.'

The back garden, seen through the window, was eerily still. All the animals had been killed for the funeral meal. There was only one chicken left. It circled the garden, flapping its useless wings.

This had all happened so quickly. Perhaps things would have been different if I'd managed to come home sooner, if I'd convinced Father to go to another doctor or to a health resort. 'When did you find out he was sick?' I asked Pani Wedel.

She glanced at the crucifix on the kitchen wall and then said, 'A little while ago.'

'When?'

'I don't know exactly … It was probably around the time of that show you put on in the woods. He made me promise not to tell you. He didn't want you to worry.'

I shook my head. All this time? 'I should have realised.'

Her fingers curled into the palm of her hand, then stretched out. 'That's how it is when we love a person. We don't see them properly.'

Heaviness settled over me. I left her in the kitchen and went to my room, closed the door and leaned against it. Sobs pushed out of my stomach and chest. Shuddering and exhausted, I slid down to the floor.

I woke in bed. With no memory of how I'd got there, I pulled on a jumper, wandered out to the work shed and switched on the lamp. Father's tools were in their pouch.

I picked up the first chisel he'd ever bought me. For all these years, I'd kept its wooden handle polished and its blade free of rust.

Even after what Dominik had done, I wanted him here with me. I wanted him to comfort me.

No. I placed the chisel back on the bench.

Dominik could have got word to me from prison, but didn't. Instead of finding out my side of the story he went to the paper and exposed my shame for all the world to see.

Pani Wedel was right. There was nothing left for me here.

I travelled by train from the village to Warsaw. It was the first time I'd been to the capital. I went for a walk, carting my luggage with me. This city had none of Wrocław's elegance. Here, concrete buildings towered through smog, competing for space in the dirty sky. Stalin's Finger, the ugliest of them all, dominated the horizon. I went back inside the station.

As I sat on a steel bench, waiting for the Chopin Express, my eyes watered. If only I could have gone back to Wrocław to see Krzysio one last time. I was too ashamed to face him and, even more than that, it wasn't safe. Though I had no intention of spying on my friends, I was afraid of being tricked or coerced into doing so. As long as I remained in Poland, those papers would continue to have power over me.

This was the worst way to leave the country, with no one left to say goodbye to. No one except Pani Wedel, who had arranged matters for me in exchange for some furniture and other household items. The travel documents were tucked in my coat – forgeries, of course. An uneasy feeling came over me as I wondered how Pani Wedel had procured them. What if this was a trick? What if she had told the militiamen about my plans to escape and they were waiting for me?

Stop.

There was a copy of *Trybuna Ludu* on the bench, and I opened it. I was simply a girl going on a holiday to Austria.

I would be away for one week and then I would return. That was the story.

The seat dug into my backside and I rearranged myself on it. Father's jewellery hung from a long rope around my neck and whenever I moved, the velvet pouch knocked against my chest. I also had złoty in my shoes and one small suitcase packed with essentials. A few changes of clothes, the chisel Father had given me, photos and feathers and letters. A stone from the cemetery where Mother and Father now lay, side by side.

The Chopin Express pulled in with a great huff of steam. Its whistle blasted the ceiling. Around me, people stood with their suitcases, staring resolutely ahead. Militiamen patrolled the station.

A conductor stepped off the train and signalled that we could now board. Some people rushed on but I made myself wait. I refolded the newspaper and then picked up my bag and stepped onto the train, trembling as I placed one foot in front of another. I looked for my seat and my heart ricocheted in my chest when I saw that someone was in it. An older man. Was he here for me?

'Excuse me, Pana.' I held out my ticket. 'I think this is mine?'

He glanced at it and grunted. 'Idiots. They've allocated the same seat twice.' He checked his ticket and then got up and sat in the opposite seat, nodding to the one now empty. 'It seems I was in the wrong one,' he said, looking embarrassed.

I thanked him and swung into my seat, which was by the window. Pani Wedel had given me instructions for my journey: *From Warsaw the Chopin Express will take you to Austria, where you need to get on a bus and go to the police station. Follow the other Poles, they'll be going there too. You tell them at the station that you're claiming political asylum. It's very important that you use those exact words, 'political asylum'. The police will take you to Traiskirchen. This is a camp for people who are refugees.*

Five minutes until departure time. I tried not to think about that word, *refugees*. Two more people sat down in my compartment, nodding politely.

Outside on the platform, a militiaman was inspecting the passports of a young couple and their two children. He shook his head. The father pointed to the train and for a terrible moment I thought he was pointing at me. I moved my head back so I could see them, but they couldn't see me. The mother put a hand over her mouth and pulled the children to her.

Movement. The train let out a fierce bleat and rattled to life. We pulled out of the station, away from the family on the platform, their bags piled around them.

A fist smashed through my dreams. 'Passport control,' someone yelled. Alert now, I sat straight as a militiaman charged out of my carriage and banged on the next one. 'Get your papers ready for inspection!'

The old man opposite me snapped open his suitcase and retrieved some documents. I held my visa in my lap, my palms dampening the paper.

The lights on the train switched on, searing my vision as the militiaman returned and stuck his boot in the carriage door. He inspected my papers, flicking through them and then directing his gaze at me. My hands started to tremble and I dug my nails into my knees.

'What's in the bag?' he said.

I opened my suitcase and he prodded it with his rifle before digging through the assortment of treasures.

He picked up a rock and gave me a look of suspicion and scorn. 'Why are you carrying this junk?'

'I'm an artist.' I hadn't known I was going to say that, but the words had come out of my mouth. *I am an artist.*

'No wonder.' He turned to the old man opposite me. 'Next.'

The old man displayed the contents of his suitcase: some neatly folded clothes and a peach.

A young woman in our carriage had her hands stuffed in the pockets of her black jacket. She took them out when the militiaman demanded her papers. 'The bag,' he said. 'What's in it?'

'Clothes. Cheap old things.' She unzipped it to reveal a folded pair of denim jeans. The girl smiled quickly, too eagerly perhaps. The militiaman wrenched the bag from her and upended it, spilling the contents on the floor. When it was empty he ripped out a layer of vinyl. A fake bottom. He tossed it aside and then pulled out wads of American dollars and waved them at her. 'Where do you think you're going with these?' He shoved her with his rifle. 'We've got some questions for you.'

The girl gave us a desperate look. Though I wanted to say something, I remained silent. As did everyone else.

I, Anna Izabela Skowrońska, pledge to cooperate with the People's Republic, alerting them to any criminal or suspicious activities undertaken by people of my acquaintance ...

The militiaman hauled the girl off the carriage and then the train pulled away, its wheels screeching against tracks of steel.

Water

1

Australia, January 1983

Before I arrived in this country I didn't know it was possible to drink air. Even at the peak of summer in Poland, the atmosphere was always thin. Yet when I got off the plane in Brisbane, bleary-eyed and sore-limbed, I didn't so much step onto the tarmac as plunge into it, a wave of humidity forcing me to gulp for breath. No wonder everyone moved slowly here. It was like living underwater.

My Polish clothes were souvenirs from another planet. I wrapped my jumpers and coat in newspapers and sealed them in a plastic bag. A woman who worked at the hostel gave me a white blouse and blue skirt made of the lightest cotton. They had belonged to her daughter, who didn't need them anymore. 'You know young girls,' she said, 'they're always buying new things.'

The staff members at the hostel were friendly and my room was comfortable, if plain. It had a pockmarked wooden floor and two single beds separated by a small table shared by my roommate and me. Despite the Brisbane heat we were given blankets for our beds. Their orange and pink flowers lent a sense of optimism to the room.

This morning, I retrieved my blanket from the floor. I tugged it over the bed and then crept out to the balcony to retrieve my clothes from the washing line, breathing in the river at dawn and the faint smell of rotting fruit that permeated everything here. When I stepped back inside

I dressed in the dark so as not to wake my roommate, Rahel. She was a Hungarian girl who pressed teabags against her eyes each morning to relieve the puffiness, and who undid these efforts at night by crying for her family in her sleep. When I first came to the hostel, I would wake to the sound of her moaning *Anya, Anya* and I thought she was calling my name, until I realised it was Hungarian for *Mother, Mother.*

Rahel had also been in Traiskirchen, though I hadn't met her there. She was granted asylum a few weeks before I arrived at the camp. Despite this, Traiskirchen became part of our shared history. We reminisced about the kitchen lady who gave us extra helpings of white bread rolls and ham, the table tennis Olympics that took place each Friday afternoon and the small living room where everyone gathered to watch reruns of *Ein Echter Wiener Geht Nicht Unter*, a television show about an Austrian family whose problems offered us relief from our own. I got the sense that Rahel also missed Traiskirchen. Most people in the camp prayed to hear their names called over the loudspeaker (*Will such-and-such report to the main office for their interview with immigration*). They all wanted to go to America. However, Rahel told me she'd been in no hurry: Traiskirchen was as good a place to live as any. I knew how she felt. When I was in the camp, I could tell myself that any day now, I could go home.

Exhausted and consumed by grief, I couldn't bring myself to care what happened next. For me the world was divided into Poland and not-Poland. So I applied for visas to all the countries I could think of and waited to see which, if any, would take me. One of the men in the camp, a nightclub owner from Romania, ran a bookmaking system in the single men's quarters. He took bets on all of us. A rumour circulated that I – *the Polish artist*, as they called me – was going to Afghanistan, and he made a profit when it turned out I was going to Australia instead.

A church sponsored my trip here. They said they could get me into a migrant hostel in Brisbane, but if I wanted to move to Sydney or Melbourne I would have to wait. It was all the same to me.

Now that I was living in Australia, I grappled to understand the choices and chance events that had brought me here. A country as far away as the moon.

Rather than listen to Rahel cry in her sleep, I took a walk by the river. As my sandals slapped the concrete I repeated to myself the strange new names I was learning here, so different to the English I was taught at school. *Yungaba*, the name of the immigration hostel where I was staying, an enormous wooden building that gleamed white against the faultless sky. *Jacarandas*, the purple and red flowered trees that shaded the hostel garden. Here, where I was walking, was *Kangaroo Point*. And there, stretching across the river, was *Story Bridge*.

I settled on a bench that overlooked the murky water and slapped insects from my legs as a man and a woman in flimsy shorts jogged past, offering me their smiles. I wondered what Father would make of this place, with its insistent cheer, its abundance of heat and light. It was beautiful, there was no doubt about it. But nothing here was mine. I longed to be back in familiar surroundings, where I could say, *That was the forest where Father and I used to collect mushrooms.* Or, *That was the park where Dominik kissed me, his ink-stained fingers linked with mine.*

The space in my chest got smaller. I steadied my breath by focusing on the river, the shimmer of light on the water reminding me of the Odra back home. When I could breathe, I took out my notepad and tried to sketch the scenery around me. The trees that sprang from the sides of the cliffs, setting their roots in rock instead of earth. The horizon of buildings made of steel and glass. My drawings didn't work. There was too large a gap between what I saw in my head and what transpired on the page. I put my pen down, shook out my hand and tried again.

By eight o'clock, steam rose from the ground. The morning heat had arrived. Clutching my notebook of awful sketches, I made my way back to the hostel for breakfast, walking through the elegant garden and into the dining room. This was a high-ceilinged space with open windows that let in the breeze. One of the walls was fitted with a corkboard that displayed notices about apartments and jobs. Above it hung a picture of the Queen of Australia, a pretty young woman who was weighed down with diamonds and a blue sash. Her cool gaze rested on the morning bustle. Around her, people toasted bread, clattered dishes and poured milk onto flakes of wheat.

As I sat down to eat, Rahel joined me at the table. She yawned and then tugged at her blunt fringe. Her eyes, veined with red, betrayed her restless night. Nonetheless she gave me a sardonic smile and said, 'It's cold,' giving an exaggerated shiver. Rahel had decided that she was sick of everyone at the hostel always saying, *It's hot, it's hot* ('Why must they say this? It bores me.'). So now she liked to announce that it was cold, that the food here was delicious, and that she'd had a wonderful night's sleep.

'It is very cold,' I agreed with her.

Though Rahel and I had French in common, we spoke in English the way the people at the hostel wanted us to. 'This is your language now,' they had said. 'You need to get as much practice as you can.' Trusting this was the best way to adjust, I used English most of the day. However, at night I closed my eyes and repeated Polish words. Songs or poems or simply the names of foods: *barszcz*, *zapiekanka*, *kapusta*, *gołąbki*, the rustle of s's and z's taking me on a brisk walk through an autumn forest. I missed the shedding of golden leaves and the dignified branches of the trees.

'Do you think there is real autumn here?' I asked Rahel as I spread butter on my bread.

'They don't have,' Rahel said. She told me she had read that the seasons didn't exist in Australia, not the way they did back home. As she talked, I dipped a teabag in my cup, jiggling it like a marionette before offering it to Rahel for her eyes. She squeezed out the liquid and placed it on a saucer. Then she nudged me with her spoon. 'See this lady?' She tilted her head in the direction of a woman who was sweeping into the dining room.

Bizarrely, the woman was wearing a fur coat. She gripped the hands of the two children by her sides and then, steadying herself against the communal scrutiny, positioned herself at a table next to mine and Rahel's. Although my own clothes were light, I was perspiring – just looking at the fur made me uncomfortable. Everyone waited for the woman to realise her mistake. Instead she brushed down a fur sleeve. 'Go get breakfast,' she said to the children in Polish. They scurried to the counter, returning with various food items and implements for breakfast. She made them straighten and re-straighten the cutlery before they were allowed to eat.

In a low voice Rahel said, 'This lady, she thinks she is an aristocrat ... Or maybe she is sick.' She tapped her head with a forefinger.

'Maybe,' I said.

Maybe the coat was important in ways we couldn't understand. I thought of all the things I'd brought with me to this country, remnants of home. The chisel Father had given me and the stone I'd taken from the cemetery where he and Mother were buried. Though I'd sold the jewellery from Father, I couldn't bring myself to part with Dominik's ring. I wore it on my marriage finger, where he'd placed it. As I twisted the gold band, my skin caught on the break. I held up my hand up to rearrange it.

The woman in the fur coat passed by our table with a glass of water. 'That's a nice ring,' she said in Polish.

'How did Pani know I was Polish?' I asked.

'The cheekbones.' The woman stroked her finger along her own cheeks. She placed the water on the table and then clamped her hand beside it. 'Emerald.' She pointed to the stone on her ring, much larger than the one on mine. Then she asked, 'Is Pani's husband also here?'

'*Nie*,' I told her.

The woman reached for the fur at her throat. She nodded and then picked up her glass and walked away. When she was back at her own table, Rahel looked to me, wanting to know what we had said.

'Nothing,' I told her, reverting to English. Rahel didn't press for details. We had an unspoken pact not pry, not to ask questions about the past. This was probably why she'd never brought up the ring. Even so, I could see that it was ridiculous to keep wearing it.

I pulled it off and dropped it on the table, the gold landing softly on the plastic cloth. Immediately, I missed the weight of it and pushed it onto my middle finger instead.

2

After getting a job in a bar, Rahel moved into a proper
house in a district called West End. We sat on her verandah, which overlooked the city, drinking our beer cold
the way Australians did, and eating the fried *lángos*
she'd prepared. It was late afternoon and the sky was
streaked with veins of red. The air smelt of sunshine
and storms. A small lizard crawled across the ceiling, its
movements staccato-like. Low mumblings came from
underneath the verandah and I thought that Rahel's
roommates must be talking among themselves until
she told me these were the sounds of bush turkeys. The
turkeys were a pest, she said, but apparently the locals
didn't eat them.

I took another bite of my *lángos*, a Hungarian bread
that I hadn't tried before today. I liked its sharp taste of
garlic and its fresh notes of parsley. It left smudges of sour
cream on my fingers and I cleaned them with a pretty
napkin embroidered with green thread. As soon as I did
so, I realised that Rahel must have brought it with her
from Hungary. I wiped the remaining cream on my skirt
instead.

Rahel finished her beer and inspected the label with
its curious string of X's. 'It's too weak,' she said, crin-
kling her nose in distaste. For once she wasn't being
sarcastic.

'Add some vodka,' I said.

Her laugh was like the tumble of church bells and
I felt that familiar tug towards home. Memories of

the exhibition that Małgorzata and I had held at the Church of Three Saints. The night that Dominik proposed.

'Beer with vodka,' Rahel said. 'If you live with me, we will do this.'

Earlier that afternoon, Rahel told me that one of the Chilean men in her house was moving out and I could have his room if I liked. With my small allowance from the government, I could afford it. But I couldn't summon any enthusiasm about moving in. It was the same problem I'd had in Traiskirchen: I couldn't make a new life without burying the one that came before.

Rahel had felt the same way during the month I lived with her at Yungaba. But now she appeared ready to move on. She had a home of sorts and even, she'd confessed over *lángos*, an Australian girlfriend called Carla. As she told me this she narrowed her eyes, waiting for my reaction. When I said I was happy for her, she gave an open-mouthed smile, revealing even teeth that were interrupted by two pointed ones on the upper row. These teeth, together with her black hair and compact frame, made her look like a sleek dark cat.

'You will like Carla,' Rahel said. 'She is artist, like you.'

'Me?' I shook my head. 'Not anymore.' I picked at the label on my beer, scratching the damp paper. 'All this is gone.'

Ever since I was a child, I had made things. I longed to be the way I was before, always learning through my hands. But I didn't have that now. Art had abandoned me in this country. It was like losing the deepest and most private part of myself – the worst type of exile. Without art, I didn't know who I was.

Rahel reached over and rested her palm on my leg. Her skin was very warm. 'You will be artist again. Carla says –' At that moment a large white car roared up the hill towards us and took a sharp turn into the driveway. Rahel pulled back from me. 'Ah, she is arrived.'

With a slam of the door a slim girl got out and pushed her sunglasses on top of her head, nesting them in her spiked hair. She took the verandah steps two at a time. I watched as she kissed Rahel full on the lips, trying to remember how it felt to be kissed like that. And then, trying not to remember.

When they pulled apart, Carla wiped her hand on her singlet and reached out to shake mine. Then she flopped onto a beanbag, setting off the rustle of polystyrene balls. 'So you're a sculptor, hey? Rahel's told me about you.' I strained to decipher her Australian accent, which gave generous emphasis to the vowels and skimped on the consonants. She repositioned herself on the beanbag and said, 'You should come check out our studio.'

'You have a studio?' I asked.

'Kind of. There's a few of us working there, rent's practically nothing. We've got an old warehouse that's going to be demolished to make way for another high-rise. Till then it's ours.'

'See?' Rahel gave me a meaningful look. 'This will be good for you.'

'I don't know …'

There was nothing worse than sitting inert in a studio while other people were absorbed in their work. But then, my attempts to make art on my own had come to nothing. Ever since I'd left Poland my days had lacked purpose and shape. I was unmoored. Perhaps this was what I needed.

My reluctance gave way. 'All right.'

This settled, Rahel and Carla started to talk about a party they'd been to the night before. As they swapped stories about people I didn't know, I drifted away from the conversation, away from the verandah in West End. I slipped to the bathroom and pulled out a folded piece of paper from my pocket. It was a letter that Father had sent me when I first moved to Wrocław. Though I'd memorised it, I took comfort in holding it, in seeing the elegant, evenly spaced letters of his handwriting. My fingertips tracing his words.

My *słoneczko*,

It pleases your old *tatuś* to hear that things are going so well for you in the big city. Here the chickens stopped laying eggs for nearly two weeks. Or so I thought until I discovered a fox was stealing them. I soon put a stop to that. I shot the old devil and sold the fur to the new manager of the brewery. My guess is he'll turn it into a coat for that mistress he keeps in the neighbouring town.

I have filled many jars with honey from our hives. Some of these I traded for a tin of real coffee, which I am saving for you.

Yesterday I found a tree lying dead in your forest. I hacked off its branches and with help from some of the local boys, carried it home. Perhaps you can do something with it when you come back?

This is all I can think of to say. I am afraid my tales from the village must be very boring for you.

With love, Father

P.S. Remember to wear an extra pair of socks on these cold days!

I looked down at my feet, pale against the brown tiled floor. *Oh* Tatuś, *if only you were still here.*

I wiped my eyes and folded the letter. The sound of laughter floated in from the verandah. I unfolded the letter, smoothed the thin paper and read it once more.

3

The studio on Charlotte Street was in a warehouse that, until recently, manufactured men's clothes. Fixed to the pale brick façade was a metal sign that read, *Parantelli's Fine Shirts, Made in Australia*. I ran my finger over the curve of the 'p', the straight line of an 'l', the tactile letters reminding me of the carvings that Father and I used to make.

'This is nice,' Rahel said, surveying the building. 'You will do good work here.'

I gave her a quick smile.

It was cool inside, the heavy bricks shutting out the midday heat. We walked through a narrow corridor to a small room that smelt of damp laundry. I pictured rows of women, their heads bent over, sewing shirts.

Carla was kneeling on the floor next to a canvas filled with yellow dots of paint. She smiled broadly when she saw us. 'It's a work in progress,' she said, getting up. As she twisted the row of studs in her ear, she told us that a range of artists worked in the studio, printmakers and painters and sculptors, and that most of them made art from whatever materials they could find. Cardboard, tin cans, plastic bottles and magazines. The aim was to keep things low cost. 'That's the whole ethos of the place,' she said. 'It's an art cooperative with a non-hierarchical structure.'

Her words made no sense to me. 'What does this mean?'

'Basically,' she said, 'it means everyone gets a say in everything. We're all equal.'

'This is nice idea.' Rahel raised her eyebrows so high they disappeared under her fringe.

'Well, we try,' Carla said. 'That's all you can do, right?' She shepherded us to a small room at the back of the warehouse, empty except for a chair, a bucket, and some stiff sheets of newspaper on the ground. 'This is it,' she said. 'Rain got in the other day. Should air it out.' She climbed onto the chair and wrenched open a small window located by the ceiling.

As I looked up at the window, I got a sense of vertigo, reminded of my cell in prison. I hadn't told Rahel about that. Or the papers. There was a lurching sensation in my stomach.

Carla was talking. 'Anyhow, if you want the space, it's yours. Free of charge.' To my relief she dismissed my protests that I should give her money, saying that the rent, minimal to begin with, was paid for the next month. 'We're stoked to have our first international artist at Charlotte Street.'

'Stoked?' The word tasted strange in my mouth.

'Happy,' Carla said. 'We're happy you're here.' She told me about an exhibition that the artists had planned, *From Nowhere*. 'It plays with the perception that Brisbane's a backwater kind of place.'

Rahel and I looked at each other in confusion.

'You know, that it's a big old country town,' Carla clarified. 'You reckon you can produce something for it?'

Without hesitating I told her, 'Yes.'

'Excellent.' Carla clapped her hands together. The gesture reminded me of someone. I tried to place who, before realising it was Małgorzata. How odd. They looked nothing alike. However, Carla's easy manner, her confidence, reminded me of my friend.

If we were still friends. Małgorzata would certainly have heard about Dominik's article by now. Even so, I was overcome by the desire to reach out to her. She was part of my past, which meant that she was part of me.

216

When the others left, I cleared the sheets of newspapers from the floor, sat down and took out my notebook. I started to write a letter, the Polish words soothing me, taking me home again.

That afternoon I went to the post office. The clerk, a fleshy man with an accent so thick I could barely understand it, licked the backs of the stamps and fixed them to the envelope I'd given him. As he did so, I imagined Małgorzata getting the letter and the look of disgust that would come over her face.

This was a mistake. I waited for the clerk to hand back the letter. Instead, he tossed it on the bench behind him, and said something about 'sorted' and 'love'. I tried to tell him that I had changed my mind but my English came out jumbled with Polish.

He said, 'What's that now?'

Mortified by his look of pity, I grabbed my change from the counter and rushed away.

4

Though I now had my own studio space, I was unable to put it to good use. My hands, which used to be so quick, always working two steps ahead of my mind, seemed to belong to someone else. Instead of working I spent the hours learning about this new country I was in, reading old copies of the local newspaper, which didn't strike me as being any better than *Trybuna Ludu* back home. I wondered whether Pani Wedel was tending to Father's and Mother's graves like she promised.

After a few weeks of sitting uselessly in the studio, I grew depressed. I decided to spend the day at the hostel. While other people busied themselves learning English or looking after their children, I went to the garden. Here was a plant that I liked for its spectacular flowers as well as its wonderful name: *Flame tree.* Its red petals crushed beneath my feet as I spread a blanket on the grass. The smell of marzipan hung in the air. I tried to devise a sculpture for Carla's exhibition but my head became muggy with heat (the days were all too hot here) and I put down my notebook. As soon as I closed my eyes, I fell back into Poland, to the picnic that Dominik and I once took at the Stobrawski forest. It was a spring day and we lay underneath the pine trees, Dominik resting his head on my chest. His breath was hot through the fabric of my shirt. He edged his way down and kissed my knees, tracing the underside of my legs as he told me he loved me, *Kocham cię*, Aniusieńka, *kocham cię*.

'Yoo hoo, Ania!'

With a start, I pushed myself up, rearranging my skirt. One of the hostel workers advanced towards me. As she drew near she waved something above her head. 'Letter arrived for you, chook.' She passed it to me. 'Looks a bit exotic.'

It was a blue envelope fixed with three stamps: two were of an iron-masked figure wielding a sword and one was a sketch of a seaside town. In the top left corner of each stamp was written, *République Française.*

The woman placed her hands on her hips. 'Who's it from?'

'Thank you,' I told her firmly. When she made no sign of leaving, I thanked her again. She marched back to reception, shooing some magpies out of her way.

I checked the back of the envelope. My hands weakened – I hadn't been expecting a reply so soon. I dropped the letter on the blanket, resolving to read it later.

No. The sooner I received the bad news, the sooner I could try to forget it. I wedged a thumbnail under the seal and tore it open.

Dear Ania,

I've thought of you often since I left Poland and was heartened to get your letter. From Australia! I read it to myself three times before reading it aloud to Ryszard and baby Tomasz. What a faraway country you find yourself in. It must be very inspiring for your art. I can only imagine the incredible sculptures you're making.

As it happens I've decided to try my own hand at sculpture. I've sent you clippings about the show I had at the Museum of Modern Art. My agent (I have an agent can you believe it? They're all the rage here in France) says the show will do well in New York. To think it all started as a bit of fun!

Dominik is out of the sanatorium – but what a habit of speech, I keep forgetting I can write what I like! Dominik got out of prison a few months ago. Of course, he was safer in there than he was on the outside as the Americans still visit Barczewo to make sure the prisoners are looked after. Dominik's prison diaries are very popular and he is quite the famous writer now, so the Solidarność movement raised funds for him to move to London. He's living there and is writing articles for *Świat Kultury* and other magazines. I hear he's even been commissioned to do a book.

I wanted to tell you that I'm very sorry about your father. Krzysio told me what happened. He went to your village to see you and discovered a large family living in your house. They didn't know anything about you. He asked around and eventually went to the abattoir. The manager told him that your father died and that you were gone. She wouldn't say where.

Krzysio seems better. I told him he should move to Paris and try to put what happened behind him but he insists on staying put. He is back at university and has joined this Orange Alternative lot who are staging happenings around the city.

There is one last thing I wanted to say and that is, I understand. I know how close you were to your father. Dominik understands this too. He just got carried away, you know what he's like. He writes first and thinks later.

Take care Ania and send me more letters about this strange hot land you have found yourself in. And your art – I want pictures!

With love,
Małgorzata

So Małgorzata knew. She knew about the papers I'd signed and she said she understood. But what did she write next? *Dominik understands this too.* A sharp twist in my chest. Had she spoken to Dominik about me? I remembered the first time I met Małgorzata, the way she and Dominik had exchanged those cosy smiles and jokes. How was it that the three of us lived in different countries and yet the same dynamics played out across oceans?

I sighed. *Enough.* The important thing was that she forgave me. I didn't need to hide any longer.

I went over the letter again, trying to extract as much information as I could. My second reading left me confused. Since when had Małgorzata been a sculptor? I located the clippings she'd included, translating a headline from French: 'Pole Brings Mother Sculptures to Paris'. A quote from Małgorzata: "My work is a reaction against the tradition that says sculptures must be dead monuments to dead men. My sculptures say yes to life. They are moving, breathing things."

Another clipping contained a photo of her standing on a pedestal in a gallery, completely unclothed. One arm hung by her side, her fingers curled next to her thigh in the manner of Michelangelo's *David*. The other arm was bent, elbow jutting out to accommodate an infant who I assumed was her baby, Tomasz. Loosely swaddled, the baby suckled at Małgorzata's breast. The swaddling trailed down her stomach, stopping above her naked pubis. In the photo, an older couple gazed up at her, the man cupping his chin while the woman clutched the strap of her handbag with both fists. From their expressions I found it difficult to decipher whether they were impressed or simply as stunned as I was.

Breastfeeding naked in a gallery ... This was sculpture?

Ever since I'd met Małgorzata, I had accepted her as the real artist. Yet the lines had been clearly divided: she was the photographer, painter, performer and all-round star. Sculpture, on the other hand, was mine. At least it had been. Małgorzata had taken the form and made it her own. She had even, in this short time, made a name for herself in Paris.

I shook out my picnic blanket, anxious to get back to the studio.

5

When midday came, I realised that I'd been gripping my pencil in the manner of an arthritic old woman. I massaged my sore hand. After six hours in the studio, all I had to show for it were a few scribbles, the pencil lines faint on the page. *From Nowhere* was opening in a week and I had nothing to exhibit.

I shifted on the damp concrete floor, wondering if Małgorzata was ever stuck for ideas. Probably not. She was her own source of inspiration. I envied her ability to take the raw material of her life and turn it into art. What would be the reaction if I stood on a pedestal at the Charlotte Street exhibition and took off my clothes? If what Carla said was true, I would probably get arrested. She'd told me about some friends of hers, theatre students, who used nudity in a performance at university. The next day the police – *pigs*, she called them – descended on the campus and arrested not only the students but their professors too. 'We're living in a police state,' Carla had insisted. I nearly laughed. The streets in Brisbane were lined with palm trees, not army tanks.

Even so, a nude performance was out of the question. Not because of the police but simply because I lacked Małgorzata's boldness.

I thought back to the sculptures I'd made in the past, wondering if I could adapt any of them for this exhibition. There wasn't time to make a piece from clay and using blood was impractical for many reasons, not least of all the heat. Then I remembered something: the nettle dress that had caused such a sensation when it was exhibited in Paris at *The Ones to Watch*. It wasn't my sculpture, that was true, but I could be inspired by it, surely. There was no harm in that. All I had to do was take the idea of the nettle dress and make it my own.

That afternoon I walked back to the hostel, where I had an appointment with a man who was going to get me a job. Back home, the only jobs I'd had were carving for Father and tutoring, now and then, for kids in the village. I was nervous about working in this new country, especially after learning what Rahel had gone through. She'd quit her bar job after discovering she was getting paid less than the Australians. Now she worked as a maid in a fancy hotel and had a boss who demanded that she should polish the toilet seats so thoroughly the guests could eat dinner off them. Rahel told him that if people wanted to eat off a toilet seat then the germs were part of the attraction. They would be doing the guests a favour, she said, if they left them intact.

My delight at Rahel's comeback sustained me as I panted uphill, my clothes dampening with sweat. Although I'd done a lot of walking in Wrocław, its flat streets didn't require this type of exertion. The hills of Brisbane, together with its perpetual sun, were changing me. My body was turning brown and my limbs were hardening with muscle.

As I walked past a man who was watering his garden, I caught sight of a tall figure coming towards me, his eyes shaded by round glasses. Dominik! My mouth made a gasping sound and, at the same moment, I realised it wasn't him. The boy glanced at me, smiled, and kept skidding downhill. I turned to watch him go. My elation gave way to shame. Even now, I didn't know how to stop myself from wanting Dominik.

To distract myself, I thought about my sculpture. For this piece I wanted to use a plant that captured my impressions of my new surroundings. The shape and smell of gum leaves were appealing but they would be difficult to weave. My legs strained as I climbed uphill, the palm trees offering scant shade. I stopped to stroke a frond, testing its narrow leaves.

As I continued walking, I collected palm fronds that had fallen to the ground. I turned up to my appointment laden with an armful of them, the leaves camouflaging my body.

The employment man stood up from behind his desk, giving me a smile of amusement and concern. 'What have you got there?'

'This is for art.' I deposited the palms on the floor.

'Is that right?' He tightened the elastic around his grey ponytail. 'Well. It's good to stay busy, isn't it. Now, your case file says you're an artist. I might have a job for you at the new gallery that's opened. Nothing flash, mind. They're looking for a cleaner.' He must have registered the disappointment on my face, because he added, 'You can always work your way up.'

I thought of how Pani Wedel had once offered me a job at the village abattoir and how dismissive I'd been. Working as a cleaner was hardly better but what choice did I have?

'This is okay,' I told him. 'I'll take it.'

With a laugh, he informed me that you didn't *take* a job here, you had to apply for it. I had to prove I was the best person to mop the gallery floor. 'Interviews are next week,' he said. 'Oh, and here's the other one.' He surveyed a sheet of paper. 'This artist, John Papa, is looking for an assistant. He's a sculptor, pretty well known apparently. Only problem is he's not in Brisbane. You'd have to move up north.' He showed me on a map, his blunt nail inching along the ragged coastline.

'Is this a nice place?'

'Never been there myself. I hear it's a bit feral, but. Wouldn't be many of your sort up there, I'd imagine. Still, no harm in having a chat to the bloke. Treat it as a practice run.'

224

He called the number and spoke to the person on the other end before cupping his hand over the receiver. In a loud whisper, he said, 'We're in luck. Now introduce yourself like I said.' He handed me the telephone and as soon as I said hello, a male voice gabbled away, the line crackling from time to time.

'Please speak more slowly,' I said. 'My English ...'

'Sorry, I'm getting ahead of myself. Where are you from, anyway? My last assistant was Yugoslavian. Nice girl but she took off to Sydney and left me in the lurch. I need your help preparing for a show I've got overseas, think you can do that?'

Instead of waiting for an answer he kept talking. Again, I had to ask him to slow down.

'Your materials,' he said, 'what materials do you use in your work?'

The employment man nodded at me encouragingly.

'I use many things,' I said, 'whatever I can find. Trees, metallic. Even blood.' On hearing this, the artist sounded excited and wanted to know more. I told him about my exhibition, *Burning*. I recounted the fires that melted the blood sculptures, the crows that circled overhead and the two blindfolded musicians who played the violins. My chest tightened at the thought of Dariusz.

There was silence. When I thought the phoneline must have cut out, he said, 'When can you get here?'

'First I will decide if to go.' I asked, 'What is this like, where you live?'

'It's wild. Like nothing you've ever seen before.'

Wild ... I didn't know if I wanted that, especially given the employment man's scepticism. As though sensing this, the artist changed his tack and said that up north was paradise, a place where the rainforest cradled the sea. 'Promise me you'll come, Ania.' Unlike other Australians, he pronounced my name the Polish way, his 'a's' as soft as a sigh.

The employment man spoke to the artist once more and then hung up. He gave me two sheets of paper outlining the details of the jobs in Brisbane and in the north. I asked what he thought of the artist.

'Sounds a bit eccentric,' he said. 'That's what they're like up there. If I were you I'd stay put. Take the cleaning job in the gallery. Even Picasso had to start somewhere, right?'

6

I worked in the hostel's dining room when it wasn't being used for meals. The Queen watched over me as I cut palm leaves into strips and arranged them in horizontal rows on a table. It was easier to do this here rather than in the studio, with its damp concrete floor. As I threaded a vertical row of leaves through the strips, I thought of that other sculpture, the nettle dress that had been exhibited at *The Ones to Watch*. To the critical acclaim of Paris, just like Małgorzata's Mother Sculpture.

A sip of water moistened my lips. Lots of artists were inspired by the work of their peers. There was nothing wrong with that. Brushing away dirt from a palm leaf, I kept weaving, creating a grid-like pattern of green and yellow leaves that was wide at the bottom and narrow at the top. Next I created two sections for the sleeves, stitching them to the body of the dress with long fibres of palm. When I was finished I held the dress up. It was a little taller than me, with stumpy sleeves and a slightly misshapen hem. Had the nettle dress looked like this? I couldn't remember. Quickly, not wanting to think about what Professor Jankowski would say, l rolled up my sculpture and stuffed it in a black plastic bag.

On the morning of the opening I caught a bus to the studio, my legs sweating against the plastic bag wedged between my legs. When the bus reached Charlotte Street, I slung the bag over my shoulder and hopped off. As I neared the warehouse my footsteps quickened. A wire fence had been erected around the building and men in hard hats were swarming around it. They were armed with clipboards and walkie-talkies.

I spotted Carla and ran over to her, dropping the plastic bag to the ground.

She was standing on the street-side of the fence, arguing with a man in an orange vest. As he stomped off, I heard him say, 'Bloody hippies.'

'Fuck.' With her fist, she whacked a sign on the fence. *Danger, Do Not Enter.*

'Carla?'

'They're tearing it down.' She hooked her fingers in the wire diamonds of the fence. 'Rent's been paid for the rest of the month but they're kicking us out. Reckon we can go to court if we don't like it.' She turned her attention to a man who was rolling yellow tape around a tree. 'We have to phone everyone. Tell them the show's cancelled.'

I pressed my face to the fence. The warehouse looked to be intact. 'When is it broken?' I asked.

'Most likely tomorrow. Maybe the day after.'

'This is not a big problem.' I told Carla that we would hold the exhibition for one night, before the building was destroyed. We simply had to be careful not to get caught. 'We used to do this in Poland,' I said. 'When the galleries shut down, we made our exhibitions in apartments, church, wherever we could find. One boy I heard of made exhibition in a hole. No, not hole. Under ...' I put one arm in front, horizontally, and buried my other hand beneath.

'A tunnel?' Carla said.

'Yes, an old tunnel. He showed his pictures in it. This here,' I gestured to the building, 'this will be good.'

Carla unhooked her fingers from the fence, regarding me. 'I've never heard you talk about that before. About where you come from.'

Turning my attention to the fence, I said, 'When it gets dark, we must cut so people can enter.' I gave the wire a shake. 'For this we need big scissors.'

'Pliers,' Carla supplied me with the word. 'We need pliers.'

When the workmen left in the late afternoon, we dissected the wire fence, pulling it back to make an opening about half my height. The warehouse electricity had been cut off so we strung Christmas lights from the ceilings and positioned candles along the bottom perimeters of the walls. We worked quickly to set up our pieces. I hung the palm dress in a back room. Carla gave me a battery powered lamp to illuminate the dress. I left it for someone else to switch on.

That night, people entered the exhibition on their hands and knees, crawling through the hole in the fence. They brushed dirt off their skin and laughed as they compared scratches.

'Much more exciting than just walking in through the door,' Carla said drily. She tipped back her drink and then darted over to rescue a kinetic sculpture from a young man with a mohawk who was backing into it, waving his arms as he entertained a couple of girls with a story about his drunken antics.

The evening was warm and Rahel arrived at the exhibition wearing a loose black singlet that could have been one of Carla's, and a short denim skirt that was streaked with bleach. There were red marks on her knees from where she'd crawled through the hole. 'If you told me this I wear trousers,' she said, picking some gravel off her leg.

'You're here.' I hugged her tight. I didn't see much of Rahel now that she was working long hours at the hotel.

'Where is your art?' she wanted to know.

Plastic cups of wine in hand, we made our way through the exhibition. Past a collage of a naked woman that had been put together from magazine clippings of meat. Next to this was Carla's piece, an intricate painting consisting of tiny dots. When I stood close to the canvas, it was ochre. When I took a step back I could see hues of yellow and even blue. The more I looked at it, the more I wanted to *keep* looking at it.

'Your girlfriend is very clever,' I said.

Rahel squeezed my arm. 'I know.'

Then we came to my sculpture. At the last minute I'd threaded a few skeins of red and white wool through the palm leaves. The wool zig-zagged to the floor, ending in three balls that were arranged in a nest made from newspaper. At a loss as to what to call the piece, I'd named it, *Untitled, 1983*.

Rahel stared at it, her arms crossed. Then she straightened up and said, 'It's good.'

I shone a torch on the dress, trailing the light up and down, from one side to the other, regarding it critically, the way Professor Jankowski would have. It was terrible. I could see that even in the dim light. Either Rahel didn't know anything about art or she was playing her old game where cold meant hot and good meant bad. Carla, on the other hand, had said nothing about my piece.

'I must drink,' I said to Rahel. I drained my plastic cup and went to the bar, which we'd constructed from a plank of wood that was elevated with bricks. After tossing some coins into the saucepan, I squirted cask wine into my cup, gulping it down and then pouring another.

The palm dress was a forgery. That's why it had no life in it – it didn't come from me. The whole time I had been making it, I hadn't looked at it. Not *properly* looked at it, with my entire self, the way I would my own work. No wonder I had put it together in the secret of the hostel dining room. I didn't want the other artists asking me any questions.

From where I was standing, I could still see the dress and I switched my attention to the exhibition. The warehouse was filled with people my age who wore torn jackets and jeans and threadbare dresses and laughed loudly as they drank their beer and wine. The whole scene reminded me of Poland.

The thought, which should have brought me comfort, was unsettling.

Ever since I left Poland, I had been chasing the past. The existence I'd fallen into here was nothing but a pale imitation of the life I'd left behind. What was I hoping to do, keep drifting until I found another Dominik? Tag along with Carla, the way I had with Małgorzata? All that was gone.

I swigged my wine. As my vision blurred, things started to make sense. If I wanted to make art again I couldn't stay here.

The next day I returned to Charlotte Street to watch the studio be demolished. The artists had rescued their works from the building. My piece was the only one left behind. I was glad to be spared the humiliation of dragging it out and deciding what to do with it next. Burn it? Stuff it in the bin?

Carla was squatting on the footpath next to the fence, shading her face from the sun. When she saw me she pulled herself up and enveloped me in a damp hug.

'They found the hole,' she said. 'Can't prove it was us but they're pissed off. We're supposed to stay two metres back or they're calling the pigs.'

On the other side of the fence a yellow machine rolled towards the warehouse. Dust rose from the ground, making me sneeze. The machine unfurled its neck and struck a window with steel jaws. The middle of the pane smashed and then the outer edges fell in small pieces, glass tinkling to the ground. The machine swung around and directed its blows at the brick wall.

'We'll find somewhere else,' Carla yelled over the noise. 'There are plenty of empty office blocks around. We'll start again.'

There was an insistent beeping as the machine backed away from the warehouse. When it subsided, I said to Carla, 'I'm leaving Brisbane.'

'Not you too.' She massaged the back of her neck. 'All the creative types are taking off. Where are you headed, Sydney or Melbourne?'

'Not there,' I said. 'I'm going to the north.'

'Up north …' Her eyes widened. 'For real? You know what you're getting into, right? There won't be art exhibitions and stuff. It's extremely isolated.'

I kicked a bit of rock towards the fence. The hole had been mended with wire. Above it was a new sign: *Vandals Will Be Prosecuted.*

I said, 'I liked your painting. You made me look at red and yellow and blue like I was seeing colours for the first time.'

Carla thanked me, saying she'd been nervous about displaying the piece. 'Yours was good too, Ania. It's just … I hope you don't mind me saying this, but it was a bit unfinished. It was missing something.'

Though the criticism hurt, it was a relief to hear it said out loud. 'Yes,' I said. 'I know.'

The yellow machine swung its jaws towards the warehouse and there was a tearing sound as the façade tumbled away. The final sounds of destruction were anticlimactic, as though the building was made of matchsticks rather than bricks.

7

For two days and two nights I sat cramped on a bus, my neck sweating against the velour seat-cover. As we hurtled past small towns and across stretches of umber track, my exhilaration gave way to stiff-boned fatigue. The employment man had warned me that the north was far away but I didn't imagine it was so far as this.

At last the driver announced my destination, pulling up near a tin shack that displayed crates of pineapples. Wedged between a pineapple and a rusty can was a hand-written sign that said *Honesty Box*. Standing on the gravel track, I coughed up fumes from the departing bus. My new leather suitcase by my side, I stared up at the colossal sky. The afternoon was hot and bright and I could smell the sea.

Behind me came the trundling sound of plastic wheels being pulled over dirt. A woman in a yellow pantsuit approached, her luggage in tow. 'Where you headed, darl?'

I showed her my map, the location of my accommodation circled in red. The artist, John Papa, had arranged for me to rent a bungalow on a citrus farm.

'Tom's Oranges,' she said. 'It's not far from here. I'll take you.'

The town centre had one main road. Palm trees grew from garden plots in the middle of the asphalt. The rain-forest loomed behind the town, overshadowing the tin-roofed buildings. There was so little keeping the rainforest at bay. I got the sense that if people vacated this place for a week or two, the plants would soon take over.

As we walked, the woman pointed out the local landmarks: the post office, the grocery store, the school. She showed me the pub: a pale yellow, double storeyed building with hanging-plants adorning its wooden terrace. She stopped to greet a couple of passers-by, towns-people with ruddy complexions and inquiring smiles; who was I, they wanted to know, and where did I come from?

Tom's Oranges was a huge citrus farm that looked onto the rainforest. The farmer and his family lived in the centre of the property, in a wooden house that was elevated on stilts. My bungalow was further back, on the outskirts of the farm. That evening I fell into bed exhausted, expecting instant sleep. Instead I was awake all night, terrified by the shrieking and scrambling and heavy breathing coming from the roof. In the morning I located the farmer and told him that a person, or perhaps a bear, had been trying to get in. He laughed and said, 'That'll be the possums.' He explained that they were a bit like rats, but larger, with long curled tails. When night came again I waited outside the bungalow with a torch until I saw one. It fixed its red eyes at me, hissed, and then scurried away.

Now that I knew the possums couldn't hurt me, I was grateful for their presence. Their awful noises distracted me from the visions I had at night. Father was always there and he was always dying. Sometimes there was Dariusz, or Krzysio lying beaten on the street. And then there was Dominik, telling me over and over that he loved me. I would have given anything to sleep so deeply I couldn't remember my dreams.

My first day of work was a week later, on a Friday. John Papa, who had been in Sydney, was now back. I called him from the payphone near the farm and he gave me directions to his house. 'Number fifty-seven. Big place on the hill,' he said. 'If you get lost, ask someone to point you the way. Everyone knows everyone around here.'

It took me about twenty minutes to walk from the citrus farm to the centre of town. The main street offered islands of shade from the morning sun. Beyond the street, to my left, were the emerald folds of the hills. To my right was the sea, its steady rush, rush accompanying me on the muggy walk. Incredibly, it was hotter here than in Brisbane and the air was wetter, too. As I walked, the itch of my plait against my neck became unbearable and I stopped to pin it around my head. The town centre behind me, I finally reached a ragged plank nailed to a tree. It was painted with the number fifty-seven. I wiped the film of moisture from my cheeks and then panted up the hill, up a set of concrete stairs that were so large and uneven that I didn't dare lift my gaze from my feet.

'Hey!' someone yelled.

When I looked up, I came face to face with a shark. Startled and dizzy from the heat, I nearly tumbled back. An arm reached out to steady me. There was a laugh as a man appeared from behind the shark, which I now saw was not real. Bare chested, the man clutched the shark under a sinewy arm and gave it an affectionate pat on the head.

'You must be the Polish sculptress. I'm John and this is Sisyphus.' He spoke faster than the other Australians I'd encountered, and despite the shark, used more hand gestures.

'Sisyphus. The one who must push the rock?' I asked.

'That's right.' He moved the shark, tucking it under his other arm. 'She keeps me company while I'm engaged in that masochistic pastime we call *making art.*'

'What is this? Mas, masor ...' I struggled to recapture the word.

'Mas-o-chis-tic. It's someone who likes pain. I reckon that's a pretty good definition of an artist, hey?' He chuckled and with his free hand, helped me up the stairs. 'Now that you're here Sisyphus can have a holiday. Isn't that right, Sissy?'

When we reached the top, he tossed the shark to the grass. 'This is where I live.'

Hands on his hips, he stood before an enormous egg-shell coloured building, the grandeur of which had slipped into decay. Cracks shot up the concrete walls and purple flowered vines pushed through them, winding their way around the Romanesque columns at the front.

I stroked the furred leaf of a vine. 'You have a big house.'

'What can I say, I'm Greek.' John caught my look of surprise. 'Second generation that is,' he said. 'When I started making art, twenty-odd years back, no one could pronounce Papageorgiou so I shortened it. I'm half regretting it now that ethnic art's all the rage. You'll do well with your name. Ania Skowrońska, that's got a nice ring to it.'

He held the door open for me. I had overdressed for my first day of work, in dark trousers and a white collared shirt. I was grateful to go inside where fans whirred on the high ceilings, slicing through the heat.

'I'll fetch us some drinks,' John said.

In the kitchen, he shooed a bird off the window sill and then leaned against a wooden bench, his eyes focused on a point behind my head. He was tall and thin, with thick dark hair on his head, and smatterings of curlier hair on his chest and legs. Was he going to put on a shirt? Part of me thought him uncivilised for being so scantily dressed. The other part of me was envious: my own clothes were clammy and claustrophobic and I longed to get back to the bungalow where I could take them off.

John had deep lines on either side of his mouth, like parentheses. He traced these, one at a time, with his index finger. Then he exclaimed to himself and grabbed an envelope from the bench and proceeded to scribble on the back of it. Having done this he seemed to return, fully present, to the room.

Bottles of beer in hand, we walked downstairs to his studio. Standing side by side, we examined a folio of sculpture designs. Sweat dripped from his chest onto a plastic-covered sketch and he wiped it off with his thumb. Something about his sketches bothered me. However, he flicked through them too quickly for me to determine what it was.

'You're a lifesaver,' he said. He turned another page in the folio. 'I don't even want to think about how many sculptures we've got to assemble for my exhibition. *White Water* ... How do you like that as a title? It's showing in London so that's quite a coup.'

The mention of London sent a jolt through my spine. I tried to put aside thoughts of Dominik to concentrate on what John was saying.

He told me that he needed me to make a series of sculptures from clear plastic sheets. Others were to be constructed from wood or glass. 'That should keep you busy,' he said.

'And you? What will you do?' My words came out blunter than intended.

John didn't seem to take offence. He laughed. 'Right now I'm going to feed you, that's what I'm going to do.'

He led me upstairs to a large verandah that overlooked the rainforest. Tree tips pierced through the decaying wooden planks on the floor. We sat at a hardwood table that was marked with water rings and ate the food he'd prepared. There was a fried fish that John said was called barramundi, followed by exotic fruits for dessert: mango and papaya and bananas, their flavours as sweet as their bright skins suggested.

A green coil burned in the mouth of a beer can, its heady smoke drifting my way. I tipped my face back to meet the oncoming breeze. A mobile tinkled; it was made of metal screws and nails, their heads bitten with rust. I thought back to the time that I had worked with metal.

'This reminds me of something I made,' I said, pointing to the mobile. 'A sculpture of car pieces.'

'Oh yeah?' John brought his foot to his chair, bending his leg so that his knee was near his chin. 'Car parts?'

Memories came to me of the exhibition that Małgorzata and I held in church. Before I knew it, I was telling John about my sculpture, *Flight*. I even sketched it on a paper napkin. He asked a lot of questions and so I told him about the discovery of the clutch discs, the closure of the galleries, and the night we gathered in Małgorzata's apartment after learning martial law had been declared. I recounted the smell of hashish in the air, the militiamen with their guns, and the fish floating placidly in the bath. I even told him about the picture I drew, *Portrait of Dominik as a Carp*.

At last I stopped talking and took a breath, startled by this flood of stories. I glanced at John.

He shook his head. 'Amazing.' He pushed back his chair and said, 'I love this idea of making art as a fuck-you to the state. It's different. Just what we need around here.'

I followed his rush of words from the verandah, down to the studio.

'I've got some new ideas,' he said. 'I have to pin them down before they escape.'

Like butterflies, I thought, picturing a collection of ideas in a glass case. Their bodies speared with silver pins.

8

The following day, when I was in the studio alone, I examined John's sculpture designs in more detail. Now it was obvious what the problem was: the drawings gave no consideration to issues such as volume and weight. They simply wouldn't work in three-dimensional form. Professor Jankowski would be disgusted if a student handed in this type of work. Though I felt embarrassed on John's behalf, there was nothing for it but to bring these flaws to his attention.

I went upstairs to find him lying on a hammock on the verandah, scribbling in a notepad. 'This sculpture is not good,' I said, brandishing one of his designs. 'If it is like this it will fall over.'

He looked up at me. 'That one's a draft. It might need a few modifications.' He brought the tip of his pencil to his tongue and then said, 'I reckon you can handle it.'

Down in the studio, I began working on the designs. When I was satisfied with them I re-cut the materials according to my own specifications. As well as making these technical changes, I went on to adapt some of the pieces so they would look more pleasing to the eye, expanding their dimensions or shrinking them. I even altered the colours in subtle and not-so-subtle ways. If John noticed these changes he said nothing about them.

A few weeks later, I completed one of the key pieces for John's exhibition: a pyramid of clear plastic, edged with blue, that would sit in a pool of water on the gallery floor.

When I showed it to him, he examined it from all angles, stretching his arms to test the boundaries of the piece. Then he said, 'Excellent. That's how I imagined it. You have a way of bringing my work to life.'

I bristled at those words, *my work*, but then shook away my possessiveness. I was getting paid to do this. And it was better than being a cleaner in a gallery. 'Good,' I said.

John rested his hand on the tip of the pyramid. 'I've got some exciting news.' He let go of the sculpture. 'You're coming with me to London. The gallery's paying for it. I managed to convince them you're indispensable – and so you are.'

'Oh.'

London was Dominik's city. Everything there would remind me of him. I would be plagued by all those useless memories, all those desires and regrets. It would be unbearable walking down the streets and thinking of nothing but Dominik.

John pulled up the waistband of his shorts. 'You don't seem very excited.'

I explained my reluctance by saying that I'd moved halfway across the world and felt too uprooted to get on a plane once more.

He breathed out and said, 'You've been through a hell of a lot. I can't imagine leaving everything behind like that. Look, don't come if you don't want to. No pressure. But this is *London* we're talking about. You'll meet some bigshots, people who run the artworld and all that. And we make a good team, don't we?'

I made a noncommittal sound. There was a smudge on the plastic sculpture where he had touched it. I wiped it away.

The thought of London set my nerves on edge and I left the studio early.

The afternoon was thick with heat. John's house was next to the rainforest and I retreated there for coolness and calm. I followed a gravel path into the wilderness, the tangle of trees and ferns getting denser as I went. One tree, its base covered in moss, had roots that protruded from the ground, forming narrow walls that, if I wished, I could have hidden in. Above my head a bird took flight, its feathers a smattering of purple and blue. A fat spider crept along the branch of a tree. I could see no other animals but I could hear the high notes of the bird calls and the occasional croak of a frog.

As I walked, I breathed deeply. I was restored by the smells of damp soil and vegetation, of decaying plants and fruits.

About half a kilometre along the path, I came across a tree, about my height, that had spectacular red flowers with yellow stamens shooting from their middles. The flowers, which I hadn't seen along this walk before, seemed uncannily familiar. As I neared the end of the path, I realised why. I had painted similar ones on a mural once, back in Poland, thinking they were more ostentatious than anything that existed in real life.

The gravel path ended and I walked on the rainforest floor, branches cracking underfoot. I reached a green creek that hummed with dragonflies. I sat on a rock and dipped my legs in the cool water. From my satchel, I pulled out a note that Dominik had once left for me at the studio in Wrocław. I took in its hurried scrawl.

> Aniusieńka. I just got back from a job in Katowice, and I want to tell you so many things. I've been running around with factory workers and madmen and drunks and I miss the sweet sound of your voice, the pine-cone smell of your hair.

He wrote that at the beginning of our time together, back when everything was hope. I read the note once more. It was easier to be angry at Dominik than to remember him like this.

No one here knew about Dominik's article. And yet the shame of it had followed me. This was no way to live: shrinking my life to accommodate someone who used to love me.

Here in the outdoors I felt braver than before. I could trick myself into believing that Father was with me. *Go to London,* słoneczko, I heard him say, *show those foreign galleries what you can do.*

241

9

One of John's ideas was to make a sculpture that looked
like a waterfall spilling from the corner of the gallery ceiling. It was to be made of chairs. This was a technical challenge I enjoyed: manipulating wood so that it took on the
properties of water. I adjusted his design to give the chairs
a more free-flowing appearance. Some of the chairs I left
intact and others I broke up so I could use their parts indi-
vidually. I was proud of this piece. I wanted to be there for
its premiere.

I wasn't going to turn down this opportunity because
of Dominik. In my past life, I had missed out on going to
Paris. This time I wasn't saying no.

When John wandered in to check my progress, I said,
'I'm going.'

'London?' He let out a whoop. 'I'm declaring today a
holiday.'

I touched up a section of paint on the sculpture. 'There
is still much work.' It amazed me that John was content
to delegate so much to me. I'd never come across such
a hands-off way of making art. Though I liked John and
was learning a lot in his studio, I found it hard to respect
a man who didn't make his own sculptures.

He took the paintbrush from me and deposited it in a
jar of water. 'Art is more than just work, you know. It's
about the ideas. And you won't find them sitting around
in here. Why don't I take you to the cove?' He pulled
me up from the floor. 'Hang on. You know how to ride
a bike?'

I jabbed him in the ribs, leaving a trace of white paint on his skin. 'We have bikes in Poland.'

'Just checking.' He hurried me away, talking about how much fun we were going to have. As we walked up the stairs I took one last look at the sculpture. From this perspective it wasn't quite right. I reminded myself to fix the angle of the top chair.

Now that I had a bike in my hands, riding didn't seem as easy as I'd remembered. I clenched the handles, unsure of how to get on. I didn't even want to think about how I was going to get the bike down the steep hill from John's house to the road below.

'I'll do that.' John took the bike from me, hopped on, and then tore down the hill. I hurried after him on foot. He skidded at the bottom, nearly crashing into a palm. 'Now you.' He pushed the bike towards me.

'I have no memory of how,' I admitted.

'As it happens, riding a bike is like making art, you never really forget how to do it.' John helped me on. Though he was a reckless rider, he proved to be a patient teacher, holding the bike steady while I practised.

'You can let go,' I said, wobbling along the grass.

He clambered back uphill to get his own bike, which was larger and rustier than mine. Then we wheeled slowly out to sea.

The emerald afternoon stretched before us. As I pushed my feet down on the pedals, my confidence grew. Soon I was hurtling past John, laughing with the salt air in my mouth.

'Left!' he yelled. 'Go left. Here!' He sped in front, directing me down a gravel track. We threw our bikes onto the sand.

Waves raced to shore, dissolving into white foam. There was the flicker of wind at my shoulders and the heat of the sun on my back. John and I were the only ones on the beach. We walked along the damp sand. Broken pieces of shells crunched under my bare feet. I breathed in the smell of the sea.

'Tell me something.' John threw a stick to the water. 'Tell me something about yourself.'

'This is your turn to talk.'

'You don't want to hear about an old fart like me. Tell me about where you used to live, the cottage by the factory. And the bees! I want to hear about the bees.'

The memory of the bees put me back in Poland and despite myself, I started to talk. 'My first pain from a bee –'

'Your first bee sting?'

'Yes, my first bee sting. This was on my tongue, when I was little girl …' As I told him this story, I shaded my face to get a better look at the sprawl of beach ahead. In the distance, the white sand was dotted with grey rocks. The day was large and bright and as the wind threaded through my hair I felt a sense of optimism that I hadn't had in a long time.

'What happened then?' John asked.

Remembering the story, I said, 'My tongue swelled so much I couldn't speak …'

As we kept walking, I saw that what I had taken to be rocks were actually birds. Behind me, John exclaimed, 'Bloody hell!'

I knelt on the sand and reached out to stroke one. Its eyes were open to the sun. There were no marks on its grey feathers, nothing to give away how it had died.

'Don't touch that. It's disgusting.' John knocked my hand away. 'This place is normally so beautiful.'

'This also is beautiful.'

'It's not how I wanted you to see it. I wanted it to be perfect.' He looked like a school boy who'd taken home a bad report card to his parent.

I brushed the sand off my knees. 'Show me the cove.'

We left the birds behind and walked until we reached a barrier of rocks, about two metres tall, that stretched from the sand into the sea. John climbed them and I followed, scraping my palms and my feet. When we reached the top, he leapt down to the other side. Standing up, he held his hand out to me.

'It's okay.' I closed my eyes and jumped. When I hit the ground my knees collapsed onto the sand.

'This is it,' he said.

The sea was silver green. The rocks cradled the water, taming it, so that the roar of the waves subsided to a gentle hiss. John wriggled out of his shorts and tossed them aside, running into the sea in a black bathing costume. He disappeared in the water and then bobbed up again, his hair slick against his skull.

I took my clothes off, readjusted the straps of my costume, and waded in. I tipped my face to the sun. This was nothing like the freeze of the Baltic Sea. Here, the water was warm and forgiving.

John floated on his back, his hands supporting his head as I swam towards a rock by the edge of the cove. I climbed onto it and when I closed my eyes, the sound of the sea got louder. Something squelched against my leg and I gasped. John laughed and threw another piece of seaweed, which landed in the water.

'You look like a mermaid,' he said.

The water rippled as he swam towards me and pulled himself onto the rock. There was just enough room for the both of us, our thighs almost touching. The proximity of his skin, the glare of the sun in my eyes and the thirst in my throat were disorienting. The rock seemed far higher above the ocean than it had a moment before.

John looked at me, checking. Then he leaned in, bringing his salt mouth to mine.

Our lips met. Desire pulsed through my fingertips. As soon as I was aware of it, it morphed into revulsion. This was my employer. I pulled away. 'What are you –?'

'I like you, Ania.'

A sick feeling crawled in my stomach. I cursed him for kissing me and cursed myself for letting it happen. What did he think he was paying me for? I recalled Rahel's stories from the pub she'd worked in in Brisbane, the way that her boss had always been trying to grope her. She told me, *He thinks I will put up with this because I am not from here.*

245

'Ania?'

I struggled to order my thoughts in English. Finally I said, 'This is not what I am for.' I plunged into the water and swam away.

By the time we got back to our bikes, the rays of the sun had weakened. How long had we been gone? Three, maybe four hours? My throat was parched and I was weak with hunger.

'We have not even a bottle of water,' I said. 'Nothing.' I threw my bike on the sand in frustration and then picked it up again.

John steadied my bike. 'Did I get it wrong? I mean, I thought you wanted me, too.'

I remembered the Yugoslavian girl he told me about, the one who'd worked for him before me. 'Why did she leave?' I asked. 'Your last assistant?'

He looked away from me and then said. 'We broke up.'

'Your girlfriend ...' With difficulty, I started to push my bike through the sand.

'It's not like that,' he said.

We didn't speak as we rode our bikes back to town. The sky darkened above our heads. It happened quite suddenly, as though a door had been closed on the bright afternoon. There was a wet smell in the air.

'Storm's coming,' John said. 'Look, do you want to come back to mine? It's closer, is all.'

'*Nie*,' I told him. As I cycled away, black clouds consumed the horizon and thunder shook the sky. This was not rain as I knew it, but enormous fistfuls of water that hurtled down and fizzed on the hot concrete. I dropped my bike to the ground and stood by the edge of the road, breathing in the storm. A car honked as it drove past.

When the rain subsided I continued riding to the bungalow, my wet clothes clinging to my skin. I hurried inside before the farmer caught sight of me.

Warm air sieved through the wire mesh on my kitchen

window. With a towel wrapped around my head, I put the kettle on. I took down two glasses from the cupboard. Realising my mistake, I put one back. For the rest of the afternoon, I decided, I would sit on the front step of the bungalow and read my letters from Father.

I was dripping. I unwound the towel from my head and tossed it on the ground. My feet on the towel, I shuffled to the bedroom to retrieve the letters.

As soon as I opened the door I saw that something was different.

The room was flooded. A damp stain on the ceiling revealed a hole that had let in the rain. My knees skidded on the wet floor as I crawled under the bed to retrieve the cardboard box. The lid was soaked. Inside, the letters were stuck together in a clump. When I peeled them apart I discovered that the ink had bled, making the words unrecognisable. I desperately sorted through the letters, trying to find one that had survived.

The wet paper gave way in my hands.

10

A sense of despondency settled over me. I had trouble sleeping and lost my appetite. On slips of paper, I wrote phrases from the letters. Writing and rewriting the words until they were as true as I could remember. I threw them out. They only served to remind me of what I had lost.

With no one around to talk sense into me, I felt a desperate need to know what Dominik was doing with himself, whether he was sorry. I went to the post office and with the help of the owner – a woman who had blue-tinged hair and generous arms – subscribed to the famous journal that Dominik wrote for. Despite the expense I bought back editions. A few weeks later a large paper parcel, bound in string, arrived for me at the post office. I rushed it back to the bungalow and tore it open.

The journal was printed on thin white paper, with its name, *Świat Kultury*, emblazoned across the front. Aside from a few earlier copies, each edition contained a piece by Dominik. He wrote mostly about politics, but also about poetry and art. Each of his articles was accompanied by a black and white headshot. Dominik met the gaze of the camera with a world-weary air, no hint of the teasing smile he used to give me.

I searched the articles for clues as to what was going on in his life. All I learned was that he was publishing a book about totalitarianism. It was both a relief and a disappointment to find that the articles contained no mention of me.

I read his articles every day. It was wrong and it was doing me no good but I didn't know how to stop.

After our trip to the cove, John adopted a formal politeness towards me. If he needed to walk past me in the studio he left a generous distance between our bodies. We discussed work but he no longer asked me questions about my life.

Today he sat at a desk doing paperwork while I polished glass bottles for a sculpture. The silence allowed me to submerge myself in unwanted thoughts and I was overcome by the beginning of tears. Angry, I wiped my eyes with the polishing cloth. I didn't even know what I was crying about – was it the letters or everything else?

'Hey.' John got up from his desk and sat next to me on the floor. He raised an arm, as though to put it around me, and then retracted it. After a moment he said, 'Sorry Ania, I shouldn't have done it. It's just, it was so good to have someone to talk to. About art and stuff. I lost my head but it's screwed back on now, see?' He clamped his hands on his face and twisted it to one side, then the other.

Despite myself, I laughed. 'I miss home.' I dabbed the polishing cloth to my nostrils.

John dug into the pocket of his shorts and surprised me by pulling out a neatly pressed handkerchief. I blew my nose on it.

'My parents were like that,' he said. 'Even after living here all these years, they still kept referring to Greece as home. Everything was better over there – the food, the weather, everything. When they finally went back for a visit, you know what happened? They couldn't stand the place! Still, it didn't stop them from missing it when they got back.'

My laughter gave way to tears at the thought that maybe I would end up like that. I told John about the letters.

'Why don't we give them a proper burial?' he said.

I nodded and wiped my nose with the handkerchief before giving it back. He held it reluctantly between his fingers and then tucked it in his pocket.

We finished work early and rode over to my bungalow. John sat on the kitchen bench, swinging his legs back and forth, looking around the sparse room. 'Why didn't you say you don't have any furniture?'

'I don't need.' Though I'd cleaned the bungalow on arrival, I'd done nothing to make it feel like a home.

'Still,' John said, 'seems a bit extravagant of me, using chairs for a sculpture when you don't have any to sit on.' He hopped down from the bench and swung open the cupboard doors, revealing neatly stacked tins. 'At least you have food.' He made a show of counting. 'Eight cans of peaches. Eleven – no, *twelve* tins of ham.'

I shot him a dark look and he closed the cupboard.

Looking repentant, he zipped open his backpack. 'I wanted to give you this. For the letters. You don't have to use it if you don't want to.' He handed me a small wooden box. The lid was painted with an intricate picture of a tree, its roots reaching deep into the earth. 'I made it a while back.'

This was the first time I'd seen an object that John had made with his own hands. I lifted the lid, testing the hinges. The box was well made. It smelt like talcum powder and spice. I thanked him. 'This is just right.'

Outside, the falling sun cast an orange glow on the horizon, making the hills look like they were on fire. We walked between symmetrical rows of trees that were specked with small oranges, making our way to the far end of the grove where a steel fence kept the rainforest at bay. Here was a tree that was different from the others: it grew knobbly green fists of fruit. The farmer had told me that the fruit were called *Custard apples*. I wondered if he was having a joke with me. If he was, I didn't care. I was enchanted with the idea of apples that grew their own custard.

John crouched by the tree and dug at the earth with a small spade. I placed the box of letters inside and packed the dirt back over. We stood and I crossed myself and murmured a prayer. When I glanced at John, his hands were also clasped together.

As the light departed from the sky, we walked back to the bungalow.

'See you tomorrow, then,' John said. He hopped on his rusty bike and rode away. If it wasn't for what happened at the cove I might have asked him to stay. I needed the company. The ritual with the letters was supposed to make me feel better but instead I was emptied out, as though I'd buried Father all over again.

The evening before I left for London, I went down to the beach for one last swim.

At this hour the water took on the dark sheen of a crow. I discarded my clothes and walked into the sea. Something bumped into my leg – a fish, perhaps. I dipped my hands in, trying to find it.

I waded further out. When the water came up to my stomach, I closed my eyes and plunged under. My ears filled with the gurgling sound of my exhale. I gasped to the surface, the taste of salt in my mouth.

Lying on my belly, I pulled my hands through the water. Bright specks of phosphorescence trailed through my fingers, tiny stars that had fallen to the sea.

11

England, September 1983

'Rumour has it there's a Basquiat going for a steal.' John rolled up the catalogue and pointed it in the direction of the stall. As we hurried through the art fair, he nodded to other passers-by before turning to me and hissing, 'A Basquiat! Can you believe it?'

The white-domed ceiling glistened with fluorescent lights. Its high, curved structure reminded me of the train station in Wrocław. We were on the ground floor of the art fair, in an enormous rectangular room that was sub-divided into stalls. On the level above us, people leaned over balcony railings, clutching glasses of champagne. On the ground floor, at the back of the room, was a video installation: a middle-aged woman wrapped a length of white bandage around her body, mummifying herself. I watched as she wrapped the bandage around and around and around.

Exhaustion rolled over me. Unlike John, I was still suffering from jetlag. Breaking my gaze away from the video, I plucked a couple of glasses of champagne from the tray of a waiter. He gave me an indulgent smile and then whisked the tray towards a thin man who was examining a painting through a monocle.

I took a sip of the liquid. Bubbles dissolved sour on my tongue. 'This champagne is like lemons,' I said to John.

'Oh yeah?' He was inspecting a painting of a naked woman kneeling by a bucket. To my disappointment, there were few sculptures at the fair and none of the paintings struck me as being particularly inspiring. Perhaps I was simply tired. Taking in all this art demanded more energy than I had.

'Wait here.' John beelined for a nearby coffee table and returned with a small packet of sugar. Grinning, he sprinkled the white crystals into my champagne. The liquid fizzed and bubbled over. 'That'll perk you up.'

I brought my lips to the glass, sucking the excess. Particles of sugar dissolved on my tongue.

'Better?' He straightened his jacket and then directed us to the stall he wanted to see. A couple of people had to exit before there was space for us to go in.

Finally, here was a painting that excited me. It was of a bulky male figure, a white skeleton superimposed on his black skin. The man gritted his teeth as he pulled a fish from the water by its tail. The tangled brushstrokes had an energy, wild and direct. It was as though the artist had removed his paintbrush from the canvas the very moment before it was hung on the wall.

'This one is alive,' I said.

John consulted his catalogue. 'Damn … Not what I'm after. I thought it would have a crown on it. That's what he's known for.'

'A crown?' I gave a laugh. 'You can add one yourself,' I pointed my champagne glass to the top of the painting.

The stallholder, who had been talking to a woman with a small dog in her handbag, cleared his throat. I backed away.

'Can't win them all,' John said.

His exhibition, *White Water*, was opening tomorrow night. When we visited the gallery earlier today, one of the sculptures was still in a wooden crate plastered with stickers that read, 'This Way Up.' I had told John that I wanted to help the gallery staff prepare for opening night. 'Impossible,' he'd said. 'I need you with me.' During our four days in London, I'd accompanied him to interviews with journalists in hotel dining rooms, to the apartment of an underfed woman who collected art, and now here.

'If this painting is no good,' I gestured to the black figure, 'we can go back to the gallery. See it's okay.'

'No,' he said quickly. 'They've got things under control.' He pushed back his sleeve and consulted his watch. 'It'd be great if you'd do me a favour and pick up my suit from the dry cleaners. I'll need it for the opening.' He lips made a sucking sound. 'Speaking of which, what are you going to wear?'

'I have not thought of this,' I said.

'Look.' He dug his hand into his pocket. 'You can say no if you want to, but how would you like to buy yourself a dress?' He handed me a plastic card with his full name on it: John Bautista Papageorgiou.

I handed it straight back.

'It's a business expense. Take it,' he pressed the card on me. 'You'll be meeting a lot of important people tomorrow and we're not in Kansas anymore.'

'What?'

'Just an expression. It doesn't matter.'

Outside, the cold gnawed at my cheeks. My jetlag ebbed away and I felt alert. I considered going to the gallery to check that the sculptures were properly installed, but decided against it. John had made it clear that we would get in the way of the staff. Besides, it was exhilarating to be on my own in a foreign city. The last few days had been spent indoors and now I finally had the chance to take in London, with its rush of black-clad figures, its enormous red buses and pale oyster sky.

An ambulance sped past. Its siren blared but no one else looked its way. The noise receded and then there was punk music as a young man with coiffed hair strode towards me, cradling a tape deck on his shoulder. With a cigarette in his mouth, he mumbled something indecipherable.

I walked on, staring up at the red brick buildings before colliding with a sign on the footpath. I stopped to fix it, my hands grasping a cartoon woman in a tight orange dress. Painted across her middle was the beguiling instruction, "Try Our Macs 'n' Mash." As I rearranged the sign, a tall lady with dark skin walked past, a beautiful purple and gold material fluttering around her. Nearby was a boarded-up shop. On the planks nailed across the windows, someone had spray-painted music notes, together with the words, "Don't Cry For Me Maggie Thatcher."

After the languid pace of North Queensland, the city made my fingertips tingle. Dazed by the noise and the traffic and the people, I lost my bearings. I looked around for a shop where I might buy a map, the moan in my stomach reminding me that I hadn't eaten since breakfast. I passed a few clothes shops, then a cinema, and then, as if by magic, I saw a sign that announced: *Polski Sklep*.

The shop was cosy and smelt of rose-jam doughnuts. A man with a fuzz of grey hair stood behind the counter, wearing a red and white apron. As I walked in he smiled broadly and said, '*Dzień dobry.*'

'Good day,' I greeted him in Polish. The shop was decorated with pictures of the Tatra Mountains, Wawel Castle and the Pope. The shelves were lined with jars of pickles, sauerkraut and herring, and the deli counter was packed with cold meats and cheese – far more food than we'd ever see in a grocery store in Poland. I bought a doughnut. Its warm jam filled my mouth as the shopkeeper asked me questions about Poland. He nodded as I told him about the curfews and the protests, the censors listening to our telephone calls. To my relief he didn't ask why I'd left.

When I finished eating, he said, 'Pani must have another.' Using a pair of tongs, he extracted a doughnut from the display cabinet and put it on a ceramic plate. He set it on the counter by a photocopied flier for the London Solidarność movement. Next to this was a Polish newspaper and also a religious magazine. Then I spotted the journal that Dominik wrote for, *Świat Kultury*. My hand rested on the matte cover and without intending to, I bought it. As an afterthought I remembered to buy a map.

I sat at a plastic table in the corner of the shop. My fingers left spots of oil on the pages as I flicked through the journal, searching for Dominik's face. I found him on page ten. He had, incredibly, got an interview with Miłosz, who was one of his heroes. Miłosz was quoted as saying that anyone could fall in love, but being able to *act with love* towards another person was an entirely different matter. It was this acting with love that was so dangerous in politically repressed societies. To this, Dominik's response was, "You're right. Love humanises us. It offers a radical force for change. That's why they're so scared of it."

My heart quickened. In the opposite mirror, I could see I was flushed. How could Dominik write so eloquently about these things and yet know nothing about them?

The next page contained details about the book that Dominik had published, together with information about a speaking tour he was doing to promote it. There were events taking place every couple of days; at universities, in bookshops, and at Polish associations across the country. Casting a glance at the shopkeeper, who was now occupied with a woman buying bread, I used a pen to mark Dominik's speaking engagements on my map, plotting out his movements for the next couple of weeks. I imagined turning up, startling him, armed with everything I wanted to say. Which was what? That I was angry? That I missed him every day.

'*Dziękuję,*' I thanked the shopkeeper on my way out.

He beckoned me over and slipped me something. It was a sweet wrapped in pink and silver foil.

Back on the street, a group of school children passed me as I consulted my map. Turning it this way and that, I navigated my way to a nearby shopping district.

Glass doors opened to a room that rustled with taffeta and tulle. I checked the price tag on a simple black dress and pulled away, astonished. As I was walking out, I noticed a rack that read 'Half Price.' The clothes had various faults such as missing buttons and torn hems. I was drawn to a soft, fibrous material. This turned out to be a long-sleeved evening dress made of velvet. There appeared to be nothing wrong the dress, and it was a beautiful colour, the same green as the hills at home. But that couldn't be right. The hills in Poland were dewy green, not emerald like this. Then it dawned on me. When I'd thought of 'the hills at home', I had meant the ones in Australia.

12

My plans to get to the exhibition early were thwarted by John. He insisted that we go together, and one hour after I had knocked on his hotel door, he still hadn't found anything to wear. The dry-cleaned suit was lying on the bed, sheathed in plastic. John had decided that it was 'all wrong' for the opening. My temples pricked with irritation. His room, though bigger than mine, felt too small for the both of us. He sat on the bed sorting through his clothes while I stood at the other end of the room by the window. On the street below, a police car sped past, its lights flashing on the wet street. John wandered over to the mirror. He held a striped shirt to his chest and then a plain one. On the bedside table, the digital clock flipped its digits to 19:00.

I paced the room, kicking a couple of balled-up socks out of my way. 'I think you are scared for your exhibition,' I told him. 'That's why you are … What's the word? Wasting of time.'

John scraped his fingers through his hair and looked around. He snatched a dark green shirt from the floor. 'I'll wear this one.'

I waited on the bed while he got dressed in the bathroom. When he came out I clapped my hands. He looked distinguished in his formal trousers and shirt – in Australia I was used to seeing him in just a pair of shorts. 'We go now,' I said.

He lassoed a tie in my direction. 'Give us a hand with this?'

I flicked the tie back to him and stood up. Making his sculptures was one thing, I wasn't going to dress him as well. 'You must do yourself. And hurry. We are late.'

John looped the tie around his neck, struggled with the knot and then cast it aside.

As I'd predicted, the gallery was crowded by the time we arrived. I stood on my tiptoes and caught sight of the waterfall of chairs flowing from the gallery ceiling. 'No,' I said to John. 'It doesn't belong like that. It needs to be more curved.' *Curved?* That didn't seem to be the right word.

John said, 'Ania. Things have been so crazy I haven't had a chance to thank you properly. And I've got a surprise for you. Truth is, I'm a bit nervous about it.' He paused in his tracks and then massaged the deep lines on either side of his mouth. 'The thing is ... Actually you'll find this flattering –'

The gallery director approached us. Her evening dress made the swooshing sound of a plastic bag. She enveloped John in her long arms and then pulled him away to meet someone. He turned back to me, indicating I should follow.

'Go,' I mouthed. I wanted to see the sculptures by myself. Even though they weren't my pieces, I had still made them.

Standing under the waterfall of chairs, I looked up at the fretwork of white wood, the black-painted walls showing through the gaps. The sculpture wasn't arranged quite the way I wanted. I would speak to the staff about adjusting its position. I continued through the gallery, coming to the cube of clear plastic with a triangle fitted inside. There wasn't much to the piece and I had discouraged John from exhibiting it. Yet as I regarded it, an older man stage-whispered to the younger man at his side: 'I love it. I have to have it.'

Behind the plastic cube was a piece that I quite liked for its audacity as much as anything. It consisted of a row of glass milk bottles, mounted to the wall, each filled with clear liquid. Holy water from the churches that John had visited in various countries: Greece, Yugoslavia, America, England and Australia. In the process of being transported here, the water from the Yugoslavian church had leaked into the packing crate. Together, John and I had come up with the idea of replacing it with tap water. He gave the piece a new title, *Spot the Fake*. A woman in a polka dot skirt stood in front of it, consulting the exhibition catalogue. 'How much?' the man by her side wanted to know. She showed him the catalogue and he snorted. 'If you want a bottle of water, I'll buy you one at Tesco.'

The exhibition catalogues were displayed on a nearby table. They were magazine-sized and printed on thick glossy paper. I hadn't yet had a chance to look at them. Perhaps because my English wasn't very good, John hadn't asked for my help in producing them. I picked one up and opened it, marvelling at the incredible asking prices for the sculptures. For the cost of one artwork I could live for a year in Australia – two if I was frugal. I ran my finger down the names of the pieces and then came across one that was unfamiliar. *Portrait of the Artist as a Carp.*

A sharp sensation gripped my stomach. I tucked the catalogue in my bag and hurried through the gallery, nudging my way between people until I found a small room at the back.

When I saw it, there was a folding in of time.

It was me. Or rather, it belonged to me.

My mind scrambled, trying to figure out how this had happened, and I remembered the stories that I had told John when we first met. About the night my friends and I had gathered together after martial law was declared. He had been so interested, and it had felt so freeing to finally speak about these things, that I told him everything. About the tanks and the militiamen, the hashish in the kitchen and the carp swimming in the bathtub. I even told him about that little picture, *Portrait of Dominik as a Carp.*

I stepped closer. Here in the gallery was a bathtub. It was chipped at the sides and a yellow carp swam in the shallow water. On the edge of the bath was a gun. I pushed aside the woman next to me and lowered myself onto the tub. I dangled my fingers in the water. The carp nibbled at my skin and in that moment, I was sitting on the other bathtub, the water turning black with ink. The smell of burning coal came to me and I could hear Jaruzelski on the television, feel the pulse of Dominik's heart as he held me in his arms.

A couple of people – gallery staff – rushed towards me, their faces contorted with alarm. 'Don't touch the art!' A hand grabbed my shoulder, cold fingers slipping under the velvet. Digging in.

Then there was another hand, gentler, on my back. 'It's okay, she's with me.' John helped me up. The gallery staff edged away.

'What have you done?' I shielded my face as John manoeuvred me through the crowd. Everything was swirling: faces, wine glasses, the ceiling and the floor. In reception, I clutched the desk, needing something tangible in my hands.

'It's an homage,' he said.

A strangled noise emerged from somewhere inside me.

'I can see you're upset.' John spoke slowly, as though he'd been struck by a pain in his jaw. When I didn't reply, he said, 'I wanted to tell you.' Then he stiffened and said, 'The sculpture was my idea.'

This wasn't an *idea* – this was my life. I tried to tell John, but the words clogged in my throat. So I spoke the way I knew how.

'*Ty kłamco i oszuście. Wszystko mi ukradłeś! Ty durniu, ty nic nie rozumiesz, nic nie wiesz o życiu. Ani o sztuce, ani o życiu, o niczym co się liczy. Nic nie wiesz! Nawet swoich własnych rzeźb nie potrafisz zrobić!*'

The outpour left me shaking. I hadn't known I was going to call John those things – a liar and a thief and a fake. A man who knew nothing. A man who couldn't even make his own art.

John was pale. He lifted his hand to the top of his shirt as though to straighten a tie. Finding none, it fell to his side. 'We'll talk about this later.'

Gallery staff and other onlookers circled us. There was the flash of a camera our way. I rushed out the doors and into the night. Chased by the image of myself, yelling at John.

In my hurry I had left my coat behind. My neck burned with shame and I welcomed the rain that dripped between awnings. I slowed down the pace of my walking, tugging at the hem of my dress. John had taken what was mine and used it in the most public way. The only time I'd been so humiliated was when Dominik wrote that article. *A woman I once considered my wife …*

A car sped past and I leapt back from the road to avoid the avalanche of water. How much time had I spent measuring myself against Dominik, against the life we'd once had? Though I'd moved all the way to Australia, to a small town by the beach, I was still plagued by the past. The only way it was going to release its hold on me was if I confronted Dominik myself.

13

The next day I was supposed to meet John at the gallery for a meeting about the opening. There was no way I was going. I left the hotel early and sat in a cafeteria for workers, a little like our *bar mleczny*, and sipped weak tea. Soon enough it was time to leave. My hands shook as I packed my map and then made my way to the bus stop.

The university was surprisingly easy to find. I got off the bus with the students, following them to a severe-looking building made of white bricks. I stood in the courtyard, wondering where to go next, when a girl in a beret took pity on me. 'Are you lost?' she asked. I told her the room I was looking for and she helped me find my way.

Inside, I waited in a dank corridor, tossing up whether I should go back to the hotel. A dishevelled-looking guy strode towards the lecture theatre, an anarchist symbol drawn in black marker on the back of his vest. When he held the door open for me, I swallowed my anxiety and went in.

I'd expected the lecture to be teeming, the way it would be in Poland. However, there were only half a dozen people scattered in the room. I positioned myself at the back, where I wouldn't be noticed. My body was out of kilter: my palms were damp and my throat was dry. Images came to me of last night. The way I'd lost control and yelled at John. It had felt terrible and cathartic and I was ready to do it again.

Taking a deep breath, I focused on the audience members. They appeared to have grouped themselves according to dress. Those with spiked hair and ripped jeans sat at the back, while those with spectacles and shirts in muted colours were at the front. As I looked at them I realised that, aside from a handful of men, they were all female.

My resolve weakened. Maybe I shouldn't have come. My being here would only tell Dominik how important he was in my life. He probably had a girlfriend. For all I knew, he had a wife. Despite my anger there was nothing I could say to him that wouldn't sound desperate.

I reached under my chair for my satchel. Then someone tapped a microphone and the room went quiet. Despite myself, my gaze was drawn to the stage.

It wasn't Dominik, but a man with neat hair and sunken cheeks. Although it was warm inside, he had a scarf draped around his turtleneck sweater. He tapped his microphone again and said, 'Before we begin, ladies and gentlemen, I want you to come closer. Don't be shy.' The man, who was English, spoke beautifully, as though with each word he was giving us a gift. Around me, people began to gather their bags and notebooks and shift towards the front. If I left now, I would only draw attention to myself. I positioned myself in the middle row.

When the man was satisfied that the audience was sitting close enough, he said, 'We're fortunate to have with us today a Polish writer who is well known for his pioneering journalism, for his willingness to speak truth to power if I can use that dreadful cliché.' He paused for the chuckles and then continued. 'Just as he is known for the incisive manner in which he shows us that there can be a thin line between democracy and totalitarianism. Exiled from his own country, he is now a resident in London, where his first book, *Spring Will Be Ours: Polish Lessons in Resistance and Revolt*, has been published to critical acclaim. Please put together your hands for Dominik Duwak.' The man stumbled a little over Dominik's last name but the girls were already clapping.

And then there he was. Smiling and ducking his head as though embarrassed by this praise. His familiarity was overwhelming. I had expected him to look different, but though his hair was shorter and his clothes were nicer, he was undeniably Dominik. Tall and strong-necked and handsome. That same satiric twist of the mouth.

Anger flooded through me and my vision blurred with tears. I wiped them away and, unbidden, the memories came back. Dominik and me taking long baths together while he read me Mickiewicz. The two of us assembling the blood sculptures in the forest. And the first time we met, when he slipped me the forged number for my coat.

Dominik settled down on a sofa next to the facilitator. He picked up a microphone from the nearby table and said, 'My friend here is making a lot of hot air. How do you call it when someone says big things about you?'

'Exaggerating,' someone called.

'Yes, thank you, exaggerating.' He unleashed a smile on the audience.

I slid further down my seat. Hoping that he wouldn't see me, and hoping that he would.

The facilitator asked Dominik questions about his book, and about his life in Poland and here in London. Dominik answered in a halting English that was so different to the ardent way he spoke in Polish.

Then the facilitator said, 'How do you feel knowing that this book of yours – this very important book – won't reach the people who need it the most. It's been censored in Poland hasn't it?'

Dominik scratched inside his shirt collar and said, 'I am grateful to Polish government for banning my book. This means it will be bestseller on the black market.'

There was a titter in the room. Then the interviewer said, 'In all seriousness though, you of all people know that writing can be a dangerous thing. You were imprisoned in Poland for your journalism, isn't that right?'

'Yes, yes.' Dominik switched the microphone from one hand to another and began to recount his time in Białystok. He talked about how he and the other prisoners were watched day and night, about the lack of food that left them near starvation point, and about the violence.

265

On one occasion, he said, he'd been dragged from his cell to the toilets and beaten by three guards. They punched and kicked him in the stomach and face until his nose and cheeks were broken. All because he refused to sign a paper declaring his loyalty to the government.

My heart skipped a beat and then started up again with a loud thumping noise I was sure everyone could hear. But the girls didn't notice: their notebooks remained closed on their laps and their gazes were fixed on Dominik. I made myself listen to what he was saying.

'Inside or outside prison, this is not so different. Poland is an occupied country and so everyone in Poland knows we are not free. But we too are lucky. There is nothing we take granted. *For* granted, yes? We are not lazy with our lives because we know that all this,' he made a sweeping gesture with his hand, 'can be taken away. And we have much to teach the rest of the world if they would like to listen.'

At the end of the speech, the facilitator quietened the applause and announced that it was question time. There was a long silence before someone asked, 'Will Poland ever be free?'

'I am optimist.' Dominik raised his hands in a gesture of helplessness. 'This is my biggest problem.'

This first question paved the way for others. 'It must have been horrible being locked up in prison like that,' a girl said.

Dominik nodded and then shrugged. 'I could put up with being in prison, but you know what I couldn't put up with?' A look of mischief came over his face. 'Not enough vodka. This is bad for an aspiring alcoholic such as myself.'

Afterwards there was a book signing. People lined up in order to have their time with Dominik. He was sitting at a small table, his head bent over as he scribbled. I hovered by the back of the theatre. Maybe just seeing him was enough. If I left now he didn't ever have to know I was here.

The small crowd dispersed and, with no idea of what I wanted to say to Dominik, I made up my mind to leave. A person in front of me opened the doors, releasing a gust of cold in the theatre and then someone called, 'Ania?'

I turned around. Confusion passed over Dominik's face. He unrolled a sleeve of his shirt and then pushed it back up. The instant I decided it was a mistake, he traversed the space between us and wrapped me in his arms.

14

It was dark inside the pub and the counter was sticky against my arm. Dominik knew the proper words to order our drinks, asking the barman for *pints*, rather than glasses, of beer. Standing beside us, a couple of wide-bellied men laughed loudly. When a slim girl in a short yellow dress walked in, their laughter drained away, their eyes assessing her. I took a sip of the frothy beer, waiting for Dominik's gaze to be pulled towards her. Instead he looked at me.

We sat at a booth by a small window, its pane smudged with fingerprints. Dominik fidgeted with the plastic flowers on our table and when he saw me watching, he stopped. I had been so anxious about seeing him again that I hadn't imagined he would be nervous too.

When he spoke, he cast aside English. 'I had this idea,' Dominik said, 'this adolescent fantasy, that one day I would go somewhere, an art exhibition or a bar or wherever, and you'd be there.'

I took a sip of the creamy beer. The murky window made the outside world look shabby and indistinct. There were a couple of wasps on the windowsill. They lay on their backs with their legs in the air.

'Father was sick.' Now that I'd summoned the courage to bring it up, I kept going. 'He was sick, that's why I did it. When I read that article of yours, I ... It's like the world stopped. I couldn't believe it.'

Dominik steepled his hands and placed them next to his mouth, breathed through them. 'I didn't know about your

268

father – not then. They didn't tell me. They just showed me the papers you signed and said you'd confessed everything. They said you were working for them now. I told them they were lying but then ... then I got word it was true.'

That was probably Elżbieta, the dentist from my cell. After my interview with the Colonel, I had told her they said that Father was ill. That he was dying. Didn't it occur to her, when I signed the papers, that this was the reason why?

'Once they had those papers,' Dominik said, 'the guards harassed me non-stop. One night they pulled me out of my bunk while I was sleeping. They dragged me outside and put my feet in freezing water and said, "She's told us everything. You're done for." After that, I couldn't eat. Couldn't sleep. You know what they can do with that type of information.'

'You were scared ...'

Stupidly, I hadn't considered what impact those papers might have had on Dominik. I had only been thinking of myself. And Father, of course. But I had always regarded Dominik as being invincible, somehow. Not like the rest of us.

'Scared, yeah,' Dominik said. 'I also had the guys in Białystok, the other prisoners, breathing down my neck. "He's a traitor like his fiancée," they said. They roughed me up in the courtyard while the guards turned a blind eye. Then I got word that the newspaper didn't want me to work for them anymore. I was damaged goods. Unless I took a stand, they said. Made a public statement of some sort. They needed to know where my loyalties lay.'

I pressed my thumb to a damp beer coaster. A tiredness seeped through my skin. 'It was his lungs,' I said. Then I said, 'I miss him.'

At that moment, Dominik seemed to get smaller. His shoulders hunched, he looked at me and said, 'He was one of a kind. Who else has a father that would help them drag buckets of blood through an abattoir – all in the name of art?' He tipped his head back. 'I feel like such an arsehole.'

A waitress came to our table asking if we wanted more beers. We shifted apart and Dominik thanked her. He said, 'I only found out about your father when Małgorzata wrote to me. She gave me your address at a hostel in Australia. Yung … something? I can't remember what it was called, now. You never replied to my letter and I can understand why. But I want to tell you in person that I'm sorry. For what I did. For ruining things.'

'A letter … You must have sent it after I'd moved.'

'It doesn't matter. You're here now and I want to tell you I've never stopped thinking about you.' He opened his mouth, hesitated, and then said, 'Will you stay?'

'In London?'

'In London. With me.' He inched his fingers towards mine and then stroked the ring. 'You still have it.'

In Queensland the heat had caused my hands to swell, so I didn't wear the ring. Before I left for London I put it back on, thinking it would be safer to travel under the guise of a married woman. Now I wondered if that had been the real reason.

The thought of Dominik's article still stung me. But I understood, now, why he had done it. Perhaps it was like Father had said, the situation in our country was rotten and any one of us could be compelled to do things we weren't proud of. I remembered how Elżbieta had given me a disgusted look when she saw the guard escort me out of prison. How I wanted to tell her that she would have done the same thing. Who was I to judge Dominik? Perhaps I would have written an article like that if I had been in his place. There was no way I could honestly say that I *wouldn't* have done it.

Dominik and I sat for a while, our arms resting on the table, almost touching. I gestured to his clean nails. 'Your hands were always stained with ink. Remember?'

'That's right … Because of that old American typewriter. All I had to do was look at it and I'd be covered in the stuff. I've got an electric one now. It's much better. It has Polish letters and everything.'

Given Dominik's success, I was surprised to see that he lived like this, in a small flat above a butcher's shop which he shared with three other men. The only common space was the kitchen. The living room had been cordoned off with a sheet to make a bedroom. The attic, which Dominik lived in, had a ceiling that slashed diagonally across the space, cutting it in half. His bed was positioned at the side where the ceiling was highest and there was a desk at the other side. I stooped so as not to hit my head. What was I doing here?

There was a copy of Dominik's book on his desk and I flicked through it while he watched. 'I'll have to read it,' I said.

He smiled.

It was disorienting seeing him again. At one moment I felt incredibly close to him, as though the past was of no consequence. The next moment, the words from his article came back to me and I felt myself harden once more.

He came over. I put the book down as he stroked a loose hair away from my cheek. Our lips met. The softness of the kiss becoming hungrier, more vital. I pressed myself against him, shifting him towards the bed, tipping him back so that he lay beneath me. He pulled the elastic band off the end of my hair and unplaited it. I watched him, rediscovering his forehead, his cheeks and his nose. I still knew his face so well. Which was strange, given what had happened in prison.

Dominik pulled me towards him, unbuttoning my shirt.

'You must have had a good doctor,' I said.

'A doctor?' He tugged my shirt off and tossed it to the floor.

'Those injuries you spoke about in the lecture. The guards broke your nose, your cheeks. And yet ...' A note of cynicism had crept into my voice.

271

He went to kiss me and then caught my look. He edged back, sitting at the end of the bed, his gaze locked with mine. Then his defensiveness gave way and he shrugged helplessly. 'Call it poetic license.'

'You lied?'

'I didn't lie. The guards were rough. They were total pricks who loved nothing better than humiliate us.'

'Did they beat you?' I asked.

'Like I said, they were pricks. They roughed me up, alright.'

I tried to understand what he was telling me. 'Did they break your bones?'

There was a guilty caught-out look on his face.

I traced the stripes on his bedspread and asked, 'What about the way they harassed you because of the papers I'd signed? Was that poetic license, too?'

'Of course not!' He dragged his fingers through his hair. 'I've never lied to you. That stuff about the guards beating me up – that was true, even if it didn't exactly happen in that way. The thing is, you've got to make things entertaining for people. It's like you need to present them with a bigger version of the truth. A version that they can really get behind, if that makes sense.'

Frowning, I looked at him once more, at his strong shoulders and the lines of muscle in his arms. His perfect, never-broken nose. Prison was his success story. It had made him a hero, all the girls lining up to hear his tales of bravery and honour. No one wanted a story like mine, that was bent in all directions. In my life, the good things I'd done were all mixed up with the bad.

'Ania.' He moved closer and brought his lips to my shoulder, making me shiver. He tipped my head gently to the side and kissed the nape of my neck, his fingertips light against my back and then firmer as he pulled me in. I let it happen and then met his embrace with vigorous kisses of my own.

This was what I wanted. For things to be the way they were before.

272

I moved down and breathed in the warmth of his chest. The smell of his skin was masked with cologne. Aniseed and spice.

The niggling thought returned: Dominik wasn't the person I thought he was. Or maybe the trouble was that there were two Dominiks. There was the lover I'd had who smelt of tobacco and ink, who kissed me in forests, who held me in his arms in his tiny bed, and who sat with me in my Father's house while we talked about our lives until it got dark outside. And then there was this other one. The Dominik who was able to lie about the things that mattered the most.

'Are you okay?' he asked.

My heart skittered in my chest as I pulled away. 'This belongs to you.' I took the ring off my finger and placed it in the palm of his hand.

'No ...' He tipped the ring onto the bed.

My smile pressed back my tears. 'Yes.'

In my life, and in my work, I wanted to move closer to what was true. Dominik, on the other hand, seemed intent on moving in the other direction. I reached for my elastic and divided my hair into three sections, threading them into a plait.

15

Australia, September 1983

The morning sun was fierce, striking down on the citrus
farm and the sweep of rainforest behind it. When I closed
my eyes the insides of my lids were flecked orange, the sun
finding me even in darkness.

After what happened in London, I wrote to Małgorzata
and confessed everything. I told her how ashamed I'd
been about the signing of the papers, how terrible it was
to flee Poland like a criminal, and how I'd lost my way
with art. I admitted, at last, that I was in awe of her and
that it sometimes made me petty. This morning I received
a reply, written in her extravagant hand, a picture of the
Eiffel Tower on the top of the page.

> It's funny you say you envied me, because I always wanted to be
> you. You've never put on airs. If that sounds condescending I
> don't mean it that way. I mean you have something in you that is
> rare and heartfelt and true. You are an artist and soon the world
> will see it and the rest of us will be able to say we knew you. (Your
> Mother Sculpture was better than mine. Remember? The one
> made of clay.)

I hadn't thought about that sculpture since Poland. I didn't
even know where it was now. Languishing in the studio at
the Academy perhaps? My chest ached as I recalled how I
had promised Father I would bring it home.

You say that art has left you and I refuse to believe it. You need a change of environment, that's all. Come stay with me in Paris. There's plenty of room in the apartment. Ryszard is in America making another film, leaving me with the baby. I'm torn between being lonely and being thankful for a break from him. He's a different person in Paris or maybe I'm the one who has changed. Anyway, I want you to come! It will be good for your art and good for me, too.

There was no reason I couldn't go. There was nothing to tie me here – nothing to tie me anywhere, in fact. A notion that made the skin on my arms tingle with exhilaration and fear.

An insect fell into my glass of coffee. I picked it out and flicked it to the ground, where it lay sodden and still. A shadow inched towards it. As I looked up, John approached, his sandals scraping against the ground. He stood before me, his hands stuffed in the pockets of his shorts. He was wearing a buttoned-up shirt.

I focused my gaze on the rainforest behind the citrus farm. John and I had barely spoken since the night of his exhibition. He'd left London a couple of days after the opening, claiming that the city was making him crazy. He went to Greece while I stayed in London, as planned, for another week. I spent my days at the big galleries, drawing the sculptures and the people who flocked there seeking art.

'Can I sit?' John positioned himself next to me on the step. He dragged a twig through the blades of grass by his feet. After a long pause he said, 'I'm sorry, really I am. I've spent a lot of time thinking about what happened. I had to get away and sort myself out. I was losing the plot a bit. You don't know what it's like, the pressure of those shows. Having all these hot young artists clambering to take your place. I needed something big for the exhibition. I got scared. In my own head, I managed to justify it. Tell myself that what I was doing was okay. Not that it's any excuse, mind.' He sighed. 'You know, in a way I miss the old days, when I was working in private, making art for no other reason than because I wanted to.' He skewered the twig in the ground. 'Tell me what I can do to make it up to you.'

'Did it sell?' I asked. 'This bath with fish?'

'Yeah.' He looked away. 'An American collector snapped it up. The critics loved it too. One of them said it captured the *existential pain and isolation of the artist.*' He raised the pitch of his voice at these last words, emphasising his sarcasm, but I could see he was proud of the review.

I wrenched the twig from the ground. 'The pain of the artist …' I said. 'And this artist, it is you or me?'

'Ha.' There was a sharpness to his laugh.

I recalled what Dominik had said to me in London, to justify his lies. That he had to make the truth bigger for people. John, on the other hand, had taken someone else's truth and presented it as his own. Did everyone stoop to these lows?

As soon as I asked myself this, the thought came to me, unbidden, that I had stolen too. Like John, out of desperation, with no ideas of my own, I took the nettle dress and remade it from palm. The difference was that my sculpture hadn't been a success. That, and I hadn't been caught.

'I'll give you half,' John said. 'Half of what it sold for.'

I recalled the incredible prices that his pieces had commanded. By comparison, the wages he had given me were paltry. I had made his sculptures with my own hands. And the one I hadn't made – the fish in the bath – that came from me, too.

In making that sculpture, John had taken something from me. However, I was beginning to see that he had given me something as well. I knew, now, that I had in myself what it took to be an artist. My stories, my ideas – these were good enough to show in a proper gallery in London. And, unlike John, I had the technical skills to make my own sculptures. I wanted to work again, and with the money that John was offering, I would have the time to do it. For a year, maybe two, I would be my own boss. The way Father had been.

'Okay,' I said to John. 'The money for the sculpture, I have half. And I will tell no one.'

John nodded slowly. Then he said, 'Let's seal the deal.' He shook my hand in his. 'Will you come back and work for me?'

'No,' I said. 'I will make my own art.'

He flicked an ant off his leg. 'That's good, you've got something in the pipeline? I mean, you've got an idea for a sculpture have you?'

'Maybe.'

There was a pebble by my foot and I picked it up. Its surface was smooth. Like a headstone, waiting for a name. I was transported back to Father's work shed, to the song of our chisels as we worked together, dust motes floating in the air. I shut my eyes for a moment, getting closer. I needed to get hold of some rocks that were big enough to carve on, big enough to hold my memories.

'What is it in Polish?' John asked out of nowhere.

Confused, I turned to him.

'What's the Polish word for carp?' He shrugged and said, 'I should learn a bit of your language, right?'

'It's the same,' I said. Using my finger, I etched the letters on a patch of dirt, *KARP*.

In a way, the fish had bought me independence. For a year or more, I would own my own time. I had John and the American collector to thank for that. However, I was puzzled by the logistics of the sculpture. 'This man who bought the bath, must he fly the fish all the way to America?' I asked.

'Nah,' John said. 'It'll be a different fish. The one we used for the exhibition is dead.'

'It died?'

'Yeah, because of the water. Too much chlorine in it. For a fish, it's like breathing in poison. Stupid, I didn't even think of that until later. I guess I heard your story and figured that regular water would be fine.'

I remembered how the carp in Małgorzata's bathtub had darted around furiously for the first day or two, before it became despondent, floating listlessly in the water. It wasn't tired or bored by its enamel cage. It had been dying all along.

I wandered through the citrus farm, towards the large house where the farmer and his family lived. Their verandah was set at ground level and was fenced off by a latticework of wood. The farmer's wife was there, watering the pot plants that were crammed onto the verandah. The hem of her dress fluttered around her ankles as she directed the nozzle of a hose towards a flowered plant hanging from a pole. Water dripped from its basket onto the concrete floor.

I spoke to her about the limestones I had seen piled at the back of the house, leftover from a spa-bath that the farmer had installed in their garden. 'Can I buy them?' I asked.

'That dusty pile of rocks?' She folded the hose in half, cutting off the water. 'You're welcome to them.'

I piled the limestones into a wheelbarrow and transported them to my bungalow, unloading them under the mango tree. It was heavy work in the heat and my skin grew damp with sweat.

From inside the bungalow, I retrieved the chisel that I had brought with me from Poland. Its comfortable weight in my palm, I sat under the mango tree and examined the limestones.

The stones were relatively flat and ranged in size. The smaller ones I could cover with two of my hands, while the larger ones were about the size of a clutch disc. Beautiful, organic shapes, no two the same. I picked up a rectangular stone in both hands. It was heavy, weighing as much as three or four tins of food. I put it down and then selected a triangular stone with a curved base. This one was smaller and light enough for me to lift with one hand. I had grown up surrounded by stone, by granite, marble

278

and slate. How odd that I had never used it in a sculpture before. I thought back to the lessons Father had given me, when he told me about the different properties of rocks. Limestone, I remembered, was formed from tiny pieces of marine life, such as coral. It was a stone that came from the sea.

Wiping the perspiration from my forehead, I selected a rectangular stone, lifting it with both hands and checking it for fissures and cracks. I secured it on a sandbag on the ground. Then I slipped on a pair of goggles and a facemask, held a hammer in one hand and a chisel in the other. It had been a long time since I'd carved, but when I brought the chisel down to the stone I wasn't nervous at all.

16

When the tide was low I began to install my sculpture, laying the stones down on the sand. Arranging them in a curved line that stretched out to sea. Each one was carved with words from my memories, some in English, some in Polish.

Crouching down, I rested my palm on a stone that was carved with a slanted script like Dominik's: *I want to tell you so many things.* I placed it on the firm, dry sand. Then I took a few steps forward, where the sand became damp, and placed down another. *I, Anna Izabela Skowrońska, do hereby confess.* Two steps towards the sea, where I rested a stone that was carved with elegant writing like Father's, *These tales from the village must be very boring for you.* On another, I had engraved the inscription from Mother's headstone, *Remembrance is ours.* Then another, more recent memory, *Pin down the ideas before they escape.* And then, *I wanted it to be perfect.*

The lick of the water transformed the stones, bringing them to life. They glimmered in the afternoon light.

There was one stone that was special. I held it in my palm. It was much smaller than the others and darker. I'd brought it with me from Poland, taking it from the cemetery where Mother and Father lay. On it, I'd written, *słoneczko.* I nestled it by the water's edge and then stepped back.

At the sea-end of the sculpture, water shimmered on the sand, filling up my footprints. The water flowed over the rocks and then dragged back towards the horizon. It left behind a trail of seaweed and froth. When it rushed forward again, it came closer to shore.

I sat by the mangroves. Using a twig, I sketched the name of the piece in the sand, first in Polish, then in English, *Dom Jest w Pobliżu/Home Is Nearby*. I knew, now, that I belonged to this. No matter where I ended up in the world, no one could take it away.

People appeared on the beach, taking their evening walks. As the sun began its descent, orange and pink light rippled through the sky. An older man and woman dragged their dog away from the mangroves and led it to shore. They glanced at the trail of rocks before stepping over them. Then a small girl in her underwear ran towards the sculpture. She tumbled to the ground and scooped up a stone in her hands, holding it to her bare chest.

'Mum, look!' she yelled to the woman in a white bathing suit who was hurrying after her. The woman caught up with the girl, looked at the sculpture and then at me. She scolded the girl, taking the stone away from her and positioning it back in the sand.

My instinct was to speak in Polish, and I corrected myself, stumbling over my words. 'It's okay.' I brushed the sand off my hands and stepped towards the girl. 'You can touch. You can take.'

The mother glanced at me. 'Say thank you,' she told her daughter.

The girl held out the rock towards me, tracing the Polish letters. 'What does this mean?'

'It is "little sunshine,"' I told her, pressing the rock in her hands. In English, it sounded wrong. '*Słoneczko*,' I said slowly, sounding it out.

The girl repeated the word and then, grinning, raced off with the stone.

Other people on the beach were watching. After the example set by the girl, they overcame their caution and approached. They strolled up and down the line of stones, stopping now and then to cast me a questioning look and when I nodded *yes*, they handled the sculpture. Sometimes they took a stone with them. Other times they examined a stone and then placed it in a slightly different position to the one I'd chosen.

When I had told John about the sculpture, he wanted to photograph it for my portfolio. 'Otherwise it'll be gone,' he said. 'Kaput.' I told him this was what I wanted. The importance of this piece was in the making, and then the letting go. My work would appear in galleries. I knew that now. This piece was for me. Of all the sculptures I'd made, it was my favourite. When I looked back at the blood sculptures I made for *Burning*, it was with tenderness for my younger self. All my brashness and elation and uncertainty had gone into that piece. Now, I could feel myself moving closer to the direction I wanted to go. Closer to *my own vision*, as Professor Jankowski would put it.

Standing up, I followed the path of stones towards the horizon. The tide was coming in and dusk was starting to fall. As I stood watching the sea, salt water welled around my ankles, submerging the stones. Soon enough, the water came up to my knees. I remembered how Father had told me that Mother loved to swim and standing here in the ocean, I felt close to her. Close to them both.

I plunged my hands into the sea and a tiny fish darted towards my fingers and then slipped away. As the sun faded I was overcome by a sense of ease. Everything was here.

Everything loved and everything lost, here in the water.

Sources

Though a great deal of research has gone into this book, it is a work of fiction. In writing this novel I have tried to identify those instances in which, I believe, it is appropriate and ethically sound to 'make things up', and those instances in which it isn't. While I have aimed to stay faithful to the broad sweep of historical events of the period, I have taken license with certain details where these have served the aims of the story (for example, to my knowledge the film, *The Blue Lagoon*, was never released in Poland). However, even 'staying faithful to the broad sweep of historical events', is not as easy as it may sound. Historical facts are themselves contested and always privilege some voices and perspectives over others. This, coupled with the fact that the events described in this book form part of people's living memories, inevitably means that my understanding of this period in history will differ to other people's. I believe that we need to hear a multiplicity of stories from this period – particularly the stories of people who have been traditionally overlooked by mainstream history.

My knowledge of Polish history was shaped by a research trip I took to Poland, personal narrative accounts of the period, online sources, and books such as: *God's Playground: A History of Poland* by Norman Davies, *Paradise in a Concrete Cage* by Leszek Dziegie, *Solidarity's*

Secret: The Women Who Defeated Communism in Poland by Shana Penn, *The Private Poland: An Anthropologist's Look at Everyday Life* by Janine Wedel, *The Polish Revolution: Solidarity* by Timothy Garton Ash, *Letters From Prison and Other Essays* by Adam Michnik, and *The Spring Will Be Ours: Poland and the Poles from Occupation to Freedom* by Andrzej Paczkowski.

The following sources were indispensable for my understanding of Polish art and culture: *The Wild West: A History of Wrocław's Avant-Garde* exhibition organised by the Wrocław Contemporary Museum, *The Wild West: A History of Wrocław's Avant-Garde* edited by Dorota Monkiewicz. *Political Upheaval and Artistic Change*, edited by Claire Bishop and Marta Dziewanska, *Fate and Art: Monologue* by Magdalena Abakanowicz, *Freedom on the Fence*: *A Documentary about Polish Posters and the Power of the Creative Spirit* produced by Andrea Marks, *Polish Realities: New Art from Poland* edited by Christopher Carrel and Andrew Nairne, *Lovely, Human, True, Heartfelt: The Letters of Alina Szapocznikow and Ryszard Stanislawski, 1948–1971* edited by Agata Jakubowska, *Something Flashed, Something Broke, Something Remained: Consciousness Neue Bieriemiennost* edited by Kasia Redzisz and Karol Sienkiewicz, *The Politics of Literature: Poland 1945–1989* by Carl Tighe and the Culture.pl website.

My knowledge of Australian art, history and culture was informed by *ephemeral traces*: *Brisbane's Artist-Run Scene in the 1980s* curated by Peter Anderson, *Journeys North* organised by the Queensland Art Gallery: Gallery of Modern Art, *The Hillbilly Dictator: Australia's Police State* by Evan Whitton, *Joyful Strains: Making Australia Home* edited by Kent MacCarter and Ali Lemer, and the Remix.Org.Au website.

The 'singing canary' anecdote referred to by Ania and her fellow prisoners was taken from a book of stories by Marek Nowakowskim, *The Canary and Other Tales of Martial Law*, published by Dial Press.

'The Crossing' is the title of the Adam Mickiewicz poem referred to in this book.

The first epigraph in this book is a quote by Czesław Miłosz which appears in *The Polish Revolution: Solidarity* copyright by Timothy Garton Ash, Yale University Press. The second epigraph is taken from Martin Herbert's essay, 'The Broken Arm', in *Thinking is Making: Presence and Absence in Contemporary Sculpture Hardcover*, edited by Michael Taylor, copyright by Martin Herbert, Black Dog Publishing.

Acknowledgments

It takes a village to write a book. This is especially true when you decide to produce a book and a baby at the same time, and I'm profoundly grateful to my family and friends for their support and encouragement on both fronts. Particular thanks go to Grazyna McGuire (Babcia) and Glenis Allen (Nana) for taking time out of their lives to fly to Melbourne and look after baby Miro so I could work on my novel.

For their input into the manuscript, I am deeply indebted to Chandani Lokuge, Marko Pavlyshyn, Grazyna McGuire, Kerrin O'Sullivan, Sue Robertson, Angela Savage, Kali Napier, Karen Lee, Laurie Steed, the Writers Victoria Short Story Clinic, Julie Twohig, Ruth Clare, Elisabeth Hanscombe, Anton Allen, Baden Allen and Rachel Singleton.

For providing advice on matters relating to art and/or history, thanks go to Lis Johnson, Tony Hulbert, Peter Anderson, James Tizzard and Marek Będkowski.

It would not have been possible for me to write this manuscript without the assistance of a Research Training Program scholarship. In this respect, I am indebted to Chandani Lokuge for taking a chance on me and championing my transition from law to creative writing. Thanks also go to Monash University for providing a stimulating environment in which to learn.

I am grateful to the wonderful people at Impress Books, particularly Rachel Singleton, for helping me realise my dream of publishing a novel.

By far my greatest thanks go to Anton Allen, whose wisdom and support make everything possible.

About the Author

Magdalena McGuire is an award-winning writer who was born in Poland, grew up in Darwin and now lives in Melbourne with her husband and son. Her short stories have been published by *The Big Issue*, *Mslexia*, *Margaret River Press* and *The Bristol Prize*. She was the winner of the 2017 Mslexia Short Fiction competition. *Home Is Nearby* is her debut novel.

WHITE HAVEN WITCHES (BOOK 8)

VENGEFUL MAGIC
TJ GREEN

Vengeful Magic
Mountolive Publishing
Copyright © 2021 TJ Green
All rights reserved
ISBN 978-1-99-004720-6

Cover design by Fiona Jayde Media
Editing by Missed Period Editing

You can get two free short stories, Excalibur Rises and Jack's Encounter, by subscribing to my newsletter. You will also receive free character sheets of all the main White Haven witches.

Details can be found at the end of Vengeful Magic.

To my readers, thank you for being so supportive, enthusiastic, and generally fantastic!
You're the best xx

$\mathcal{T}$he smell of sizzling meat drifted through Avery and Alex's walled garden, and their guests chatted and laughed as they filled their plates with the food spread out on the patio table.

It was a Saturday night in early June, and they had gathered to celebrate Cassie, Dylan, and Ben finishing their postgrad studies, and Dan completing his master's degree. The White Haven witches, plus Newton, Sally, and Shadow were there too, the drinks were flowing, and the weather was balmy.

Reuben was wearing his loudest pink Hawaiian shirt that clashed with his yellow board shorts, and despite the fact that his clothes were partially covered by an apron stuffed with barbeque tools, Avery still winced when she looked at him.

"Who wants more sausages?" he asked, as he placed another dozen on a plate and ferried it to the large wooden table, setting them down next to some steaks and chicken wings.

"Good grief, Reuben! Are you trying to fatten us up?" Cassie asked.

"Don't complain!" Dylan said, already leaning forward to top his plate up. "This is brilliant! You're doing a great job!"

Reuben grinned and pulled up a chair. "I aim to please. Besides, it's the least I can do, since I'll eat most of it."

Alex raised his beer bottle. "Cheers, Reuben. Saves me some work, seeing as I've been slaving away all afternoon!"

Avery just looked at him, knowing he'd spent a couple of hours on the preparations, at most. "Exaggerator! Besides, you were enjoying yourself. I could hear music blasting!"

"It's still work, Ave!" Alex leaned over and kissed her cheek, looking very smug, and eased back in his seat again. "So now that your studies are over, what's the plan?"

Ben groaned. "A couple of weeks off would be nice. I'm knackered!"

"I wish," Dan said, laughing. "Avery is a hard task master."

"I'm not," she said, mock-outraged. "I'm very generous! If you want a holiday, just say so!"

He winked. "I'm kidding! But maybe in early July, before the school hols begin and the place is inundated with hoards of kids."

"Yeah, I might need some time off for the school holidays," Sally said. She raised an eyebrow at Dan. "Are you going away with Caroline?" She was referring to Dan's girlfriend of only a few weeks.

Dan winced. "Maybe? It might be too soon."

"Why didn't you bring her tonight?" Shadow asked, finishing her conversation with El. They had been leaning close in an animated exchange, and Avery wondered what they had been talking about. "I was hoping to meet her!"

"That's precisely why I didn't bring her. The poor woman would have been interrogated by all of you! Besides, I haven't shared some of the more *interesting* things about you yet, so I wasn't sure it would be wise."

Briar laughed. "Did you think we'd get a bit witchy and start casting spells? We're very discreet, you know!"

Dan gave Shadow a knowing look. "It was more Shadow's habit of pulling a knife at any minute that had me worried."

Shadow looked affronted. "I don't attack people at random!"

"But you do carry weapons—always!" Dan pointed out. "Regular people don't do that."

She shrugged, a mischievous glint in her eye, and a ripple of glamour made her hair shimmer. "I like to be prepared. Besides, they're hidden, most of the time."

"That's worse," Briar said. "You whip them out of thin air. It's so unnerving!"

Newton just shook his head. He was sitting next to Briar, and Avery was pleased to see their old friendship had resumed. "Twelve months ago I can honestly say I didn't think I'd be sitting at a barbeque with five witches, one fey, and three paranormal investigators." He shot Sally and Dan a grateful look. "Thanks for being normal!"

"I hate to break it to you, Newton," Sally said, smiling, "but seeing as you're the head of paranormal investigations for the Devon and Cornwall Police, you're not that normal anymore."

"Yeah, well, I keep trying to forget about that." He looked at Shadow. "Your friend, Maggie Milne, has phoned a couple of times."

Shadow looked suspicious. "Maggie is *not* my friend! Was she asking about me or the boys?" By 'boys' she meant the Nephilim—and they were far from boys.

"No, don't worry. Whatever you've been up to lately seems to have escaped her. Although, she did mention something about a missing necromancer."

Shadow shuffled uncomfortably in her seat. "He's dead, not missing, and we reported that."

"*Dead*?" Avery asked, shocked. "A necromancer? Did one of his demons kill him?"

Shadow looked up at the darkening sky where the faint pinpricks of stars were already appearing, and grimaced. When she looked at Avery again her eyes were wide. "It's sort of complicated—but essentially, it was a test of sorts and he failed."

Avery crossed her arms, sensing more to this story than Shadow was sharing. "Ah! That's the thing you needed Alex and El for, in the Mendips!"

She nodded. "We were on the trail of an unusual tomb. He was the competition."

Cassie leaned forward, intrigued. "What sort of tomb?"

Alex gave a short laugh. "They were hunting for angels."

"*Angels*?" Cassie's face filled with disbelief. "I know we've been busy swotting, but how did that happen?"

"Long story," Shadow explained, "to do with lost maps and weird visions, and Harlan's boss." By now, the clusters of separate conversations had dwindled as everyone looked at Shadow, and she appeared uncomfortable as everyone watched her. "What? The necromancer's death had nothing to do with me! But, there are many, many occult organisations out there." She gestured wildly. "Far more than I thought. No wonder Maggie is kept busy in London. You've got it easy here, Newton." She took a slug of her beer as she watched his reaction.

"Depends on your definition of busy," Newton said, caustically. "But Inez's brother-in-law works with Maggie, so I know what you mean. Besides, Maggie has a bigger team than me. She certainly needs it."

Shadow nodded. "I remember him. He took my statement."

Ben, Dylan, and Cassie glanced at each other, clearly baffled, and Ben said, "I feel we have some catching up to do!"

"So, now that you're going full-time with the business," Reuben said to them, "what are you going to call yourselves?"

Cassie groaned. "Don't ask. We can't decide. Ben wants to keep it simple, but I think it should have more of a ring to it!"

Ben glared at her. "We don't want to put people off by having them think we're fruit loops! We need to sound professional."

"But we don't want to sound boring!" Dylan put in.

Reuben laughed. "Is Ghostbusters too obvious?"

El rolled her eyes. "Yes!"

"I thought you had a name?" Avery asked, confused. "You set up last year, didn't you?"

Dylan shrugged. "Sort of. We capitalised on the Walk of the Spirits," he said, referring to Samhain. "But we still didn't really name ourselves, and of course now we have to for what is essentially our re-launch."

"Are you still based out of your flat?" Alex asked. Ben and Dylan were renting together in Falmouth, and they had moved all of their equipment there the previous year when they could no longer use the university campus.

Dylan nodded. "Yep. I think we need to clean it up over the next couple of weeks, sort out an office for clients."

Cassie sniggered. "And maybe just stop living in squalor?"

"It's not squalor!" Ben said, crossly. "It's just slightly messy!"

"Yeah right," Cassie said, shooting Avery an amused look.

Avery laughed. "So, you're still living with your friends in Harbour Village, Cassie?"

"Yep. They've got local jobs, so that works out for me."

Briar sipped her wine and said, "I can give you some hours in my shop again, if you need extra money."

5

"Cheers, I might take you up on that," Cassie said gratefully. "I take it things have settled down here after all the excitement of Beltane?"

The witches glanced at each other, relieved, as Alex said, "Yes, fortunately. The Goddess seems to have gone, and we're just left with the Green Man doing his usual thing."

Dylan topped up his plate and asked, "What do you consider *usual*?"

"I guess my definition would be that he's a regular presence now," Briar explained. "I feel him all the time, especially in all the green spaces, and particularly in Ravens' Wood. Although, thankfully, that place doesn't feel anywhere near as weird as it did on Beltane." She turned to Shadow. "I keep meaning to ask—did you go that night?"

Shadow looked wistful as she turned her beer glass in her hand. "I did…on my own. It was both amazing and heartbreaking."

"What else did we miss?" Ben asked, confused.

"The Otherworld was allowed through—but I couldn't cross." Shadow shrugged, frustrated. "It was a taste of home. But, I can't complain. This is home now. It's different, but it's fun." She grinned mischievously and winked. "Very fun."

"Don't tell me anything else," Newton warned her as he put his empty plate on the table. "The less I know, the better."

Shadow had a fixed smile on her face. "You really need to learn to trust me!"

"No, I really don't." Newton's phone started to ring, and he groaned. "Damn it. Excuse me."

He stood and walked to the far side of the garden, and Avery watched him with a sinking feeling. He'd said he was off that night, but she knew that meant nothing. If something really odd happened, he could get a call. With luck, this call wouldn't be the police.

They all fell into an easy conversation while Newton was

absent, and Avery started to stack the plates. It was fully dark now, and the fairy lights that were strung around the trees and the candles she'd placed in lanterns gave them enough light to chat by. Reuben had lit the fire in the small brazier at the centre of the gravelled area, and Alex added some logs, sending the flames flaring. They all rearranged their chairs as they topped up drinks, and settled themselves closer to the fire.

"What will you do for the Litha celebrations?" Cassie asked, as she took a sip of her wine.

El spoke up first. "We're celebrating with the coven at Rasmus's place in Newquay." She looked a bit guilty. "We sort of blew them off for Beltane."

"Yeah," Briar grimaced. "We should keep our coven happy. Besides, it was fun with them at Imbolc."

"As long as I don't have to run around a circle with a broom," Reuben complained.

Avery was so busy laughing at her memory of Reuben holding a besom broom she almost didn't notice the faint shimmer of movement at the edge of the seating area. She turned to look at it, wondering if she'd had too much wine, and with horror realised the disturbance in the air was expanding.

"Shit!" she shouted. "Something's coming!"

She dropped the plates on the table and raised her hands, summoning her magic, and heard the clatter of chairs as the others turned to look.

Alex started to speak. "Avery, what are—"

A wave of power flashed out from the centre of the disturbance, and *something* flew at her.

Avery sent a blast of air ripping through whatever was manifesting, and the window in her shed beyond smashed with its impact. But whatever it was counterattacked, knocking Avery off her feet.

With lightning-quick reflexes, she threw air around her, cushioning the impact so that she floated rather than crashed into the ground, and simultaneously heard a disembodied shout. A shower of coins rocketed towards her, bouncing off Avery's protection and ricocheting across the garden, and then a face emerged in the darkness.

Helena.

CHAPTER 2

*A*lex jumped to his feet, overturning his chair, and ran to Avery's side, ready to join her attack, but whatever had manifested out of the darkness had gone.

He hugged her as she lowered herself gracefully to the ground. "Are you all right?" He examined her swiftly for signs of injury, but although she was pale, and her hair streamed across her shoulders from the wind that had buffeted around her, she was otherwise unharmed.

"I'm fine," she said, but she was already distracted, her eyes turning to the dark corner of the garden. "Did you see that?"

"I saw something! What the hell was it?"

"And what is *this*?" Shadow asked, holding up a golden coin, her knife in her other hand. She was already standing by the shed, and Alex blinked. He hadn't even seen her move.

By now the others were on their feet, Reuben and El already heading purposefully to where Avery had directed her magic, while Briar scanned the garden with narrowed eyes.

"Is that a coin?" Cassie asked, looking confused. She

crouched and picked up something shining in the gravel. "Look, here's another!"

"Bollocks!" Ben said, looking annoyed. "Why the hell didn't I bring my EMF meter?"

"It's in the van!" Dylan said, already running out of the gate.

Sally, wide-eyed with shock, grabbed Dan's arm. "What happened? I don't understand. And Avery flew!"

Of course she was shocked, Alex realised, suddenly feeling very sorry for Sally. She knew they were witches, but she'd never been this close to any action before. Even when they rescued her from Caspian, she'd been in the cellar, well away from the fight.

Avery looked guilt-stricken. "Yes, sorry, I do that sometimes. Just ignore me."

Dan helped Sally to a chair again. "I'll get you another drink."

Sally nodded, her face vacant, as Newton emerged from the garden.

"I've been away for minutes only!" Newton said, shocked. "What the hell has happened?"

Avery shook her head. "I'm not exactly sure, but I think I saw Helena."

Alex thought he was surprised before, now he was doubly so. "Helena! Where?"

Avery gestured to the area that Reuben and El were investigating. "There! I don't know how to explain it, but the air sort of shimmered, as if something was manifesting." She looked frustrated. "Sorry. That sounds ridiculous, but that's what I saw!"

Shadow reassured her. "I saw it too, but I couldn't make out anything in it."

"But you saw Helena," Alex persisted.

Avery grimaced. "Yes. Initially, it was just swirling darkness, but right at the end, for just a split second, I saw her face."

Alex's anger was building. "I knew we should have banished her! I'm going to do it—tonight!"

"*No!*" Avery turned to him, alarmed, her hand restraining his arm. "I think she was in trouble!"

"She attacked you!" Alex had always been frustrated by Avery's inexplicable loyalty to Helena. He understood family ties, but she had tried to kill Avery. "We can't trust her!"

Her mouth was set in a stubborn line. "But she's helped us, too—you know that! And besides, she wasn't attacking me."

"How could you possibly tell that in a split-second?"

Briar had joined them, and she shot Alex a warning look before speaking in her gentle, reasonable tone. "Why do you say that, Avery? I think we're all a bit confused right now."

Avery took a deep breath and exhaled heavily. "I think there was something else there with her. Did you hear the shout?"

Alex met Briar's worried gaze and glanced at the others, who all shook their head. "No, we didn't," he said. "What did it say?"

"Nothing! It was just a scream, or a cry," Avery said crossly, "and I'm pretty sure it was female. What if she's in trouble?"

At that moment, Dylan came running, the EMF meter in one hand and his camera in the other. He thrust the meter at Ben. "Quick, we might get residual readings!" He took in their tense faces. "What did I miss?"

"Nothing but confusion," Alex said, resigned. "Whatever you can get will be great." He turned to Avery, knowing she was annoyed with him. "Come on, let's sit and talk while these guys do their thing."

"Yeah!" Shadow said. She and Cassie were now striding

around the seating area, collecting coins. "Let's talk about these, too!"

Newton rubbed his face with his hands, his mood clearly growing grim. "Not me, I'm afraid. I have to go. There's been a death in Fowey—a suspiciously paranormal one, obviously."

Not something else, Alex thought as he asked, "How weird this time?"

"A body was found on the beach just beside the town, close to the mouth of the estuary." Newton's mouth was set in a thin line. "Every bone in his body was broken. Every one! That's not normal!"

Briar frowned. "But the cliffs are high there. He could have fallen. Surely that would explain it?"

"Maybe, but I have a feeling there's more to it." Newton looked at everyone's tense faces. "I hate to leave after this, but I can't wait. I'm sure you'll be hearing more from me about this. Is there a witch based there?"

Alex shook his head. "No, but Oswald and Mariah are close. I suggest dealing with Oswald, if you need to. He's a good man."

"But we're happy to help," El said quickly. "Fowey is really not that far."

Newton nodded. "Thanks, but perhaps you've already got your hands full." He met Alex's eyes, a knowing look in them. "I'll call you tomorrow."

Alex watched him go, a sinking feeling already settling into the pit of his stomach, and then encouraged Avery into a chair, the others sitting next to them, while Ben and Dylan started their investigation.

"All right," Alex said, forcing himself to be patient. "What did you think you saw?"

"I didn't *see* anything—I felt something. Something malevolent."

"A demon?" El asked.

"No, I don't think so. Although, it was sort of portal-like."

"A spirit, then," Reuben said, catching Alex's eye.

"Maybe." Avery looked frustrated. "I couldn't tell. It was just the feeling of *something*—and Helena's face. But she didn't look evil, or mean. If anything, she was appealing to me."

"But you only saw her for a moment!" Alex reminded her.

"That was enough!" Avery told him. "And we haven't seen her for weeks! Not since before Beltane. I've actually been worried about her. Where has she gone?"

Sally shook her head as she clutched her wine like her life depended on it. "Do you need to worry about Helena? She's a spirit."

"Yes!" Avery said forcefully. "She's my relative, and she could still be influenced by other spirits!"

"Okay!" Sally held her hand up, palm outwards. "Just a question!"

Alex looked at Avery, surprised. Something had touched a nerve with her tonight. She wasn't normally this tetchy. "Maybe I should try and summon her, see what I can find. Not tonight, obviously, but tomorrow? If you think she's in trouble, then I'm willing to help her. I guess I could consider entering the spirit realm, if I can't summon her."

Avery smiled at him, and he felt his heart catch. "Would you? That would be great!"

"Whoa!" Reuben said, alarmed. "If there's something malevolent, you need to be careful, mate! You shouldn't walk in there alone. I could help."

Alex shook his head. "No, it's easier on my own, and I'm pretty good at this. No offence to you, but you're not as comfortable with the spirit realm as me."

"I could be your anchor, here."

Alex had often used the other witches for their power,

and to ground himself while he communicated with spirits. "Okay, let me think it through and I'll let you know."

"And now," Shadow said, a clutch of coins in her hand. "What about these?"

El reached over and took one from her. "Gold coins! Wow. These look old. Are they English?"

Shadow shrugged. "They're not fey!"

"Unfortunately," Cassie said, holding one up to the firelight, "I know nothing about coins, but these must be valuable."

She started passing them around until they all had one.

"How many have you found?" Dan asked, squinting at his coin.

Cassie and Shadow did a quick count, and Cassie said, "We're pretty much all holding one—about a dozen. Not many."

"We should take these to an expert," Dan suggested. "Get them valued, and maybe find out some history on them."

Shadow shook her head. "Oh, no. You'd have to declare them and everything! How are you going to explain that they came from some weird, ghostly portal?"

Dan's face fell. "Good point. Is there someone we can trust?"

El grinned. "Dante! He might know. And if he doesn't, we'll rethink."

"He owns a forge! That doesn't make him a coin expert," Reuben pointed out.

"But he studied art history, and worked in a museum, a million years ago," El said. "It's worth asking him."

Briar had fallen silent as she examined her coin, but she finally spoke. "I think the most important question is, why are they here? Are they a warning to us? A clue to finding Helena? Or something else entirely?" She looked at them all one by one, as the whine of the EMF meter finally fell silent. "What has the power to carry a physical object in the spirit realm and then eject it? Whatever these mean, it isn't good."

Ben and Dylan joined them, Ben looking grim. "I agree with you, Briar. I may only be picking up residual energy patterns, but they're strong. I'll analyse them properly tomorrow, though."

"What about you?" Alex asked Dylan. "Anything in thermal imaging?"

"Nothing," he said, looking disappointed. "But again, I'll look properly tomorrow. Maybe we should take a coin—run that through some tests, too."

"Great idea," Alex said, passing him his. "And now I think I need a beer. I'm hoping that's the end of our excitement for the night!"

Reuben laughed. "Yeah. This time last year we were battling demons. I really hope we're not in for a repeat of that."

"True." Avery looked as if she was starting to relax, and she leaned back in her chair and sipped her wine. "We were still hunting for our grimoires then."

"And Newton hated us!" Reuben reminded her.

"And we," Dan said, gesturing to include Sally, "had no idea how powerful your magic was. This year has been quite the ride! And tonight, Avery," he said looking at her pointedly, "was quite the demonstration!"

"Sorry." She looked chastened. "I didn't mean to scare you. It was instinctive."

He smiled. "That's okay. I'd rather you did that than get injured. What we all need after a nasty shock is sugar. Didn't you say you'd made some cake, Sally?"

Sally groaned. "Some things do not change. Yes, I did. It's on the table."

"Allow me," he said, leaping to his feet as he headed to get everyone a slice, and Alex was suddenly very grateful for Dan's affability.

Alex took a deep breath, relieved that some normality seemed to be descending on their evening again. But nevertheless, he couldn't really relax now, and neither could anyone else. An air of watchfulness had settled on them all, and expectation. And what about Newton's dead body? Alex feared that whatever had happened tonight was just the beginning.

CHAPTER 3

*N*ewton looked at the body at his feet and inwardly groaned. *Christ.* The man was smashed to a pulp. It didn't look as if there was a single bone in his body that wasn't broken.

Moore's deep voice rumbled next to him. "A few kids spotted it while they gathered firewood." He gestured to where the remnants of a fire smouldered a short distance away among the rocks at the back of the beach.

"Bloody hell. How old?"

"Mid-teens. At least they weren't younger."

"Could the fall have done this?" he asked, studying the cliff top above them.

"I doubt it…not unless he bounced off every single rock on the way down."

Newton grimaced as he crouched to examine the dead body. The man's limbs were splayed awkwardly, and his head was an odd shape, partially crushed on one side. Newton had a hard stomach, but he could feel his recently eaten food rising and he quickly stood and took some deep breaths. "Who was first on scene?"

"PC Marshall." He gestured to the officer on the edge of the beach a few minutes' walk away, where the path led from the car park. "The kids were good. They called it in and said they hadn't touched the body."

"Are they the ones I saw on the car park?" Newton had parked and headed to the crime scene quickly, nodding to Inez who was talking to three boys.

"Yeah. Coroner and SOCO will be here soon."

"I thought they'd have been here before me."

Moore ran his hand through his red hair. "Saturday night. There was a stabbing in Helston."

Newton nodded, distracted. "Any ID?"

"I waited for you."

Moore had recently been promoted to sergeant and seemed wary of overstepping his bounds, which was unusual. Most newly promoted officers couldn't wait to flex their new powers. Newton pulled his gloves from his pocket and, crouching again, felt in the man's pockets, finally pulling a wallet free. He quickly found the driver's license.

"Miles Anderson, twenty-eight years old, with what looks like a Carlyon Bay address."

Moore frowned. "Not far from home, then."

Carlyon Bay was about 15 minutes from Fowey. He could have been there visiting friends, or a girlfriend. "We need to search along the cliff top," Newton said, quickly assessing their options. "Let's see if there's any sign of a struggle." Newton squinted up again, but it was too dark to see anything. "The light will be poor. Is the coastal path close?"

"I think it's set further back from the cliff top at this point," Moore speculated, "but I'm not sure. It could be hazardous now. St Catherine's Castle is on that point, too."

Newton nodded, remembering the ruined castle on the headland. "We shouldn't wait. We'll seal off the path and get lights up there so we can start looking straight away." Every minute lost meant evidence could be lost too.

Moore folded his arms, his face grim. "So, if it's not an accident, what kind of supernatural creature could do this?"

"It might not be one," Newton said cautiously.

"Oh, come on, Guv. Have you seen the look on his face? I know he's badly damaged, but he looks terrified!"

Newton followed the line of Moore's torch and realised he was right. He hadn't taken much notice of the man's expression until now, but his face, what was left of it, was frozen in horror.

"Fair point," Newton said, nodding. "I have no idea, but I'll probably consult with our friends on this."

Moore knew exactly who Newton meant. "Good. They're useful. Does Inez know much about them?"

"Not yet. Although, I'm sure she suspects," Newton said. "I suppose I should share their unique abilities with her. She has been on the team a couple of months now."

Moore laughed. "She suspects, all right. She's on the team for a reason, Guv."

"True." Newton still felt he needed to protect the witches, wanting to keep their abilities known only to a few, but Moore was right. Inez was on the team now, and wasn't going anywhere. Part of his reticence was to protect himself, too. "I'll inform her tomorrow." More torches flashed at the end of the beach, and Newton sighed with relief. "SOCO is here. With a bit of luck, we might get some sleep tonight."

Alex rolled over in bed the next morning, and grinned. Avery was half-hidden under the duvet, her red hair sprawled across the pillow, snoring softly. He leaned forward and kissed her outstretched arm, and her eyes fluttered before she settled into sleep again.

Avery was not an early riser, especially after a late night, so rather than make her grumpy, he rolled out of bed, pulled his shorts and a t-shirt on, padded across the bedroom, and headed down to the kitchen to make coffee.

Circe and Medea, their two cats, circled his ankles, threatening to trip him up on the stairs, and he hissed at them. "Bloody hell, kitties, if you kill me, you starve!"

As usual they took no notice of him at all, and he fed them first before making his drink. He headed to the balcony, throwing open the French doors to a pale blue cloudless sky, and sat at the small table to enjoy the early sunshine. It was going to be another warm day; there was hardly any wind, and the sea was calm and flat for miles. It was probably already busy on the seafront, despite the early hour. Some of the boats would leave early to take visitors on day trips, depending on the tide. He sighed, wishing he could take the day off, but he had to head to his pub for the afternoon shift, and he had a feeling it would be busy.

Alex put his feet up on the chair opposite him and wondered if they'd hear from Newton today. If the death reported last night was suspicious, what type of creature could break every bone in someone's body? It was more likely that Briar was right about the fall, but maybe Newton knew something else he hadn't told them yet. He grabbed his phone and pulled up the local news, seeing that the death had already been reported on, but the coverage was light on details, not surprisingly. The only thing it said was that the victim was a young man.

They had speculated on it the night before after Newton had left, but without any details to go on it had been fruitless. Fortunately, the mysterious swirl of energy that had manifested hadn't returned, either. They ended up suggesting ridiculous names for the three parapsychologists' business, before they'd finally all headed home in the early hours of the morning.

His phone rang, jolting him out of his reverie, and he answered it quickly. "Hey, Newton. I guess this is bad news."

"You could say that. They weren't joking about this poor guy's state. He was pulp." Newton sounded cranky.

Alex groaned as a horrible image entered his mind. "Shit. Not a fall, then?"

"He'd had have to have fallen from a plane to be so injured."

"Shit," he repeated, wondering what might follow, because he doubted this would be an isolated incident. "Have you been up all night?"

"No, fortunately, but I've been at the station since six this morning."

"We were talking about it last night," Alex said as he made himself more comfortable, "but have no suggestions as to what could do this, I'm afraid."

"That's okay." Newton sounded distracted and his voice muffled for a moment as he turned away. "Sorry about that. We did find something odd, though. The victim had an old gold coin in his mouth."

"What? Placed there?"

"I reckon…like a warning."

Suddenly, Alex wasn't seeing the view anymore. He was picturing the gold coins that had spread across the gravel in the garden the previous night. "I hate to say this, but two appearances of gold coins in one night is not a coincidence! What kind of coin?"

"A very old one. A doubloon."

Alex nearly spat his coffee out. "Isn't that Spanish?"

"Yep. Maybe it's pirate gold. Don't ask how it came to be there, because I don't know! What were yours?"

"Honestly not sure, but English, we think."

"Mmm," Newton mumbled. "It would be good to know. I wonder if they're related?"

"Herne's balls," Alex said, using Shadow's favourite curse, which seemed to have caught on. "Is this to do with smuggling?"

Newton sighed. "Maybe. Look, I don't need you to do anything right now. I just wanted you to know."

"What about the victim?"

"His name is Miles Anderson, he's twenty-eight, and he lived in Carlyon Bay. But we haven't announced that yet, so keep it quiet."

"Of course."

"Anything else happened with you after I left?"

"Nothing, fortunately."

"Well, that's some good news," Newton said, obviously relieved. "I have to go, but I'll call you later if I find anything else. Let's hope this isn't the start of some summer madness."

He rang off abruptly, and Alex finished his now cold drink. A doubloon? This was going to require more coffee.

By the time Avery woke up, the scents of bacon and coffee were drifting through the house. She stretched, easing the kinks from her neck, and wished she'd had a better night's sleep.

Dragging herself out of bed, she wrapped a light summer robe over her long t-shirt and shorts and then padded downstairs, smiling at seeing Alex cooking at the hob, the radio low in the background. She walked up behind him and wrapped her arms around him, leaning into his back.

"Something smells fab. Is there enough for me?"

"Of course!" He twisted around to kiss her. "Egg and bacon sandwich on crusty bread sound good?"

"Perfect!" She headed to the coffee machine and made herself a drink, but Alex was watching her with a worried expression on his face.

"Did you sleep okay after last night?"

She nodded. "I did, eventually, other than a few weird dreams. I am really worried about Helena."

"I know. I have to work this afternoon, but I can search for Helena afterwards. I find that communing with spirits is more effective at night."

She smiled. "Do they have a night?"

He laughed, a little ruefully. "I don't think so. I think it's better for me, not them." He paused, a wary look on his face, as he said, "I didn't mean to doubt you last night, or piss you off."

"You didn't," she said, knowing he'd been concerned about her welfare, and understanding his feelings about Helena. "I was just worried…and a bit shocked. That attack came from nowhere. In our garden!" She shook her head. "Something punched straight through our protection spells. That will be one of my jobs today—I'll reinforce them."

"Just promise me you won't try to find Helena on your own!"

"Witches' honour!" Talking to spirits was Alex's specialty, not hers. "Any news from Newton?"

"'Fraid so. The guy was pulverised." He updated her while he cooked, and then steered them both to the outside table with their breakfast.

Avery brushed her hair back from her shoulders as she settled at the table. "I feel I should have lost my appetite, but I'm afraid I'm still starving." She took a bite, swallowed and said, "Do you think a witch attacked him?"

"It's possible, I guess. It would have to be a pretty nasty spell to break every bone, and I can't see it being one of the Cornwall Coven, but we shouldn't rule it out."

Avery shuddered. "I just hope his death was sudden. I hate to think he'd have suffered. But the doubloon is odd!"

"The Spanish attacked Mousehole and a few other towns farther along. Not the Armada…it was a few years later than that. I looked it up after Newton phoned."

"Wow. That's like over five hundred years ago!"

"It's even weirder when you consider the gold that was thrown at you last night. We've still got a coin here, so I'll see if I can get a timeframe on it."

"They have to be connected, surely," Avery reasoned. "We all know how popular smuggling was in Cornwall years ago. It makes me think they must be part of a treasure hoard."

"Maybe more than one," Alex suggested. "Newton was very sure his coin was Spanish, but if ours is English, are they from the same place?"

"And why would the Spanish hide their own gold?" she asked, puzzled, before taking another bite and speaking through a mouthful of food. "Shouldn't they have been stealing it?"

"In theory, yes. But they burned entire towns then—Mousehole was completely destroyed, except for the pub."

"Wow. They burned everything?"

He nodded. "And then moved on to Newlyn, Penzance, and Paul. A few locals were killed, and they took prisoners. Fortunately, they were released unharmed when they left."

Avery finished eating and pushed her plate away. "So there were a lot of them?"

"Four galleys, according to what I read. They were planning to take England, eventually." He laughed and sipped his coffee. "But failed."

"I guess trade would have meant their coins would have

been circulating here too." Avery groaned. "So many questions for a Sunday morning. One night and everything changes!"

"Typical White Haven."

Avery tried to dispel her worry, especially about Helena. "With any luck, this is just a horrible one-off."

He grabbed her hand and kissed her fingertips. "Ever the optimist! I hope you're right. Apart from doing protection spells, what are you getting up to today? You know I'm working later."

"Gardening, I think. Going to take advantage of this beautiful weather."

He grimaced. "Great!"

She laughed, knowing he hated gardening. "Grinch."

"Like you want me grumbling around you," he pointed out.

"Ha! True." As much as she wanted to disagree with him, he was right. Once she was in the garden, she lost hours, just as Briar did.

"I shall do something useful and clean the attic!" he said, rising to his feet. "We've been making a lot of mess lately, practicing our spells."

Avery drained her cup. "Deal."

By the time Alex arrived at The Wayward Son at just after one in the afternoon, the pub was already packed, and his staff were busy.

Alex didn't waste time, heading into the kitchen to see how everything was going. His head chef, Jago Hammet, a big burly man in his late thirties, was generally good-humoured and loved his work, in a sharp-tongued way. He had a quick wit and was very impatient, and although he was inclined to shout when busy, the other staff loved him. He looked up as Alex walked in, a cloud of steam billowing around him. "He finally arrives! About time!"

"Cheeky sod," Alex said, nodding in greeting to the other three staff that were busy preparing the meals. There was a young man barely out of his teens called Jake, Georgie, who was in her mid-twenties, and the sous chef named Larry who had four kids. He constantly looked knackered, and Alex wasn't sure if it was the job or the kids. He suspected the kids. "How's it going?" he asked them.

"Like clockwork, of course." Jago glanced outside at the weather. "The sun always brings the punters out in force. Doesn't stop them from eating acres of roast beef, though."

Alex winked. "It's Sunday lunch! Not the same without it." He inhaled deeply. "Smells amazing."

"That's because it is." Jago never doubted himself. "Tell Anna out there to get a move on—and that bloody big unit, Zee. Next lot of food is up."

Alex nodded and left them to it, narrowly avoiding Anna as she swung through the door as he exited. She'd been working at the pub for a few months and was a good find. Dark-haired and feisty, she was a single mother in her thir-ties with teenage sons. She worked hard and was reliable. "Hey, boss. Newton is in. You in trouble again?"

"Funny," he said dryly. Everyone knew Newton by now. He made himself comfortable at the bar and watched the football if Alex wasn't around, and Alex was pretty sure if he focussed less on the match and more on his surroundings, he might actually get a date.

"And Reuben's here, too." She lowered her voice and looked hopeful. "Is he still with El?"

"Of course."

"Damn it. A girl can hope. That big hunk of muscle." A

dreamy expression passed across her face, and then she disappeared to grab the plates on the counter.

Alex shook his head as he headed into the bar, half wondering why Zee wasn't on her hit list. If she wanted 'a big hunk of muscle,' Zee was it. He banished the thought from his mind, vowing never to refer to his friends like that again. Instead, he thanked the Gods that his employees were cheerful and upbeat, which made his life easier. He often envied Avery for her small number of staff; running the pub was hard work and usually busy, and sometimes the bar staff turned over quicker than he liked. He was lucky with Simon, his manager. He was calm and organised, which allowed Alex time to pursue some of his more unusual activities. He spotted Zee further along the counter and went to relieve him, nodding to Kate, his barmaid, as he passed her.

"Hey Zee, finish this order and then head to the kitchen. I'll cover this."

"Sure thing," Zee said as he finished pulling the pint, placed it on the bar, and took payment. As soon as the customer had gone, he said, "Shadow said there was a problem last night."

"That's one way of putting it." Alex reminded himself he shouldn't be surprised by Shadow's masterful understatements. He lowered his voice. "They found a man dead on the beach by Fowey last night. It's been on the news. And it's probably paranormal. Hopefully Newton can tell us a bit more today."

Zee nodded. "Good, keep me informed."

He disappeared into the kitchen to start carrying dishes as Alex continued to work, finally making his way to Reuben and Newton's spot on the bar.

"Didn't expect to see you today, Newton. Do either of you need another pint?"

"Not for me," Reuben said, wiggling his half-full glass.

"Just a coke, please," Newton said. "I needed a break, and time to think, and the drive has given me that." He checked his watch. "I'd better be getting back, though. I've just told Reuben we can't find anything on the cliff edge."

Reuben's eyes were narrowed as he watched Newton. "The cliff path isn't close at that point though, is it?"

"No. There's a patch of open ground and a few stunted trees, all sloping towards the edge—but the ground is undisturbed." Newton shook his head, perplexed. "It doesn't make sense. We should have found *something*!"

"He wasn't washed ashore?" Alex asked.

"No. The victim was bone dry. Time of death is estimated to be between eight and ten last night."

Reuben sipped his pint. "I take it you searched a good distance?"

"Yep, on the beach and the cliff top, a half a mile on either side. There's no sign of a scuffle, or his car."

"The cliff path runs a long way. Maybe it was parked further than you think."

"Maybe." Newton sipped his coke and grimaced. "Not quite Doom, is it? Anyway, with luck we'll find his car today somewhere."

"Has he got family?" Reuben asked.

"An older sister who lives in Penzance, and parents who live in St Ives. I went to see them this morning." He frowned. "Unfortunately, they can't tell us anything. They have no idea what he was doing there. He lives with his girlfriend, so I really need to find her, but so far she's not at their house, or answering her phone…and that's worrying."

"Do you think they've been up to something dodgy?" Reuben asked.

"Possibly. He had a very unpleasant death." Newton stared into his drink. "Something feels off. I don't suppose you've thought of anything that could smash someone to a pulp?"

Alex shrugged. "Not really." He looked at Reuben. "I guess this could be demonic?"

"It's possible," Reuben said, nodding. "They are violent!"

Newton groaned. "I hope it's not! We might find something useful when we search his house. I'm heading there now." He drained his glass. "I had to get the identification confirmed first. His father did that. His mother was hysterical. Horrible."

Newton rarely shared the details of his job, and Alex suddenly felt sorry for him. He'd never even considered the things such as victim identification. "Sorry, Newton. What a crap way to spend your day."

"You never get used to it," he said sadly. "Anyway. Must go, and I'll keep in touch."

Reuben and Alex watched him leave, and Reuben said, "Demon is a good suggestion."

Alex felt a heaviness settle in his stomach. "But that means someone is controlling it. I'm really hoping it's something else."

"Like what? An angry spirit? A poltergeist?" Reuben looked uncertain. "Sounds dubious. And I can't see it being anything to do with a witch."

Alex glanced down the bar to make sure no one was waiting to be served, and with relief noticed Zee was back, serving again. "No, hopefully not."

Reuben pushed his empty pint glass to Alex, and he topped it up absently, saying, "I think we should call Oswald. He's a bit closer than us. We can see if anything odd has been happening up that way. I'll ask Avery to call him, she'll have time."

"*I've* got time!" Reuben said, looking slightly affronted.

Alex slid his pint in front of him, and laughed. "Well yes, but you don't have Avery's winning ways."

"Are you saying I'm not charming?"

"You know exactly what I'm saying," Alex said, deciding to lay it out. "Your dry sarcasm and general scepticism doesn't always win friends and confidences."

Reuben gave him a sly grin. "I suppose when you put it like that, maybe Avery should call him." He paused for a second and then asked, "How is she today? She was a bit...*sensitive* last night."

"I guess sensitive is one word for it," Alex admitted, unwilling to criticise Avery but also feeling the need to confide. He wiped the counter down, even though it was perfectly dry, and saw Reuben still watching him. He gave up. "She's unreasonably protective of Helena. I don't get it! I'm glad to see the back of her! Damn spooky ghost just manifesting around the flat. And I'm used to spirits!"

"I'd hate it, too," Reuben admitted. "And Helena did try to kill her. I'm with you. I'd put my foot down with El if she had a spirit lurking around."

Alex gave him a long look. "You say that, but I think we both know where she'd tell you to get off. We are both blessed with feisty women."

Reuben grinned. "Well, yes, but you do live there, too!"

"It's not that simple though, is it?" Alex said. "It would be like suggesting I get rid of the cats. I can't! Helena isn't just any spirit, and she has this odd sentience, too."

"So did Kit, but you got rid of him well enough!"

"Yeah, well, he was actively hurting people. And Avery has a point. She has helped us in many ways since. I guess I was hoping she'd just quietly disappear, but now it seems as if she's trapped in some kind of spirit prison." He rolled his eyes. "Just my bloody luck! It's like having to rescue my mother-in-law!"

"Ha!" Reuben threw his head back and laughed. "Let's hope you get rewarded for your services."

"But seriously, what's with the gold coins? What is this, some kind of smugglers' revenge?"

They both stopped laughing then and Reuben's eyes widened. "Maybe Helena's past needs more investigation."

"The smuggling was well after her time!"

"But were the Spanish?"

CHAPTER 4

*A*very finished weeding her herb beds with the aid of a little magic and stepped back, pleased with her progress.

In the last couple of weeks, since the risk of frost had gone, she'd planted lots more annual herbs, trimmed the existing ones, and had harvested some to dry. A trug was on the gravelled path next to her, filled with cuttings. She filtered through her favourite gardening spells, decided on one that was best for this occasion, and said it softly under breath. Her magic rolled around her, and she smiled as she saw her plants respond.

Satisfied, she headed back to the patio table where they had partied the night before, pulled the phone from her pocket, and called Oswald, as Alex had asked, smiling at hearing his warm but slightly old-fashioned mannerisms.

"Avery, I'd like to say this is a pleasure, but I sense trouble."

"You do?" she asked, surprised.

"I have a sixth sense for these things sometimes, especially when I'm relaxed. Which I was. And besides, you don't normally phone for a chat."

Avery felt horribly guilty for disturbing his afternoon. "I'm so sorry Oswald, but we thought you should know about the death they reported this morning."

He groaned. "The young man found on the beach outside Fowey? Go on."

Avery updated him as succinctly as possible, but as soon as she mentioned the doubloon, she felt Oswald's excitement. "A *what*? How very unexpected, but exciting too! Terrible though this death is, the doubloon does lend an air of intrigue, and the suggestion of smuggling, dare I say!"

"I guess so," she said, surprised by his response. "I must admit, we thought of smuggling, too."

"It's a natural assumption when you hear of treasure, and a doubloon is undoubtedly just that. We all love a pirate story, and there's plenty of smuggling tales around here, too!"

Avery leaned back in her chair, looking over her garden, but not really seeing it anymore. "Well, true, but a doubloon is from a couple of centuries before the smuggling industry became really big in Cornwall."

"But it doesn't mean they're not connected in some way." He fell silent for a moment and then said, "I'm going to have to do some smuggling research."

"But how could that be connected to the poor man's death? It was so violent!"

"Early days for that, Avery, but I'll have a think. No sign of any more treasure?"

"Well, actually yes," she confessed, relating the events of the night before.

After a moment's shocked silence, Oswald said, "That's fascinating. And your ancestor?"

"I got the impression she was in trouble."

"Well, I have no idea what to do with that," he murmured.

"Nor us, but we were wondering if you've noticed anything odd in your area lately?"

"Nothing, but you can be sure I'll be keeping a close watch from now on. I'll tell Ulysses, too."

After they said their goodbyes, Avery headed up to the attic with her herbs, surprised by how clean it now was. Alex had done a good job, and he'd opened the windows, allowing a light breeze to drift through the room. She placed her herbs on the table, and took her time tying them together before hanging them from the rafters overhead. Then she turned to her bookshelves, looking for something on supernatural creatures.

She pulled one book after another, but frustrated at having nothing really suitable, decided to search her shop instead. Rather than walk downstairs, she used witch-flight, and materialised in the occult section.

It was hot and stuffy in Happenstance Books; dust motes hung in the sunshine that slanted through the windows, and yesterday's residual incense mixed with the scent of old and new books. Avery searched the magic section, noting the new books that Sally had ordered in. There were lots of new spell books, and books on the history of witchcraft, and they continued to add to their selection regularly. Ever since Rupert had started his occult tours, they had increasing interest in witchcraft and had decided to capitalise on it. However, there was nothing that listed supernatural creatures specifically, and instead she decided to check the shelves stocking books on myths and legends, pleased when she found a few about Cornish folklore. "Bingo," she said softly, as she pulled them from the shelves.

Then she felt a breeze across the back of her neck, and the temperature around her dropped.

Avery whirled around, her hand raised, ready to either defend or attack. "Helena? Is that you?"

A shimmer in the air to her left had Avery turning swiftly, but nothing appeared, and the cold air disappeared as quickly as it had arrived. *That was odd.* Was Helena trying to contact her again, or was it something else? One good thing, she reflected, was that at least nothing had been thrown at her. But where the hell was Helena?

At six that evening, after a couple of hours of research, Avery arrived at The Wayward Son and found that Reuben, El, and Briar were already in the back room at the pub, chatting over drinks. She grabbed a glass of wine at the bar, unable to see Alex, who she presumed was in the kitchen, and joined them.

The small room at the back of the pub was, as usual, quieter than the main area, spelled by Alex to only encourage locals to loiter. The patio doors were open, and a warm evening breeze flowed inside, carrying the sounds of voices and laughter from those seated in the courtyard garden.

"Hey, guys," she said, sipping her wine and taking a seat. "I hear Newton has had an interesting twenty-four hours."

Reuben nodded. He had a half-empty pint glass in front of him, and his arm was slung across the back of El's chair. "Yeah, unfortunately. We haven't heard from him since lunch, though. I guess he's very busy."

Avery frowned at him. "Have you been here all afternoon?"

"No! I've been surfing, obviously! Trying to clear my head after a few too many beers last night."

El laughed. "Like that ever puts you off. You're a freak. What have you been up to, Avery?"

Avery reached into her bag and withdrew a small, slim book with a few pages marked, placing it on the table. "I've been doing some reading this afternoon, and have a few ideas of what could have caused that man's death."

"Have you?" Briar asked, looking hopeful. "I've been completely tied up with making new stock for my shop."

"I have news, too," El confessed, looking pleased. "I've been at the forge with Dante for a couple of hours. The boys want enhanced weapons, so I've been working on them in my downtime."

Avery was momentarily sidetracked. "As in the Nephilim?"

"Yeah—I'm making swords and daggers with enhanced powers. They've all decided they want some. Nahum wants throwing knives, so that's a challenge." She grinned. "Fun, though. Anyway, while I was there, I showed him the coin… but you first!"

"I've been reading up on piskies, púcas, spriggans, and other Cornish creatures, trying to decide if they have something to do with that man's death, but to be honest, I'm a bit bewildered," Avery said, her hands idly flicking the pages of the book. "I need to chat to Dan. There are so many legends to consider."

"That's a good idea," Briar agreed. "Reuben said you were going to phone Oswald. Did you ask him about supernatural creatures?"

"No, actually," she said, telling them what they'd discussed. "But he will keep an eye out for anything odd."

Reuben pulled the book towards him and started leafing through it. "What sounds most likely then, according to this?"

Avery frowned. "Púcas are a possibility—they have a reputation for being menacing. Or, more likely, spriggans."

"Like what our beach is named after?" Reuben asked.

She nodded. "Among the many stories about them, they apparently hang around old ruins and cairns, guarding buried treasure. They can become very mean when disturbed."

El looked baffled. "Aren't they supposed to be like little old men?"

"Yes, though that doesn't sound particularly threatening," Avery confessed.

Briar rubbed her face, bemused. "This is a crazy conversation to be having—and I know that I've been possessed by the Green Man—but this just sounds mad!" She leaned forward. "Are we actually entertaining this discussion?"

Reuben tutted. "Briar! Of all the people who should be the most accepting of this! You go out with a shape shifter! How is he, by the way? He hasn't been down for a few weeks."

"He's fine," she said, a flush colouring her cheeks. "Just involved with pack business. And I know exactly what you mean. It's just that piskies, of all things, and other little creatures sound, well, make-believe!"

"You're right," Avery admitted. "I've been wrestling with this for the last couple of hours, persuading myself that I'm already mad just thinking about it."

El laughed. "You live with a ghost, and we've banished mermaids, spirits and demons, *and* seen the Raven King! Surely it's not that far-fetched?" Her finger tapped her pint glass. "Maybe we should speak to Shadow. She's fey, and might know far more about them than what's written in that book."

"I hadn't considered that," Avery said, nodding. "By the way, talking of ghosts, I had another odd experience this afternoon." She started to relay what had happened in the shop, and Alex arrived halfway through, taking a seat opposite her.

Once she finished, he frowned. "But you didn't actually see Helena?"

"No, not this time." Avery took another sip of her wine. "But I'm even more worried about her now."

"I wish I could say I miss her," Alex said, "but I don't. However, I will look for her tonight, as agreed."

"Thank you!" Avery hadn't wanted to make such a big deal about it, but now that he'd offered, she couldn't wait to see what he found. Realising he hadn't heard her update about Oswald, she said, "And I spoke to Oswald. He's going to make inquiries, but there's nothing much going on that he's noticed."

"Well," Alex said, looking pleased with himself. "I've found out that our very own White Haven Museum has a new exhibition on smuggling. It starts next weekend, and is only open for a short time, but it will be worth seeing."

"I've never been in there at all," Reuben confessed, slightly sheepish.

Alex laughed. "Well, that's not surprising. You're not exactly known for your love of museums and research."

"I could be persuaded to go, though," he said, "if there's a pub lunch at the end of it."

"I'm sure we could manage that," Avery reassured him. "I wonder if there'll be something about the West Haven tunnels there?"

The passages they had found that led from Rupert's House of Spirits connected to a network of tunnels, and they hadn't followed most of them, focussing only on finding vampires.

El looked thoughtful. "I'd love to know how far they go. There are smuggling tunnels all over Cornwall. But where has that doubloon come from?"

"And what's its message?" Briar asked. "It would have been better off leaving the man dead with no doubloon. Now we have a clue!"

"Is it, though?" Reuben said, ever sceptical. "Or is it a diversion?"

"So, what have you found out about our coins?" Briar asked El.

"They are guineas, British, and the one I have is eighteenth century—King George, I think Dante said, though not sure which George." She shrugged. "But guineas were made in the seventeenth century too, so we may have a mixture."

"Are they worth anything?" Alex asked.

"Sure! Not millions or anything," El said brightly, "but a few hundred pounds, depending on the guinea. The quantity of gold in them varies, apparently, and they're worth more than their value to a collector."

"So," Avery reasoned, "these are obviously a very different timeframe to Spanish doubloons. I guess the question still is, are they connected? Is the death of the man in Fowey and Helena's odd appearance connected?"

"Surely, they have to be!" El said, appealing to them all.

The others looked around the table blankly, and Avery realised that with so little to go on, they were speculating wildly. But at this stage, there was nothing else they could do.

"If we're going to look into smuggling," Briar said, interrupting her train of thought, "we should go to Bodmin and see the Jamaica Inn Smuggling Museum, too. That's supposed to be good." She rose to her feet wiggling her glass. "Another drink, everyone?"

CHAPTER 5

*A*lex sat in front of the fire in the attic, in the centre of a circle of protection, with a single candle burning in front of him. Avery sat opposite him, cross-legged. She'd watched his preparations silently, her lips pressed tightly together.

He tried to reassure her. "Avery, I'll be okay."

"You don't know that! You've never done this before!"

She was right, and he was worried, too. He had just spent the last hour trying to summon Helena, seated outside a summoning circle, but she had failed to appear. He'd sensed some kind of block, and unable to work out exactly what it was caused by, he'd opted to travel into the spirit world to find her.

He squeezed Avery's soft, warm hands that were in his own. "My own magic is now stronger than it ever was."

"I know. So, I just ground you—give you some power, like when you spoke to the Nephilim in All Souls' Church?"

"Sort of. Just remember, I might take quite a while, but don't freak out."

The candlelight flickered across Avery's face as she

nodded, the rest of the attic in complete darkness. The potion he'd drunk to help him enter the necessary mental state was already taking effect, and as he started to utter the spell that would bring him into the spirit realm, the darkness seemed to get more absolute. Within seconds, Avery's face disappeared completely, and he was surrounded by a shadowy void.

Alex felt weightless, his body left behind, but still he felt Avery's warm presence, like a kiss on his consciousness. But she wasn't just there to support him; she was there to help him find Helena. Whatever he thought about their connection didn't matter; the important thing was that their connection was strong.

He'd noticed similarities in their looks, around the eyes and slim build, not to mention a certain stubborn set to their features, but there was more than that. Helena was of a similar age to Avery when she died, something that had upset Avery more than anything, especially as she had two young children. But where did she go when she wasn't in Avery's flat? And how had she corralled so many spirits on Samhain to walk through the town? Helena was unusual in that she wasn't a spirit at rest; she still visited the real world, and had managed to retain some kind of control of her actions.

For a few moments Alex tried to orientate himself, and felt a tremor of unease as he realised that was impossible. There were no landmarks here, just shadowy presences that he sensed rather than saw. He was in a grey void. Was this what spirits saw? Or only him, as a live being moving in a place where he probably shouldn't be?

Enough. Time to move. He willed himself forward, feeling presences brush past him, mostly harmless and curious. But the further he travelled, the stronger their curiosity grew. His spirit was bright in their realm, like a beacon. He paused, trying to detect Helena's presence, calling out to her with his spirit voice, but he couldn't feel her at all. Every now and again he felt an echo of her presence, but still pushed on, frustrated at her nebulousness.

Something wasn't right, he knew it. He was deeper now, and the atmosphere had changed. Spirits fled before him, but with a flash of recognition and a feeling of victory, he picked up Helena's energy—but following it was like following a fine thread. She was so elusive.

And then he felt something else, something that watched him, waited for him. No, there was more than one presence —there were many more—and he picked up a distinct feeling of resentment from them. He ignored them and called for Helena, projecting his power outwards, and finally heard a cry. A glimmer of light flashed from what seemed to be a long way away before vanishing again.

He was close, he knew it, and he continued on, regardless of the brooding menace of those watchful presences that were too close for comfort. Then he summoned his magic. Using magic here was very different to using it on the Earthly plane. Spells didn't work as effectively, but his power would be visible to those around him. He flexed it now, so that it pulsed as a warning to others, and then pushed on, Helena's presence growing closer.

Out of nowhere, something hit him, like a punch to the gut. It sent him spinning away, leaving him confused and disorientated—and feeling smothered.

And worse still, Avery's presence had vanished.

Alex tried not to panic; that was the worst thing to do. Getting lost in the spirit world was a sure way to die, but the feeling of being restrained was stronger now, as if a bag had been thrown over his head. He was suffocating—which should be impossible—but it was happening.

It was a trap. Was this Helena's doing?

Anger surged through Alex and he flexed his power again, feeling a wave of magic roll around him. For a moment, he could breathe, just before he felt rough hands on him and smelt something sour and fetid. Alex fought back, desperately trying to break free, but with every struggle, his bonds grew stronger.

What the fuck was happening?

Real panic kicked in then. Something malevolent was here with him, gleeful with his capture. Alex's spirit struggled wildly, his magic now rolling off him in waves, but nothing seemed to work. He was stuck, and the sour smell returned, thick and oily, filling his mind with death.

And then he felt someone else, someone so familiar that he almost forgot the trouble he was in, and a wave of different power flashed from a point close by. The hands that restrained him weakened, and Alex broke free.

"*Alex,*" the presence whispered in his ear.

Alex jerked back. "Gil? Is that you?"

Gil's shimmering face appeared before him, its kind, comforting lines so familiar to him that Alex could have cried.

"*It is, old friend. You have ventured too far, Alex. It's dangerous here. Go back.*"

"But why? What's happening? How did you find me?"

Gil glanced behind him, at nothing that Alex could see, but a hardened resolve appeared on his face. "*Another witch, strong like you, has walked these paths, but whoever it was knew exactly where they were going. They've been helping old spirits who want revenge. They're the ones who attacked you. Let's go.*"

Gil sent another flash of power behind him, and then before Alex could comprehend what was happening, Gil propelled them both away. They were travelling swiftly now, streaking through dark, shadowy realms he hadn't even realised he'd passed through, and so fast that Alex was dizzy and sick by the time they finally stopped. He felt Avery again, a candle in the dark.

Gil looked around once more. *"We've lost them for now—but you have to go!"*

"What witch? Tell me. It's important."

"I don't know who it is. I can't even tell if they were male or female! It was just their energy that made them stand out."

"You're sure it's not the spirit of a witch?" Alex asked, desperate for answers before he left. "I'm looking for Helena —Avery's ancestor!"

"Helena?" Gil gave a hollow, empty laugh, his eyes filled with a mixture of sorrow and joy. *"Why are you looking for her?"*

"It's a long story, but ever since we regained our grimoires, she's been with us...until recently."

"No wonder she feels different," Gil said, nodding as if things were making sense to him. He looked behind him again, fearful of pursuit, and then focussed sharply on Alex. *"Yes, I have felt Helena, but she's trapped, and you won't get her free—not yet."*

"And you're sure she's not the witch you sensed?" Alex was confused now.

"No. The other witch was as real as you are, not a spirit. Causing trouble with the ones who attacked you. You were far deeper than you realised—and you don't know this place like I do. Skilled though you are, you travelled too far." Comprehension dawned. *"Helena was a lure. You must go—they're getting closer!"* Gil's spirit pushed Alex again, shepherding him away, and Alex felt desperately sad; he didn't want to leave Gil so soon after finding him.

"But Helena!" Alex persisted. "I can't leave her trapped."

"You must leave her to me, and instead deal with the witch in your world. I'm just sorry I can't tell you more." Gil gave him one final push. *"Go! Give my love to the others, especially my brother."*

And then he vanished.

For a moment, Alex hung in the dark, and then feeling the vengeful spirits once more, he returned to his body with such speed that his breath left him. He opened his eyes to find Avery staring at him with surprise and relief.

"Thank the Gods!"

But there was no time to rest. "Something's coming!" Alex leapt to his feet—or tried to. His legs felt numb, and it was more of stagger, but he stood in the dark attic, lit only by the flickering fire and single candle. "Don't move from the circle!"

"Why?" Avery asked, standing as well and raising her hands, magic balling in her palms.

The words had barely left Avery's mouth when a whirling object appeared out of nowhere, clattering against their wall of protection and falling to the floor. It was followed by a hollow-eyed spectre wearing rags, and then another, and another. Instead of attacking them, they ransacked the room, causing mayhem.

Alex cast his strongest banishing spell, and with a crack like thunder and flash of white light, he sent them back to the spirit world. For what seemed like endless minutes, they stood there, waiting, just in case something broke through again, but when nothing happened, Alex dropped his hands, satisfied that the door to the Otherworld was sealed.

He turned to Avery and sighed. "Well, that was all kinds of unexpected."

She looked at him with utter shock. "*Unexpected?* What the hell happened in there? You've been gone for almost two hours!"

Exhaustion hit him as his adrenalin ebbed, and breaking the circle, he dropped on the rug in front of the fire.

Avery sat next to him, her hand resting on his arm. "Alex, what happened?"

He lay flat, his chest heaving up and down, and reached for her hand. There was no way to sugar-coat what had happened. "I saw Gil."

Avery froze, her eyes wide, momentarily silenced. Her mouth worked as she tried to form words, finally saying, "*What*? How?"

His heart was filled with sorrow it could barely contain. "Come here."

She lay next to him, and he pulled her close, glad of her vibrancy, and immensely grateful she was part of his life. Her arms trembled and he kissed her forehead.

"Was he okay?" she mumbled into his chest. "Sorry—that's a stupid question."

"It's not." Alex's breathing had settled, and she placed her hand on his chest as he said, "He seemed well, for a spirit. But it was a shock to see him."

Avery propped herself on her elbow, watching him. "I don't really understand how the spirit world works. Why haven't you seen him before?"

"It has never crossed my mind that I should even try to contact Gil. It seems wrong somehow. But," he admitted, feeling guilty, "I travelled too far into the realm, deeper than I realised. I was so intent on finding Helena, I didn't stop to think. I guess I was too sure of myself, too. I got into trouble."

"Alex! I trusted you. You could have died!"

"I'm sorry. It won't happen again. But I found her—sort of. She's a prisoner. Don't ask me how, because I've no idea. They used her to lure me to them."

Avery was clearly more confused than ever. "What do you mean? Who are *them*?"

"Whoever those spirits are who followed me here." He rolled over to face her. "Gil said they're seeking vengeance."

"On you? Us?"

"I don't know, and neither did Gil. But he said another

witch has been there, strengthening them…stirring their anger." He lifted his hand and ran his fingers across her cheek. She was so precious to him; he hated to see her upset. "Gil sends his love."

Avery's tears welled up. "It's almost a year since he died. I can't believe it. What happened in there?"

"The spirits who have trapped Helena tried to trap me— or kill me. Gil saved me." The feeling of being lost filling him with horror, but he tried not to show Avery that. "I had no idea how far I'd travelled. I'd lost sight of you. I was an idiot. And what's worse is that I didn't even tell Gil how much I missed him. I was so focussed on Helena. What a jerk."

"You're not a jerk, and Gil knows that. I will be forever grateful that he brought you back to me. But what about Helena? I don't want you to go back there again—obviously —but how do we rescue her?"

"Gil said to leave it to him. We have another job to do. We need to find the witch who travelled there."

CHAPTER 6

*B*ehind the counter in Happenstance Books the next day, Avery was enjoying a mid-morning coffee and biscuit while updating her friends on Sunday's activities.

"What do you mean, you were attacked by ghosts?" Sally asked, horrified.

"They whirled around our attic, making a bloody mess," Avery said crossly. "It annoyed the crap out of me!"

Dan looked at Sally, and then back at Avery. "They followed Alex? He actually walked in the spirit realm?"

"Well, not exactly *walked*, but I know what you mean." Talking to Dan and Sally in the cold light of day, the enormity of what Alex had done hit her. "It was nuts, really. I get so used to the odd stuff we do that I didn't even worry too much." She looked at their expressions of disbelief, and tried to explain. "I mean, I know it was dangerous, and I *was* worried, but not much. I trust Alex's power!"

Dan lowered his voice. "It's the realm of the dead, Avery! I didn't even know that was possible!"

"Mediums do that kind of thing all the time!"

"No, no, no!" He wagged his biscuit. "They summon spirits to them—in *this* world. They don't enter another! That's very different."

"He's right, Avery," Sally agreed, looking at her like she'd grown two heads. Actually, Sally had been looking at her like that all morning, and Avery had the feeling that was because she'd seen her float during the barbeque. "I don't think you realise quite how unusual your life is—compared to us mere mortals, at least!"

"Don't be ridiculous," Avery said. "I'm a 'mere mortal' too, I just happen to have a few special skills. And besides, I can't do what Alex did!"

"We're getting sidetracked," Dan said, breaking up what could have become an argument. "Who were they?"

"We don't know! But Alex banished them pretty quickly."

"Interesting," he said, nodding abstractedly. "Why are they targeting you?"

"They're not!" Avery said. "Not really."

Dan rolled his eyes. "Avery! Something appeared in your garden and threw coins at you. They lured Alex away by using your ancestor! I don't think that's a bloody coincidence."

That reminded her of something else. "They threw something else yesterday—an old dagger. Fortunately, it hit our wall of protection, but that was worrying."

"A dagger!" Sally said, almost squealing. A few customers turned and stared, and Sally immediately lowered her voice. "How can an object materialise out of nowhere?"

Avery shrugged. "We've been debating that for hours, but think it's because they're abnormally strong."

"Good grief, Avery!" Sally said crossly. "Your capacity for trying to make *nothing* out of *something* is amazing!"

Avery looked at Sally with alarm. She really was cranky.

But once again Dan waded in, asking, "How old was the dagger?"

"Not sure, but it looked very old. I'm going to ask El to take it to Dante."

He nodded. "To return to my previous point—this must be connected to Helena or you."

"But Helena has been gone for weeks!" Avery pointed out. "I think her disappearance was something entirely separate—for a while, at least."

"Huh!" Sally grunted in a very un-Sallylike way. "Tenuous, at best!"

"Whatever it started as," Dan said, "you are now connected to it—big time."

Avery groaned. "I know. It's really messy. Gil said another witch had walked the spirit realm, too—a mortal, not a dead one. He suggested they were deliberately stirring up the ghosts who had imprisoned Helena, however that works!"

Dan and Sally exchanged worried glances as Dan said, "That's quite an important point, Avery, because it absolutely suggests you *are* being targeted. Who have you pissed off?"

"No one!"

"Oh, come on! I thought there were a couple of witches in the Cornwall Coven who resented you being there?"

Avery sagged in her seat. "Yes, there's Zane and Mariah, but just because they don't like us doesn't mean they would act against us!"

"Well, someone is!"

Avery wanted to change the subject. It depressed her to think that another witch was responsible for Helena's capture and the attack on them. "I need your brains, Dan."

He nodded encouragingly. "Of course. With what?"

"I've taken some of those folklore books off our shelves. I was trying to find out about supernatural Cornish creatures that could kill or cause mayhem. What about Púcas or spriggans?"

"Well, they're about as Cornish as you can get! Like any fairy-style myth, the creatures are untrustworthy, mischievous, and sometimes deadly. But why them?"

"The man that died had every bone in his body broken. It could be spirits—the ones we've encountered this weekend are particularly violent—but we're considering other options. And," she added, "spriggans are said to guard buried treasure and burial sites."

Dan looked thoughtful. "Well, that's true, and spriggans are also said to be the ghosts of giants, so are very strong."

"Giants?" Sally's voice rose again. "Now that sounds like a fairy story!"

"But Cornwall is renowned for its giants!" Dan reminded her. "Jack the Giant Killer is supposedly based on a Cornish giant."

Avery blinked. "Hold on—did you say ghosts of *giants*?"

"I did." He scratched his chin thoughtfully. "It's like the essence of a giant has been distilled into the wizened form of a grumpy old man."

"Well, whoever killed that man would have been very strong," Avery reasoned. "So maybe our vengeful spirits—whoever they are—are working with them, or at least one of them." As weird as that idea was, Avery felt a glimmer of intrigue. "Is there such a thing as a pack of spriggans?"

Dan laughed. "I hope not, but I wouldn't put it past you to find one. I think they should have a better collective name, though."

Sally looked disbelievingly between them both. "I can't believe you're making light of this! A man is dead… pulverised. It's horrible!"

"Yes it is," Avery said quickly. "Sorry, Sally. I'm not making light of this, but all of this is really odd!"

A fire began to smoulder behind Dan's eyes. "And you said there was a doubloon in the dead man's mouth?"

"Yes!"

"And you had guineas thrown at you, and a dagger… maybe the dead guy actually found buried treasure, and someone's not happy about it."

"That's why we're going to look into smuggling," she admitted. "It must be related. We thought we'd take a trip to Jamaica Inn, and our very own White Haven Museum."

"Of course," Sally said. "They have a new display. It doesn't open until the weekend though, so you'll have to wait."

"That's okay," Avery said, nodding. "We've got plenty to keep us going."

"What are you going to do about Helena?" Sally asked.

"I don't know. I hate the thought of her being trapped, but equally I'm terrified that Alex could be, too. I guess at the moment I have to trust that Gil will help."

Sally crossed her arms. "And will you tell Reuben about Gil?"

Avery nodded nervously, knowing how upset Reuben would be. "Yes. We're inviting the others around tonight. I don't want to tell him in the pub."

"Maybe you should be a little less blasé when you tell him," she said, before draining her coffee and marching across the shop, leaving Avery looking after her, dumbstruck.

Reuben looked at Avery and Alex and felt a lump forming in his throat. "You saw my brother? In the spirit realm?"

Alex nodded at him, his eyes narrowing with concern. "Yes. It was completely unexpected. I promise I didn't go looking for him, he just swept in to save me."

"Are you sure?" Reuben asked, suddenly suspicious. "Because when I offered to help you, you refused. Was this why?"

Alex jerked back in his seat like he'd had an electric shock. "Of course not! Bloody hell, Reuben. I would never summon Gil to do my bidding!"

Reuben felt sick and suddenly hot, and he stood up abruptly, almost upending his chair as he stalked to the small balcony off Avery and Alex's living room. It was Monday evening, and they had just eaten dinner together, but for the last hour he thought they looked worried about something, and he couldn't work out what. Now it was obvious.

He leaned on the balustrade, taking deep breaths and trying to blink back tears. He'd done enough crying over Gil's death, and didn't think there could possibly be any more, and yet…

El appeared at his side, sliding under his arm and wrapping hers around his waist. "Are you all right?"

He looked at the sea in the distance, the waves sparkling in the evening light, but he wasn't really seeing them. Instead he was seeing Gil's broken body on the ground in the cave on Gull Island.

"Reuben, please talk to me," El said softly.

He blinked away his tears and looked down at her. "Sorry. I'm in shock."

"Don't apologise. You have every right to be upset." She reached up and kissed his cheek, and the warmth of her skin and familiar scent of patchouli and musk steadied him. "But equally, you know Alex would never use Gil like that. I'm upset, too, and so are the others."

He nodded, unable to speak. *Great*. He'd just accused one of his best mates of being a dick. *He could make such a mess of things sometimes.*

El continued, her tone light. "I'd hoped he was sipping Mai Tais on a beach somewhere in the spirit realm."

He laughed, despite the situation. El could always cheer him up. "There's a beach there? And Mai Tais?"

"There better be! I'm banking on it."

"Maybe he does that in his downtime." He kissed El's forehead and then rested his cheek against her silky hair. "It's been almost a year, El. I thought his spirit would be at rest. I wanted it to be."

"And maybe it is," she murmured. "Maybe it was just Alex being in trouble that attracted him. But isn't it lovely to feel that he's out there, watching for people...like with Shadow and Gabe beneath your family's mausoleum?"

"I guess so." He grunted. "He's like some avenging angel."

"Maybe he's in Valhalla—a hero!"

"He *was* a hero. Bloody Caspian." And suddenly, all of Reuben's hard-fought magnanimity came crashing down as his anger surged. "Fucking Faversham bastard. It's his fault."

El squirmed in front of him, her back to the railing as she gripped his arms tightly and stared at him. She was so tall that she was almost at his eye level, and her blue eyes challenged him. "No. Don't go there. He apologised, and then saved me—don't forget that."

"Gil was too sodding young to die, El."

"Of course he was. But Caspian said he didn't mean it! It was a horrible accident, and a warning to us all to be careful of our magic. We take it for granted," she said, trying to appeal to him. "We're powerful witches! Caspian unleashed his strength in his effort to get our grimoires, and so did we when we retaliated."

Guilt hit Reuben like a punch. "And I have squandered my magic. Gil wouldn't have."

El looked confused. "You don't squander it!"

He met her gaze belligerently. "Yes, I do. I don't practice my magic, or use it half as much as you do."

"You use it more than you used to. You wield it more confidently now. You know you do."

"Not like you, or the others."

"But you can, when you try." She cupped his face in her hands. "Remember the wall of mist you conjured behind the Crossroads Circus? That was brilliant. And how you found the mermaids' cave. Stop doubting yourself!"

She was humouring him, and he dismissed her comments. "You know I'm right."

"All right. I admit you don't use it as much as we do, but that's because you choose not to! And that's okay. You're ambivalent about it, and we're not. But you always help, and we—*I*—can always count on you!"

Reuben suddenly felt incredibly weary as his normally enormous amounts of energy seemed to drain from him. Gil's reappearance had hit him hard, and so close to the anniversary of his death. It made him realise how very little real progress he had made with his power. "I need to go home and think."

Concern flashed across El's face. "Think about what?"

"Me. My future and my magic and my place in this coven."

El gripped him with surprising strength. "You'll always have a place in this coven. You're part of us. Don't you dare think that you're not!"

"I'll think what I need to," he said, gently but firmly. "I'm going home now—to my home—and I'll call you tomorrow."

He turned, but El didn't let go. "You shouldn't be alone tonight."

"That's exactly what I need to be." Reuben extricated himself from her grip, lifted her hands, and kissed them.

"Don't worry. I'll be fine. And no, I won't try to drown myself doing some kamikaze-surf thing."

El's eyes filled with tears and Reuben felt horrible that he'd upset her, but he knew he'd be awful company that night.

He entered the large, open living area of Avery and Alex's flat, and found that they and Briar were sitting on the sofa, talking quietly. All three looked up at him, obviously worried, and he smiled wanly. "I'm heading home, guys. I just need to think." He could feel El at his back, and he couldn't look at her, so he headed to the stairs, grabbing his jacket on the way.

They leapt to their feet, Briar saying, "Don't go, Reuben. Stay and talk."

"You talk. You can fill me in another time." He didn't wait, and almost ran down the stairs and out of the back door, pausing to take a deep breath in the lane behind the house, but within seconds, Alex was next to him.

"Reuben, I meant it. I didn't do it deliberately."

Reuben looked at his old friend, similar to him in so many ways, and noted the lines of worry etched around his eyes. They had grown up together, but had never been as close as they were now, partly because Reuben had ignored his magic for years and kept apart from the witches in White Haven. "I believe you—sorry about earlier. I was shocked. But I just need to go home now."

"I'll call you tomorrow, then?"

"Sure." And with that, Reuben walked away, feeling Alex watching him until he turned the corner.

CHAPTER 7

"*I* feel like shit," Alex said to the others when he re-entered the living room.

The girls sprang apart from where they had been conferring, heads together on the sofa, as Avery said, "So do we."

Alex continued through to the kitchen. "I need beer. Anyone else?"

"Me, please," El called.

When he returned, carrying two open bottles, El was pacing, and she gratefully accepted the drink. "Thanks. Now I'm going to be worried about him all night."

"Sorry," Alex repeated, feeling doubly guilty. "I swear I didn't summon Gil."

"I'm not blaming you, you twit! Gil was always generous and helpful. It makes sense he still would be after death. But this has just brought everything flooding back for Reuben."

"Of course it has," Avery agreed. "For all of us! I dreamt about Gil last night. Just weird, random stuff. And I know it's unexpected, but I'm so grateful that he helped Alex."

Alex dropped into the squishy armchair. "I'm sure Reuben needs time—just like he said. We need to respect his space. In the meantime, we've got plenty to think about. Like who our mysterious spirits are, and who the witch could be." He looked at Avery. "Any news from Oswald?"

"Not yet. We should go to the Jamaica Inn Smuggling Museum. I'd actually love to know a bit more about smuggling. I've lived here all my life and heard so much about it, but I know so few details!" She flopped back, huffing. "What a day. You know, I upset Sally today, too. She looked so cranky about Gil."

"It's hardly surprising though, is it?" Alex said, wishing they could change the subject. "It's one thing to meet with a random spirit, but it's totally different to hang around with someone you know!"

Avery looked offended. "She said I was blasé! I was anything but!"

"We do take this stuff for granted," Briar pointed out, and then added hurriedly, "not that you did it intentionally, I'm sure!"

El clapped her hands like a tour guide, as much, Alex thought, to distract her than anyone else. "Come on! Let's make a plan. That will cheer us up. Tomorrow is Tuesday, and I can definitely spare a few hours to go to Bodmin." She looked at Avery hopefully. "Shall we go together? It's only half an hour to get there."

"Absolutely! We can grab lunch, too." Avery turned to Briar and Alex. "Do you two want to come?"

"Not me, sorry," Briar said, shaking her head.

"Nor me," Alex replied. He groaned at the thought of his busy day. "I'm interviewing a couple of new bar staff with Simon, just to tide us over the summer."

El winced in sympathy. "Ooh, fun."

Briar settled herself into the corner of the sofa. "You know, you haven't shown us the knife that came out of the spirit world. I'd like to see it."

"Great idea," Alex said, rising to his feet. "It's upstairs, give me a sec."

He bounded up to the attic, grabbed the knife and quickly returned, examining it again before handing it to Briar. It was made of a dull metal, with two sharp edges, and a bone hilt with no discernible markings on it. "Here you go. It doesn't give us a clue as to where it came from, unfortunately."

"I don't feel any magic in it," Briar said as she examined it. "Looks horribly sharp, though. El?"

She held it out and El took it from her, heading to the window to see it better in the fading evening light. "It's simple and cheap, so clearly not belonging to a rich man. And it's quite dirty. Would you mind if I cleaned it up?"

"Not at all," Alex said. "Whatever you can find out about it would be good."

El wrapped it up in her cotton scarf and tucked into her leather bag, while Briar asked, "Did the spirits do much damage?"

"Everything was tossed off the shelves," Avery said, still cross. "Fortunately, nothing was broken, but some of our books were damaged. Bloody heathens! At least the grimoires were too heavy to be lifted by them."

Briar cradled her glass of white wine, rolling it between her hands. "And you said they wore rags?"

Alex tried to remember what he'd seen as they whirled around the attic. "I think so. I'm pretty sure they were male, and I think they wore long, loose trousers—"

"No," Avery interrupted. "A couple had three-quarter trousers, and one wore a kind of bandana."

"How many were there?" El asked.

"Four," Alex said, very sure.

"They looked unkempt," Avery added, "with long hair and scraggly beards. I mean, Helena always looks clean and wears her long dress, despite the manner of her death, so I presume this means they were unkempt in life?" She wrinkled her nose. "Am I making assumptions?"

Briar laughed. "Maybe. But the three-quarter trouser is interesting. They could be sailors."

"True! That would fit with smuggling!" Avery agreed.

"Or it could be that they were wrecked sailors, killed by pirates, who are seeking revenge," El suggested. "Yes! Maybe they are seeking revenge on the townsfolk who abandoned them and let them die!"

Alex tried to recall what he'd sensed of them in the spirit realm. "They smelt sour—like I could smell their breath. That was horrible, actually. I could feel them pressing around me."

"Ugh!" Briar shuddered.

Alex rubbed his cheek, feeling his stubble and realising he needed a shave. It felt more like a beard. "I can't see how one spirit can imprison another, but I guess it comes back to the other witch who walked the spirit realm."

Avery looked distracted and worried. "Dan said I should consider Zane and Mariah, seeing as they are openly resentful of us."

"Unfortunately," Alex said, hating to admit it, "I think he's right."

"I bet it's freezing here in the winter," El said to Avery as she exited her Land Rover on Jamaica Inn's car park.

Jamaica Inn was actually a collection of grey stone buildings in the middle of one of the highest points of Bodmin Moor, situated on the main road with a large car park and a sign with a scowling pirate on it. Outside the main pub was a cobblestoned area filled with tables and benches, and hanging baskets were overflowing with flowers, bright against the grey building. It was full of 'olde world' charm, and huge cartwheels were propped in plant beds to add to the theme, as well as a set of stocks.

Avery nodded. "Yeah, I bet the wind howls over the moor."

"It's very atmospheric. Maybe I should persuade Reuben to stay here one night." She said his name lightly, but she was actually worried sick about him, and didn't want Avery to know. They had avoided the subject in the car, talking about anything else.

"Have you heard from him?" Avery asked.

"Just a text," she admitted. "Saying he's fine. I'm just giving him some space."

"That's good." Avery hugged El briefly as they found the entrance to the museum. "It was inevitable he'd take it hard—especially considering the timing."

"I know."

El was grateful she didn't ask any more questions. They headed through Pedlars Restaurant to get their tickets, and she admired the low roof with dark timber beams and stone walls. It was cosy, and because it was mid-week, not too busy.

"Did you know it has a farm shop," El said, "and a gift shop, too? We must go before we leave. And get a pub lunch, of course!"

Avery laughed. "I'm sure we can manage that. They're advertising cream teas, too!"

The museum focussed on the smuggling scene of the late 1700s and early 1800s, and was filled with wooden and glass cases displaying weapons, examples of smuggled goods, and even small scenes depicting wrecking crews. For a while they split up, and El drifted around on her own, fascinated by the displays and the history. Smuggling was a cutthroat business. While it may have originally been opportunistic, started by looting wrecked ships on the shore, it quickly escalated, and soon looters were luring ships in with false lights instead. El shivered to think of the poor men drowning or being murdered by the bootleggers. But, she had to admit, it was a hard life. The crown had increased taxes on brandy, gin, tea, silks, and salt in order to fund expensive wars, and it came to a point where ordinary folk couldn't afford them. The museum also had old wanted posters on the wall, and a couple caught her eye. They mentioned the names of boot-leggers who were wanted, and rewards were offered, but from what El could tell, most of the locals were involved.

She found a display about the Carters of Prussia Cove, and she called Avery over. "Have you seen this?"

Avery nodded and started to laugh. "John Carter, the King of Prussia! Self-styled, I guess. He and his brother, Harry, really put smuggling on the map here. They had two huge ships, and plenty of crew. I wonder if these could be our spirits?"

El shook her head. "Doesn't sound like they came to a sticky end, though, so maybe not." She moved on to another display. "What about this guy? Cruel Coppinger. His gang was ruthless, and his ship was called Black Prince." Her eyes widened as she scanned the text. "Wow. He sounds like a nightmare. There aren't many details here, though."

Avery took her phone out and snapped a few pictures. "Something to look into though."

"And this inn was the central hub," El said, "to store all smuggled goods before they were moved out of Cornwall. Apparently, they estimate that there were potentially a hundred hidden routes to get here from the shore."

Avery's mouth dropped open in shock. "A hundred!"

"Yep. It was totally isolated in the eighteenth century, and the moor was boggy and wild. Can you imagine how dangerous this place would be?" El had a vision of the moor under moonlight, clouds scudding across the sky and the wind flattening the heather as men made their way with their goods. Were they excited or scared? Did their blood race, or were their feet like lead in their boots, the threat of pursuit ever present. "And the inn is rumoured to be haunted. Why the hell don't I come here more often?"

"Good question," Avery had to acknowledge.

El spun on her heel, looking around the room. "This has been really fascinating, but I don't feel any closer to finding out about any mysterious buried treasure."

"Me neither." Avery pointed to Daphne Du Maurier's memorial room. "Come on, let's have a look at that before lunch. I love the book, *Jamaica Inn*."

"I love *Rebecca* more," El admitted, heading across the room. "Lots of gothic mystery!"

She was almost on the threshold when she realised she'd lost Avery. El turned, wondering where she'd gone. Avery was staring at a poster and plaque on the wall, and El hurried to her side, curious as to what had caught her attention.

"What's up?" And then she too stared at the picture of a middle-aged man standing next to a familiar figure, and her mouth fell open in shock.

"El, it's Mariah! And that's Ethan James, the man who had oversight of the modernisation of the museum!"

El was still reading the text. "It says that Mariah donated an old ledger that belonged to Zephaniah Job, the smugglers' banker." She scanned the room again. "I saw those, but didn't see Mariah's name." She grabbed Avery's arm, tugging her to where a collection of papers were displayed in a glass cabinet, and squinted at the writing on a card. "No wonder I didn't see her name. The writing is tiny."

"According to this," Avery said, reading it too, "Job was based in Polperro, and most of his records were burned after his death. No wonder they were excited to find one of his ledgers."

El straightened up, biting her lower lip as her mind raced with possibilities. "Intriguing. This was several years ago, but it means Mariah has a link to smuggling that we can't ignore. Come on, let's see this memorial room and then have lunch. I can't think on an empty stomach."

Almost two hours later, after they had eaten lunch in the Smugglers Bar, stocked up on local produce in the farm shop, and indulged in the gift shop, where Avery bought a couple of interesting-looking books on smuggling, they headed home, still musing on their findings.

Avery's phone rang, and she quickly answered it. "Hi Oswald, any news?"

El focussed on the road, half listening to Avery's conversation, and half wondering if Reuben was feeling any better. She'd wanted to call him many times but had resisted, knowing that Reuben hated being crowded, and she was desperately trying to respect that. But she also knew that underneath his devil-may-care exterior he could be incredibly vulnerable, and she hated knowing that he thought he was letting them down. She was glad when Avery broke her train of thought.

"Oswald said there have been some unusual incidents around Fowey lately. Strange, paranormal events such as lights on the moor and unusual noises," she told her without preamble. "Some of the older folk are talking about piskies and spirits haunting the town, too."

"For how long?"

"Just the last few weeks, from what he could tell." Avery laughed. "Good old Oswald. He just sat in a pub and started chatting. He said the locals were intrigued, especially the older ones, thinking it was part of Cornwall's charm, but they do admit something odd is happening."

"I guess the advantage of being old is that you can gossip with impunity!" El said. She noted the moors streaking past, still wild and remote once away from the road. "And what about the death?"

"The victim had been spotted in the area a lot, hanging around St Catherine's Castle with another man who no one has seen in days."

"Wow." El glanced across at her. "That's great. Any local theories?"

"He said that everyone knew about the doubloon, and they reckon he'd found a hoard of gold that had been cursed. No specific spot was suggested, though."

"Ha! More gossip!"

"They found the victim's car, though. Did you hear?"

"No. Where?"

"On the National Trust car park, just out of the town. The Goddess knows why he ended up on the beach," Avery said, and she fell into a thoughtful silence, allowing El to start worrying about Reuben once again.

CHAPTER 8

*A*very wound through the stacks at Happenstance Books, greeting some of the regulars, before heading to the counter to talk with Dan and Sally.

"Hi guys, anything thrilling happen while I was away?" she asked.

"Haven't you heard the news?" Sally asked, surprised. "There's been an incident in Looe."

"Looe?" Avery shook her head. "We weren't listening to the radio. What happened?"

"There was a cave-in on the cliffs above the town—"

"A sinkhole, really," Dan corrected, and Sally shot him an impatient look.

"Whatever. Anyway, it's lucky no one was killed, because this massive area just collapsed, revealing this huge cave beneath."

"Oh, wow! Was anyone hurt?" Avery asked. Looe was a beautiful Cornish town situated on the south coast, further north than White Haven. It was a popular spot for tourists, too.

"Fortunately not," Dan told her, "but it was what they

found at the bottom that had more interest."

There was a speculative look on his face that worried Avery, and warily she asked, "What?"

He raised his eyebrows. "Three skeletons, rotting casks, and a few empty chests."

"Holy shit! Smugglers' remains?"

"Looks like it!"

"Well let's hope so, or it could be their victims," said Sally. She still looked disgruntled, but Dan was trying to suppress his excitement—probably so as not to annoy Sally.

Avery sank onto the spare stool as she considered the implications, and it was Dan she addressed next. "Do you think this is linked to—"

Dan didn't even wait for her to finish. "Absolutely! Something has been set in motion, Ave!" He lowered his voice. "*Something wicked this way comes*!"

"Oh, good grief!" Sally said, exasperated. "How can you be excited about potential disaster?"

Dan just rolled his eyes dramatically, and Avery had the feeling she had arrived in the middle of a bigger discussion. "Get over it, Sally! A man died in Fowey! Horribly, yes, but why? What was he doing? He—and others—are meddling in something that should have been left alone." He crossed his arms like an old fish wife. "You mark my words."

Now it was Sally who rolled her eyes. "Drama queen."

"Slow down, you two," Avery said, interrupting their squabble. "When did this happen?"

"Middle of the night, apparently," Sally said. "Not far from the coastal path."

"The police and the council have been onsite to secure it," Dan added. "Once they made sure it was safe, a couple of climbers headed down there. But guess what was more interesting!"

"There's more?" Avery said, surprised.

Dan nodded. "Oh, yes!"

Sally butted in, her excitement now clearly overriding her irritation. "Someone was in there recently! It looks like whatever was stored down there had been recently stolen."

"But how can they tell?" Avery asked. "Surely the fall of rock and earth would have covered up all the evidence."

"Something about specific damage to the chests," Dan said. "They were to the side of the cave, beneath an overhanging bit of rock, so they were relatively protected. And there's a passage leading off the cave that shows signs of recent use."

"Wow. I wonder why the cave suddenly collapsed?" Avery mused on her earlier conversation. "You know, Oswald phoned me this afternoon. Apparently, Fowey has been experiencing paranormal events recently. I wonder if Looe is as well."

Sally opened the drawer and pulled a pack of biscuits out, took one, and then offered them around. "Is there someone representing the council in Looe?"

Avery knew she meant the Witch Council, and nodded as she accepted a cookie. "Mariah. She's a sour-faced puss. Well, with me at least."

"One of Caspian's old cronies?" Dan asked.

"Yes. And a friend of Zane from Bodmin. He hates us, too." Avery crunched her biscuit. "We did find out something interesting about her this morning, though! She donated one of Zephaniah Job's accounting books to Jamaica Inn!"

"Bloody hell!" Sally said. "That's an impressive name. Who's he?"

"He was the smugglers' accountant. Got very rich himself, too. He was based in Polperro."

Dan's eyes lit up. "Fowey, Polperro, Looe. They are all very close, and very entwined in smuggling back then. How did she find the ledger?"

"In old family papers, apparently. Not that her family was in any way linked, of course!" Avery laughed. "The museum was very keen to point that out."

"Doesn't mean she's not your spirit-walking witch though, right?" Dan said softly.

Avery nodded. She'd been debating that since finding out, but didn't want to accuse her just yet. She didn't like Mariah, but that was no reason to vilify her unjustly. "Nothing supernatural reported on the news, I presume?"

"Nope," Dan said, having a second biscuit.

Avery thought for a moment, and then said, "I'll wait, see if Newton or Genevieve call, and if not, I'll call them."

They paused their conversation when Mary, one of their older regulars, appeared at the counter with a stack of books. She smiled apologetically. "Sorry to interrupt your chat, but I'm just topping up my romance selection!"

"You never interrupt us, Mary," Sally said, starting to serve her. "That's what we're here for! We're just gassing about Looe."

Mary's hand flew to her chest. "Such a terrible thing. That poor man!"

Confused, Avery asked, "What poor man? I thought there'd just been a cave collapse?"

"Didn't you hear the lunchtime news? A man was walking his dog along the cliff path this morning and never came back. They found his body just before lunch." She lowered her voice conspiratorially. "He'd had his throat cut!" Despite Mary's age and very proper appearance—her blue-grey hair was rigidly set in a perm that hadn't changed in decades—she looked morbidly fascinated. "Ear to ear! It almost beheaded him!"

"Bloody Hell!" Dan exchanged a nervous glance with Avery. "That's terrible."

"I know. My cousin is in a right old flap about it. She lives close to the coastal path, at the top of Looe. Heard the big rumble in the night, and a very strange, bloodcurdling cry."

By now, all thoughts of the sale had vanished as Mary leaned forward on the counter, eager to impart gossip. She was quickly joined by Fred, another local who was a very similar age.

"You talking about the murder, Mary?" he asked, leaning in next to her. "Bad business, that. Very bad. Doesn't do to go disturbing smugglers' remains. They'll have their revenge, they will!"

Avery could barely believe her ears, and she almost stumbled over her words. "Well, dead men can't kill people. Someone else must have killed that poor man."

Fred fixed her with his steely blue eyes. "You should know better than that, my dear! You more than anyone!" He wagged a finger. "Spirits are walking this coast now. Two deaths in two days. Won't be the last of them, either!"

"Be away with you, Fred," Sally said impatiently, her accent broadening as she chatted.

Mary chimed in, settling shoulder to shoulder with Fred in solidarity. "Don't be so foolish, girl. These are smugglers we're talking about. They lived violently, and they died violently. That makes for a restless spirit. Mark my words, there's more to this than meets the eye." She raised an eyebrow at Avery. "You need to look after White Haven. We had our fair share of smugglers; one of Coppinger's places, this was." She shuddered. "We don't want him back. Evil bastard. Anyway," she smiled at Sally. "Ring me up dearie."

Coppinger. Avery had read his name only hours ago.

"You free for a pint of stout down at the Bootleggers Arms?" Fred asked Mary as Sally fumbled through the sale, obviously flustered. "We can catch up on some gossip."

"Sounds lovely," she said, handing Sally some cash, and then turning to Avery, she waved her hands above her head in some vague gesture that encompassed the room. "Mind what I said, now. Whatever it is you do, do it bigger!"

And then she and Fred cast beaming smiles at them before heading out the door together.

Avery's head was swimming. *What had just happened? Was she just outed as a witch by two of her most regular customers?*

Dan grinned. "Your face is a picture."

"I'm glad you find it funny," Avery said crossly. "'Whatever it is you do, do it bigger!'"

He shrugged. "I keep telling you, people love you for it."

"Aren't we missing the point here?" Sally reminded them, her tone sharp. "Another man is dead. Spirits are walking the coast—horrible, vengeful, restless spirits!"

"That settles it," Avery said decisively, "I'm calling Genevieve."

Newton's hands were on his hips as he surveyed the coastline below him. Looe was to his left, and it looked bright and welcoming in the afternoon sunshine. Further along on his right was the crime scene where the man had been found, and now the whole area was crawling with forensics.

Boats bobbed on the sea, white freshets breaking its smooth expanse, and he had a sudden longing for an ice cream. That, however, would have to wait. *Another coastal town, another violent death.* He sighed heavily, and then turned to survey the expanse of green behind him, unable to see from here the deep pit that had opened in the night. "Bollocks," he muttered to himself.

"What was that, Guv?" Inez said, as she finished her phone call and joined him.

"I'm just swearing. Bloody paranormal bullshit."

Inez laughed, her wide smile illuminating her face. "You

71

could always apply for a transfer. But once you know this stuff, you can't un-know it."

"I know. And to be honest, I'd rather deal with this than some snivelling little thief or sex offender."

"Oh, I'm sure restless spirits or other paranormal creatures could be those things, too." The victim's body had already been removed, but Inez gestured to where the white suited team, tiny from this distance, searched for clues. "Are we sure this is supernatural? It could just be a vicious murder."

"It could. But it's close to the cave, and the coroner reckons he was already dead before his throat was cut."

"Does he? Why?"

"Very little bleeding. There should be arterial spray everywhere, but there isn't. Maybe a heart attack?"

Inez was shorter than Newton, and she squinted up at him now, shielding her eyes from the sun with one hand and restraining her hair from whipping around her face with the other. "Well, that could be natural!"

"Then why slit his throat? And did you see the look on his face?"

She winced and nodded. "Just like the other victim. Horrified."

Newton recalled the wide-eyed stare and silent scream frozen on the man's face. "And there was rust in the very ragged wound."

"A dodgy knife. That happens." She paused at Newton's sceptical expression. "I'm playing devil's advocate here."

"He's the last thing we need." Newton looked inland again. "Come on, let's see this cave again."

Inez fell into step beside him and they walked across the springy turf on the cliff top. "Where's Moore?"

"Interviewing the victim's wife, but I doubt if he'll find much out."

"Is the dog okay?"

He smiled as he cast her a sideways glance. "He's upset. We found him whimpering at his master's side, but is otherwise unharmed."

Within minutes they ducked under the police tape and after a short walk reached the sinkhole, looking down the rubble-filled sides. The whole area was an uneven circle with a sheer drop on some sides, but in front of them was a gentler gradient, allowing for a safer descent to the cave itself. On the far side was the section that had been least affected because of the over-hanging rock that sheltered the remains and the old chests.

The area had been thoroughly checked that morning and declared safe—to the police, at least—which was why a couple of police climbers had descended to investigate. A safe route had been marked out, and Newton glanced at Inez. "I'm heading down there."

"Newton! There could be a bigger collapse."

"Maybe, but I want to see it for myself. Stay here if you want."

"I don't think so!" she declared, gesturing to her trainers and jeans. "I can manage."

Inez Walker dressed smartly most of the time, but Newton noticed she had a distinct leaning towards jeans, trainers, and sweatshirts whenever she could get away with it. That was fine with him. If he weren't the inspector, he'd be more informal, too.

"All right—after me. And be careful!"

They both edged their way down the rocky slope, gently testing their way, despite the assurance of the marked path, and Newton sighed with relief when he reached solid ground. The cave was a decent size and about fifty feet down from the surface, well above the shoreline.

Inez examined the cave with a critical eye and pointed at

the rubble they had descended. "Do you think there's a passage here from the beach, hidden under that?"

He nodded. "This coastline is riddled with tunnels from smuggling days, so there must be. But," he pointed to the other side, "there is one leading away from here." He made his way carefully across the debris to a narrow tunnel entrance. Extracting a torch from his pocket, he illuminated the darkness.

"You're not going down that, surely?" Inez asked, startled.

"Nope. Not yet, anyway, but I'd love to know what's down there."

"Me too," she admitted, "but death by suffocation doesn't appeal to me."

Newton wondered how safe it would be. The tunnel looked clear—from here, at least, the ground churned up around the entrance. But Inez was right; being buried alive under a mountain of earth was not appealing. However, he had other options. "I might try it with one of our friends."

"I presume you mean *your* friends, the witches?"

"No, I meant *ours*." Inez looked amused at his response. "What? They are. They have been very helpful to our investigations."

"I know they have, but they are good friends of yours, too. Personally, I mean. And there's nothing wrong with that."

When he'd told Walker about the witches a couple of days ago, she had taken the news quite well. "I take it you don't object to witches, then?"

She shrugged. "It depends on the witch. I've only come across a couple with real power and haven't really liked them, but your guys seem okay."

"Where was that?"

"The witches? Brighton."

Newton wasn't usually so chatty with his work

colleagues, but now he was intrigued. He leaned against the rock wall. "Really? Did you meet them with a case?"

"Yes, but they weren't helpful. They were on the periphery of an investigation into illegally shipped items, but it turned out they weren't involved."

"And you came here after Brighton?"

She gave him a tired smile. "I'm going through a divorce. Getting away from Brighton seemed like a good idea. This job came at the right time."

"Oh," Newton said, genuinely surprised. "I had no idea. Does your soon-to-be ex work in paranormal policing, too?" Newton, for some reason, presumed her husband was a policeman.

"Ha! No. He's hates it—calls it mumbo-jumbo! Only Ted does that. Mike works in drugs."

"Well, I'm sorry to hear about your divorce." Newton turned away to walk back to the broken wooden chests. "Any kids?"

"No, thank God. It's complicated enough." Inez followed him, crouching down to move the shattered wood of the old chests, pulling aside earth and stones. "Damn it. There's nothing left in these. Do you think they'll find prints on the old locks?"

Newton knelt next to her, sifting through the rock. "Maybe, but I doubt we'll be so lucky." A couple of hours ago, they had removed the old, broken locks from the two chests that provided evidence they had been forced open recently, and they were being processed by the lab. But this wasn't urgent, and they couldn't really connect it to the murdered man on the path. They had also removed the skeletal remains for examination, certain they were very old. "I'd love to know where that passage goes, though. From the churned up ground, I think they had to have come in that way!"

"So, it should be safe—in theory," Inez said. She sounded excited, and looked at him with a hopeful expression.

"I thought you said going down there was a mad idea?"

"I've changed my mind! Woman's prerogative. What do you say?"

"We haven't got hard hats or anything sensible!"

"We've got brains and a torch, and if the tunnel forks, we head back. We can't risk getting lost in there."

Newton had to admit that now that they were down here, it seemed stupid not to head into the tunnel, at least for a short way. He grinned. "All right. You text Moore and let him know what we're doing, and I'll call Alex."

CHAPTER 9

*A*very leaned against the doorframe and looked out onto the lane behind her shop while she talked to Genevieve, enjoying the warm breeze that lifted her hair and caressed her cheek as if it knew her.

In the end, she hadn't had to phone Genevieve; she had instead called her, just as she arrived in the back room. It was uncanny.

"This situation could get a lot worse," Genevieve admitted, sounding more exasperated than worried. "The spirits of bloody smugglers sounds annoying! And I'm trying to plan Litha!"

"And of course two people are dead," Avery reminded her.

"Of course," she answered crossly. "I can hardly forget that!"

Sounded like she had. "So, what now?"

"We meet at eight tonight, at Oswald's. I doubt everyone will make it, but I've let them all know—or left messages, at least." She hesitated a moment, and then said, "Would you try Caspian again for me? It's so unlike him not to answer, and I've called three times already."

"Of course I will," Avery answered, feeling uneasy. It was unlike Caspian. He was a very reliable communicator. "I can even head to his house if he doesn't answer. Have you tried his work?"

"No, actually. Could you? I need to pick the kids up from school and I'm running late already."

The idea of Genevieve, their statuesque High Priestess, doing the school run was so incongruous that Avery almost laughed, but instead she said, "No problem."

As soon as she rang off, Avery called Caspian, hoping Alex wouldn't complain. His phone rang and rang before his voicemail kicked in, and she left a message before ending the call. Straight away she called his office, asking to be put through, but was told he was working from home due to office renovations. Maybe he was just busy, she reflected, trying to quell her concern. And besides, his sister would be around, or his uncle. He *must* be fine.

Heading into the kitchen, Avery filled the kettle and turned it on to make tea, but she couldn't dispel the niggling thought that something was wrong. If Caspian was at home, she could check on him. Without waiting to question the wisdom of her decision, or whether Alex might be upset— she was, after all, seeing Caspian on her own, and she knew Alex's opinion on that—she summoned air, and using witch-flight was in his extensive front gardens in seconds.

Caspian's velvety lawn stretched ahead of her, the borders bursting with summer flowers. More importantly, no one was in sight. Avery headed to the front door and knocked, gently at first, and then with increasing strength, ringing the doorbell, too. It echoed through the house, but no one responded. He could be at his warehouse, or maybe even the docks. Avery recalled that Shadow and Gabe said that he was very hands-on with the business.

She waited by the front door for a few moments more

and then strolled around the house; on such a warm day, maybe he was in the back garden. She headed to where Caspian's study was, and paused. The house was ominously quiet. There were no open windows or doors, and peering through his study window, she noted it was empty. But something felt weird.

Avery stepped back and looked at the upper floor. She remembered Caspian's bedroom from when she was practicing witch-flight and had accidentally ended up there. She could head straight there. Or, she chided herself, use witch-flight to cross the short distance to the study—if she could get through his protection spells.

And that's when it struck her. She couldn't detect any spells on the house at all.

Something was very wrong.

Without a second thought, Avery manifested into Caspian's study and paused, listening. The house was utterly silent. Keeping her power raised and magic crackling at her fingertips, she walked into the hallway, following it to the main reception area. She couldn't detect any other energy, but why wasn't the alarm on, and why couldn't she feel any spells?

"Caspian!" she called out. But her voice echoed around her. She knew it was unlikely his sister would be here, but… "Estelle?"

Still no answer. Tempting though it was to go upstairs on her own, if Caspian had been injured in some way, whatever had hurt him was clearly very strong. If the house were empty, she'd feel like a bloody fool. She pulled her phone from her pocket and quickly called Alex. He answered straight away. "Alex, I'm at Caspian's, and something is wrong."

"What the hell are you there for?"

She explained the call from Genevieve and how Caspian hadn't answered his phone.

"For fuck's sake, Avery. Come and get me. Now."

"What?"

"Come to my flat, pick me up by witch-flight, and take me back there with you."

"But—"

"Do it." And then he hung up.

Half annoyed, and half relieved, Avery flew to Alex's old flat, and within seconds the door burst open and he was there, his lips pursed as he stared at her. "I can't bloody believe you went there alone."

"There are no protection spells on his house, Alex, and he's not answering his phone. It's odd!"

"Why are you phoning him?"

"I told you! Genevieve asked me to. There's a meeting tonight, and she can't get hold of him."

He gave her one final, impatient look, stepped behind her, and wrapped his arms around her waist. In seconds, Avery had flown them back to Caspian's hall.

In the brief time since she had left, nothing had changed, and after a few deep breaths to control his nausea, Alex straightened and looked around, his annoyance disappearing.

"I see what you mean. Have you checked the ground floor?"

"Not that half," she said, pointing to the other wing of the house.

"Call him again, while we search." Alex marched down the hall, but Avery waited for a second, hoping Caspian would answer or she'd hear the phone, but neither happened, and she hurried after Alex.

"He's still not answering."

"What's worrying me," Alex said, pausing on the threshold of a large lounge, "is that I can't even feel any residual magic. What if he's…" He looked at her, his gaze serious.

"Don't even suggest that," Avery said. Not feeling any remnant of magic might mean Caspian was dead, and Avery didn't want to entertain that thought at all—and she was glad to see Alex didn't, either. For all that Alex resented Caspian flirting with her, he would never wish him ill.

By now they were almost running through the ground floor of the enormous house, and they raced upstairs, finding the next floor as quiet as below. But this level was cold; far colder than it should be on a warm June afternoon, and they paused on the landing, wary of what they may find.

"Something's here," Alex whispered. "Something is watching us."

Avery felt a prickle down her spine and a cold draft on her neck, and she whirled around, hands raised, to find a knife whirring towards her. She batted it away with her magic, shouting, "Alex—duck!"

The dagger smashed into the wall, but it was followed by more, shooting out of nowhere like darts. She ducked and rolled, and immediately smelt brine and seaweed as a shower of coarse sand hit her, almost blinding her.

A wave of Alex's magic rolled above her, and she heard him cast a banishing spell. But he couldn't finish it. A dark, shadowy figure hit him, throwing him to the floor, and together they rolled down the hallway, smashing into the wall and upending furniture.

Avery leapt to her feet, bewildered as to what to do. If she mistimed a fireball, she could hit Alex, and she wasn't even sure if it would be effective against spirits. And then icy cold, wet hands slipped around her throat, and started to choke her.

She used witch-flight and manifested behind the spirit, just in time to see the shade of a ragged-clothed man spin and jab at her with a knife, a rictus grin revealing blackened teeth and vacant eyes. She leapt back and smacked it with a lightning bolt of energy. It sizzled through the spirit, hitting the wall behind with a burning smell, and the spirit vanished.

Hoping there weren't many more ghosts to contend with, she raced down the hall to where Alex was still fighting. She could see the figure clearer now. Like the other spirit, it was wearing old-fashioned, ragged sailor's clothing. He sat on Alex's chest, pinning him to the floor. His arm was across Alex's neck, and Alex struggled to get his hands free. Without hesitating, Avery propelled a powerful wind at the spirit, picking it up like driftwood, and tossing him down the hall. Alex leapt to his feet, and with a sure and commanding voice, banished the spirit into the void.

For a few seconds, they both stood there poised for further attacks, but an eerie silence descended on the house.

Alex swept his tangled hair back, and glanced at her. "Are you okay?"

"Yes, you?"

"A bruised ego, but that's all." He rubbed his throat. "He felt all too real."

"I know. I was attacked, too, and I'm not entirely sure that it's gone." Avery headed to the closest door, nudging it open to check the room beyond. It was a bedroom, but no one was in there. "Empty," she said, relieved. "I'm really worried, Alex."

"Me too," he said, already checking the room closest to him.

Avery headed down the passage, giving the rooms she passed a cursory glance before rushing to Caspian's room, Alex right behind her.

"This is his room," she told him, summoning her courage before she opened the door.

Alex froze and his eyes hardened. "How do you know

that?"

She knew that admission would make him suspicious and she laid her hand on his arm to reassure him. "When I practiced witch-flight I accidentally ended up here. That's all."

He nodded, his expression relaxing. "Yes, of course. Sorry."

Avery opened Caspian's door, peering inside cautiously, and saw a crumpled heap next to the bed. "Alex! He's hurt!"

They both ran in, Avery abandoning all caution as she raced to his side. Caspian was lying on the floor wearing track suit bottoms and a dirty, sweat-soaked t-shirt. His face was bloodied and bruised, and she only saw the knife in his side once she was kneeling next to him. Blood pooled on the floor, already thick and sticky.

"He's been stabbed!" She reached for his pulse, his skin cold beneath her fingers, and relief swept through her as she felt its faint, thready beat. "He's still alive, just barely. I have to get him to a hospital!"

Alex knelt next to her, half watching her, and half scanning the room. He laid a calming hand on her arm. "Briar first! You know she's better."

"But—"

Alex's phone was already in his hands and he called Briar, while Avery gathered her power. Alex was right, but Caspian might need a blood transfusion, or surgery, or… She could barely think straight, and was hardly listening as Alex summarised the situation before hanging up.

"Take him to the back room of her shop, then come back for me later. I'm going to search the house."

For the first time since she had entered the room she took in the damaged furniture that indicated a chaotic fight, terrified that the same fate could befall Alex. "It's not safe for you on your own."

"In that case, don't be long." He kissed her cheek. "Go!"

CHAPTER 10

*B*riar watched Avery manifest in the middle of her herb room situated at the rear of her shop, and hurried to Caspian's inert, pale body lying twisted on the floor, quickly assessing his condition.

"By the Goddess!" she said, falling to her knees and examining his wound. "He's lost a lot of blood!" She held his wrist, feeling for his pulse.

"He's been stabbed by a ghost!" Avery looked beside herself, her green eyes wide with shock. "How can a spirit do this, Briar?"

"I'll worry about that afterwards. I want him on the table. Can you lift him?" She needed to keep Avery focussed.

"Yes, of course."

They both stood as Avery summoned air, sending it under Caspian and lifting him gently until he was deposited in the middle of Briar's large, wooden table that she'd dragged to the middle of the room. Avery had arrived so quickly that Briar had only had time to boil water, but she had more than enough herbs to deal with this situation. She rolled him gently onto his back and eased his t-shirt out of the way to inspect the wound. The knife was still embedded in his side.

"It's an old knife. It has a weird hilt," she observed.

"But his wound? Is it deep?"

Briar glanced up at Avery's pinched expression. "It's hard to say until the blade is out."

It was low on his left side, and caked in blood, but there was only one stab wound. He was lucky there weren't more. But as her eyes travelled across his hard, muscled physique, she noted a myriad of cuts and bruises across his chest and face. He'd been beaten severely.

She pointed to his throat. "Finger marks. It tried to strangle him, too." That was odd. "I don't understand why they left him alive."

Briar heard the door open and shut as Eli came in, crossing quickly to her side. "I've locked up," he said, his tall frame dwarfing her. "What do you want me to do?"

"Make a poultice using yarrow and shepherd's purse," she instructed him. "When I pull the knife out, I want to be able to fill the wound with it. Avery, pour some hot water from the kettle into a bowl, grab the cotton gauze, and bring it here."

Within moments, the hot water appeared next to her, but rather than use it straight away, Briar wanted to scan Caspian's body first and assess his energy levels. However, Avery's anxiety was washing off her in waves, and Briar looked at her, perplexed. She knew her and Caspian's relationship was complex, and respected her silence on it, and her wish to keep Caspian as a friend. It was pretty obvious to all of them that Caspian wanted more than that. But Avery's mood wasn't helping now.

"Where is Alex?" Briar asked her.

"Still at Caspian's. I need to get back to him."

Briar smiled. No wonder she was anxious. She was

worried about Alex, too. "Go. I have Eli now, and we'll be fine."

"Are you sure?"

"I'm sure."

After a moment's hesitation, in which Avery cast another worried look at Caspian, she disappeared in a swirl of witch-flight, and Eli crossed the room to stand in her place. Eli was one of the seven Nephilim, with honey brown hair and gentle brown eyes, and was charm personified. He was also a very good apothecary, and had taught her things about herbs that had long been lost to time. That was one advantage of working with millennia-old Nephilim. He was also calm, competent, and kind.

He reached for Caspian's wrist, taking his pulse. "It's weak. He could have internal bleeding. I'll prepare a herbal drink when we've finished."

Briar nodded, pleased with the suggestion. "I'm going to scan him now."

She held her hands over Caspian's abdomen. She could feel his blood flow as well as energy levels, but she needed to concentrate, and she fell silent for a few minutes as her hands travelled across him, inches above his skin. He was covered in a sheen of sweat, his breathing shallow and quick. She detected swelling around his windpipe, and could feel the sluggish flow of blood around the wound where it had already clotted. His energy was low, too, his natural magical powers stunted somehow, and that was just as worrying as his physical injuries.

She dropped her hands as she glanced across at Eli. "He's weak, but I don't think the wound is deep." Briar dipped the cloth in the hot water and started to wipe the blood away. "I don't understand why the spirit attacked him, and once it did, why it didn't kill him. From what Alex told me, it sounded like he'd been lying there for hours—with the spirit still there."

"It is odd," Eli admitted. "Maybe it's a warning." He took the bloodied cloths from Briar, and moved next to her to inspect the wound. "It's a dirty knife, too—old and tarnished."

Suddenly fearful for all of their safety, she asked, "Do you understand how a spirit can manifest with a weapon?"

He shook his head. "I can only presume it's very powerful." He must have picked up on Briar's hesitation because he looked at her, eyes narrowed. "Why don't I pull the knife free? I've done this before."

"You have?" Briar prided herself on being level-headed, but she also hated violence, and the thought of pulling the knife out of flesh and muscle made her feel nauseous.

He was already gripping the bloodied hilt. "Too many times. You stand ready with the poultice."

"Okay, but I have a spell to say first. Wait one moment." Briar dipped her hands in the bowl of hot water, cleansed them with a spell, and then placed them either side of the knife. "I'm ready."

As Eli carefully withdrew the knife, Briar uttered a spell to clean the wound and reduce inflammation, speeding up the healing of flesh and damaged blood vessels. The knife was about four inches long with wicked-sharp edges that had been buried to the hilt, and she sighed with relief that it was a short blade. Fresh blood welled as the blade exited the wound, but Briar continued the spell, watching as Eli pressed hard with thick cotton cloths. They both worked calmly, full of intent, and when Briar nodded to say she'd finished the spell, satisfied that flesh had started to knit together, she reached for the poultice and filled the ragged hole. Then, for the next half an hour, they worked on Caspian's neck, reducing the swelling there before moving on to the other cuts and bruises covering his battered body. Eventually, they both sighed and stood back, Briar happy to see that Caspian already looked better.

She gave Eli a grateful smile. "Thank you. You were fantastic. Can you carry him to the sofa?"

She had a small couch in the corner of her room, under the window where it caught the afternoon light, and Eli nodded, scooping their patient up effortlessly and then gently positioning him. Briar wrapped a blanket around him, anxious to keep Caspian warm, before turning to boil the kettle once more. She leaned against the counter, watching Eli clean his hands at the sink, his shirtsleeves rolled up to his elbows.

"Caspian is a powerful witch, Eli. He has strong protection on his house. This shouldn't have happened."

Eli shrugged. "We're all caught unawares sometimes. Maybe he has a weakness that someone knew about."

"Maybe. Mind you," she said, recalling the events at the barbeque, "it happened at Avery's place, too. A spirit appeared in her garden, bursting through the protection spells."

Eli dried his hands and threw the cloth into the basket of dirty laundry. They were both scrupulous about cleanliness. He leaned his hip against the counter, mirroring her actions, and folded his arms across his chest. "Sounds to me like the ghost—or ghosts—have something to prove." He jerked his head at Caspian. "He's been beaten up! I think whoever did this wanted him to remember it."

"Like a warning?"

"Exactly. Maybe there's more violence to come." Eli's gentle eyes darkened. "Maybe he'll target someone close to him next. His sister? Avery?"

"Avery's not his girlfriend, Eli."

"But he loves her."

Briar jolted in shock at his words. "I'm not sure it's love."

"You're brighter than that, Briar. Of course it's love—as much as he tries to hide it and she tries to ignore it. I've seen enough of that in my lifetime. But, we should warn Estelle." And then he grimaced. "We need to tell her about Caspian's injuries, too. She might want to be here."

"I haven't got her number," Briar admitted, now worrying about Estelle, even though she didn't like her.

"We do. I'll get one of my brothers to call her. But what are we going to do with him?"

"I'll stay here for a few hours," Briar said, watching Caspian's deepening breaths. "I think he's stable, but even so…" She looked at Eli to find that he was staring at Caspian, too. "You can go. I can get Avery to take him to my spare room later."

"Oh, no," he said, grabbing some cups and starting to make tea. "I won't let you wait alone. I'm waiting, too. But I'll call Gabe first. He can have the pleasure of finding Estelle."

Briar smiled, relieved. She was used to being the healer in the coven, and was happy to do it. It gave her great satisfaction to make someone well, and she enjoyed drawing on the Earth's power to do so. But, it was nice to have someone to bounce ideas off. "All right, thanks Eli. I hope you're not disappointing any ladies tonight," she added, teasing him.

He winked. "Absence makes the heart grow fonder."

Reuben stood at the threshold of the cave beneath Gull Island, his heart pounding, as he wondered what had possessed him to come *here*.

His mouth was dry and he felt dizzy suddenly as grief threatened to overwhelm him. Almost one year ago they had been searching for his family grimoire when Gil died. *No, when Gil had been killed by Caspian Faversham.*

Reuben's legs buckled beneath him and he collapsed in a heap as he surveyed the gloomy cavern. He'd thrown a couple of witch-lights up, and they faintly illuminated the old crates stacked at the side of the cave and the stones strewn across the hard ground. Opposite was the lip of rock that hid the entrance to the passage leading to the narrow rocky strip of beach on the far side of the island.

He leaned back, feeling the cold stone behind him, and remembered how optimistic he had been when they first arrived here, sure that he and Gil would find their grimoire and their old family spells. Instead, there had been disaster and death, and his life had changed forever. Now he was the head of the family business, Greenlane Nurseries, and the owner of the family's manor. He had responsibilities he'd never wanted but had assumed anyway. And sitting in the dark, damp cave, all of his doubts about his abilities were magnified. He wasn't doing any of it as well as he should be.

He looked at the spot where he had found Gil's crumpled body. After all that violence, the grimoire hadn't even been there. And if it wasn't for Avery taking Caspian unawares, there might have been more deaths, too. He rubbed his face with his hands, trying to be rational and reminding himself that Caspian had apologised, that he had been under as much pressure from his father as they had been to find their grimoires. But he couldn't subdue the sharp spike of anger that was always so close to the surface. Yes, he tried very hard to bury it, and most of the time he did, but now wasn't one of those stronger moments.

Bollocks. He was being morbid. He needed to get out of here. This wasn't the way to remember Gil's life. He was also being unnecessarily negative. The business was fine, and he had El, who despite everything had stuck with him. What was bothering him more than anything was his magic. Hundreds of years of the Jacksons' magical legacy was swirling within him, and he wasn't doing it justice. Rather than go to work that day, he'd popped in for a couple of hours and then left, heading straight home, where he'd immersed himself in both grimoires, familiarising himself with the magic that resided in their pages. El had been right; he was improving, and had pulled off a couple of great spells when pushed, but he generally lacked discipline…for magic, at least. He had plenty of discipline for surfing.

The cool stone against his back was soothing, calming his thoughts as he regarded the jumble of old crates and barrels. Another of his ancestors' secrets was smuggling. Maybe his subconscious had known what he needed after all. He remembered the coins that had been thrown at Avery on Sunday, and the death of the man on the beach. *Were those events really related to smuggling?*

Reuben stood and headed to the old wooden crates, lifting the lids on a few to find nothing but dust and sand. These would have been here since the late 1700s or early 1800s. His family must have been heavily involved in the local smuggling industry; after all, the access to this cave was under the glasshouse. They'd joked about it last year, and then he hadn't really given it a second thought. But now he wondered who was involved? It would be easy enough to find out. Anne Somersby had done the family trees of all the witches. He could match up the dates to known names.

Seized by a sudden urge to look at the sea, he left the cavern and trudged up the narrow passage to the smaller cave. No one had been down here since the events last year, and he could still see the jumble of footprints in places in the earth. He quickly found the mechanism that released the door into the next cave and pushed it open, stepping onto soft sand. A strip of daylight pierced through the gap in the wall opposite him. The sound of crashing waves reverberated in the bare space, and he inhaled the strong smell of the sea, smiling as it lifted his spirits. He felt his magic respond to the water, his natural element, and was about to walk to the beach beyond, when he felt *something*.

Reuben paused, feeling as if someone was watching him. He pressed his back to the rock wall behind him, scanning the space, but there was no place to hide here.

His peripheral vision picked up a flicker of light to his right, and he whirled around, seeing the faintest outline of a lantern containing a warm, yellow flame before something struck his chest. His head cracked off the wall and he fell, winded, to his knees. A strong, weather-beaten hand materialised in front of him, grabbing his t-shirt at the throat and lifting him up so that Reuben's feet were swinging off the ground. Bad breath hit him like a punch, and without waiting to see what happened next, Reuben lashed out with his magic, sending a blast of pure energy at his unseen attacker.

It retreated, and Reuben fell awkwardly. Remembering one of the basic banishing spells Alex had taught them, he cast it at the shadow that hovered on the far side of the cave.

Unfortunately, the spell wasn't strong enough, and the spirit hadn't finished with him yet. It swelled, broad-shouldered and malevolent, and from the middle of its bulk, Reuben saw a flash of steel as a weapon came whirring across the cave.

Reuben rolled and tried to cast a circle of protection around him, but he wasn't quick enough. The dagger embedded in his shoulder, skewering a tattered, ragged piece of paper. The blade burned like fire, and gritting his teeth, Reuben wrenched it out of his flesh to use in defence.

But before the shadowy figure could advance any further, another figure manifested between them, a shape so familiar to him that Reuben froze in shock.

Gil.

He swiftly advanced on Reuben's unknown attacker with a whirl of darkness and magic. They clashed, melding into one, the fury of their encounter reverberating around the cavern. Stunned, Reuben struggled to identify who was winning before they suddenly vanished, leaving only a scattering of gold coins behind in the sand.

Reuben just sat there, wincing with pain and breathing heavily, adrenalin keeping him poised to attack, but only the sound of the distant surf broke the silence. Blood poured from his wound, but he ignored it. The pain in his chest was far worse as the tightness of grief took over, so powerful he suddenly couldn't breathe. When he did finally inhale, it was a shuddering, ragged effort that shook his entire body.

For what seemed like endless minutes, he just sat there, shaking. Gil had saved his life. And he couldn't even thank him. As he wrested control of his body, Reuben took deep breaths to steady his nausea, and then leaned forward to pick up the paper that had fallen next to him. A wave of dizziness dulled his vision, but he staggered to the far exit that was bathed in daylight. Inhaling the fresh sea air, he looked at the blood-stained paper in his fingers.

Written in an ornate script were the words: *Blood will be my vengeance.*

Newton shone his torch along the dark tunnel and frowned.

"Inez, I'm not sure we should go on. The walls are crumbling quite badly here."

She paused next to him, her own torch flashing around the roof and along the ground. "But look, footprints. This is the way they came."

He turned to look at her determined face. "That doesn't

mean it's safe. They were after treasure. We aren't. I quite like being alive."

They had been walking through the uneven, musty passage for about five minutes, moving steadily inland from what Newton could tell. The tunnel turned in places, disorientating him, so he wasn't completely sure, but the slope was ascending, hopefully towards a near exit.

"But Newton, it can't be much further," Inez argued. "This could give us a real clue as to who broke into these chests."

"Could it? Or will their transport and any sign of them be long gone?"

"Yes, that's likely, but they might have left evidence at the other end. We might even get a clear footprint! Not like these sludgy ones that we can see here. They're so trampled, they're unusable."

Inez slipped past him, taking the lead, and although Newton felt he should order her back, he was also torn. He liked Inez's enthusiasm. She was very different to Moore's calm and even-tempered approach.

In places there were trickles of water down the tunnel walls, and the air was damp and stale. Newton couldn't help but wonder how often this place had been used in the past. At intervals he paused to examine the thick, wooden beams overhead, and the sturdy supports along the side. This passage had obviously been shored up at least once. But, he also thought that it had started out as a natural rock passage that had been enhanced over time.

The sound of Inez's footfalls vanished, and he shouted, "Inez, wait!" He hurried to catch up, noting the passageway had turned up ahead. He couldn't even see Inez's torchlight.

A scream broke the silence and Newton ran, forgetting any pretence of being careful. He rounded the corner, but the passageway snaked onwards, and over the sound of his pounding feet he heard an ominous thump and the slither of falling rock.

Shit. Had she triggered a landslide? Had the tunnel collapsed? Suddenly wary of being buried alive, he slowed, rounding the bend ahead cautiously, and then blinked with shock.

The passage had widened, and outlined in the bright beam of light from Inez's fallen torch, something small dashed across his path, rasping and wheezing in a distinctly non-human way. He whipped around, trying to see the figure. It leapt at him and he instinctively swung his torch, his only weapon, connecting with something hard. He heard a solid crack and the impact shuddered up his arm. An anguished grunt and hiss made his skin crawl, and then the figure skittered away. Without stopping to think of what he'd just encountered, Newton dashed forward, seeing Inez's body lying on the ground beyond her torch.

He crouched over her, shouting her name. But as her head flopped heavily towards him, he saw that her skull was crushed and her eyes were lifeless.

Inez was dead.

CHAPTER 11

*A*lex searched the first floor of Caspian's house, hoping he would find something to indicate who had attacked Caspian while Avery was gone.

However, so far he'd found nothing, and his attention wandered as he searched. The last time he'd been in this house was when Sebastian, Caspian's father, had still been alive. They'd broken in to get Reuben's grimoire and Sebastian had died at Helena's hands. It was hard to believe that was almost a year ago. So much had changed since then. For a start, Caspian had been their enemy, and now he was a friend...of sorts. Alex doubted he would ever really consider him one, especially since he'd made it pretty clear he wanted Avery. Alex was a confident man, always had been, within reason. But there was no doubt that Avery was flattered by Caspian's attention. She was far from shallow, but the big house and impressive bank account was something he couldn't compete with. Caspian was also a powerful witch, and clearly charming enough when he wanted to be. *Bastard.*

Alex tried to subdue his worry. He loved Avery, adored

her, and he knew she loved him. He hoped that would be enough.

Her voice startled him as she called from the hallway. "Alex, where are you?"

"In here—one of the bedrooms," he shouted, heading to the door.

But in seconds she'd entered the room, looking at him with concern. *Avery was truly beautiful*, he reflected. Her pale skin and red hair were stunning, and she had the sweetest, gentlest smile—plus a wicked temper, on occasions. She was also clever and sharp-witted. He liked that. He didn't want a simpering girlfriend, he never had.

"How's Caspian?" he asked her.

"I didn't linger. I waited until Eli arrived to help Briar and then left them to it, but he didn't look good." She grabbed his hand. "I didn't wait because I was worried about leaving you alone here."

He brought her hand to his lips and kissed it. "I'm fine.

"No more spirits?"

"None."

"Have you found anything?"

He shook his head. "No, not really. Any protection spells Caspian had on this place have vanished."

"Maybe they were overloaded? Or another witch destroyed them?"

He grimaced. "Maybe. It's weird. I can't even find a trace of them."

Avery wrinkled her nose. "I can smell brine! And I see there's sand down the hallway." She tried to laugh. "At least Helena is not this messy."

Alex noticed a mark on Avery's neck, and pushed her hair back. "There are finger marks on your throat! What happened?"

"While you were being tackled, I was attacked from

behind." Her hands touched the marks and she shuddered. "Horrible, cold hands. Helena can't touch me! How are these spirits so strong?"

"Good question," he said. "And one I have no answer to—yet. I presume that witch is making them stronger than normal, and is potentially behind this." He'd been pondering that ever since Avery had left. Of all the witches, he was the most skilled at banishing ghosts and negotiating the spirit world, but right now, he felt inadequate.

Avery glanced around the richly appointed room, looking uneasy. "We should leave. I feel like we're snooping, and if we can't find anything…"

"You're right," he agreed. "But before we go, follow me. It's a good job you came to look for Caspian when you did." He walked across the room, down the hall, and back into Caspian's room, Avery trailing behind him. He pointed at the jeans and t-shirt on the bed. "He was wearing his gym gear, wasn't he? I reckon he'd gone running or something, and he'd been attacked after that. Maybe just before lunch."

"That makes sense," Avery said thoughtfully. "But who would attack him? And why?"

"Something else I have no answer to," he told her. "Is the council meeting tonight? You said you'd spoken to Genevieve, right?"

"Yes, of course!" Avery looked surprised. "I'd almost forgotten that. We'll meet at Crag's End as usual. Bloody hell, Sally and Dan will have no idea where I am!" She checked her phone for the time. "It's after four. I'll ring them in a minute, but I'll take you to the pub first?"

"Please," Alex nodded. He took her hand, realising he'd been very abrupt with her on the phone. "I'm sorry if I shouted earlier. I was worried that you'd get hurt coming here alone. And," he voiced what he really thought, "I hate you being alone with Caspian. But you know that."

"I know you do. Don't you trust me?" Her eyes narrowed with a spark of anger, and disappointment too, he realised.

"Of course I do!" He didn't know how to describe what he felt. And then it struck him and his anger boiled to the surface. "I just hate the way he flirts with you all the time. It pisses me off! It shows an utter disrespect for *me*. He's point-scoring, and he uses you to do it. I hate that, too."

Avery nodded, and her expression softened. "You're right, he does. Sorry. I won't let him do that again. But he is still our friend, and right now he's in a bad way at Briar's. With luck, Eli will have found a way to contact Estelle, and we need to go. Ready?"

He pulled her close and kissed her, leaving her breathless, and then he grinned, happy to know he could still bring a flush to her cheeks. "Yes. Let's get out of here."

Within seconds they were back in Alex's flat, and he fell to his knees as the expected nausea and dizziness hit him. At least it lasted only mere seconds now. Her hand appeared in front of his face. He grabbed it, and she hauled him back to his feet, saying, "Come on, cowboy. We must be due a glass of something after that."

"All right. I'll stand you a glass of wine."

Before the words had even left his mouth, Alex felt his phone buzz in his pocket and then it started to ring, and at the same time so did Avery's. He frowned and headed across the room to answer, telling Avery, "It's Newton."

"I've got El," she said, answering quickly as she turned away, too.

"Hey Newton," Alex said, looking out at the sea from the kitchen window. "How's it going?"

"Badly. Very badly."

Newton sounded grimmer and angrier than he'd ever heard him—in recent months, at least. He'd yelled at Alex often enough when they first met. Alex's stomach twisted and he glanced at Avery, hoping his friends were okay, but she was still talking too, her brow furrowed.

"What's happened?"

"Inez Walker is dead."

"*What?* How?" An image of Inez flashed into Alex's mind, replacing the view in front of him, and he leaned against the counter behind him in shock.

"Something jumped us in the tunnel; she was alone and *I wasn't there.* Fuck it! Fuck, fuck, *fuck!*" Newton sounded on the edge, as if his voice was about to break.

Alex overcame his momentary shock. "I'm so sorry, Newton. What can I do?"

"You can find what the fuck this damn creature is that crushed her skull!" he shouted.

"Of course! But I meant, what I can do for you? Where are you?" Alex was more worried about the living than the dead at this moment.

Newton took a deep breath and exhaled heavily. "I'm with Moore, at the station, but I've only just arrived here. I've been at the bloody site all afternoon."

"What site?"

"The place where the sinkhole collapsed into the cave. Looe."

"Come to the pub when you're done. We can talk. Pints are on me."

"I don't think I'll be good company."

Alex knew Newton wouldn't have called if he wanted to be alone. "You can stare into your pint all night if you want. Just come. I have news for you, too."

"What is it?" Newton asked, his voice suddenly sharp.

"Not now. Later." If anything, he knew that would make Newton come round. "You've got enough to worry about now. And look, I really am sorry. She seemed a nice woman."

"She was, and she didn't deserve that. I'll see you later."

Alex ended the call, but he barely had time to get over his shock when Avery shouted to him across the room. "Alex!"

He turned. "What else has happened?"

"Reuben has been stabbed by a ghost! Just like Caspian."

"*What*? Is he okay?" Reuben was his best mate. The knot in his stomach tightened.

"Yes, he's with Briar now. Want to come with me? It's just a shoulder wound," she added, "so he's okay-ish." Avery crossed the room to him, frowning. "What did Newton want?"

That needed to wait. "Let's get to Briar's shop first."

And in seconds, his guts were in his boots as they used witch-flight once again.

Avery took in Briar's herb room, sighing with relief when she saw Reuben sitting on a chair, shirtless. El was next to him, pale and distracted, pressing a dressing into his right shoulder. Briar and Eli were working at the counter.

"Reuben! Are you okay?"

He smiled ruefully. "Not too bad, considering I've been stabbed." He nodded at Alex behind her, and then to Caspian lying prone on the couch. "I think I'm doing better than those two."

"Cheeky sod," Alex said, bent almost double as he inhaled deeply. "I bloody hate witch-flight. Who did you piss off?"

"Some hulking bloody spirit on Gull Island." He started to shrug and then winced. "*Ow*. Bastard threw a knife at me and I wasn't quick enough to block it." He looked across at Caspian again. "At least I fared better than him."

Briar had been measuring out dried herbs, but she paused and glared at him. "You've still been stabbed!" She nodded at

Eli. "It's a good thing we closed the shop. We've turned into a hospital."

Eli laughed grimly, but concentrated on whatever he was making in a bowl, his hands grinding something with a pestle.

"It wasn't all that happened, though, was it, Reuben?" El said, her eyes serious as she watched him. "Gil appeared."

Reuben stiffened, his gaze falling to the floor, and when he spoke, his voice was thick with emotion. "He saved my life."

"Gil?" Avery's voice sounded shrill with surprise, and she made an effort to calm herself. "He actually appeared?"

"Sort of." Reuben looked broken, although he was trying his best to hide it. "He was a barely-there shape, to be honest, but I recognised him straight away. He tackled the other spirit and then they just disappeared. I couldn't even thank him."

Avery struggled to find the right words, but Alex said, "I'm so sorry, mate. But at least he's looking out for you."

"Yeah, I guess so. I shouldn't need him to save me though, should I?"

"He's your big brother, that's what he does."

"But why now?" Reuben asked, genuinely confused. "I haven't seen him all year!"

Alex leaned against the counter. "I don't know either, but there's obviously a disturbance in the spirit world, enough to shake up lots of things. I'm glad we have him on our side."

"But I don't want him battling other spirits!" Reuben said, annoyed. "I want him resting in the afterlife…whatever that may be!"

Briar lifted her head from her task and watched Reuben. "I think Gil's doing what he needs to do right now. Hopefully when this is over, we won't hear from him again."

Reuben just nodded, his eyes firmly on the floor again.

El's hand was resting on his arm, to comfort both of them, Avery thought, and she squeezed it gently. She was trying to be calm, but Avery could see she was struggling. "What were you doing on Gull Island? If you'd been seriously injured, we would never have found you!"

He looked sheepish. "Reminiscing about Gil, actually. Hearing about him yesterday made me want to see the cave again, so I went." He glanced at Caspian. "I got a bit angry, and then I started thinking about smuggling, and who exactly would have been involved in our family. Anyway, I headed to the cave by the beach. Remember it, Avery?" he said looking at her.

She nodded. "Of course. It had the hidden catch in the stone door." She remembered how Reuben had found the mechanism, allowing them to enter the cave beyond that led to the rocky beach.

"That's where I was jumped." His eyes took on a far away expression. "I saw a lantern—a ghost lantern. Who knew there could be such a thing? And then I was hit in the chest and lifted clean off my feet. That's never happened before!"

Avery imagined not. Reuben was a big guy.

"And then," he continued, "a knife came out of nowhere—with this." He reached into his pocket with his left hand and pulled out a blood stained note. "It says, 'Blood will be my vengeance.'" Avery was relieved to see his humour finally return as he attempted a smile. "Ominous, isn't it? And it left a handful of these." He reached into his pocket again and produced a couple of gold coins, which he handed to El. He added, "I'll give you the knife later."

Alex strode forward, taking the note and scanning the message. "Vengeance? For what?"

Reuben shrugged and winced again. "I have no idea."

Alex looked from the note to Caspian, who appeared far

better than he had earlier, even though he was still unconscious, and frowned. "Why were you two stabbed?"

"I don't know," Reuben said. "You're the one with the
crystal ball."

Alex looked at him impatiently. "Thanks!" He started to
pace. "If restless spirits want vengeance on you, then it
suggests that your families must have pissed them off in the
past."

Reuben looked at Caspian suspiciously. "I hardly think
we'd have worked together."

"You might have," Avery said. "Remember all that stuff I
found out about Helena? Our families were all merchants in
the sixteenth century, and potentially yours were still in the
eighteenth. You could have been affected by smuggling and
decided to combat it together."

Reuben shook his head, his face wrinkling with disdain.
"But *we* were involved in the smuggling business, from what
I can tell. That doesn't make sense!"

"Intriguing," El said, "and worrying. You could be
attacked again."

Eli stopped grinding herbs and leaned on the counter to
look at them all, arms crossed over his broad chest. "Potentially, you could have been more badly injured than you
were, if not for Gil. The spirit certainly could attack you
again. Caspian, too. It's odd that he could have been killed,
but wasn't. Sounds like the spirit is biding his time...or *their*
time. This could be just the start."

Avery saw Alex flinch. "I have some bad news too, I'm
afraid. Inez Walker was killed today."

Everyone gasped, and Avery asked, "How?"

"Her skull was crushed by some kind of creature. She was
with Newton in the tunnel that led off that cave collapse in
Looe." He held his hands up. "That's as much as I know."

Briar's voice was sharp. "And Newton?"

"He's uninjured—I think—but upset. Angry, actually. I told him to come to the pub later."

Avery's legs suddenly felt weak, and she needed to sit down. She sank onto a stool and used the table to prop herself up. "I had a weird conversation this morning in the shop, after we came back from the museum, El."

"Of course. I'd forgotten to ask about that," Briar said, pouring hot water onto the herbs they'd prepared, and releasing their pungent scent into the room. She dropped the cotton cloths into it, keeping busy as she tried to hide how upset she was. "Did you find anything useful?"

"A few interesting things, but my customers mentioned a smuggler that I read about at the museum—Cruel Coppinger."

El nodded. "I remember that name."

"According to them, he was very active in White Haven, maybe Harecombe too. I think we should focus on him. I'll ask Dan to help."

"And Oswald had news," El reminded her before addressing the group. "They found the victim's car, the one in Fowey. It was on the National Trust car park, out of town."

"That's not close to the beach!" Alex said.

"Exactly," El said darkly. "What does that mean?"

Just then Caspian stirred and groaned, sending Briar hurrying to his side, and Eli picked up the dressing and started to treat Reuben's wound. At the same time, a loud banging sound came from the front of the shop.

"That's probably Estelle," Eli said. "Gabe managed to tell her about Caspian."

"I'll get her," Alex said, already leaving the room.

Within seconds Avery heard raised voices and Estelle appeared in the doorway, dressed in a smart skirt and silk blouse, her long hair brushed back from her shoulders. She looked coolly professional, but her eyes blazed with a mixture of fury and worry. "Where is he?"

"I'm here," Caspian said weakly, as he struggled to sit up. A ray of afternoon sunshine illuminated his pale face, showing dark shadows beneath his eyes.

Briar laid her hand on his shoulder, pushing him back down. "Don't move. You've been stabbed."

Confusion clouded Caspian's face, and he glanced around the room, trying to orientate himself. He finally saw Avery, but he looked quickly away to Estelle, who was now at his side.

In typical Estelle manner she hadn't bothered to greet anyone, instead striding across the room as if they didn't exist. She dropped to her knees next to Caspian, examining his injuries. He was bare-chested, partially covered by the blanket that had slipped as he struggled to sit. His bruises looked worse now, and a large one bloomed across his cheek.

"What the hell happened?" Estelle asked, her voice sharp as she looked first at Briar, and then the rest of them suspiciously.

"He was attacked by ghosts," Briar told her calmly. "Avery and Alex found him, and they brought him to me."

Estelle's eyes narrowed and her voice dripped with disdain. "Spirits? A likely story. Did one of *you* do this?"

Avery was so astonished at the accusation that she couldn't speak, but Briar's voice was hard and her dark eyes sparkled with an emerald light as the Green Man rose in her. "How dare you! I have spent hours tending to him. We've saved his life, you ungrateful bitch!"

Estelle recoiled in surprise, and then she stood, clenching her fists as magic sparked around her. Briar stood too, the scent of earth and old magic pouring off her. Estelle took a quick step back.

Before either could say or do anything else, Eli intervened, stepping between them, his bulk shielding Briar. "You should be more grateful, Estelle. I suggest you apologise."

Estelle squared her shoulders and looked up at Eli as if about to speak, but Caspian interrupted. "Estelle, please stop. I feel like death, and can do without you fighting the people who helped me."

Estelle stared at Eli for a moment longer and then turned to Caspian. "You remember what happened?"

"Vaguely. Will you please sit down?" Despite his obvious pain, his voice was firm.

Estelle glared at them all once more, and then her shoulders dropped. "Go on."

The tension in the room eased, and Eli returned to finish Reuben's dressing, as Avery exchanged a worried glance with El. Briar perched on the sofa next to Caspian, as if to protect him from Estelle, her hand resting on his. Her voice was gentle as she said, "Don't overdo it."

He smiled at her, albeit weakly. "I couldn't if I tried. Everything aches." He pressed his hand to his side. "And this feels like a red hot poker has been stuck in my side."

"That's where you were stabbed."

"What happened?" Estelle repeated sharply.

"I'd just been for a run around the grounds and was heading to the shower, when my protection spells on the house suddenly collapsed and I was struck from behind. The next thing I know, I was fighting for my life against some surprisingly strong ghosts." He rubbed his face and then winced with pain. "It's a bit of a blur, actually. Something struck my head, and I don't remember anything else. I certainly don't remember being stabbed." He looked confused. "I don't understand how I'm here now."

"Genevieve couldn't get hold of you," Avery explained. "She asked me to call you to tell you about tonight's council meeting. When you didn't answer me, and your office said you were at home, I headed to your house. I knew something was wrong when I realised your spells were gone. I called Alex for backup."

Alex was standing next to Avery now, his warm hand on her shoulder, and he gave it a reassuring squeeze as he answered. "It's a good job she did, too. You still had two spirits in your house. They're both gone now. We found you in your bedroom, unconscious and bleeding."

Caspian looked shocked, and so did Estelle. "What could do this?" he asked, struggling to sit up again. "And why?" He tried to laugh. "I know I piss people off, but not usually the dead."

"I was attacked, too," Reuben told him, as Eli finished bandaging him up. "More spirits. I think we're being targeted." He passed the bloodied message to them and Estelle frowned at it, pinching the paper between the end of her finger and thumb like it carried a disease. "'Blood will be my vengeance?' Is this a joke?"

Reuben shook his head. "Nope."

Estelle looked between him and Caspian. "You two? Why?"

Reuben gave her his most charming smile. "I have no idea, but I aim to find out. And if I were you, Estelle, I'd watch my back. Because if our families are being targeted, that means you might be next."

CHAPTER 12

*A*very examined the grim faces of the members of the Witches Council who sat around the long, wooden table at Crag's End.

Not all of the members were present. Claudia had sent her apologies, as had Charlie from Polzeath, Hemani from Launceston, and Gray from Bude. Estelle was there in place of Caspian, her eyes narrowed with annoyance. The windows were open, allowing a warm breeze to circulate around the room, and it carried the scent of roses and lavender from the garden.

Avery had just related the events of the afternoon, and every single member was looking at her, most exhibiting worry, but Mariah and Zane clearly showed dislike. She shifted in her seat, uncomfortable with the level of attention she was getting.

Genevieve spoke after her, swinging her gaze to Estelle. "How is Caspian now?"

"Better," she conceded, "but still weak. I've settled him at home, and renewed all of the protection spells—for whatever good they may be worth. My uncle is with him."

"I'm glad to hear it." Genevieve looked back at Avery. "It's good you checked on him when you did. He might have died."

"It's lucky you asked me to," she answered. "He was very weak. But it *is* odd. The spirits could have killed him at any time, and yet they didn't. I don't understand what's happening."

"Of course," Zane said sharply, "there is only *your* word to go by on this."

Avery was too tired to argue and just glared at him. "Oh, shut up, you idiot."

Her disdain was more shocking than if she'd argued, and Zane's mouth fell open in surprise.

Rasmus's gravelly voice broke the stunned silence. "Well said. We trust each other in this group, and Avery has more than proven her worth here, as have the other White Haven witches, which is more than can be said for you, Zane." Ignoring Zane's furious face, Rasmus turned to Oswald, who was trying to conceal his amusement. "Oswald, I understand you have been looking into the death in Fowey?"

Oswald nodded. "The victim, a young man called Miles Anderson, was found on the beach, with pretty much every bone in his body crushed. His car was parked out of town, not too far from the coastal path."

"Someone could have picked a fight with him and then pushed him over the cliff," Eve suggested.

"But," Avery said, "Newton thinks the fall wasn't enough to have broken so many bones. And there was no sign of a struggle at the top. They searched quite a large area, I gather."

Oswald continued. "The locals also report an increase in supernatural activity. Nothing concrete, of course, and certainly no ghosts looking like sailors! Just rumours about piskies. But they did say that the young man had been seen about town recently, and hanging around the castle ruins."

"He could have been looking for something," Rasmus suggested thoughtfully. "But it really doesn't give us much to go on."

Eve was sitting opposite Avery, and she looked at her sadly. "I'm really sorry to hear about the policewoman. That's awful."

Avery had updated them on all of the recent news, and she smiled at Eve. "Thanks. I hardly knew her, but it is terrible, and it sounded as if Newton was upset. I'm hoping he's at the pub now, speaking to Alex."

"There are several things worrying me," Genevieve said. "Obviously, these unnaturally strong spirits, and what could be a very destructive supernatural creature. They both seem to have appeared very recently. Simultaneously." Her arms were resting on the table in front of her, and she leaned on them, staring at Avery. "Tell me what Newton saw, again."

"Well, I only know what I heard via Alex, but he said that something scuttled down the tunnel, something small. He hit it with his torch, but didn't get a clear picture of it because it was too dark. But if he hit it, then it's not a spirit."

"But you said you felt the spirit's hands around your throat earlier," Zane said, "and that one picked Reuben up. Therefore, it must have some physical presence. It could have been a ghost that Newton encountered!"

Avery looked at Zane's accusatory glare and nodded. "It's possible. But Newton is a policeman, which makes him very observant, and he reacts well under stress. If he thinks it wasn't a spirit—and he's seen enough of them—then I trust him."

Jasper intervened. "We can't forget that these events are linked to treasure. Guineas were thrown at Avery, there were some at Caspian's house, a few were left when Reuben was attacked, and one was placed in Miles Anderson's mouth. It's seems pretty obvious to me that someone has found buried treasure and disturbed some spirits…and they are seeking revenge."

"Miles?" Genevieve asked. "Or someone else?"

"It could have been Miles," Oswald said. "Potentially he, and maybe someone else, found the buried treasure, and that's why he was killed. This has to be about smugglers! We all know there were a lot of them in Cornwall."

"Absolutely," Genevieve agreed, nodding.

Oswald looked puzzled. "I'm confused that there are both doubloons and guineas, but there must be a connection."

"What about witches?" Rasmus looked at Estelle. "Why was Caspian targeted? Did your family clash with smugglers in the past?"

Estelle rolled her eyes. "I have no idea, Rasmus! You're talking about a few hundred years ago. It's possible, I suppose."

"You were, and are, shipping merchants," Avery told her. "I think it's very likely you would have clashed about shipments." She turned to the rest of the table. "Reuben has caves under his grounds, and a long passage leading to Gull Island. We know his family was involved in smuggling. But, we don't know if they clashed with a particular group. Reuben has already started to look into it."

Rasmus grunted. "I think you should do the same, Estelle. Your life may depend on it."

She nodded, stiffly. "I will, but I'd be very surprised if we worked with the Jacksons."

"So would Reuben," Avery said, dryly. She caught Eve's eye and suppressed a grin.

"Mariah," Genevieve said abruptly. "What do you know about the cave collapse in Looe?"

Mariah looked surprised at being addressed. She normally remained as quiet as possible. "Only what has appeared on the news. The locks on the wooden chests found in the bottom of the cave were recently smashed, and there were the remains of three bodies found—very old ones, obviously. Looe, like everywhere else, has an extensive smuggling history. One of our most notorious smugglers was Cruel Coppinger."

Avery watched her while she talked, not wanting to reveal that she'd seen her photo at Jamaica Inn's Smuggling Museum. She also hadn't told the group about a witch walking the spirit world. If it was someone around this table, she certainly didn't want to alert them to the fact that she knew, or that Alex had walked there, too. She glanced around the rest of the table, but no one looked guilty or worried at all.

Mariah was warming to her subject as she continued to address the group. "He didn't earn the name 'Cruel' for no reason. He and his posse beheaded a revenue officer. He was considered almost supernatural. His gang was called the Cruel Gang, too. They controlled much of this part of the coast."

Avery recalled her earlier conversation with her regulars at the shop. "Including White Haven and Harecombe."

"Yes," Mariah confirmed.

"Why was he considered supernatural?" Eve asked.

"He arrived in the middle of a storm, his ship breaking up on the shore. The locals had come to watch the wreck, as they often did, hoping for bounty, and he strode out of the waves, leapt up behind a local woman on her horse, and absconded with her. This was on the north coast, not the south. She became his wife—somewhat unwillingly, I gather," she said, eyebrows raised. "Anyway, he was huge, Danish—a Viking striding out of the past. Some called him a demon."

"You seem to know a lot about him," Oswald said. "Do I recall correctly that you gave something to the Smuggling Museum once?"

She nodded, unconcerned. "One of Zephaniah Job's ledgers. He was the smuggler's banker, and very good at it apparently. My grandfather was fascinated with smuggling, and an old friend left him all his papers when he died. He found the ledger in the collection and was determined to donate it. Most of them had been destroyed in a fire after Job died, probably deliberately. I just organised it. He told me all sorts of tales as a child. And of course, Cruel Coppinger is well known in Looe. We have a pub named after him." Mariah smiled, looking at everyone's expectant faces. "And what's more intriguing is the manner of his end. He just disappeared into the sea one night, and was never seen again."

"Drowned?" Eve asked.

Mariah shrugged. "A ship was seen anchored offshore, and he rowed out to it on a small boat."

Avery leaned back in her chair. "That's intriguing. So he has no grave here?"

"No. But plenty of his gang would have had burials here. I'm just not sure where they would be."

"This could be related to him, even with that enigmatic exit," Genevieve said. "I'm just wondering what could have set this whole thing off. Something must have happened recently."

Avery said, "White Haven Museum is putting together a new exhibition about smuggling. It's not open to the public yet, so I have no idea what they're planning to show, but maybe that has something to do with it."

"Very possible," Genevieve said, nodding. "Perhaps a researcher discovered something they shouldn't have." She looked around the table. "We need to work together on this. Anything that we can find out could be valuable. Reuben and you, Estelle, should check your family histories carefully."

Estelle didn't look impressed at being given instructions

by Genevieve, and she gave an abrupt nod of acknowl-
edgement.

Genevieve's gaze swept around the table. "Is there anything else before we go?"

The council members shook their heads, and Avery noticed many of them appeared worried by the turn of events.

"All right," she said with a sigh. "In the meantime, I suggest we all watch our backs, and enhance our protection spells until we know what we're up against."

Alex poured Newton another pint and set it in front of him, concerned about his friend. Concerned about both of his friends, actually.

Reuben sat on the barstool next to Newton, nursing his own pint. He was stoic regarding his injury, but every now and again he winced, and he used his left arm to pick up his pint, not his right. El sat next to him, casting him surrepti-tious, worried glances. Briar was next to Newton, her dark eyes that were now ringed with emerald fire, were full of concern.

On Tuesday nights the pub was usually half-empty, and tonight was no different. They had the freedom to talk easily without being overheard by anyone other than Zee, and Alex didn't mind him listening. Newton had arrived an hour ago, looking more depressed than Alex had ever seen him, and he leaned on the bar, struggling to maintain his composure. Since he'd arrived, he'd run through a range of emotions, from fury, sadness, and frustration, to feeling like a failure, and now he'd settled into a brooding determination to avenge Inez's death.

"And worst of all," Newton said, talking to his pint rather

than meeting their eyes, "we didn't even find one scrap of evidence to indicate who might have broken into those old chests. It was all a fucking waste of time."

Briar squeezed Newton's arm. "It feels like that now, but we will find out what did this."

Newton turned his troubled grey eyes on her. "We better. I feel sick."

Alex glanced up as he saw Avery arrive, her face pensive but also determined, and he relaxed at the sight of her. He turned automatically to grab a wine glass and pour her favourite red wine, and by the time she'd drawn up her stool, he slid it in front of her. She smiled at him and murmured her thanks before turning to Newton. "Newton, I am so sorry about Inez."

He brushed it off. "Thanks, but I won't rest until I've caught who did this." He shook his head. "She was starting a new life, post-divorce. She should have been safe here."

Avery nodded. "Yes, she should have been. I have a feeling though that this could escalate even further."

"Why? What happened at the meeting?" El asked, alarmed.

"Nothing there, particularly," Avery confessed. "It's just this general feeling I have. However, Oswald told everyone about the supernatural events around Fowey."

"What events?" Newton asked straight away.

"Just local accounts of the feeling that spirits are in the area, and the idea that piskies are stirring up trouble. Oswald did say that most people thought it was just Cornish stuff and that it wasn't anything to worry about, but…" She shrugged. "He did say there was a lot of speculation about the Spanish raids in the sixteenth century. Not surprising, really, after the doubloon."

"But they were much further down the coast," Alex said.

"Doesn't stop them from talking!"

"Any issues anywhere else?" Alex asked, sensing that Avery had other news.

She smiled at him, a gleam in her eye. "No one else has noticed anything unusual in their area. But Mariah told us about Cruel Coppinger."

El nodded. "The smuggler we read about this morning?"

"The very same. He was a violent man with a violent gang, and she agreed with what a couple of my customers told me earlier. He *was* particularly active around here. He also had supernatural associations." Her eyes widened with intrigue. "He arrived in a storm, a hulking Viking striding out of the waves, and left by the sea too, never to be seen again!"

"Viking?" Briar asked, confused.

"He was Danish, and also reputed to be demonic," Avery added for good measure. "Although, that may have been to do with his size. He was massive, apparently."

"Maybe 'demonic' is more to do with his cruelty," Reuben suggested. "Either way, it's interesting. It gives me something to look into in my own history."

"*Interesting* is not the word I would use," Newton said crossly. "Sounds like a bloody nightmare! Three people are now dead."

The witches all fell silent, chastened, and Alex calmly said, "We haven't forgotten that, Newton. But it is important that we have something to work on. We are as keen to avenge Inez's death as you are."

Newton nodded, briefly meeting his eyes, before staring into his pint.

"There's something else," Avery said quickly. "Oswald asked Mariah about the donation to the museum. She says her grandfather found the ledger, and she didn't seem the slightest bit concerned at the question. In fact, apart from

Zane being his usual grumpy self, no one looked remotely guilty or shifty."

"You were thinking about the witch walking the spirit realm," Alex said.

Avery nodded, slumping over the bar with her chin in her hands, and Alex realised what a long, busy day it had been. "I was," she admitted. "But everyone looked normal!"

Newton drained his pint. "I can't do this right now. I'm beyond tired and I need to sleep." He stood, his stool scraping across the floor. "I also need to work out what was in that tunnel."

"I hope you're not planning to go back out there alone?" Briar asked him, suddenly alarmed.

"No. I'm going to bed. Aren't you listening?"

"I mean tomorrow. Or the day after?" she said, trying to keep the impatience from her voice. "Whatever it was could still be there!"

"The whole place is lit up like a sodding Christmas tree now," he said impatiently. "A police officer died! SOCO have been tramping around there. It's been searched from top to bottom, and there's nothing there. *Nothing*!" Newton was almost shouting, and Alex shot him a warning look. Suddenly aware of his surroundings, Newton lowered his voice again. "If you want to help me, find out what that creature was and how to kill it."

Without waiting for a response, Newton left, and Briar made as if to move. "I should go after him."

Alex leaned forward, placing a hand on her arm. "He needs to be alone. He knows we care."

"Does he?" she asked, looking upset. "He didn't look like it."

"Of course he does," Alex said softly. "Men deal with things differently. We rage and stomp about, but he knows. He just needs some time."

"So, what are we going to do?" El asked. "I certainly don't want to wait around and let Reuben get attacked again. I've finally persuaded him to stay at my flat!" She shot him an annoyed glance.

"For tonight only," he told her. "I need to look at my family history, and I can't do that at your place."

"You could bring your books!" El said, continuing what was obviously an earlier argument.

"It's not just my grimoires. It's a whole load of books. I have a library, you know!"

"Do you?" Avery asked, looking surprised.

"Yes. I barely go in it," he conceded, "but I figure there must be something useful in there."

Alex couldn't help but laugh. "Only someone who doesn't like reading could look so underwhelmed at having his own library."

He shrugged. "Sorry. I don't even know what's on the shelves."

Avery's mouth hung open, emitting a strangled cry. *"What?"*

"Wow. You've just committed the cardinal sin in Avery's eyes," Alex told him. He rubbed Avery's shoulder. "It's okay, babe. Don't have a stroke."

Avery looked at Reuben, horrified. "But Reuben, you could have first editions in there, and leather-bound masterpieces…"

"I could. I admit it, I'm a heathen. Feel free to check it out sometime." He smiled at Avery, an attempt to appease her.

"This isn't helping," El said, narrowing her eyes at Reuben. "We need a plan! How do we find out what's happening?"

"Well," Alex said decisively, "I think this new exhibition in White Haven Museum is worth looking into. Let's see if we can find out more about it; the theme, who's organising it, etcetera. I know it's not open yet, but we could visit the museum anyway, look around the other exhibits, and ask a few questions. I can go tomorrow morning."

"Good idea," El said. "I'll come with you, while Reuben here fulfils his family history obligations."

Alex was aware of Zee's looming presence next to him, as he sidled closer. "May I make a suggestion?" he asked.

"Sure," Alex said.

"You mentioned supernatural creatures. Why don't you talk to Shadow? She's kicking her heels around now, and driving us all mad," he said, rolling his eyes. "She sees piskies on the moors. Perhaps she sees other things."

"Piskies!" Briar said, amazed. "She's never told us."

Zee shrugged. "She doesn't like to advertise it—and may not thank me for mentioning it—but it sounds like you need help."

Briar nodded. "Thanks, Zee. I'll call her first thing tomorrow."

"In that case," Avery said to Reuben brightly, "guess who's helping you tomorrow?"

Reuben groaned. "You're going to be such a task master!"

"Yes I am! It's your own fault," she admonished him, and Alex tried to suppress a smirk at her peremptory tone. "You should never have mentioned your library!"

CHAPTER 13

*C*aspian reclined on the cushioned sofa in the informal lounge that overlooked the back of his house, watching Estelle pace back and forth in front of the unlit fireplace.

The patio doors to the garden were open, and the night sounds carried inside—the hoot of an owl, the tinkle of the fountain, and soft sough of the warm summer breeze through the leaves. Caspian had been waiting anxiously for his sister to return from the Witches' Council meeting, and he'd been forced to listen to his uncle moaning about their obligations. He'd been too tired to object, and could only hope that Estelle hadn't alienated everyone. He'd worked hard to make connections over the last year, separate from those of his father. He wanted friendships that were on a more equal footing.

However, Caspian also knew that his Uncle, Maximilian Faversham, resented Caspian's approach, and so did Estelle. He didn't care. They could complain all they wanted. He was the head of the family and the business, and he called the shots. Even now, while recovering from his attack.

"Estelle," he said, more aggressive than he should have been, "you're making my neck ache. Will you please sit down and tell us what happened?"

Estelle shot him a look of pure loathing. "I don't know how you stand that group! We don't need them, we never have! Listening to them planning and plotting all night was excruciating. What do we care about the other covens, or bloody smuggling?"

Caspian couldn't believe her short-term memory; he was still bloodied and bruised in front of her. "Have you forgotten already, Estelle, that I was half-dead when Avery and Alex found me earlier? If it weren't for them, there'd be no *half* about it! And," he continued when she fixed her steely glare on him, "Avery only came looking for me because of Genevieve!"

Max looked sheepish. "That's true, Estelle. They do have some uses." Max was his father's younger brother, shorter in stature, with a thinning head of dark grey hair. Like his father, he had a mean streak in him, but he was also cautious. Years of doing business had taught him that. He headed up their overseas branch, and spent half of his time in France. Like all of them, though, he was a skilled witch, and his strongest element was fire.

"I should have known you'd take his side," she said scathingly, before stalking to the drinks cabinet and pouring a stiff gin and tonic. *That was a joke in itself,* Caspian thought, catching his uncle's eye. He almost never took Caspian's side. They both still seemed to blame him for his father's death.

When Estelle finally turned around, she looked more composed, and she sat down in a deep armchair, opposite their uncle and next to Caspian. "There seems to be some consensus that Cruel Coppinger could be behind this—or should I say, his spirit."

"The notorious smuggler?" Max asked.

"Yes. It seems he had control of this area, although I can't see what that has to do with us!"

Caspian gestured to their old family grimoire on the side table next to him, which he shared with Estelle. "I've had a cursory look in that, in case there's any reference to smuggling, but found nothing so far."

His uncle snorted. "It's a grimoire! Did you really expect to?"

"It's possible," Caspian reasoned. "Spells are annotated in there, suggestions squiggled in corners. There may have been a reference to a useful spell, but," he fell silent as he considered the vast number of spells in there, and the almost indecipherable writing in places, "I admit it's a long shot. Tomorrow, when I have more energy, I'll look in the study. There are some local histories in there that might be of use." He appealed to both of them. "If our business was threatened, we would have retaliated. I take it, Uncle, that you don't remember any family stories about smuggling?"

Max shook his head. "None. But you're right. We would have hit back if our livelihood was threatened."

"But," Estelle countered, "we would also have *led* any smuggling enterprises in this area if there was profit in it. Maybe Coppinger wanted a cut? Or wanted to take over our area?"

Caspian tried not to roll his eyes, and failed. "We were—are—legitimate business men. We couldn't have been thought to be smuggling! We were rich. We had a position in society to maintain."

"So how do you explain the Jacksons' involvement? Avery mentioned that cave today, the one where you killed Gil. They were clearly involved in it!"

Caspian winced, and not from the pain of his stab wound and all of his bruises. "His death was an accident. I didn't mean to kill Gil!"

"Whether you meant it or not doesn't matter. The fact is, you did kill him!" Estelle looked at him almost triumphantly, rubbing his nose in something he so deeply regretted. Something he would never forgive himself for.

"You shouldn't look so pleased about it. I hate that I did—and you should, too."

"If I was in your position I'd have done the same thing, and been proud of it," she sneered.

"Don't be ridiculous!" Caspian struggled to sit up and wished he hadn't as a searing pain pierced his side, and he broke out in a cold sweat. "You have no idea how it feels. I wouldn't wish that on anyone!"

"Maybe Avery can come over and comfort you," Estelle said, uncaring as to the pain she was causing him, physically and emotionally. "Although, she actually can't. She loves Alex, not you. Thank the Gods."

Fury flashed out of Caspian, rising up like a cobra, and before he could even think, he had willed her mute. He watched as Estelle struggled to speak, her hand at her throat, and her lips pressed closely together as if stitched by an unseen hand. Her eyes flashed as she tried to hurl a spell back at him. But he was ready for her; his protection spells were strong after what had happened that afternoon, and more than ready for her magic. Estelle moaned, her face contorting as she stood, and her fists clenched.

Max leapt to his feet. "Caspian, stop that now!"

He ignored him and glared at Estelle. "I've had enough of your vicious tongue. Say one more word against Avery and I'll rip it out!" Caspian blinked at the force of his own anger, but he wasn't about to back down now. Although he couldn't stand up, power radiated from him, and he noted both Estelle and his uncle took a step back. "You have never known love, Estelle, but one day you will. Then you'll understand. You'll know how it feels to have your heart ripped out when you're rejected because you're such a miserable, spiteful bitch. I wonder if that will be Barak." He smirked, even though what he said gave him no pleasure. "I've seen him watch you, and you watch him. But he's far nobler than you can ever be. I hope I'm there to see him break your heart. Now, get out. When I hear your car leave the drive, I'll release the spell."

For a moment, Estelle didn't move, looking at him wide-eyed with utter shock, and then those eyes narrowed with a calculating look that promised revenge. She turned, grabbed her bag, and stalked out. His uncle stood, uncertain.

"You'd better go, too," Caspian said. "Talk her down from taking her revenge on some poor, unsuspecting bugger. I'll be fine."

"I know she can be difficult, but she is your sister. And you're injured."

"Go," Caspian insisted, suddenly eager to see the back of both of them, and realising he could always call Gabe for help. "I need to be alone."

His uncle gave him a long look, as if about to say more, and then he shook his head, put his glass down, and left. Caspian waited, tense, listening to the sound of slamming doors and the whine of retreating engines as they drove down the drive. When silence finally fell, Caspian dropped back against the pillows behind him, releasing the spell on Estelle.

What had he done? He'd crossed a line, and he doubted that Estelle would ever forgive him. He recalled the fury in her eyes. *Would he have to protect himself from her now?*

And all because she'd taunted him about Avery.

He thought he was over her. That he'd buried his feelings too deep for them to hurt him again. But he was a fool. Love didn't work like that. And it was love, as much as he hated admitting that to himself. He had never said the word aloud, especially not to Avery, but she knew. She had to. He'd hidden it for months behind flirting and sarcasm, but the night of the Crossroads Circus, it had broken free, and he couldn't help himself. He looked out at the dark garden, but he saw only Avery, swirling in the centre of the crossroads, majestic with power. And he saw her pity when she looked at him. No, not pity. *Sorrow.* She loved Alex; that was obvious. There was no place for him in her life. Another time, another place, maybe.

What burned more than that, though, was the fact that Estelle knew of his feelings! And Alex knew, too. Alex looked at him with wariness and resentment, maybe fear too, at the possibility of losing Avery. He shouldn't, he was sure of that. But at least he didn't crow about his victory. Alex was too classy for that.

And that meant that probably everyone knew how he felt. Caspian hated that. He felt exposed, raw. And the only way he could deal with it was to embrace the pain of his rejection. At least he knew he was alive.

He shook his head and sipped his whiskey, feeling its warmth softening his despair. At least he had something to distract him now. He wanted to solve the mystery of why his family had earned the enmity of unknown spirits, and how they were strong enough to have breached his very strong protection spells.

With the help of his uncle, Caspian had layered them again on his return, making them stronger than before, and adding in specific protection against ghosts. But he should do the smart thing and call Gabe. Extra help wouldn't go amiss, and maybe he should add additional security to the warehouse, too. It was a huge place, stocked with all manner of shipments and equipment—and his staff. If he'd been targeted here, they could be, too. He reached for his phone.

"Sorry about yesterday," Avery said to Sally. "Everything went a bit mad after I called Genevieve."

They were in the kitchen of Happenstance Books, making their first coffee of the day, and as Sally pulled the mugs from the cupboard, her face was etched with worry.

"I'm just glad that you're okay," Sally said. "But I'm sorry to hear about Reuben. It sounds like he had a lucky escape."

"Very! Caspian wasn't so lucky."

Sally's face tightened with disapproval. "Well, as you know, I'm not a fan of Caspian, but I am sorry he was injured. But," she reached for the milk, "I'm so sad to hear about Inez Walker. Poor Newton. Is he okay?"

Avery sat in a chair at the table, recalling his anger the night before. "Not really. He blames himself, which is ridiculous, but also understandable. I would, too."

Sally finished their drinks, and bringing the cups to the table, sat down next to her. "You really have no idea what could have attacked her?"

"I keep coming back to spriggans—you know, the ghosts of giants I talked about with Dan. But, it's just a theory. Did you know," she leaned closer, "that Shadow sees piskies on the moors?"

"No!" Sally's eyes widened. "Really? That's amazing. Then the stories are true!"

Avery grinned, pleased to see her friend seemed to have forgiven her for the flash of magic that had scared her the other night. "I know. Briar is going to call her to see if she's seen any other faerie creatures. She could help us find out what Newton's mysterious attacker was."

"Good." Sally blew on her coffee, sending an eddy of steam up, and then sipped it, closing her eyes briefly. "Oh, that's lovely. Just what I needed. I must admit, I didn't sleep too well last night. Events seem to have escalated very quickly."

"They have," Avery admitted. "Three attacks in one day, three deaths, and other than vague guesswork, we're still in the dark about why. And of course, Helena is still missing, imprisoned somewhere in the spirit world." She rubbed her face, overwhelmed by the sum of it all. "I didn't even know that was a thing!"

"I'm not magical, Avery, so it has me worried, for me and my family, and Dan. If Reuben and Caspian were attacked, despite their magic, we would have no chance."

Avery reached forward and grabbed Sally's free hand. "I genuinely don't think you need to worry. The spirits seem to be targeting specific people, for now."

"What about the man walking his dog?" Sally reminded her. "He was just going about his business, and now he's dead."

"Wrong place, wrong time."

Sally shook her head, releasing her hand from Avery's hold. "And that could happen to any of us, too."

There was no denying that. Sally had an excellent point. "You're right. He didn't stand a chance. But we're working hard on this."

"Do you think it's Cruel Coppinger, like Mary and Fred said yesterday?"

"It's certainly possible, but still just a theory. I'm going to help Reuben search his library today. I may know more then." She smiled at Sally with what she hoped was a reassuring expression. "I'll go mid-morning, if that's okay."

"That's fine," Sally said, rising to her feet. "I'll go and open the shop up, and hopefully Dan will be here soon. As far as I'm concerned, Avery, you take as much time as you need, because I think this violence is only the start."

El stood in front of a glass cabinet, looking at the objects displayed within it: evidence of White Haven's rich history.

Strictly speaking, White Haven Museum was more than just educational. It was situated in a Georgian building on the hill looking over the town, and in addition to displaying White Haven's history, it housed an art gallery, a gift shop, and a very busy café. The artwork they displayed was a mixture of paintings, watercolour and oil, charcoal and pencil drawings, and prints, all depicting the surrounding countryside and Cornwall in general, and mostly created by local artists.

The room El was currently in was an exhibition about the local industries. It featured archaic farming implements found in the soil in the hills around the town, old fishing equipment, and black and white photos of the farming and fishing communities. White Haven had always been a fishing village, and of course a trading one. Compared to some of the other museums in Cornwall, this one was small, but its displays were impressive, and it was a popular attraction.

The room was bathed in morning sunlight, and as it warmed her, El took a deep breath, feeling the heat ease the knots in her shoulders. The knots of anxiety that had accumulated by worrying about Reuben. She wasn't just worrying about his stab wound; she was also anxious about his lack of confidence in his magic, and the nearing anniversary of Gil's death. Reuben, despite his confident swagger about many things, was deeply unsure of his magical abilities, and although he'd made great headway over the past year, was still nowhere near as proficient as he wanted to be. Or *should* be, considering his family. A couple of months ago she thought that was all in the past, but it seemed not.

El shook herself out of her worry, and looked around the

room once more. It was pointless being in here, interesting though it was. It shed no light on smuggling, or anything pertaining to their current problem.

She decided to find Alex. They had arrived together about half an hour ago, but had split up to search the exhibits. She headed through the stately rooms converted to exhibition halls, finally arriving in the art gallery, and found Alex looking at a large painting of a stormy sea, on which a rigged ship with tattered sails floundered. Huge waves crashed on a rocky beach, and men clustered on the sand, watching and waiting. *Smugglers, waiting to plunder the wreck.*

Alex looked lost in thought, and she gently nudged him. "It's impressive, isn't it?"

He looked at her and grinned, looking slightly piratical himself with his long hair and swashbuckling goatee that he was currently sporting. "It is. Very atmospheric." He turned back to it. "It depicts smugglers, though. I'm wondering why it's here, if they're setting up a smuggling exhibit."

"Maybe they plan to move it?" El stepped away from him, idly looking at the other artwork. She stopped to admire a watercolour of White Haven in bold purple, black, and grey, thinking how good it would look on her wall. "Did you see the entrance to the new bit?" She jerked her head towards the other rooms. "It will be in the room at the back of the building."

He nodded, and pushed his hair away from his face, wrinkling his nose with annoyance. "I did. It doesn't give much away, does it?"

"No. But we could ask someone."

"Before we do, come and see this."

Alex led the way across the gallery to the image of a man with a scowling face, a heavy beard, red-rimmed eyes, and dressed in old-fashioned sailor's clothing. His hair was as black as night, and he stood on the deck of the ship, staring, it seemed, right at El.

She shivered. "He's unpleasant looking."

Alex raised an eyebrow. "I'm not surprised. It's Cruel Coppinger. Or an artist's representation of him, at least." He pointed to the small printed card on the wall.

"Wow." El looked at the image with new appreciation. "So that's the demon pirate. I feel he's looking right through me."

"Maybe we should talk to the local artist. It's the same one who's done many of the seascapes, including the one I was just looking at."

El looked at him, perplexed. "I suppose we could, but why?"

"They might have done some research that could help. Could save us some time."

El shrugged. Avery and Alex loved their research, but she was a bit more like Reuben. She found it time consuming and annoying. But, Alex was normally right about these things. "I guess we could try," she conceded.

She saw movement in the corner of her eye and turned, momentarily alarmed, to find it was an older woman in a museum shirt. She smiled at them. "I notice you're interested in our painting of Cruel Coppinger. It's brooding, isn't it?"

Alex stepped back to allow her room. "It is. We were just admiring the artist's other work—like the seascape over there."

The gallery assistant nodded. "Anthony Carter. He lives quite close to here. He's kindly agreed that we can display these in our new exhibition that opens next week."

"We were wondering about that. Will Cruel Coppinger be part of that exhibit?"

The woman smiled, excited. "Oh, yes. The curator has been doing some wonderful work!" She bounced on her soles, a curiously childish gesture, El thought, for a mature woman. "We actually had a remarkable find a few months ago when we cleared out some of our basement areas. I'm sure you know that many museums have so much stock that they can't possibly display it all?" They nodded, wondering where she was going, but she ploughed on. "We found more documents about Zephaniah Job working with Coppinger, which was amazing, because it was presumed that it had all been lost, as well as some other items I'm not familiar with! We can't wait for it to open. This painting will move at the end of the week."

"Wow," Alex said, eyes wide as he glanced at El, and she knew he was trying as hard as she was to hide his excitement. "So you actually found new material?"

"Yes! Such good fortune, and we were so lucky that Ethan was released to help us!"

"Ethan James?" El asked, recalling his name from the photo she'd seen the day before. "Did he assist with Jamaica Inn's Smuggling Museum, too?"

The woman looked surprised. "Yes, he did. He's well known for his expertise on the subject, so it was natural to ask him to help us. He's actually based at Helston's Ship-wreck Treasure Museum, so he's here only for a short time, you understand. It means he could incorporate some items that haven't made it into the other museums, too."

El nodded at Cruel Coppinger. "So, he's a big figure in our local history, then?"

"Absolutely! He caused so many problems for everyone. Incredibly headstrong, by all accounts." Her eyes darkened as she looked at him. "And cruel, of course. That's why he got his name. There was a bounty on his head, but of course, everyone was terrified of betraying him."

"I'm not surprised," El said.

The assistant continued, unabashed. "Actually, the anniversary of his disappearance, as near as we can work out, is this weekend, so we timed the opening to coincide with it. Anyway, I'll leave you to it, but there are some leaflets about the new exhibit in the gift shop and by the entrance, so feel free to pick them up before you leave. I'm sure you'll love it."

El watched her walk across the gallery and then looked at Alex. "New material? That can't be a coincidence."

"Perhaps not. Coupled with the anniversary of his death, it all sounds ominous to me." Alex checked his watch. "Coffee time. I'll treat you to cake in the café, and we can chat then."

"You're on. And I'll get a leaflet to look at."

CHAPTER 14

*B*riar watched Shadow prowl around her herb room as if she expected to find something dodgy, energy rolling off her. Briar was exhausted just watching her.

"What are you looking for, Shadow?"

"Nothing!" Shadow turned to her, her violet eyes wide with surprise. "Why?"

"You look like you think I might have hidden a body in here!"

Shadow laughed. "I wouldn't tell, even if you had!" She sobered immediately. "Have you? Have you mashed their bones into a paste, saved their blood, and put their hair in a spell?"

Briar tried to laugh, but it came out as a strangled cry. "Of course not, you daft idiot! What kind of witch do you think I am?"

Shadow just winked. "Never mind."

Briar stopped chopping the geranium leaves she was preparing and dropped them into hot water, inhaling the scent with pleasure, and then readied the next herbs, eyeing Shadow while she worked. "Are you bored?"

Shadow wagged her head. "Maybe. But I am intrigued by your random spirit attack. And of course Caspian was attacked, too."

"You heard about that?"

"Caspian phoned Gabe last night. He wanted additional protection for his house and the warehouse."

"For his house?" Briar asked, surprised. "I can see his reasoning, but still, I'm surprised."

A mischievous grin spread across her face. "He argued with Estelle."

"Did he? Over what?"

"Her being a bitch! What else?"

That was far too simple an explanation. "She's always been one of those. Something must have happened."

"He didn't go into details." Shadow looked disappointed. "But he sent his uncle away, too. Although he renewed his protection spell, I guess the attack has shaken him up."

Briar had planned to check Caspian's wound later that day, so maybe she could find out then. She changed tack. "Was the warehouse attacked?"

"No. It was as quiet as the grave. Anyway," she said, pulling herself up onto the counter and leaning her arms on her knees, "I'm guessing you called me for a reason, so how can I help?"

"Well," Briar paused, looking forward to Shadow's reaction, "I hear that you see piskies!"

She sat up abruptly, looking shocked. "Who told you that? It was that bloody womaniser, wasn't it?"

Briar laughed. "No, it wasn't Eli. It was Zee."

"Gossipmonger! You just wait 'til I see him later."

"Why didn't you tell us? It doesn't need to be a secret, does it?"

"I guess not. I suppose I wasn't sure what you'd think about another bit of the Otherworld in this one."

"I think it's great!" Briar said, and then she frowned. "Well, if they're harmless. I guess that brings us to why I wanted to speak to you. You've heard about Inez Walker, I presume?"

Shadow nodded, suddenly serious. "Yes. I met her brother-in-law. He was the one who took my statement. "

"Well, Newton was with her when she died, and he said that there was something supernatural in the tunnel—something small and fast. Inez was hit hard, her skull crushed, and Newton was almost attacked too, until he whacked whatever it was with his torch. But, there's no evidence of what it could be. And combined with the man who was found crushed in Fowey…" She trailed off.

"You think it's something supernatural that I might be able to see?"

"Yes. Some kind of Otherworldly something."

Shadow frowned. "I'm certainly willing to try, but I've really only seen piskies so far. Well, I call them *pixies*, actually." She smiled. "They're sort of an unexpected present. They pop up when I least expect them to."

"What do you mean by 'pop up?'"

Shadow spread her hands wide. "I can't predict it. They are there one minute and gone the next."

"Where do they go?" Briar asked, confused.

"Good question. I think it's sort of like what I can do when I'm in the woods. I blend into the landscape. I don't think they actually pass between worlds. In fact," she paused, thoughtful. "I'm sure of it."

Briar nodded. "Have you heard of spriggans?"

"I don't think so, but you may have a different name for them here. What are they?"

"According to folklore, they are small, wizened men, incredibly strong, that possess—sort of—the ghosts of giants."

"Giants? Wow."

"They also guard buried treasure."

"Hence the connection to the current events," Shadow said, thoughtfully. She stared at Briar. "There were giants here, once?"

"According to our myths, yes. Cornwall is renowned for them. Were they in the Otherworld?"

"Yes, but there aren't many now, and they keep themselves isolated. I don't know about spriggans though, or if we have an equivalent." Her face brightened, and she jumped off the countertop and walked to the door. "Okay, I'll do some investigating."

"Well, be careful," Briar called after her. "They're violent!"

"Don't worry. So am I," Shadow said, before she shut the door behind her.

Reuben groaned and looked up from the old book open in front of him, the words swimming before his eyes.

He was reclining in a deep armchair in front of a large stone fireplace, currently unlit due to the summer heat. "This is so tedious," he said to Avery.

She was sitting at a table under the long windows that overlooked the gardens at the side of the house, and her red hair glowed in the sunlight that streamed in. She looked up at him, vague for a moment before she focussed. "It's great! You have an awesome library."

He looked around at the oak shelves stacked with books from floor to ceiling, the only wall not to be affected the one with the windows. The shelves were filled with paperbacks, hardbacks, and classics with leather covers and gilded titles, as well as very old books worn by many hands over time.

"I suppose it is impressive," he admitted. "Not that I've really been in here for years."

"I can tell. It has an unloved feeling. At least it's clean."

"That's what cleaners are for."

"You should get this catalogued! You could have all sorts of hidden gems tucked away in here."

"You could do it."

Avery shook her head. "I'm not a rare book dealer. I wouldn't know what I'm looking at. You need a professional."

"You sell books!"

"*Regular* books! Two completely different things."

It sounded like a lot of hard work to him, but he wanted to keep Avery happy. "Maybe I should…one day. Have you found anything, anyway?"

When Avery had arrived a couple of hours before, they searched the library and found that the shelves had been organised into categories. They had discovered a section full of books about Cornwall that encompassed a mix of history, myths, and folklore, but nothing that was particularly relevant to Reuben's family history. Nevertheless, they had pulled a few pertinent titles and started to read them.

"Not really," she said, disappointed. "Just information that we already knew about spriggans, Púcas, and piskies. What about you?"

"Only some generic smuggling stuff. Nothing about the Jacksons specifically. This book talks about Coppinger, and he really does sound like he was an evil bastard. He extorted, smuggled, tortured and murdered people, and generally terrorised the neighbourhood. North Cornwall, in particular. I can't imagine we would have worked with him. But then again, our families did some questionable stuff in the past."

"They did," Avery admitted, "but they also did good things. Maybe your family fought with him for the rights to smuggle here. You know, force him back to the north."

"It's possible." He leaned back and looked thoughtfully at the shelves again. "If we *had* been involved with Coppinger, we wouldn't be likely to leave evidence just lying around, would we?" A recollection of old boxes filled with papers in the attic made him sit upright suddenly, jerking his injured shoulder, and he winced. "Ow. I've just had a thought."

"Did that hurt your head?" Avery said, teasing him.

"Funny. There are some boxes of letters in the attic—the regular side, not the spell room. I remember seeing them when we moved some old furniture up there a few years ago. I wonder if there's something in those."

"Letters! Reuben, they sound fascinating!"

What was it with Avery and the written word? "They could be full of boring crap!"

"And they could be full of Jackson secrets!" She was already standing, her face flushed with excitement. "Come on. Let's check."

Alex watched El over the rim of his coffee cup, worried about her. She looked distracted, and although her makeup had been applied with her usual skill, she lacked her typical energetic glow. He knew she was worried about Reuben, just like him, but he also didn't want to pry and upset her.

They were seated under the window on the second floor of the museum, looking out to the street below, a glimpse of the sea visible through the gaps between buildings on the opposite side of the road.

He decided to talk about one of her favourite subjects instead—weapons. "Have you had a chance to inspect those daggers yet?"

"I have!" She dunked her marshmallow in her mocha latte

and popped it in her mouth, eyes widening with pleasure. "This is *so* good! I was so hungry, I thought I might die!"

"It's a marshmallow! How can it possibility fill you up?"

"That's what the cake is for, idiot," she said, gesturing to the large slice of lemon drizzle cake beside her cup. "This is an *amuse-bouche*."

"I have honestly never thought of a marshmallow as one of those before."

She gave him a wicked grin. "It's the sweet version."

He laughed. "You've got a hell of a sweet tooth, El. You're as bad as Reuben is with curry. Well, just about anything, really. So, what have you found?"

"Well, I popped in to see Dante earlier, and he agrees that they are late-eighteenth century. The one that was thrown at you has a double-edged blade, which is typical, and a bone hilt. Once I cleaned it up I found tiny initials on it—CG."

"Cruel Gang?"

"Could be," she said, forking a mouthful of cake up. "Or they are the initials of the owner's name."

"And the other one?" Alex prompted.

"It's far more ornate, a walnut hilt, with some lovely engraving on it. But no initials on that one."

Alex was disappointed. "Damn it. I'd hope we'd get some clues from them."

El shrugged, unperturbed. "It was always a long shot. Hopefully Reuben will find something today, with Avery. She has a nose for finding things."

"She certainly does." Alex hesitated a moment, and then took the plunge. "Is Reuben okay? I feel horrible about Gil, and I know I upset him the other night."

El swallowed a bite of her cake, and grimaced. "Hold on. This needs to be warmer!" Glancing around to make sure she wasn't being watched, she held her hands above her cake and Alex felt her magic flare as she warmed it up. She took another bite and smiled. "That's better. I can concentrate now. So, Reuben. Yeah. I think the initial shock has worn off, but it's the other stuff that it has set off that worries me."

Alex gripped his coffee cup. "Like what?"

El stared at her fork, as if she wasn't sure how much to say, and then she met Alex's eyes, resigned. "He's doubting his magical abilities again, and is consequently disappointed with himself. He feels he's failed Gil and isn't living up to his family legacy."

"That's rubbish," Alex said, angrily. "His magic is strong. He just needs to use it more!"

"I know! And I've told him that, but it's almost like he shies away from it sometimes." El rested her fork on the table, her cake half-finished. "It's like he's in denial."

"But he's done some fantastic spells! The fog he conjured at the circus, the spell to find the mermaids… And he never turns away from a fight. He tackled the vampires head-on!"

El laughed, despite her worry. "Yes, he did, with that ridiculous water gun."

"He's inventive! And I never doubt that I can rely on him."

"But it's not courage that he lacks," El pointed out. "He's strong and quick, and very loyal to us. It's his magical self-confidence that is troubling him."

"And he'll only get that by using it more." Alex groaned. "I wish I knew how to help him. He did fight off a spirit the other day, though," he said brightly. "That must have boosted his confidence."

"True." El picked her fork up and speared another piece of cake. "But I think it's more deep-seated than that."

"I doubt it helps being in that big house all by himself."

"Oh, he loves that! He doesn't use half the rooms, but he really enjoys being there." El looked at him speculatively while she chewed her cake, and when she swallowed, she said, "Do you like living with Avery?"

"I love it." He didn't hesitate. "It's the best thing I've ever done, and I'm relieved she puts up with me. I just wish Caspian would back off."

El froze. "What's he done?"

Alex almost choked on his coffee. "You haven't noticed?"

"I've noticed that he flirts with her. But that's okay. You flirt."

His anger rushed back and he wished he could control it more, but Caspian annoyed the crap out of him. "It's more than flirting. He's made it very clear that if I wasn't around…" He trailed off, his meaning clear.

El reached across the table and squeezed his hand. "It doesn't matter. Is Avery flattered? Sure. Who wouldn't be? He's rich and good looking, and is less of a dick than we first thought. But he isn't meant for Avery. You are. And she knows that. You two are adorable together."

"Adorable?" Alex winced. "I sound like a teddy bear."

"You are. In the best possible way," she teased. "Seriously though, I get that it's irritating, but that's Caspian's way." She studied him. "Don't you start doubting yourself, too. Or Avery. I've got enough to worry about with Reuben."

He smiled, properly reassured, and saluted her. "Yes ma'am."

CHAPTER 15

*D*ust clouds rose around Avery as she lifted the lid on a wooden chest and peered inside.

"Bloody hell, Reuben. I take it your cleaner doesn't come up here."

"Of course not. It's the attic."

Avery coughed, summoned air, and sent it spinning around them both in a gently revolving circle, carrying the dust away. "That's better."

"You're very practical with your magic," Reuben observed. He was a short distance away, opening up more boxes.

"It's meant to be practical. I use mine everyday for all sorts of things." She lifted a bundle of papers out of the box, setting them on the floor, and then sat cross-legged on an old, dusty rug that was probably worth a small fortune, and proceeded to sort through them, talking as she did so. "I use it for protection. I have a spell on my shop to help customers find their perfect book. I warm my tea with it when it gets cold. I use it to prepare herbal drinks depending on my mood. It helps to bolster my garden. I use it to gather herb bundles, pick my plants at the optimum times, and loads of other things." She shrugged. "I can't imagine *not* using it daily, and it certainly doesn't need to be showy." She looked up at him, and found that he was watching her, frowning. "It's like breathing to me."

Reuben shuffled to the floor and started emptying another box. "Maybe that's where I'm going wrong. I don't use it like that."

"What about in the nursery? You said you'd spelled the hanging baskets for Beltane."

"Yeah, I did that. And I head to the greenhouses on occasions at night to spell the plants, so I don't freak out the employees. Gil had a timetable. I just follow that."

Avery smiled. "Well, there you go then." She knew he wasn't as comfortable with his magic as she was, and didn't want to make a big deal out of it. "Try doing the same things around the house. Little things. Spells in your cooking, enhancing your space, that kind of thing."

"Not showy, you say?" He looked puzzled.

"No. Magic is sometimes the gentlest of things. Like when El weaves her magic into her jewellery, or Briar sprinkles it into her candles and lotions. They are both subtle, like a caress." If Reuben was puzzled, Avery was doubly so. Surely Reuben knew that. She tried to explain it better, leaving the papers she'd found resting in her lap. "The big spells we do—throwing fire and energy balls, me commanding air and making mini tornados, huge protection spells, the cleansing of White Haven—they're unusual. Until this last year, when we've been practically forced to because of everything that's happened, I hardly ever did those showy things. Personally, I feel that magic is more effective when it's subtle." She tried to make him laugh. "Sneaky, I know. And also far more dangerous, potentially, because you can do things to people and they have no idea. Which is why we don't, obviously. Blessed be, and harm none."

Reuben's expression seemed to clear, and he smiled. "I haven't thought about magic like that for a long time, but you're right. That's exactly how it should be. It's become this big thing in my head, and I don't think it needs to be."

"No, it shouldn't. But having said that, we also shouldn't forget how lucky we are. We're gifted, and we shouldn't squander that, or neglect it. Anyway," she said, not wanting to lecture him, "you have a huge collection of private papers here." She gestured to the boxes and wooden chests littered around them. The attic was huge, running the length of the main area of the house, with a proper set of stairs leading up to it. The far end had been opened up to reveal Reuben and Gil's previously hidden spell room. The rafters were high, with narrow windows set under the eaves, and lots of old heavy furniture was stored there. The place was an antique dealer's dream. "It's a good job it's so dry up here."

"Yes, it is. It's odd that these papers aren't in the library."

"Maybe they were deemed *too* personal." She winked. "I guess we'll soon find out."

An hour of searching had gone by when Avery finally found a name she wasn't expecting. Both she and Reuben were now surrounded with bundles of letters, old diaries, estate accounts, invoices going back decades, and more personal things, like party invitations. It was a fascinating insight into life at Greenlane Manor. They had called back and forth, shouting out what they'd found, and Avery was itching to start cataloguing it, wishing she had family archives this extensive.

The years were completely jumbled up, letters from the nineteenth century mixed up with those from the eighteenth, and before. Some family members seemed to have saved lots of things, and yet there were big gaps in time periods, too. But now, she suspected she'd found something useful.

"Reuben, this letter is from a Serephina Faversham."

He looked up, startled, a smear of dust across his cheek. "*What?* Are you kidding?"

"No. It's to someone called Virginia."

"Serephina?" He looked horrified. "What kind of a bloody name is that?"

"The posh kind. Any idea who Virginia is?"

"Hold on." He dug into his jeans pocket with his left hand, his right he was still hardly using, and extracted a crumpled piece of paper. "I noted down a few names from my grimoire and family tree."

"Blimey," Avery said, surprised. "That's organised of you."

"How dare you! I do take *some* things seriously. Like getting stabbed." He scanned the paper. "Yes! I have a Virginia listed, as well as Jerome, Adele, Talwyn, and Lowen. They are names across about a 70-year period—just in case. Virginia, Talwyn, and Lowen are also in my grimoire."

"Super cool names," Avery observed. "Well, this is just one letter. Hopefully there are more in this bundle."

The paper was creased and brittle, and before she handled it any further, Avery said a quick spell to preserve the paper, satisfied when she felt its effects.

"What's it say?" Reuben asked impatiently.

Avery frowned as she read the contents, and then looked up at Reuben triumphantly. "Essentially, after much polite dithering, Serephina has asked for help dealing with the troublesome *Dane* and she suggests a meeting. 'Despite our differences, we have much to gain.'" She picked up a couple of letters from the same bundle and passed them to Reuben. "I think it's pretty clear who the Dane is. Check these out. I think we're on to something."

≈

It was a triumphant group that met that night in The Wayward Son, and Reuben settled back in his chair, comforted by the reassuring presence of his friends after what had been a stressful day.

All five witches and Newton were seated around a table in the back room, empty plates pushed aside and drinks topped up, as they continued to share their news. Briar had told them about Shadow's plan to investigate spriggans, and Alex and El had updated them about their museum visit.

El placed a couple of leaflets on the table. "Unfortunately, these don't tell us much. They've kept the contents of the exhibition very vague."

Reuben watched as Avery picked one up. He'd read it earlier. It was a single-page flyer, basically saying the exhibition would highlight the complicated smuggling history in the region, and focus on some colourful characters.

"You're right," she said as she scanned it. "I doubt it can differ that much from the one we saw in Bodmin."

"I think it will be smaller," El told her. "But it will be more localised, too. They might mention the local beaches and caves that would have been used, that sort of thing."

Reuben laughed. "Maybe my family's smuggling history will be revealed. Although, I would have thought I'd be contacted if that was their plan." It wasn't something he was worried about, but he was curious to know if the tunnel to Gull Island was recorded elsewhere. "I think what's more interesting is the stuff they found in the museum basement."

"Absolutely," Briar said, agreeing with him. "Perhaps Ethan found directions that led to buried treasure…potentially *Coppinger's* treasure. Perhaps he's aiming to keep it for himself."

Avery looked sceptical. "A highly respected museum curator? I doubt it!"

"I guess we'll just have to do more digging," El said.

"I'll look into him," Newton said. He'd recovered his composure from the previous night, although a grim determination had settled over his hard features. He'd listened more than chatted, so far. "You'd be surprised what disgruntled employees can get up to."

"You two are looking very smug," Alex told Reuben and Avery. "Like you've found something exciting."

Reuben grinned. "We have. My stash of paperwork in the attic revealed that Virginia Jackson was approached by Serephina Faversham to help tackle 'the Dane.'" He said it ominously, like it was a pantomime.

"Really?" Newton asked. "Did she say yes?"

"It seems Virginia agreed, because the next letter detailed a time to meet—neutral ground in West Haven, the coastal path—and there was one more letter after that. Serephina thanked Virginia for her ideas, and suggested another meeting." Reuben sipped his beer. "That was it. No details."

"Sensible, really," Newton said. "Anything that is written can be incriminating."

Alex tapped his glass, impatient. "So, there's no suggestion of what they actually did?"

"No," Avery answered. "We searched lots of other letters, but nothing gave us any clues. And essentially, we have no idea if they were successful or not."

"Did you tell Caspian?" Briar asked.

Reuben shook his head. "Not yet. We thought we'd tell him tomorrow. I've decided to go to his place."

"Are you sure that's wise?" El asked. She was sitting next to him, and she nudged him gently, her gaze searching his face.

He knew why she was worried. He'd been furious about Caspian when he reflected on Gil's death, but he'd since pushed it aside—with difficulty. "Our families are linked together with this. We were then, and we are now. I'll show him the letters. Hopefully, he'll have family records, too."

Newton nodded. "Let's hope he has. Your old families and massive attics have probably got all sorts of secrets stored in them."

"I haven't found any others," Reuben protested. "Although, I must admit that I haven't searched all that stuff up there. I will keep looking."

El nodded, but she still looked concerned. "Do you have any idea about Virginia's magic?"

"No. Her name is in my grimoire, but I can't identify any spells that are written by her; I'll keep looking." As much as Reuben was struggling with Gil's death, he had to admit that this mystery was giving him something positive to focus on.

"Well," Newton said, clearing his throat. "I have heard from Cassie. They've started investigating Fowey and Looe, but I've told them to be very careful. I can't have another death on my conscience."

"You shouldn't even have one on it," Briar said firmly. "Inez's death is not your fault."

He shrugged, but it was pretty clear Newton wasn't letting go of his guilt that easily. Reuben also thought that Cassie, Ben, and Dylan would keep digging, regardless of Newton's advice.

"Have they found anything supernatural yet?" Alex asked.

"A few heightened readings, but nothing conclusive."

El said, "We found a local artist who painted smuggling scenes." She turned to Alex. "Do you still think it's worthwhile contacting him?"

"Yes, actually. I've looked him up. He has a small studio on the road to West Haven. It's open tomorrow, so we could go if you want to. I'll go alone, if not?"

"The shop is covered, so I can manage it." El looked at Reuben. "If you're happy to see Caspian without me?"

"I'll be fine," he assured her. And besides, it would be good to be alone for a while. He'd have time to think over the recent events. Right now, he needed space from everyone's worry. He could see it in their eyes. Not that he really wanted them to know that. He smiled and drained his pint. "I'll get another round."

Newton sighed as he looked at the body at his feet, her eyes glassy as she stared up at the cloudy night sky above. He crouched next to her and gently shut her eyes.

It was a little past three in the morning when he had been summoned from his bed, and it was now just after four. Dawn was close. He could feel the subtle change in the air, and that intense silence that seemed to fall just before the sky started to lighten.

He looked at Moore, who crouched next to him. "Tell me again who found her."

"A guy walking home from his girlfriend's place." Moore stood and pointed. Newton followed suit, staring in the direction of Moore's outstretched arm. "His girlfriend works in the caravan park, staying on site, and he lives," Moore swung around, pointing to the outskirts of Perranporth, "over there. He's a baker and has an early start. He decided to walk across the sand. It's the easiest route. Not that he'll get there on time now, poor bugger."

They were standing on the edge of Perranporth Beach, close to the Rock Bridge. The girl's crumpled figure was almost lost in the darkness at the base of the cliff face, not far from the path that led to the town. That was the only reason the man had seen her.

"Her face is completely battered," Moore observed,

shaking his head. "It's almost impossible to make out her features. Who would do this?"

"Or *what*? And her body is battered, too. It's like she's been put through a mangle," Newton added. "Where's the bloke?"

"At the top, giving his statement. He's pretty shaken up. He thought he'd be accused."

Newton stared at the cliff face towering over them, and the holes scattered across the surface; adits. *Relics from the mining industry*. "Bollocks," he said, as recognition dawned. "They'll lead away from the mines, won't they?"

Moore turned to see what Newton was talking about, and then nodded. "Yeah. The tin mining was extensive here. There'll be miles of tunnels."

Newton flashed his torch across the ground, and spotted some crumpled metal. He carefully made his way towards it, and realised it was the remnants of a grill. "Moore! This has come from one of those adits. She must have come through one of them!" He groaned and rubbed his face, horribly weary.

Moore looked horrified. "Why would a young woman be poking about in those mines? They'd be dangerous, especially if you didn't know your way. I bloody wouldn't risk it!"

A thought struck Newton, and he marched back to the victim again, crouching next to her. "That reminds me," he said, pulling some gloves on and gently opening the victim's mouth. His torch picked out a dull gleam. "Well, this confirms it." He extracted a gold coin and stood up. "Another one."

"She *is* linked to the other deaths!"

"The lure of bloody treasure!" Newton said, infuriated at what people did for greed.

Moore watched him slip the coin into an evidence bag. "Is

this her retribution for discovering gold? And is she part of a larger group?"

"Fuck knows," Newton said angrily.

"Someone has found some kind of map," Moore said. "That's the only conclusion!"

"Unless there's a serial killer around here with a gold coin fixation."

"I think we both know this is something else! Your supernatural encounter still hasn't been explained. And something forced that grill and this victim out of the adit!" Moore's head jerked upwards. "Someone has been in the mines, looking for smuggler's treasure—and maybe found it. They must have disturbed something."

"*More* treasure, you mean."

"We've only found a few coins so far, and some empty wooden chests," Moore pointed out. "That doesn't really tell us anything."

Newton handed Moore the evidence bag, frustrated with the amount they still didn't know. "Make sure that gets to the lab early. We're presuming this is a supernatural death, but what if she stumbled across the thieves and was killed? Are there more dead bodies in the mine?"

"Why highlight that her death has to do with gold at all? Wouldn't it be better to keep that a secret?"

Newton groaned. "None of this makes sense!"

Movement up above caught Newton's eye, and he realised the coroner had arrived. He watched him descend the steps, a precise but slightly shabby man, called Arthur Davidson.

He nodded at Newton and Moore. "Morning, gentlemen." He didn't waste time with pleasantries, immediately crouching to examine the girl. He swore under his breath. "She looks like she's been through a mangle."

"I know, and I can't explain why," Newton said, frowning at the horribly unnatural angles the girl's body was in.

Davidson spent a few moments examining her, and then straightened. "Hard to say right now, but the broken neck was most likely the cause of death, though obviously she's suffered severe trauma. She's covered in scratches and contusions, too. I can tell you more later, of course. What was she doing here at such an early hour?" He looked at the cliff top. "A fall, I suppose."

"Maybe," Newton said, uncertainly. "We think she came through an adit."

"Really?" Davidson looked alarmed. "She was in the mine?"

"Just a theory, so far."

"Any ID?"

"None."

"Well, I need to remove the body now," Davidson said, all business. He frowned and then added, "I'm sorry about your colleague. I'll be doing her PM today. I presume you'll be there?"

Newton closed his eyes briefly, wishing he could turn back the clock. "Yes. I'll be there."

"In the meantime, Guv," Moore said, checking his watch. "Let's grab an early coffee while SOCO does their thing." He gestured across the sand to where a café was already open-ing, ready to serve the surfers who were arriving in the dawn light.

Newton had forgotten this was a surfing beach. He nodded, knowing he needed something to fortify him for the day ahead. "Sounds good."

Ten minutes later, Newton had a steaming hot coffee and a bacon and egg sandwich in front of him. A green wash of colour lined the horizon, of which they had a perfect view. He and Moore sat in a window seat in the nearly deserted café, watching the surfers prepare themselves. Although clouds were rolling in, and the warm weather of the previous few days was cooling, it wouldn't stop them from surfing.

Newton took a bite of his sandwich and tried to organise his jumbled thoughts, but it was Moore who started the conversation.

"We need to find the connection between these deaths. A firm one. Not vague conjecture about *something* supernatural."

"But I did see *something supernatural* in that tunnel."

"I know, and I don't doubt you. But other than gold coins, empty wooden chests, and old bones, we have nothing that *really* indicates buried treasure, and nothing that suggests a supernatural creature killed the other three victims."

"What about the mangled mess of the first guy, Miles Anderson?" Newton asked through a mouthful of food.

"But the second? Although he looked horrified, it wasn't a particularly supernatural death."

"Maybe not, but Inez's was, and this could be." Newton frowned at the rock face, the early morning light illuminating the adits. "What the hell happened in there? Bloody hell. We're going to have to go in."

Moore paused, his bacon butty halfway to his mouth. "Can't we just investigate the adits from this side?"

"We will, but that won't tell us what happened inside." He could see Moore's reluctance. "Sorry. I don't want to go in either, but we need to know where she died. There'll be more evidence in there, even though we risk a supernatural attack."

Moore nodded. "I know. What are your friends suggesting it could be?"

"Spriggans. They're very strong, ghosts of giants that guard buried treasure. And perhaps some very agitated spirits. My friends have been attacked and injured by ghosts. I suppose they could be responsible for these deaths, too." He frowned as another thought struck him. "That girl was young. Mid-twenties, I reckon. You?"

"Agreed."

"I know her features are badly smashed, but she's dark-haired, like Miles Anderson's girlfriend." They had been looking for her for the last few days, and she had remained stubbornly elusive. "Let's check—just in case."

CHAPTER 16

euben looked at Caspian's shocked face and laughed, despite the situation. "I know it's unlikely, but see for yourself."

He handed him the three letters they had found, and while Caspian read them, he watched him out of the corner of his eye, while pretending to look at Caspian's study. Caspian looked better than he had two days before, but he was still pale, and he leaned back in the big leather office chair, his hand resting on his wound. There was a tightness to his lips that Reuben thought was more to do with the pain of his injuries than the letters. He had a sleek computer on his desk, and it seemed that although he was injured, he was determined to work.

It was just after nine on Thursday morning, and Reuben had set out early, wanting to find out as much as he could before the day advanced. On the way into the grounds, Reuben had seen Barak patrolling the perimeter, and he'd waved, the big man waving back before he continued his rounds. He'd thought that interesting. Caspian clearly wasn't taking any chances.

Caspian put the letters down and looked at Reuben. "Interesting. You say you found them in your attic?"

Reuben nodded. "Have you any family letters anywhere?"

Caspian's gaze drifted around the room and then finally back to Reuben. "Maybe. Not in here, certainly. We could look in the attic." He attempted a smile. "I guess, like you, we have all sorts of skeletons up there."

"Metaphorically only, I hope." He nodded to the window and the gardens beyond. Barak was now making his way towards the house, an easy stealth to his movements, despite his size. "What's with Barak? Don't you trust your defences?"

Caspian winced as he sat up straighter. "I have strengthened them considerably, but seeing as I'm moving like an old man right now, I thought it would be wise."

"Yeah, my shoulder aches. It was lucky the blade missed my lung. I probably shouldn't have driven here," he confessed. "Briar will kill me."

Caspian's hands grasped the edge of the desk, his knuckles whitening as he stood. "Needs must. I'll show you the attic." His face tightened as he tried to walk, and Reuben stopped him.

"No. Stay here." A rush of guilt flooded him. *Caspian looked like shit*. "You shouldn't be working. You should be in bed. How did you even get dressed?"

Caspian sank back into his chair, sweat beading his brow. "With difficulty. And painkillers. And witch-flight to get here, obviously. It's odd, though. My powers seem to have weakened, too. I'm not going to risk it again."

That was something to confess, Reuben thought, surprised. It was unlike Caspian to admit any weakness. He was seeing an unexpectedly human side to him, shorn of his smugness. "Where's Estelle? I would have thought she'd be helping you."

"Did you? Have you met my sister?"

Reuben had stood ready to leave, but now he sat again.

"But you're injured. What about your cousins, or your uncle?"

"I sent my uncle and my sister away a couple of nights ago. I decided I'd rather be alone." Caspian's eyes were wary, and Reuben guessed that was as much information as he would get.

"Is Briar coming to see you?"

His face softened. "She's already called. Yes, she'll be here this afternoon. I'm surprised you didn't come here together."

"I wanted to come first thing," Reuben said, lying. As gentle as Briar was, he didn't want her company, either. "Why don't I search the attic? Unless, of course, you're worried about family secrets."

Caspian shook his head. "Right now, I don't give a crap. Second floor, at the end of the hall. There's a narrow door in the panelling. I'm sure yours must be similar. Greenlane Manor is about the same era as this, isn't it?"

"It is. Nice to be a pillar of society, right?" Reuben said sarcastically as he stood again. "I'll see you in a few hours. Take it easy."

Avery finished her call with Newton and returned to the shop, trying to work out what was going on.

It was nearly ten o'clock on Thursday morning, and the week seemed to be passing in a blur of death and injuries. She sat on the stool behind the counter, barely focussing on the shop around her. It was quiet, fortunately, and both Dan and Sally were stocking shelves with new books and other goods.

She was worried about Caspian and Reuben, and the safety of the rest of her friends. *Especially Newton.* He had just told her about the death of the woman on Perranporth beach, although she had also heard about it on the morning news. Newton had managed a lucky escape when he was with Inez. If anything supernatural was still hanging around the murder scenes, Newton could be at risk. She hoped Cassie, Ben, and Dylan would be able to detect something useful.

But what could *she* do? She stared absently out of the windows, considering her options. Helena was trapped in the spirit realm, Gil had promised to help, and Alex couldn't risk going again. She wouldn't let him try, even if he wanted to. Someone was searching for buried treasure—and maybe finding it—and had unleashed terrible violence along with it. And then there was Cruel Coppinger. Were he and his gang the vengeful spirits they were dealing with? And if Reuben's ancestor had colluded with Caspian's, what kind of spell had they used? And more importantly, what spell could they use to stop all of this?

A sudden thought struck her. If someone was on the trail of buried treasure, finding caches hidden across Cornwall, then potentially they had some kind of protection; something to guard them against a supernatural attack. *Magical protection.* It brought her back to the witch Gil had seen walking the spirit world. *Was a witch helping them, and stirring up spirits? Perhaps the spirits were meant to be a distraction?*

The bell at the shop entrance rang and she looked up, surprised to see Alex entering with four coffees and a bag with *Sea Spray Café* on it. She smiled. "What are you doing here? I thought you were with El."

He handed her a cup. "She bailed. She's needed at the shop after all. Do you want to come?"

"Yes!" She sighed with relief. "I'd love to see what we can find out."

She searched for Sally, but both she and Dan were already

heading to the counter, Dan eyeing the bag. "Anything good in there, Alex?"

"Of course," Alex said, laughing. He put the bag on the counter and opened it. "I'm actually buttering you up. I need to borrow Avery."

"Ah, your penance," Sally said, slapping Dan's hand and beating him to a muffin. "We'll let you, as long as you two promise to be careful."

"Of course we will," Avery remonstrated. "We're just going to a gallery."

Dan had already taken a large bite of an éclair, and he wiped the cream off his lip. "To see what?"

"Anthony Carter's paintings at his studio in West Haven," Alex told him.

Sally rounded the counter to sit next to Avery. "I've heard of him." She looked warily between Alex and Avery. "Has he got something to do with these deaths?"

"I hope not," Avery said, shocked. "But according to Alex, he paints smuggling seascapes."

Alex nodded. "I was admiring his painting of Cruel Coppinger in the museum the other day. I thought perhaps he might know some snippets of useful information."

"I've been doing some reading on Coppinger," Dan said. "Did you know he had a son? He was born mute and deaf, and was a sociopath by all accounts. He liked torturing animals. And he was thought to have pushed another kid over a cliff."

"Really? That's horrible." Avery shuddered. "What happened to him?"

"No idea, and I've read a few accounts now. He's not mentioned. He certainly wasn't rumoured to have disappeared with his father. He might not have survived childhood, or he could have gone on to have kids."

"So there might be Coppingers in Cornwall, even now?" Sally asked, alarmed.

"Maybe it's his ancestors who are searching for the gold?" He scowled at Sally, and in an exaggerated Cornish accent cried, "Pieces of eight, Capt.!" Dan was clearly joking, but as soon as he finished the sentence, he seemed to realise what he'd suggested. "Oh, wow. That could be a thing."

Avery looked at Alex. "Yes, it really could be! What if someone discovered their deep, dark family history, and clues to his hidden gold?"

"Personally, I think it's more likely someone found something in the museum archives." He turned back to Dan. "Did he actually make any money?"

"Lots. In fact, in later years he would pay in cash for lots of things, a mixture of all sorts of currency—doubloons, dollars, and ducats, as well as guineas. And pistols. He paid his lawyer that way when he purchased a farm."

Alex almost spit his coffee out. "The doubloon found in the first victim's mouth. That would explain the link."

Avery was about to have another bite of her pastry, and it hovered inches from her mouth, forgotten. "Who did he marry? Can you remember?"

"Somebody Hamlyn." Dan's face wrinkled with concentration. "I'll have to check. But, from what I can tell—and these accounts are fantastical—no one disliked his wife. They felt sorry for her. She was a victim, too."

"Okay," Alex said, frowning. "Coppinger's body was never found, right?"

"No. He supposedly rowed out to a ship in a storm and was never seen again. His own ship was called Black Prince. I don't know what happened to that, either—or if that was the one he sailed away on."

Avery nodded. "Mariah told us that. Weird, isn't it, that he arrived and left in a storm? It sort of adds to the myth around him."

"I wonder how his disappearance ties to Reuben and Caspian's family," Alex mused.

Sally was brushing crumbs off the counter, and generally tidying the area ready for customers, but she paused, looking between Alex and Avery. "What are you talking about?"

Avery quickly filled her in on what they'd found the day before. "Reuben is going to see Caspian today, and find out if he has any letters in his family archives."

"Wow." Dan looked puzzled, and then suspicious. "The Jacksons and the Favershams working together. Wonders will never cease. Unless, of course, it was a double-cross."

"*What?*" For the second time that day, Avery looked at Dan, astounded. "I didn't even think of that!"

"You're too nice, Avery, that's why. But you should know better. The Favershams are slippery characters, even now, if you ask me. Maybe you shouldn't assume the best of them just yet."

"But Caspian was attacked—almost killed!" she reminded him.

"But he wasn't, was he?" Sally said softly. "The ghosts prowled around, waiting for you to arrive. Was it a set-up?"

Avery's thoughts whirled. She did not believe that Caspian had allowed himself to be so badly injured as a ruse. He was half-dead when they found him. It didn't make sense.

But Alex was already interrupting her thoughts. "Shit, Avery. Reuben is going there alone, this morning! He could be there now!"

He was already reaching for his phone, and he punched a number in and put it to his ear, frowning. For anxious seconds they watched him, and he eventually hung up. "No answer."

Reuben looked up from the paperwork scattered around him, and rubbed his neck wearily.

He'd spent one hour up there, and he was already over it. He rolled his shoulders and winced, wishing he hadn't. His injured shoulder still ached, and he sighed as he looked around. *Different house, same attic...almost.* It was a large room with a long, low-raftered roof and dusty gabled windows that stretched across a good portion of the house, crammed with old furniture. *He and Caspian should open an antique shop together.* He laughed at the thought. *Talk about an odd couple.*

Grey light filtered in, the sun banished by the clouds, and he looked around, wondering if there was somewhere else he should look. He was currently wading through love letters and business letters, and it was all so tedious, though intriguing. Most of the business stuff seemed to be above board, and the love letters revealed hidden passions he wouldn't have expected from Caspian's rather staid and seemingly uptight family. He put them aside quickly, feeling like a voyeur despite the fact the subjects were long dead.

He hauled himself to his feet and started to meander to the far end of the attic, hidden in shadows, noting the antique tables, chairs, and old bedsteads, all heavy oak furniture that was solid but dark, and crates of plates and glasses. Nothing looked particularly expensive; he imagined Caspian's family would be keeping the best objects on display, or had sold them.

He spied a couple of wooden chests behind a stack of rugs and old sheets, and some large objects swathed in blankets. Threading his way through, he ended up dislodging the stack of moth-eaten sheets. They slid to the floor, dragging the blankets with them, and a cloud of dust enveloped him. Remembering Avery's advice, he used his magic to clear the air, and saw that he'd uncovered several bookshelves groaning with paperwork.

Deciding that spending his whole day up here was not an attractive idea, he elected to try using magic again—a simple finding spell, using a piece of Serephina's letter and a pinprick of his blood, for the connection to Virginia. They were related, so it should work. He dropped his blood into a small silver bowl he took from his backpack, added a portion of the letter, and uttered the spell. At first it didn't seem to work, and then as the smoke eddied towards the shelves, he saw a stack of paperwork start to wobble and then slide haphazardly towards the floor. A package of letters teetered out and smacked him in the chest before landing on the floor.

For a second, Reuben could only stare at his feet, shocked. He actually hadn't expected that to work. He crouched and scanned them, ignoring the dust, and realised he'd found Virginia's responses. These letters were all business. There was no chit-chat or social niceties, and they gave no clue to either of the women's personalities, but it was clear that they were determined. Virginia confirmed her interest in meeting, but again there were no details. The next letter from Virginia said she had considered the plan they had discussed and agreed with it in principle, but suggested a different time of execution. But there was no hint of what that plan was. *Damn it, these women were sneaky.*

But before Reuben could do anything else, he smelt the strong scent of seaweed behind him, and he flattened and rolled, sending a searing pain through his shoulder. A shadowy figure lunged out of the gloom, pinning him to the floor with surprising strength, and strong hands wrapped around his neck.

Once again Alex stood next to Avery on the grounds of Harecombe Manor, quickly subduing his dry retch, as Avery hammered on the front door.

They had debated trying to use witch-flight to get inside, but neither wanted to surprise Caspian, or risk injury from his protection spell. They both had a shock when Barak answered the door, and Alex noticed the Empusa's blade was in a scabbard, strapped to his side.

His bulk blocked most of the hall behind him, and he peered down at them, his frown quickly turning to smile. "Hey, guys! Come to join Reuben?"

"Is he okay?" Avery asked, quickly shoving past him and entering the house.

Barak looked at them, puzzled. "Yes, he's fine. Why wouldn't he be?"

Avery's eyes were darting everywhere, her fists clenched, and Alex could feel her power growing as she asked, "Where is he?"

"In the attic." Apparently, Barak could feel her power building, too. "What are you doing, Avery? You look ready to fight."

Alex didn't want to accuse Caspian of deception. After all, they might be wrong. "I think we're both a bit jumpy after the events over recent days. We decided he shouldn't be alone," he hedged.

A whirling blackness manifested in the corner, and all three of them jumped, but it was just Caspian, looking sallow-skinned and clutching his side. "What's going on?" He looked between them all, and then especially at Avery. "Why are you glaring at me?"

She stuttered, and then said, "I read the cards and saw that Reuben was in danger. Where is he?"

"In the attic. He offered to search alone." He grimaced. "I'm not that steady on my feet right now."

Alex studied him. This was no ruse. Caspian looked awful. And to be honest, Alex knew deep down that Caspian had too much regard for Avery to hurt one of her best friends. If he thought he'd stand any chance with her, he wouldn't risk that.

Avery started to speak. "Maybe we should check on him, just—"

"Something's up there!" Barak interrupted her, his head jerking upwards to stare up the stairs.

In seconds he'd shed his t-shirt, revealing his muscled chest, and his wings appeared. They were enormous, the feathers so inky-black they had a blue sheen to them. He soared up through the huge stairwell to the upper floor, and in a flash Avery had vanished, too.

Alex couldn't believe she had abandoned him. Then again, he was still feeling sick from the first trip. He ran for the stairs, yelling, "Avery! Wait for me!"

Even as he was saying it, he knew it was pointless; she'd already gone. Caspian was curiously silent, and Alex glanced down at him as he rounded the landing and then skidded to a halt. Caspian was backing away from a shimmering figure that was coalescing in his hall. *A spirit.*

Caspian was in no position to fight. In fact, from this angle he looked horrified, scuttling backwards as quickly as his injury allowed. Alex wondered why he wasn't using witch-flight, but maybe he was too weak.

Alex was torn.

His girlfriend and best mate were above somewhere, and who knows what they were facing. But Caspian was here, unarmed and clearly too weak to fight back. Caspian didn't even look up at him. He either thought he'd already gone or was buying him time, because the spirit that was slowly taking shape, solidifying into the lean, weather-beaten figure of a smuggler, replete with old-fashioned clothes and a wickedly sharp dagger, hadn't seen him. The spirit scowled, showing blackened teeth, and Alex caught a glimpse of a long scar that ran down the side of his face, puckering his lip.

Alex uttered the words to the modified, rune-binding spell he'd been researching only the night before, and a flurry of runes dazzled in the gloom of the hall, wrapping themselves around the spirit. The blade flashed, tearing through them, and he stopped his advance, turning to leer up at Alex.

But Alex was already on to his next spell as he ran back downstairs, and runes again filled the air, this time composed of fire. He started to banish the spirit, but it ran towards him heedlessly, his all too real blade flashing in the light. Then the runes wrapped once more about the now snarling ghost. As quickly as his blade flashed, destroying the runes, more appeared until he became overwhelmed, and Alex advanced with his hands outstretched, a wall of power building as he pushed the spirit back, cornering it in the hall.

The spirit was thrashing now, and a low, unearthly moan seemed to come from his core, setting Alex's teeth on edge. With the final word of his spell, he thrust the heel of his hand outward, and the runes started to eat into the spirit's shimmering form. His mouth opened wide in a soundless scream as it vanished.

Alex whirled around, defences raised, wary of another attack, but the hall felt eerily empty. Caspian had collapsed on the floor.

Reuben's vision started to blacken, but he was damned if he was going to be killed by a ghost.

The spirit now felt so unnervingly solid that Reuben brought his leg up beneath him, and kneed the spirit in the groin. He wasn't above playing dirty. *Besides, did spirits even have genitals?*

It appeared they did. It grunted, emitting a powerful blast of stale breath in Reuben's face, and before the spirit could respond, Reuben punched it with his left fist that was loaded with magical energy. His attacker flew backwards, landing in the pile of blankets.

Reuben tried to grab his backpack. He'd brought the shotgun with him, loaded with salt shells, but his hand scrabbled and grabbed only air. The spirit lunged at him, but Reuben rolled to the side, vaulted to his feet, and threw a ball of pure fire, catching it squarely in the chest. It flew across the attic, its clothes smouldering on its withered frame.

But it didn't stop.

Instead it disappeared, reappearing seconds later mere inches from him. It picked Reuben up and threw him against the bookshelves. Reuben grunted, winded, and felt the bookshelves start to wobble behind him. Rolling again, he narrowly missed being hit by the falling bookcase.

But the thud as it hit the floor masked another noise. The door at the far end of the attic flew open, smashing back against the wall. Barak strode in, bare-chested and grinning with malevolence, Avery hot on his heels. The Empusa's sword slashed before him, whirling so quickly Reuben blinked with surprise. Barak didn't give the spirit a second to respond. He released the sword and it flew through the air, taking the spirit's head clean off. It rolled to Reuben's feet before both body and head vanished.

For a second, Reuben couldn't speak. He was staring at Barak, astonished, and the big man grinned. "You okay?"

"Er, I think so."

Avery ran towards him, streaking past Barak who was already checking his surroundings, and she landed next to him with a thump. "Reuben! I was worried sick." Her eyes travelled across him, checking for injuries, before finally staring at his wounded shoulder. "You're bleeding again."

"Not surprising. It hurts like a bastard." He leaned back against the wall, wincing as the pain burned through his adrenalin.

She sat next to him, taking deep breaths. "I thought we'd be too late."

"For what? Why are you even here?"

She paused, frozen, words stuck in her mouth before she finally said, "I thought it was a trap."

He considered her words, and nodded. "I think it was."

Her eyes widened, and he could see the disappointment there, before a steely resolve settled. "Caspian?"

"*No*! Have you seen him? He looks like death. No, this was something else. Help me to my feet, and let's head downstairs."

CHAPTER 17

*N*ewton was beyond tired. His head pounded from his interrupted sleep, and it wasn't helped by the pressure coming from his DCI, demanding results. And burning beneath that was the fury of Inez's death.

He was seated at his desk, which was situated at the police station in Truro in an unobtrusive corner of the building. The best place for the small but increasingly busy paranormal division, apparently. That was fine with him. The less people he saw right now, the better. But he did need to recruit a new officer to replace Inez. He shook his head. *That could wait.* What was important right now was finding who was behind this spate of deaths, and if there was a connection between the victims.

Newton started sifting through the files again, lost in the details of Miles Anderson's life, jerking his head up with surprise when Moore knocked and walked in.

"Success with the ID." Moore leaned against the frame, a triumphant smile on his face. "She's Jasmine Connelly, twenty-six years old, from Carlyon Bay."

"Miles's elusive girlfriend! That's brilliant." Newton

realised that sounded awful. "Well, not really, but you know what I mean." He stood up and started to pace his office. "Where had she been for the last few days?"

"Bunked up with their accomplices, I guess."

"If there were any. It might have been just those two. But," Newton sighed, "there'll be more. I know it." He circled back to her file, glancing through it before looking at Moore again. "Let's call her mother and arrange a visit. We need to organise a formal ID, but I want to know a lot more about Jasmine. She's our key, I feel it."

"By the great Goddess!" Briar said, glaring at Reuben. "Why don't you ever listen to me?"

"I listen!" he said crossly. "How was I to know that I was going to get attacked at Caspian's? Can you feel the protection on this place? How did they get in?"

Briar was too furious to answer, although she had to admit he was right. Caspian's house vibrated with magical protection. Briar, Alex, Avery, Barak, Reuben, and Caspian were gathered in Caspian's living room that was next to the hall, the closest and easiest place to get Caspian to. He was lying on a sofa, clearly exhausted. Reuben was pacing, holding his shoulder awkwardly, while Barak, Alex, and Avery conferred in the corner.

Briar turned her attention to Caspian, kneeling next to him. His face was covered with sweat, and he was watching her; he was scared and her fury vanished as worry took over. "You should have stayed in bed."

"I'd probably be dead by now."

"Maybe not," she said softly, sensing his frustration. "It was a good idea to get Barak here."

Caspian glanced over at Alex. "It was Alex who saved my life." His eyes looked haunted. "My magic is so weak."

"It is odd," she confessed. "I know you're physically weak, but your magic should be unaffected."

"Maybe I'm cursed."

"I don't think so. Hush a moment."

She hunched over Caspian, her hands once again on his wound, and she sent her healing powers down through his skin and muscle. She could almost feel the damage, the torn flesh that struggled to heal. Briar closed her eyes, and reaching deep into herself, accessed the Green Man. His wild, earthy energy filled her senses and bolstered her magic, and a gentle heat radiated from her palms. She started to knit the wound together, calming the inflammation. When she was satisfied that was done, she ran her hands over the rest of him, a few inches above his body, feeling his energy. She frowned, sensing it had changed.

When she opened her eyes again, Caspian was staring at her. "You found something."

"Your energy feels off. I don't know why, *yet*. But you can't stay here. You can move in with me."

"This is my home."

"I don't care. Unless Estelle will help you."

Caspian's eyes shuttered. "No."

Reuben's voice startled them both. "Your house is the size of a tea cup, Briar. Caspian can stay with me."

Caspian twisted his head to look up at him. "You want *me* to live with you?"

"Well, not forever. I'm not asking for your hand in marriage."

Despite his pain, Caspian laughed out loud. "Thank the Gods for that. I'd have had to disappoint you."

Briar smiled up at Reuben, her heart swelling with pride. *How unbelievably generous he could be. And to Caspian, of all people.* "I think that's a fantastic idea. Thanks, Reuben." Briar realised Caspian still looked doubtful, and she needed to convince him. "Reuben's place is close to all of us, if there are problems. Better than here. And I can come and see you together. Please say yes."

For a moment he didn't answer, clearly not comfortable with the idea, but eventually he nodded. "All right. If you're sure, Reuben."

"I'm sure."

"But," Briar pointed at both of them sternly, "you are not to overdo it! I'll ask El to watch over you."

Reuben moved to the end of the sofa so that Caspian could see him better. "We need to work together to find out what spell our ancestors used. With us both under one roof, we can work quicker, and protect ourselves better, too."

Barak must have overheard them, because he headed to his side. "And we can defend your place, too."

Reuben nodded. "Cheers, I think we'll need it." He looked back at Caspian thoughtfully. "I think I know why they didn't kill you the first time. The spirits hoped to get to me, through you."

"That sounds far too organised and sentient to me," Caspian protested. "Spirits don't plan, surely?"

"But they got past your defences, again," Briar pointed out.

"No, they didn't," Avery said, as she and Alex finally finished their quiet chat and came to join them. "They never left. Caspian's enhanced protection spells just sealed them in."

"*What?*" Caspian struggled to sit up, and Briar helped him, putting cushions behind him. "You mean they've been here since I was first attacked?"

"We think so." Avery glanced at Alex and said, "Alex banished one, but the one that attacked me disappeared, and we, stupidly, assumed it had gone. The one that attacked you, Reuben, looked like the one that attacked me. The other one must have been here all along, too."

"I didn't suspect a thing!" Caspian looked horrified.

"Neither did we," Avery admitted. "These spirits are getting assistance from a witch. Gil told us as much. We have to find who, and stop them."

"The good thing," Alex added, "is that the defences you've got now are solid, and we can do the same at Reuben's. Specific spells to block spirits and ward the property." He looked thoughtful. "We can cleanse your house, just to make sure, and then do the same at Greenlane Manor. I think we should all work together to protect your place, Reu. We can go over there later, get El too, and our combined powers will do it."

"Sort of like what we did on Samhain," Reuben said. "Good idea. You agree then, Caspian? You can bring anything you need, but I'd like a few papers from the attic, too."

Caspian looked surprised. "You've found the letters, then?"

"Just before I got slugged by the ghost." He pulled them out of his jeans pocket. "But I want to make sure there's nothing I've missed."

"I'll come up there with you," Barak said, already moving to the doorway, the Empusa's sword in his hand.

"And I can pack some stuff for you, Caspian," Alex offered.

"Thanks, yes please, and," Caspian looked slightly uncomfortable, "thanks for your help earlier. It would have killed me if you hadn't stopped it."

"I'm sure you'd have done the same for me," Alex answered, brushing it off. "But now, it's payback time. I'm sick of being on the defence. We need to fight back."

Avery assessed the front of West Haven Gallery as Alex parked the car.

It was situated on a side street that led to the beach, just off the main road between White Haven and Harecombe. It was technically part of West Haven village, even though the majority of the settlement was on the other side of the main road, where Rupert lived in the House of Spirits. In this part there was a small community of modern houses, many large, and a smattering of boutique shops, cafés, and the gallery. There were quite a few cars parked, and Avery could see the start of the boardwalk that led through the dunes to the beach. It was a beautiful spot, and she started to relax.

As soon as they were satisfied that Reuben and Caspian were okay, they left Barak and Briar to oversee Caspian's move, and Avery had flown her and Alex back to Happenstance Books. Alex had used his car to drive them to the gallery. Now, as she leaned back in the passenger seat, she sighed.

"What was that for?" Alex asked as he turned off the engine.

His dark eyes were watchful, and the wind caught his hair, so that it whipped across his face. They had driven with the top down, but the increasingly heavy clouds threatened rain.

She twisted in her seat to look at him. "I think my adrenalin has finally worn off. I feel horribly guilty. We should have made sure those spirits had gone!"

"We thought we had!"

"They could have died."

"At least we know Caspian didn't set a trap," Alex said. "What do you think happened between him and Estelle?"

"What do you mean?"

"He was abrupt when Briar asked him about her staying. I know she's difficult, but I get the feeling there's more going on."

He was right; Caspian had seemed cagey. "Maybe they argued about the business. Or, more likely, about us. She was so prickly during the meeting the other night. So superior!"

"Well, with luck, she'll never have to go again." He nodded towards the gallery. "We better go in. Let's hope the artist is there!"

They exited the car and entered the gallery, and Avery paused to take in the clean, white walls lined with artwork, as well as the prints, cards, sculptures, and local pottery on display. They meandered around the space, stopping and starting, idly picking up prints and cards, before coming to a section filled with smuggling seascapes. A large, stormy image caught Avery's eye. It was moody, showing a wrecked galleon half swallowed by the waves, its cargo of casks and crates strewn across the beach as figures scurried around.

Alex was at her shoulder, and he asked, "Can you imagine living in those times?"

"It sounds quite lawless, but I guess it's something you learnt to live with. But these paintings really draw you in." She moved on to the next. "They were doing the locals a favour, though. Import taxes were huge. No wonder they turned to illegal activities." For a moment, with gulls calling outside the shop, and the breeze carrying the scent of the sea and sand in through the open doors, Avery could almost imagine herself on the cobbled quays and the rough beaches as a storm rolled in. "It almost seems romantic!"

Alex laughed. "You would think that! I saw *Jamaica Inn* on the sofa last night!"

He was referring to the book by Daphne Du Maurier, and Avery looked at him sheepishly. "I must admit that the visit to Bodmin put it in my head, so I snagged a copy from the shop. If anything, that book certainly dispels the romance. It was brutal."

"I spy an artist," Alex said, nodding to a large archway and a light-filled room beyond. A grey-haired man with a large beard was seated in front of an easel, painting, oblivious to the few customers who were watching him.

They headed to his side and watched him quietly for a moment, before Alex said, "Excuse me, are you Anthony Carter?"

For a moment he didn't respond as he finished his brush-strokes, and then he looked around, startled. "Sorry, did you speak?"

"Yes, sorry," Alex said, "I didn't mean to disturb you."

He repeated his question, and the man smiled. "I am. Sorry, I get very focussed when I paint."

Avery smiled, amused at all the sorries. It was so English. She wondered how Anthony could possibly concentrate with people watching him, and asked, "Do you do all of your work here?"

"Heavens, no! I spend a couple of mornings here a week, just to be visible really, but I work mainly in my studio. I live close by."

He looked as if he really wanted to get back to painting, so Alex spoke quickly. "You have a lot of smuggling themes. Just wondered if you were an expert on the subject?"

"Not at all," he said, topping his palette up with paint. "I have a keen interest, of course, but I think the images of wrecked ships are quite evocative, and so do my buyers. They're my most popular paintings, so I keep doing them."

"I saw your painting of Cruel Coppinger," Alex told him, "in the White Haven Museum Gallery. That's what drew me here, really. Do you know much about him?"

Anthony laughed. "Oh, that old devil. I know just the folklore around him. He had quite a reputation. Obviously I have no idea whether he really looks like that, but he was supposedly a giant of a man, demonesque, with a fearsome reputation." He tapped his head. "That's how I see him."

"I gather he was active in this area," Avery said.

He nodded. "I believe so. He was expanding his territory from the north, but ran into some trouble here. I think some locals worked against him."

"Really?" Avery asked, glancing at Alex. "Any idea who?"

"No idea, but I believe they were successful—eventually. It wasn't long after that when he disappeared, swallowed up by the sea that brought him! Marvellous story, isn't it? Suitably dramatic!" He smiled at them dismissively, and turned back to his painting. "Anyway, I must get on."

"Of course," Alex said, looking disappointed. "Thanks, anyway."

They walked away, and Avery headed to the postcards and prints. "I'm going to buy a few. I think they're lovely."

"I was hoping he'd know more," Alex said, hands in his pockets. He glanced around the gallery while Avery searched. "It's frustrating. It seems like Coppinger's story is all folklore and no facts!"

She looked at him and winked. "But there's a kernel of truth in there. This was a long shot, anyway. Treat me to coffee?"

"I raise you to a pub lunch!"

She made her final selections and grinned. "Deal!"

El tried to subdue a smirk as she watched Newton stare between Caspian and Reuben, exclaiming, "Seriously, Caspian's staying *here*?"

It was just before seven in the evening, and they were in Reuben's cosy living area that was situated off the kitchen, commonly called the snug. Caspian, looking the part of the invalid, was set up in the corner of the sofa, his feet up on a Turkish-style ottoman. The other witches and Ash, the Nephilim, were seated around the room, and various drinks and snacks were placed on the central coffee table. Newton had just arrived, helping himself to a beer, and he perched on the end of an armchair, confused.

"Yes," Briar said abruptly, trying to head off an uncomfortable conversation. "It's best they're both here, and Caspian can't stay on his own."

Newton frowned. "So there was another attack today?"

El reached for the bowl of chips and grabbed a handful. "I'm afraid so. I must admit. I've been worried sick all afternoon. I couldn't get away from the shop."

"We've been fine," Reuben reassured her.

"You were beaten up by a ghost!"

"All in a day's work," he said, shrugging nonchalantly, despite the pain the movement was clearly causing him.

Idiot. El knew he was making light of it, to reassure her more than anything, but it wasn't working. Reuben was being stalked. A sudden thought struck her. "You know, both of you being here could be a bad idea. You're both being targeted, and now you're conveniently here together!"

"But it's double the magic! Triple, with you here," he said, smiling roguishly.

"Except my magic is not what it was," Caspian reminded them.

"It will be," Briar said. "I think you have residual bad energy left from the spirits, and I'm going to purge that soon." She gestured to the kit at her feet. "I have everything I need."

"And I will be here all night, patrolling," Ash told them. He was currently at the window, surveying the grounds. "With the sword, of course. But your protection feels strong."

179

"We'll add to it anyway," Alex said.

"How was the gallery?" El asked, disappointed she couldn't go. Zoe hadn't been able to work that day and she'd had to go in.

Alex wrinkled his lip, looking unimpressed. "It was a nice gallery, but not that useful as far as information went. Anthony did say that some locals banded together to get rid of Coppinger, and that they were eventually successful. I'm not sure what that means." He shrugged. "Anyway, the result was that Coppinger disappeared, getting on board a ship in the middle of a storm, never to be seen again. But we already knew that."

"What year was that?" Caspian asked.

"I was talking to Dan about it," Avery answered. "It was sometime in 1805."

"And he arrived when?" Newton asked.

"1792. Dan told us something else very useful, too. Coppinger was so wealthy by the end that he paid in cash using all sorts of currency, including doubloons!"

Newton nodded. "That helps explain a few things. I have news, too!" He had an air of excitement about him, which was unusual.

"Go on, then!" Reuben said, clearly impatient.

"The dead girl is called Jasmine Connelly, and she was Miles Anderson's girlfriend."

A ripple of intrigue ran around the room, and Avery asked, "The first victim?"

Newton nodded. "She's been missing for days. Well, avoiding us, at least. There was a gold guinea in her mouth, too. And SOCO confirmed that she came out through one of the adits—one of the bigger ones."

El frowned. "I thought they were all closed off?"

"They are. She was pushed through one, at speed, I would say, forcing the metal grill out. She looked like she'd been in a tumble dryer. Every bone broken, all scratched and bruised." Newton was pretty hardened to death, but even he looked disturbed. "The force used to get her through there must have been major."

"Not water?" Caspian asked. Adits were used to drain excess water from the tin mines.

"It's been too dry, and so was she." Newton took a deep breath. "And there's more. We investigated her background today—looked at family, friends, etcetera. It turns out that she works at Charlestown's Shipwreck Treasure Museum. Her cousin also works there, and just happens to be the curator of the White Haven Museum exhibition. Ethan James."

"Seriously?" El asked, surprised. She glanced at Alex. "We heard about him when we visited yesterday, but never met him. Interesting connection!"

"It is." Newton looked relieved to have a lead. "I'll be going to talk to him tomorrow."

"Why not right now?" Avery asked, looking annoyed.

"Because there's nothing to link him to her death—other than his job."

"But someone is obviously searching for lost treasure, and White Haven Museum did find previously lost papers on smuggling which he now has access to," Caspian pointed out.

"But there's nothing to suggest that *he* found a treasure map! It could be just Miles and Jasmine. And if I can remind you, I'm a detective. I need evidence!" Newton said crossly. And then he sighed and adopted a conciliatory expression. "However, it *is* suspicious. My angle is the coins. I'll be asking for his expert opinion on them, and questioning if his cousin might have uncovered something. And obviously I'll be watching him closely to see how uncomfortable he looks…or how guilty. I'm sure there's more to this."

"Of course there is," Alex agreed. "There's the violent,

probably supernatural manner of their deaths, the supernatural something that you saw, Newton, evidence of the old chests—"

"Dated to the late 1700s or early 1800s. We had the ones found in Looe appraised," Newton interrupted him.

Alex nodded. "There are the other paranormal activities in Fowey, too. And the unnaturally strong ghosts."

"Plus," Reuben added, "evidence that our ancestors colluded to stop a smuggler, *the Dane*, who *must* have been Cruel Coppinger."

"What are the dates on your letters?" Ash asked.

Reuben frowned and swiped the letters from the table where he'd placed them. He grinned. "1805. Same year as when Coppinger disappeared." He turned to Newton. "Is there anything fishy about Ethan?"

"Not that I can tell. We ran a quick background check on him late this afternoon. He's worked in Charlestown at the Shipwreck Treasure Museum for years. No police record. Liaises with Jamaica Inn's Museum, too. He's obviously well respected."

"Don't forget he knows Mariah, the witch from Looe," Avery reminded them.

"Only through a donation," Newton said warily. "I doubt he knows she's a witch!"

"And," Avery persisted, "Gil told us a witch has walked the spirit world! Caspian," she said abruptly, "what sort of powers does Mariah have?"

"Water. And," he sighed, raising his eyebrow, "spirits. Her water strengths make her emotional connections strong, and combined with her psychic abilities, it makes her powerful in that area."

"See! Mariah could be involved!" Avery said, appealing to them all. "She could be the witch who's stirring up the spirits."

"I know you don't like her," Newton said, "but that is pure speculation."

"And so is us thinking that this is about treasure. All we have are tantalising crumbs so far. It doesn't mean we're wrong!"

El recognised that gleam in Avery's eye. It meant that she had the bit between her teeth and she wasn't about to back down. Everyone else knew it, too.

"Where does Ethan live?" Alex asked, looking suspiciously innocent.

"Carlyon Bay, why?" Newton asked.

Alex looked dumbstruck. "The same place as Miles and Jasmine?"

"The very same," Newton admitted, but he held his hand up in a stop sign. "But I am not leaping to conclusions!"

"I am!" Alex said. "I think we should watch him tonight—very carefully, of course."

Newton sipped his beer, considering his suggestion. Finally, he said, "If you know you won't be spotted, then I think that would be an excellent idea."

Alex looked at Avery. "What do you think?"

"I like it, a lot!" She checked the time on her phone. "We could give it another couple of hours until it gets dark, and start then."

"Great," he agreed.

Caspian shuffled in his seat, looking much brighter than he had only an hour or two before, and said, "I'm worried about where the girl was found. Have you investigated the mines close by?"

There were tin mines all across Cornwall, and a warren of them in Perranporth.

Newton shook his head. "Not yet, but we will, tomorrow. Those mines have been shut down for years, and we're worried about safety, but we have a local expert who knows the mines well, identifying where we should look. A small team will go with him." He looked grim. "We have to do this, but I'm worried what we'll find—especially if there's something supernatural there."

Newton looked wracked with guilt, and El knew he was dreading a repeat of what had happened to Inez. "I'll go, too. If the team meet something odd, they'll be sitting ducks."

"El!" Rueben looked at her, incredulous. "That's a ridiculous idea. You could get hurt!"

"And so could they. I have magic on my side. The team going down there won't." The more she thought about it, the more she realised she had to go; her conscience wouldn't allow her not to. "In fact, I insist I go."

"But you might give yourself away. You know, your magic," Newton said. He looked worried, but was clearly interested in her suggestion.

"Who's going?"

"I will, obviously, plus the local mine expert, Moore, and another couple of officers assigned to my team."

"You *are* the paranormal division," El reminded him. *If there were consequences, she'd just have to manage them.* "And you told us that they know you have help, and Moore knows all about us. I'm prepared to do it."

"I'm not," Reuben said, protesting. "Unless I come, too."

Reuben's normally teasing blue eyes were fired up with a mixture of anger and worry, but El wasn't put off. "No way. You're injured, and you have stuff to do here. Where you're protected," she reminded him forcefully.

Reuben tried to keep his anger bottled. "Someone should go with you."

Before anyone could volunteer, she said, "I'll be fine! I know what to expect, which means I'll be prepared."

Alex looked unconvinced. "Are you sure you don't want

one of us to come? Or ask a witch from Perranporth? I bet they're wondering what's going on right now!"

"You and Avery could be up all night! Briar is busy healing this pair of miscreants, and I don't want another coven involved. This is the best option."

Newton turned to El. "Are you sure, considering what happened to Inez?"

"I'm especially sure because of that. I'm a witch, none of you are."

"Thanks." Newton smiled. "Actually there's something else we should check out. Miles's car was parked at the National Trust car park by the Fowey Estuary, close to St Catherine's Castle. We haven't found a thing, but Ben said they'd picked up odd readings there. Maybe," he looked at Alex and Avery hopefully, "you could check it out tonight, while you're up that way."

"Sounds like a plan," Alex said, looking at Avery for her approval and getting it. "I think you're right, El. This could be a long night for both of us."

CHAPTER 18

*A*very and Alex pulled to a halt on a quiet street in a housing estate in Carlyon Bay, just to the north of Charlestown.

It had been years since Avery had visited Charlestown, and she had forgotten what a charming place it was. They had driven through it before heading to Ethan James's house, passing the Shipwreck Treasure Museum. It was obviously closed, but it was a large place, very well maintained, and it also had a clay mines exhibit, too.

"Maybe we should visit the museum tomorrow," she suggested as she settled herself in the passenger seat of her van, ready to watch James's house. Alex had offered to drive, and she was pleased to not have to concentrate on the drive.

He shook his head. "I'm giving up on museum visits. Whatever's going on now certainly won't be advertised in there."

"I guess you're right," Avery admitted, feeling like they were still clueless. "I think this might be useless, too. What if he sits inside all night? We'll learn nothing."

"If nothing happens tonight, we come back tomorrow."

He turned to her, and she saw his frown in the light from the street lamp. "Jasmine was his cousin. It's too much of a coincidence. Potentially, if he's involved, he'll be laying low tonight."

"Do you think he was there when she died?"

"Perhaps. If he was, he might be terrified. It could spell the end of whatever's going on."

Avery stared down the street, not really focussing on the houses in front of her, instead imagining the mangled body of Jasmine. "So far, all of this is happening on the south coast. I'm a bit baffled as to why Perranporth is involved."

"It's an almost straight run across the country. Maybe whoever hid this treasure wanted to spread it around in an effort to confuse anyone who might search for it. Well, other than those who were meant to find it."

"So, you think Ethan has stumbled upon a map or clues or something?"

"He must have!" Alex barked a laugh. "This is so suburban, though. It's hard to think there's skulduggery among the hedgerows!"

"I guess his house is at least a bit more secluded," Avery noted. "But you're right. A nosey neighbour would spot something."

"I've already noted twitching curtains," Alex confessed. "Let's throw a veil of illusion over the van, before someone calls the police on us."

They combined their magic, and with a whoosh, a shadow swept over them, and by mutual agreement they fell into silence to watch the house. Unfortunately, an hour later, nothing had happened, except someone had walked past with their dog.

"I can't even see a light on in the house," Avery said, feeling restless and stretching the kinks out of her shoulders.

"Maybe he's out."

"Or we're too early for him to be going out, and he's lurking in a back room." Avery glanced at her watch. "It's close to half past eleven. Maybe we should head to Fowey and come back here later."

"Agreed," Alex said. He turned the engine on and pulled out, and Avery quickly dropped the spell.

Avery studied the isolated spot as Alex parked. The National Trust car park in Fowey was situated down a country lane, offering access to the woods, walks, and the coastal path. It was pitch black outside, and they were completely alone. When they stepped out of the van, Alex flashed his torch around. A light breeze blew off the sea, and the land seemed hushed around them.

He lowered his voice, seemingly hesitant to disturb the silence. "This will be a tricky walk in the dark to the castle."

"I could fly us there."

Alex's tone dripped with sarcasm. "Fantastic. I'm so glad you learned to fly."

She poked him in the ribs. "I'm very useful, you know that!"

"That's the only reason I keep hold of you," he teased her, kissing the top of her head affectionately. "And maybe a few other things."

"You're so cheeky, Mr Bonneville!"

"I know. Isn't that why you love me?"

"Most of the time. Your cooking helps."

He laughed at that, but a wild cry disturbed the night, and Avery whirled around.

"It's just a fox," Alex reassured her, "from over the fields."

"Of course," she said, feeling like a fool. "Sorry, I'm jumpy!"

They walked to the start of the track that led to the cliff top, and the moon edged from behind a cloud, lighting the landscape.

Alex gave a small cheer, and she could hear the relief in his voice. "We can see enough in this light. I think we should walk some of it, or at least head into the woods first. Miles was here for a reason. We need to find it."

"Agreed," Avery said, "but I also know you're avoiding witch-flight."

"So would you if it made you sick."

She laughed, and pointed in the direction of Coombe Farm Bed and Breakfast. "Let's head that way. The path will lead us through the woods to the coastal path and the castle."

Alex turned his torch off, and once beneath the trees, the night sounds erupted around them. They both draped themselves in shadows and progressed quietly, Avery raising her awareness as she searched for any sign of magic. They had been walking for several minutes when she detected a strange energy.

She placed her hand on Alex's arm. "Do you feel that?"

"I think so," he said cautiously.

She grabbed his hand. "Come on."

Their progress slowed as the path began to get harder to find in the dark, but she followed what increasingly felt like wild magic, finally plunging into the undergrowth.

"This way."

"We're going off the path!"

"The magic is getting stronger! I have to follow it," she whispered back, afraid to break the spell that seemed to have fallen around them.

Without another word she forged onwards, fighting past branches and tripping over tree roots until they came to a clearing that led to the sea. She could see the moonlight on the waves and hear the crash of the surf, and still following the wild magic, headed closer to the coast before veering back into a dense patch of trees. She finally halted in front of a jumble of huge boulders.

"What's going on?" Alex asked, turning on his torch again.

"Can't you feel it? We're surrounded by old magic—ancient magic! It's at its most powerful here!"

"I don't know how you do that," Alex confessed. "I don't feel it as strongly as you." He played his torch across the area before them. "You know, this looks like a collapsed tower to me, or a folly?"

Avery squinted at the jumble of stones. "You might be right!"

"Okay. You focus on the magic, I'll hunt around."

Avery quieted her mind, wishing Briar were with them, as she was more attuned to the earth. She slipped her boots off, wriggled her toes into the loam, and then lifted her arms to call the air, her most powerful element. For a moment, she tuned out the soft scurrying of night creatures, the barks of the foxes, and even the sounds of the surf, and enveloped herself within the two elements. The earth warmed her feet and the air caressed her cheek, carrying the promise of secrets about to be uncovered. And then she felt a current of damp, stale air trickling somewhere ahead of her, and something hollow beneath her feet.

Terrified she would lose the sensations if she moved too quickly, she waited, slowing her breathing and letting her awareness strengthen, like a signal. The scent of musty air escaping from somewhere beneath the earth grew stronger and Avery walked, almost in a dream state towards it. She ignored the sharp stones beneath her feet, winding around the rocks until she came to the far side. Again, she felt the wild magic swell around her.

Alex had completed his search and followed her

cautiously, and now he stopped too, flashing his torch around. "What have you found?"

She pointed a couple of feet away to the base of a block of stone. "I feel something hollow beneath us, and I think the entrance is there. It must be a tunnel!"

The scent of things long buried was stronger now.

Avery went to advance, but Alex's arm flew out to stop her. "Wait." He trod forward, carefully testing the ground with his weight, and examining the earth underfoot before he nodded. "Okay, it feels fine."

"Stand back. I'm going to use air to move that. I'm sure there's an entrance beneath it."

"It's huge! Are you sure you can?"

She nodded, excitement stirring her blood. "I'm sure."

They scooted back several feet, and then Avery gathered wind around her, directing it forward and shaping it like a giant lever. She had never used her magic quite like this before, but her intent was clear. Slowly, the stone trembled and moved as the edge lifted slightly. As the balance started to change, she levered more forcefully until it tipped and rolled, revealing a narrow rift in the ground ahead.

Caspian stirred in bed, wondering for a second where he was. The bed felt different, as did the space around him, and he experienced a moment of confusion before remembering he was at Reuben's place.

Ugh. Briar's potion was strong! But, to be fair, it was just what he needed. He hadn't slept well for days, and he needed deep, healing sleep. But, it was certainly too early to get up now. It was still dark outside. He squinted at the clock next to him. 1:00am. Crap. Why the hell was he awake now? He flopped back down on the pillow, relieved that the pain from his stab wound was now a dull ache rather than something sharp, and he felt stronger. Whatever residual effects the fight had caused, Briar had cleared them out. She really was an excellent healer.

Caspian squeezed his eyes shut in an effort to block out thoughts of the last few days, causing stars to speckle his vision. He couldn't believe he was sleeping in Reuben's home, or that he hadn't heard from Estelle yet. Although, he shouldn't really be surprised. He had let his temper get the best of him. He was used to her digs and scathing mockery. Nothing ever pleased her. But the comment about Avery was simply one too many.

Avery.

It didn't matter what he did, his thoughts always circled back to her. He saw her in his mind's eye. Her pale, freckle-dusted skin, red hair, and laughing green eyes. She was strong, yet so kind, and he saw a determination within her not to give up on their friendship, despite his feelings. A dull ache returned in his heart. That kind of thinking would do no good.

A strange noise disturbed his thoughts, and suddenly awake, he sat up in bed. But the room was silent, and he felt the weight of the protection spell wrapping around the house like a warm blanket. Earlier that evening, they had combined their magic, adding another layer of protection that repelled ghosts. Nothing was entering Reuben's house uninvited.

He heard the noise again, but it was coming from the garden. He got out of bed and padded to the window, pulling back the heavy curtains to look over the long lawns at the back of the house. The noise was louder there, a kind a whispering or shushing that had nothing to do with the surf crashing on the cliffs at the garden's edge. Something shimmered to his right, and he focussed on the glasshouse, dappled in moonlight. A spectral body emerged from the shadows, accompanied by a dull clinking. It seemed to limp, or rather, lurch across the garden. And then there was another, and another. They were half-formed ghosts that seemed to hover between worlds. One of them looked up and Caspian stepped back, alarmed, but it was too late. It had seen him, and it fixed him with a malignant grin as a shaft of moonlight fell on it fully.

It was the ghost of a smuggler, dressed in nineteenth-century clothes, the glint of metal in his hands, and fire in his eyes. Next to him, his fellow looters lined up, half a dozen in all, looking up at his window. Then they separated as they made their way towards the house.

Caspian's mouth went dry. *They were planning to attack.*

CHAPTER 19

*A*lex insisted on leading the way down the steep stairway that led into blackness. A witch-light bobbed ahead of him, revealing rough-hewn walls and stone steps worn smooth from the passage of many feet.

They had blanketed the tunnel entrance with a protection spell, although they hoped that in the woods in the middle of the night, no one would find it. Fire was balled in Alex's hands and he cautiously advanced, Avery on his heels. The air was stale, but every now and again he smelled the sea.

Avery whispered, "This must go down to the beach!"

"It also must have blocked access through, or everyone would know about this."

The lights caused their shadows to flicker wildly, and Alex proceeded slowly, wary of attack by a supernatural creature. But so far, nothing stirred. Eventually they reached a short passage, and there they had to make a decision. Steps headed downwards again, but another passageway branched to the left.

"Shit. Which way?" he said to Avery.

She threw a witch-light down the passage, watching as it illuminated around a bend.

Her eyes gleamed. "That could lead to St Catherine's Castle. It's the right direction—I think. If I'm not utterly disorientated."

He nodded. "I think you're right."

"But I suggest down first. Then, depending what we find, we go there next."

Alex was already pointing his torch down the steps, sending another witch-light ahead. It revealed more uneven rock walls and smooth steps, and also something else. He frowned. The darkness stirred below.

"Avery," he whispered, retreating into her, "I think there's something down there."

"There's something the other way, too. I can feel it."

"What? Where?"

Hardly daring to turn away from whatever was below him, he followed Avery's stare. Alarmed, Alex saw the witch-light still visible at the bend, and in its pale illumination, a shadow stretched and changed, becoming outlandishly large in the tight space. He glanced down the stairs, horrified to see something approaching from down there, too.

"Shit, Avery, we need to back up—"

Before he could even finish his sentence, the unknown attacker was streaking up the stairs, and without hesitation, Alex hurled a fireball.

In seconds, chaos erupted as they fought off their attackers.

A small but surprisingly strong creature had smacked into Alex's chest, throwing him to the ground. The ugliest, wizened little creature was furiously grappling with him, and wild eyes stared into his. It grabbed Alex's head between its strong hands and squeezed. Terrified his brains were about to be turned to mush, Alex thrust a powerful surge of magic under the creature, and threw it against the rocky ceiling, pinning it there while it writhed with frustration, snapping and snarling like a rapid dog.

"You didn't expect *that*, did you?" Alex yelled.

Avery was engaged in her own battle next to him, rolling down the tunnel in a blur of limbs. But he couldn't help her, not yet.

From out of nowhere, the spriggan—because that's what Alex was sure it was—produced a giant club and swung it wildly, narrowly missing Alex's head. Its shadow stretched and elongated, and its shadow-arms reached for Alex's throat. With horror, Alex realised he could feel the cold, clammy fingers on his skin, and he grasped one of the shadow-limbs with his free hand, trying to loosen its steely grip.

What the hell kind of power did this creature have?

Alex quickly decided that guile was needed, not strength. Mentally rifling through his store of spells, he uttered one to send the spriggan to sleep. At first it didn't seem to work, but he repeated it, full of intent and conviction, and with a snap, the creature fell unconscious and Alex let it drop to the floor. He turned to see if he could help Avery, but she had finally succeeded in wrapping her attacker in a twisting mini-tornado, and it whirled in place, a bundle of limbs and shrieks as it tried to break free. Alex levelled his spell at it, and within seconds it too fell unconscious, and Avery lowered the creature to the ground.

Avery was lying on the floor, covered in dirt. "Bloody hell! They are strong! They look like Gollum in *Lord of the Rings!*"

Alex laughed and pulled her to her feet. "Did it whisper *'my precious'* to you?"

"Fortunately not, but it was a vicious little thing." She

dusted herself down, and eyed their slumped bodies suspiciously. "What did you do to them?"

"Put them to sleep. I couldn't bring myself to kill them." He walked over to one and crouched to examine it. "It really does look like a little old man, except for the weirdly large baby head. They have to be spriggans!"

Avery joined him, tentatively turning it over with her foot. "I agree. Look at its scrawny little limbs. How can it be so strong?"

"Maybe they really are the ghosts of giants in some strange, miniature form? That one produced a club from nowhere and tried to smash my head with it. And its shadow could grab me, too!"

"And they can manipulate their shadows to grow. It's no wonder Inez and the other victims didn't stand a chance, if that's what they faced!" She frowned at Alex. "How long will your spell hold?"

"A couple of hours I hope, but let's bind them with magic, too."

"I hate to say this, but they're too dangerous to keep alive."

"They've lived down here long enough without causing harm. It's only because we've disturbed them."

"True." But Avery still looked worried. "Let's bind them for now, and see what's down here. If *they're* still here, then maybe there's treasure. Potentially, we could use another type of binding spell to restrict their strength long term."

They worked quickly, binding both spriggans with strong webs of magic, and hoping there were no more waiting for them, headed down the steps.

◊

El stood next to Briar, Reuben, Caspian and Ash, staring through the patio doors in the snug, out to the back garden. Briar had opted to stay over that night, weary after her healing spells.

"I can't see a thing," Reuben confessed.

"Trust me. There were at least half a dozen," Caspian said.

They had all thrown on jeans and t-shirts, and El and Ash clasped the Empusa's swords.

"I can't see them, even with my sword," El said. She stepped closer to the window, trying to see down the side of the house. "The good thing is, our protection feels strong. They won't get in."

Ash shook his head. "I still don't like it. They're planning something."

"They can plan all they want." Reuben looked coolly confident. "What are they going to do? Attack my roses?"

"They could attack the greenhouses and the nursery," Ash said, looking at him thoughtfully. "That's your livelihood, and you employ a lot of people—including me! Or, they could creep into the town."

Caspian's arms were folded across his chest as he stared at the garden. "It's interesting that they seemed to come from your glasshouse, and that there are so many of them. Maybe our ancestors wrecked the ship that supposedly carried Coppinger away and killed all of the pirates, not just him. Perhaps the wreck is close by?"

"Good suggestions," Reuben said nodding. "But, it still doesn't answer why they're active now."

El looked between them, still unable to believe that Reuben had extended his hospitality to Caspian and that they were both under the same roof. Reaching a truce was one thing, but this was something else entirely. And Caspian was different too, in a way that she couldn't quite put her finger on. But there would be time enough for speculation afterwards.

El pulled a hair tie out of her jeans pocket and quickly wrapped her hair into a high ponytail. "I don't feel comfortable knowing that they're out there and we're doing nothing. Why don't we head out, Ash, and get rid of them?" She raised her sword and grinned.

Ash smiled, lighting up his handsome Greek face. "I think that's an excellent suggestion." He looked pointedly at Caspian and Reuben. "You two must stay here. Briar can guard you."

"I don't like that suggestion at all! I'm not a bloody invalid!" Reuben said, outraged.

"Actually, that's exactly what you are," Briar pointed out, hands on her hips.

Reuben looked as if he wanted to say something very rude to Briar, but he turned and glowered at El again. "What's with you? Have you got some sort of death wish?"

She knew he felt useless because of his shoulder, and tried not to snap. "Of course not. I have magic and the Empusa's sword. We'll be able to see them! Don't you trust my abilities?" She cocked her head to the side, amused.

Reuben tried to speak, but got all tongue-tied. He glared at her, eventually admitting, "Of course I do."

"There we go, then. And besides, if they try to get in by breaching one point, you three need to stop them. This is our safe retreat!"

"Don't worry, we can handle it," Briar said, not giving Reuben a chance to respond.

Ash and Caspian watched the exchange with amusement, and Ash said, "Great. It's settled, then. Allow me."

He unlocked the door and exited. El followed, blowing a kiss at Reuben as she did. He gave her one last, furious glare before locking the door behind them.

~

Avery studied the small cave at the bottom of the steps, disappointed.

"No treasure!"

"But there are bones!" Alex pointed to a corner of the cave where a jumble of bones and a skull rested, rotten clothing still visible.

"Wow!" Avery hurried over, hoping a spirit wasn't about to emerge and attack them. "His weapons are still here!"

Next to the bones were a rusting dagger and flintlock, lying on the sand.

Alex grinned at her. "Brilliant! An actual pirate's body!" He surveyed the space and gestured to a wall of rock through which they could hear the crash of the waves. "There's no access to the sea."

"Yes, there is. Look, a pool of water at the base of the rock." It was almost imperceptible in the darkness, and they hurried over to investigate. Avery shone her torch into the water. "I bet this feeds into a sheltered cove, right under the cliff face, and I would also bet it's only a short passage. This is so cool!"

"We should come in the daylight sometime. Maybe use Ulysses or Nils to bring us here. But for now, let's go up the other passage."

After a quick sweep of the cave to ensure they hadn't missed anything, they hurried along the next tunnel, passing the unconscious and bound spriggans, soon arriving at the base of more steps leading upwards. Before Alex had time to push ahead in his protective way, Avery headed upwards, eager to see what was at the top. After a steep rise, she came to a small square landing and a heavy wooden door.

"This is old!" Alex observed. "Maybe as old as the castle. Which was what? Fifteenth century?"

"Sixteenth," Avery told him, examining the thick iron bands that bound the wood. "Dan said it was built in Henry VIII's time, like a lot of the castles in Cornwall, once we'd left the Catholic Church."

Although St Catherine's Castle was smaller than many, more of a keep really, it had served to protect the Fowey estuary and was perched on the rocky promontory, affording good views of the town and sea. It had also been used in the Second World War. While they talked they tried to open the door, but it was shut tight.

"Is there any suggestion of dungeons or cellars below the castle?" Alex asked.

"I don't think so."

"Maybe we're under another building? Or it's just a cave?"

"I think it's time to use a little magic to find out."

Avery laid her hand over the ornate keyhole and used a spell to unlock it. Then, running her hands around the edges, she loosened the swollen and buckled wood and together they pushed the heavy door open. A wave of musty, damp air hit them.

The witch-light glided ahead, revealing a cavernous space, on the far side of which were three heavy wooden chests, all bound with iron. Next to them were casks of varying sizes, and bundles of rotting cloth.

Alex couldn't keep the glee out of his voice. "Herne's bloody horns! Pirate treasure."

CHAPTER 20

*E*l and Ash crept to the left, along the side of the house, pausing to peer cautiously around the corner.

"I can't see them," Ash confessed, pulling his t-shirt off as he spoke.

For a moment, El couldn't work out what he was doing, and quite frankly was trying not to be distracted by his muscled chest. She kept her eyes fixed firmly on his face, reflecting that actually Reuben's physique was more than a match, which made her feel a little smug.

"What are you doing?" she asked him.

"Flying, of course."

In a flash, enormous wings erupted from his shoulders, and El blinked with shock. While she knew the Nephilim had wings, and had seen them from a distance, she had never been so close before.

"Holy crap. They're impressive." Ash's wings were a beautiful golden brown, or at least they appeared to be in the moonlight.

"Thanks," he said, with a knowing smile. "I'm sure I'll spot them from up there. I'll keep an eye on you, too."

"You won't need to," she said, raising an eyebrow. "But thanks, and good luck."

She watched Ash soar upwards, and then kept heading left towards the far corner of the house. Greenlane Manor has been added to over the years, so that although the main building was medieval, there were other, more modern additions, and by that she meant Elizabethan and Victorian, giving the building odd angles and a quirky layout.

For a few minutes, she couldn't see a single ghost, not even in the distance, and was beginning to think they were either at the nursery, or that the sword wasn't working. And then up ahead, in a small courtyard edged with service rooms, she spied a couple of ghosts looking as real as she did. Well, sort of. They were blinking in and out like a weak signal, and El realised they were trying to pass through the walls of the house, but were being blocked by the protection spell. The section of wall shimmered with each attempted breach, and she grinned. *Their spells had worked.*

Without hesitating, she ran, sword raised. Before they were aware of her presence, she attacked from behind, slashing across the back of one, and then as he turned, fury etched onto his ravaged face, she slashed across his belly too, before plunging the blade in. With an unearthly shriek, the spirit completely vanished. But before she could attack the second, it charged her, tackling her to the ground and raising its knife. El punched out with a ball of fire and air, knocking it backwards, and then while it was spread-eagled against the wall behind, plunged the sword into his stomach.

A whirl of activity in her peripheral vision caught her attention, and she spun around in time to see another spirit run at her from the old stables. He was short but stocky, with a full, dirty beard and ragged clothing. He hurled a knife at her and she swatted it away with magic, and then he pulled a nasty-looking sword from its scabbard. With a leering grin he rasped at her, his strong, Cornish accent and old dialect making him almost impossible to understand.

"So, young maid, ye seek to fight old Tom Trenary? I'll give ye a fight ye won't forget." He swished the blade in front of him, daring her.

For a moment, El was tempted to blast him away with magic like she had the other two.

But this could be fun.

She returned his grin and raised her sword. "All right, old man. Let's see what you've got."

Alex gazed at the hoard of gold, coins, and jewellery in the chests they had broken apart, and couldn't stop his mouth from falling open. He couldn't believe that after all their speculation they had actually found treasure.

"By the Gods! This is worth a small fortune!"

Avery dipped her hands into one of them, like a cup, and lifted out a pile of golden guineas, her eyes wide with excitement. "Wow. Actual pirate treasure!"

They had thrown several witch-lights up, and the gold and jewels glittered in their light.

"We have to declare this."

"Not yet, we don't. Not until we've solved this." She dropped the coins back in the chest. "This is what Miles was searching for."

"And was killed for—by the spriggans guarding it."

"So, why is this still here?"

"Miles was looking on his own," Alex said. "That's the only reasonable explanation."

Avery shook her head, looking perplexed. "Maybe whoever is involved is planning to come back for it. After all, they took the treasure from Looe, despite the fact that there's a spriggan there."

"Maybe. I still think we're missing something." Alex walked over to the casks, pulled a bung out and sniffed, before recoiling. "Christ. That smells rancid. I presume it was brandy."

"And these," Avery said, crouching by the rotten bundles of cloth, "would have been silks and fine linens." She lifted a few pieces, but they disintegrated quickly. She stood, wiping her hands on her jeans. "What a waste."

Alex started pacing. "Originally, these must have been hidden with the plan to come back to claim them later, and something stopped them. Either they were caught, or killed."

"Maybe they were caught by Reuben and Caspian's ancestors' spell."

Alex nodded, his thoughts racing with scenarios. "We're getting closer to working this out, I'm sure, but I don't think we should leave these here."

"Agreed." Avery looked thoughtfully around the space. "Why did Miles get attacked? The fact that he was killed by the spriggans suggests that he must have been either in here or close by. But the entrance above was sealed. He could not have got in here that way. The stone is far too heavy for him to have shifted alone, and it looked undisturbed."

Alex nodded. "He could have come in through the pool below, but he wasn't wet, either."

In their excitement at seeing the chests and casks, they hadn't explored the rest of the place, and now Alex's gaze swept around the room. It was definitely manmade, constructed from huge stone blocks, with a low, beamed ceiling, and the floor was beaten earth. It definitely felt like a cellar. The far side of the place was still in shadows, and sending a witch-light ahead of him, Alex walked over, flashing his torch across the walls, and finding a narrow doorway.

He called over his shoulder, "Avery, there's another room."

Alex proceeded cautiously. Beyond was a series of small, connected rooms, mostly empty except for some disintegrating wood. They were swathed in cobwebs, and as he walked, dust kicked up around them. When he finally reached the end, he found a narrow stone staircase leading to a hatch in the ceiling.

He turned to Avery, who had followed him. "There's the way out." He ascended the stairs and pushed the hatch upwards, but it didn't budge. "It's sealed."

"We could try to move it with magic," she suggested. "But, if it's covered with earth or rock, or even another building—"

Alex sighed. "We'd be crushed. Damn it." He studied it for a few more moments before heading to Avery's side. "I guess we'll just have to accept that it's sealed. It's certainly been undisturbed for years. The dust hasn't moved, and the cobwebs are thick. There's no way Miles came in this way."

"Come on." Avery grabbed his hand and pulled him back to the main room. "I'll use witch-flight to get these chests to my van, and then we'll seal the entrance again."

"And then I suppose we should release the spriggans," Alex said. "Let's hope they don't decide to follow us outside, or that will be a whole other level of crap to deal with."

El was working up a sweat. Tom Trenary may be old, and a ghost, but he was reasonably adept with the sword. Fortunately, El had youth on her side. Tom, however, was mean. And their fight was drawing attention.

While they circled, parried, and attacked, the clash of

their swords drew two more ghosts, and El had the feeling they were waiting to swoop in if Tom lost, ready to end her. She was surprised they hadn't already. As if he'd read her mind, Tom leered at her and gave an almost imperceptible nod to their observers. He unleashed a furious attack designed to absorb all her attention, and the other two swept in on either side.

If Tom was willing to play dirty, so was she. Still fighting, El released a wave of power and it pulsed out around her, sweeping back all three ghosts and sending them crashing against the surrounding walls. Then more ghosts arrived, fire and malevolence burning deep within their empty eye sockets, and she realised she was hemmed in.

Fortunately, within seconds Ash landed next to her, and without hesitating they tackled them all in a messy, brutal fight. Ash used his wings to sweep the spirits either out of the way or to herd them into tight spots, and then finished them off with the sword, while El used magic to compliment her blade. The spirits, however, flashed in and out, disappearing and reappearing seconds later in concerted attacks. For a few minutes it felt as if they might be overwhelmed, but the combination of wings, magic, and the swords gave them the upper hand. Eventually it was over, and the ghosts were despatched by the Empusa's swords to whatever grim fate befell them.

Ash turned to her, breathless. "Sorry. I didn't mean to interfere, but it looked too much fun not to."

She laughed. "Apology accepted. I'm just glad I managed to wipe the smile off Tom Trenary's face. And besides, taking on so many all on my own was probably a bit much."

"Oh, I don't know," he said, taking her in from head to toe. "You seemed to be doing just fine."

She returned his scrutiny, determined not to be outdone

by a Nephilim. "You, too! I guess we better make sure there are no others lurking around here."

Ash folded his wings behind his back and led the way out of the courtyard and further around the house. "There was no activity by the nursery, and besides, simple damage seems pointless, especially when you consider that both Caspian and Reuben are rich."

"But why the concerted attack?" El asked, confused. "Is it really just about revenge?"

"Revenge is always a powerful motive."

A loud explosion broke the silence of the night. They both froze, looking at each other in shock, and then El ran towards the noise, and Ash flew. As El rounded the corner at the far end of the house, she saw a plume of smoke and flames.

What the hell?

The explosion had blown a huge hole in the wall, and another half a dozen ghosts were swarming inside. Ash was already swooping down, and he grabbed one, while striking down another. El charged in, killing the one at the rear, before being caught in a powerful blast of magic that came from inside the house, propelling them all backwards. At the same time, roots exploded out of the ground like writhing limbs.

El flew through the air, landing in a heap on the ground, heavily winded, and the Empusa's sword fell from her hand. She dragged herself to her feet, panic stricken. The spirits had faded to shimmering, barely-there shapes. She lunged at the sword, getting a hand on it just as a spirit rushed at her. As soon as her hand touched the hilt she could see it clearly again, and she angled the sword upwards, impaling the ghost as it leapt. It slid down the blade, pinning her in place until it vanished with an anguished scream.

The roots snaked through the air, trying to pin the spirits

in place, but it was difficult. They moved constantly, manifesting elsewhere in the blink of an eye, trying to avoid the thrashing roots that managed to spear a couple of them, shattering bones like glass. Ash and El waded among them, ducking and dodging, finally finishing them off with the swords.

When the last one vanished, Ash and El waited, swords readied, El not quite believing that it was over. She looked at the destruction all around them. The earth was a churned-up mess of roots and fallen masonry, and a ten-foot hole had been blown in the house.

Reuben.

Her heart in her mouth, El was about to run inside when he appeared in the gap, flanked by Caspian and Briar. His hands were on his hips as he surveyed the mess, and he pursed his lips at El and Ash. "That's the last time I let you two out to safeguard the house."

Avery and Alex sat in the Bedford van, down the street from Ethan James's house, and Avery yawned, struggling to keep her eyes open.

"I'm knackered now."

"Let's just give it another half an hour," Alex said, checking his watch. "But I doubt we'll see much tonight."

Avery leaned back in her seat and chewed her lip, mulling over the recent events. "Ethan *must* have found a map in the White Haven Museum papers. That's the only explanation."

"We don't even know if it is Ethan yet." Alex shuffled to get himself more comfortable. "Or if it is, who else is involved. Or the identity of the witch who must be helping them."

"I'd love to know where the museum papers came from."

"Does it matter?"

"I guess not," she admitted with a sigh.

"They were probably donated years ago, which is why they've been gathering dust. But you'd think people check what they donate!"

"We get donated items, remember?" Avery said, shaking her head. "Or I buy books from house clearances. People don't look at what's in there. Not really. What's puzzling me, if it is him, is why would a very respectable museum curator turn into a thief?"

"Turn to the dark side, you mean?"

She giggled. "Yes. Surely cataloguing all of that stuff and having it in your museum would be huge!"

"Selling it on the black market would be bigger."

"Only if you have connections. I wouldn't know where to start."

"I reckon museum curators would know all about it. Even from the position of trying to stop it. He'd know more than we think."

The sound of a door shutting stopped their conversation, and they both froze, watching the end of the drive ahead. Avery used the binoculars, watching a slight figure wearing jeans and a hoodie emerge on to the road, the hood pulled over their head. They crossed the road, heading to a car parked on the opposite side, facing them, and Avery and Alex slid down in their seats, Avery grateful they had used their shadow spell again.

The figure looked furtively to either side. It wasn't until they passed under a streetlight that Avery got a glimpse of their face, and she groaned as their suspicions were confirmed.

It was Mariah, the head of the Looe Coven.

CHAPTER 21

*R*euben studied the hole in the wall of his billiards room and mourned one of his favourite spaces, a place where he and Gil had spent many happy hours.

"Well, what a bloody mess. I suppose I should be grateful that they didn't blow the whole bloody house up."

The dust had finally settled, but bricks were strewn inside and out, and the billiard table was upended, as were other items and furniture. Caspian, El, Ash, and Briar were with him, inspecting the mess.

Caspian's eyes narrowed as he inhaled deeply. "Gunpowder. It's very distinctive. I guess it's something they'd be familiar with." He turned to look at Reuben. "Intriguing."

"That's one word for it." Reuben looked up at the cracks in the ceiling. "For spirits, they're remarkably destructive."

"And remarkably solid!" El added. "I know I was carrying the Empusa's sword, but they had a real physical substance!"

Ash nodded. "I agree." His wings had now disappeared and he was wearing his t-shirt again. "They are certainly bridging two worlds now, and that's ominous."

El righted one of the upended chairs and leaned against

it, thoughtful. "It reminds me of when we encountered the ghosts at White Haven Castle last year. They had a strong physical presence too, and we thought that was because of our magic."

"Good point," Briar agreed, "which lends weight to our beliefs that the spirits are being strengthened by a witch." She looked a little sheepish. "Sorry about your garden, Reuben. I'll fix that in the morning."

"No need to apologise," he said breezily. "You helped get rid of them. Thank you." Reuben was always amazed by how much power Briar wielded in such a small frame.

"The important thing," El said, moving next to him and sliding her arm around his waist, "was that they didn't get to either of you. But wow, your families must have really pissed them off!"

Caspian scratched his head. "That's something I know we've been good at for a long time. And this, to me, has the feel of a curse. We were good at those, too."

Just then, a door banged at the front of the house, and Avery shouted, "Hello?"

"Down here," Reuben shouted back.

He had called Alex after the attack, taking a chance that they'd still be up, and wanting to make sure he and Avery were okay. Alex leapt at the chance to come over, telling him they had news. In a few minutes, Alex and Avery stood next to them, mouths hanging open.

"Bloody hell," Alex said. "I thought we'd had a crap night. What happened here?"

"Ghosts," Ash said dryly.

Alex looked sceptical. "With *explosives*? Or was that one of you?"

Reuben laughed. Well, he tried to; it got stuck in his throat. "Nope. That was them." He finally turned away from the hole in his wall and had a good look at the new arrivals.

They were both dishevelled, their clothes rumpled and their faces smeared with dirt. "You're filthy. What have you been up to?"

"Spriggans and buried treasure," Avery said, unable to suppress a grin.

Everyone's attention now left the smoking ruins and switched to Avery.

Briar almost stuttered. "You've found treasure?"

Alex and Avery were both grinning insufferably, but at least it was taking Reuben's mind off repair bills and feeling like he had a death warrant on his head.

Alex preened. "Yes, and if you fix us a drink, we'll bring it in."

Five minutes later, they were assembled in the snug, after plugging the hole with yet more protection spells. Ash had volunteered to keep watch, anyway. Three wooden chests were in the middle of the room, their lids open, revealing the collection of gold coins and jewels within.

Reuben stood transfixed, arms folded across his chest. "Herne's magnificent hairy balls! You actually found treasure."

In fact they were all mesmerised, standing in a circle, just staring.

"Where did you find this, again?" Briar asked.

"We think we were beneath St Catherine's Castle," Avery said, going on to explain the hidden tunnels. "I'd like to go back in the day, actually, just to check the grounds, but I doubt we'll find a thing."

"That place is a complete ruin," Caspian agreed. "If there's an entrance, it's been long buried by earth and rubble."

"How much do you reckon that's worth now?" El asked.

"Hundreds of thousands of pounds, probably," Alex estimated. He stepped forward, picking up a few coins to examine. "A few guineas, doubloons, and…" He frowned. "Something else I don't recognise."

It was as if he'd broken a spell, and they all started to pull coins and jewels out, a palpable excitement filling the room.

"But," Alex continued, "we think this is part of a larger hoard. It has to be, or why does there seem to be a few sites involved?"

Reuben looked at his old friend and nodded. "Something like this must have been in the chests in Looe. Maybe they carried it out in bags instead."

Caspian had retreated to the sofa again, the night beginning to take its toll. "Bags would certainly look less conspicuous." His hand rested gently on the site of his stab wound, and Briar immediately headed to his side to offer another healing spell.

"You should go to bed and sleep," she advised him.

Caspian shook his head. "I'm not missing out on this! Besides, I need more whiskey to get me to sleep after all this excitement."

"I know exactly what you mean," Reuben said, heading to the cupboard where he kept a bottle and glasses. His head was buzzing with the events of the night, and after passing round drinks to those who wanted one, he sat down. "Tell us about Mariah again."

Avery looked bleak with disappointment. She always thought the best of people, and no doubt Mariah's betrayal was a shock. Actually, to be fair, it was to Reuben, too. He just happened to be more cynical than Avery.

"There's not much to tell," she said, easing into the armchair. "She snuck out of Ethan's home looking very shifty. She has to be involved, and not in a good way." She looked at Caspian. "You know her better than any of us. What do you think?"

He met her eyes briefly, before glancing at the rest of

them. "I'm afraid that since I have become friends with you, she and Zane are ignoring me. They feel I've betrayed them." He gave a dry laugh. "They were big fans of my father, and our families go back many years. But, Zane and Mariah are both vindictive, narrow-minded, and spiteful. I'm honestly not surprised she's involved. She probably knows a lot more about that cave in Looe than she's letting on. What was she like at the council meeting?"

Avery shrugged. "Her normal self, really. If anything, I found her more animated than normal, but maybe that's because she was being questioned about smuggling in Looe. She certainly didn't seem awkward or guilty."

Briar's hand flew to her chest. "I hope she wasn't behind Inez's death. Or the man on the cliff top."

Alex shook his head. "I think that's the spriggans. But she must be responsible for the super-powered ghosts."

"Wow," Briar said, flabbergasted. "Should we tell Genevieve yet?"

Avery answered immediately. "No. We're sure she didn't see us, and what if other witches are involved?"

"But Genevieve wouldn't be. We can trust her," El said.

Reuben looked at his friend's pensive faces. "I think Avery is right. Let's keep this between us. Whatever her reasons are, she's involved. Maybe she's connected to pirates in some way, or maybe she's a close friend of Ethan's and is getting a cut of the treasure. I don't actually care. The important thing is working out how to stop her."

"Agreed," Avery said decisively. "And El, you should tell Newton in the morning, before he sees Ethan."

"Well," Reuben said, sipping his whiskey to fortify himself, "I guess me and Caspian must persist in finding out what our families did. Although, they seem to have covered their trail very well."

"If you struggle, I could try to summon one of their spirits," Alex suggested warily.

Avery rounded on him. "You are not going into the spirit world again!"

"I'm not suggesting I do," he said patiently. "I'll call them to me. In a full circle of protection, too. They might even have a way to help Helena."

"Okay." Reuben nodded. "We'll keep that option in mind. And now, before I collapse and my adrenalin wears off completely, tell us about these spriggans."

Avery looked at Dan and Sally's shocked faces and laughed. "It's incredible, isn't it?"

They exchanged bewildered glances, and Sally said, "I guess that's one word for it." She lowered her voice and looked around the shop, making sure it was still empty. "Where is it now?"

"At Reuben's. Neither he nor Caspian are leaving the house, and it's fully protected, so that seemed like the best place." She grimaced. "I mean, there is the slight issue of the hole in the wall in Reuben's billiards room, but I think they're trying to fix that with magic today."

They were behind the counter at Happenstance Books at just after nine the next morning, discussing the treasure. Despite the fact that Avery had slept for only a few hours, she had awoken refreshed and energised, fuelled by their success the night before.

Sally's eyes narrowed with suspicion. "I am still shocked that Caspian has moved into Reuben's place. Are you sure Reuben will be safe?"

Avery tried to reassure her. "I'm certain. He was seriously

injured. They're both being targeted, and they're helping each other."

"So you're sure now it wasn't a set-up to get Reuben?" Dan asked, referring back to their conversation of the previous day.

"Positive. I told you, if we hadn't arrived there yesterday, Caspian might be dead."

"All right, I'm convinced." Dan turned to Sally. "She *is* a good judge of character."

Sally still looked doubtful. "If a little too willing to see peoples' good sides sometimes."

Avery was annoyed. "Sally!"

Sally looked contrite and hugged her. "I'm sorry. I just worry about you. Honestly, the things you get up to lately. And I'm still freaked out by your flying thing."

Avery felt terrible and hugged her back. "I'm so sorry about that. It was instinctive. I didn't mean to scare you." She held Sally's hands and looked at her worried expression. If she'd been in Sally's shoes, she'd be worried too. Avery's life was odd, and she was lucky that Sally and Dan accepted it so well. "In fact, I apologise to both of you. I take you for granted and I shouldn't."

Sally smiled softly. "No, you don't."

Dan pretended to vomit. "Ugh. Pack it in you two soppy idiots."

"Piss off, Dan," Avery joked as she hugged Sally again.

"I'm just looking forward to gossiping about you again," Dan teased. "We'll do it over elevenses, when you've buggered off on some mad pursuit. I presume you have one today?"

Avery tried to look affronted, and then had to concede he was right. "I'm going to have a look at St Catherine's Castle in the daylight, just in case I can see where the entrance to the cellar might be."

Dan frowned. "I've never heard talk about deep, dark cellars, but maybe they were blocked up years ago, and all reference has been lost."

"Or, the entrance is in the grounds," Sally suggested, "and the cellar isn't attached to the house, but is something completely separate."

"That's actually a good suggestion, Sally," Avery admitted.

Sally looked smug. "Thank you."

"Oh, you two! Blah, blah, blah," Dan said, waving his hand airily. "Back to the pirate treasure. What's in it?"

Now they both glared at Dan, before Avery said, "Lots of gold coins, some jewellery, and some gems. I'm no expert, though. The boys will get Newton round later today to look at them."

"Can we see them?"

"I guess so. But you both have to keep this very quiet! Like *top secret* quiet."

"Witches' honour," Dan said, saluting. "Now, what about the spriggans?"

"Oh, good. I'm glad you've brought that up. They were crazy strong! They had massive shadows that could actually touch us, but they looked like funny little wizened men."

Dan's eyes lit up. "Fantastic to know that these folklore creatures really exist! I wish I could see one."

"No, you don't," Avery told him. "They are vicious and deadly. I'm convinced now that one of them killed Inez and the other two victims. We had to bind them and spell them to sleep."

"I'm glad you didn't kill them," Dan said, relieved. "And it means the lore is right. They do guard treasure. Fascinating."

"Let's just hope Shadow can communicate with them in some way. It would be nice to have them on our side," Avery mused.

"Talk of the devil," Sally said, nodding to where Shadow was striding past the window. "Here she is."

The bell jingled as Shadow strode in, and her eyes lit up as she joined them. "I have news!"

"Spriggan news?" Avery asked, feeling hopeful.

"Absolutely!" She looked around, frowning. "No customers yet?"

"No, so get on with it," Dan said impatiently.

Shadow huffed. "It's a good thing I like you. Anyway, after I spoke to Briar, I had a think about what they may be and whether they had a link to my world, but I honestly couldn't think of anything similar. I decided I had to see one first hand, so I headed to Looe last night with Gabe, and ventured down to the tunnel where Inez died." She smiled at them triumphantly. "And I found one!"

"Strange you should say that," Avery confessed. "So did we. Two of them actually, in Fowey."

Shadow's shoulders dropped and her smile faded. "Oh! Did you talk to them?"

"Talk? Ha!" Avery snorted. "They tried to kill us. We had to bind them with magic and put a sleeping spell on them."

Shadow relaxed and smiled again. "That's okay, then."

Avery wasn't entirely sure what was *okay* about her and Alex nearly being killed, but she presumed Shadow hadn't wanted her to steal her thunder.

"Did they speak English?" Dan asked, intrigued.

"A mix of English and old fey, actually."

"Hold on," Avery said, "why didn't it attack you?"

Shadow leaned her hip on the counter. "It did, initially. We went in fully armed, but Gabe was more than a match for its strength and managed to pin it against the wall so I could speak to it. It also helped that I bribed it with fey metal."

"What kind of metal?" Sally asked.

"I offered it one of my fey-made armguards from my

armour in exchange for information, and its little eyes gleamed!" She laughed. "And it was that easy!" Shadow's version of easy was very different to Avery's. "It seems that it kills on instinct. It doesn't really plan its attack. It's quite a simple creature, really. Inez and Newton disturbed it, and it lashed out. They love precious metals—it sort of calls to them, and the reason it's still hanging around that passage is because it still scents gold. " She shrugged nonchalantly.

Sally crossed her arms and huffed. "You shouldn't look so pleased about it. Inez is dead!"

"I'm not pleased about *that*!" Shadow shot back. "I'm pleased I could speak to it." She tried to make her tone more conciliatory, and clearly struggled with it. "It *is* part giant, too. That piece of folklore is correct. I could sense the spirit of one contained within it."

Dan shook his head, confused. "But how does that even work?"

"I don't know…and as I said, it's a simple creature. It is what it is, so it couldn't tell me. But it's ancient, I could tell that, too. They have probably been part of the landscape here for millennia, hidden underground, guarding ancient hoards, or even base metals in the ground."

"I felt it, actually," Avery said, recalling the ancient magic she had sensed the night before. "Old, powerful magic, and you're right. It's completely rooted in the earth. Did it know anything about the pirate treasure?" she asked. "Or had it been motivated by someone in some way?"

Shadow shook her head. "It didn't know anything. From my admittedly limited interaction with it, it's like a blood-hound. Or should I say dragon?" She nodded to herself, as if confirming her own idea. "Yes, that's exactly it. Dragons love gold, too. It calls to them, and they sniff it out and sit on it. Spriggans are the same."

"So it couldn't tell you where other treasure might be, or whether more spriggans are there?" Avery persisted.

"No. But at least we know a way to stop them from being violent."

"Have you spoken to El about this yet?" Avery asked. "She's going to Perranporth to investigate the tin mine this morning. This will be really important for her to know!"

"No. But in that case, I'll go to see her now." Shadow pulled her phone out of her pocket and quickly texted her, and then patted the messenger bag she carried. "I've got a few trinkets in here for all of you—just in case."

Dan's eyes widened. "Fey metals?"

Shadow grinned as she pulled out another armguard and some fey coins and placed them on the counter.

"By the Gods," Dan said, examining the armour. "This is amazing workmanship."

He was right. The engraving was intricate and breathtaking, but the metal was light, too.

"Not '*by the gods*', but fey masters," Shadow said, her eyes taking on a faraway look. "Such skill."

Sally looked at her, concerned. "Are you certain you want to give these away, Shadow? Surely they're precious to you?"

"They are, but I've kept the bigger pieces. And besides," she addressed the counter rather than them, "my friends' safety is more important."

Avery, Dan, and Sally shared astonished glances before Shadow looked up at them again, her violet eyes bright, and Avery once more reflected on what a contrary creature she could be. She smiled at her. "Thank you. We appreciate it."

"My pleasure," Shadow said, dropping her gaze shyly. "Anyway, I'll leave these with you, and go see El." She shouldered her bag, and then paused. "Oh, I knew there was something else. Have you seen the news this morning?"

They all shook their heads, and Avery said, "No, why?"

"That blonde reporter was on, doing a piece about White Haven Museum. She was interviewing Ethan James. It turns out that part of the stuff they found were Zephaniah Job's old ledgers. They contain a mine of information about smuggling connections and money across Cornwall, apparently."

Avery nearly spat her coffee out. "Seriously? Wow."

"Does that help you?"

Avery's mind raced with possibilities. "Yes, I think it might."

"Great! Call me if you need me!"

They watched her go, and then Dan slid her gifts under the counter as they watched a couple of customers enter before turning to Avery. "So, Zephaniah Job. His ledgers weren't destroyed after all. He could have all sorts of secrets in them!"

"I agree. Now I'm convinced that Ethan found a bloody treasure map!"

$\mathcal{C}$aspian walked around Reuben's kitchen while he spoke to Gabe on the phone, moving gingerly so as not to aggravate his injury. "Are you sure there's no damage?"

"None at all," he reassured him. Gabe had phoned him to explain that the large warehouse in Harecombe was attacked by ghosts during the night, but the protection spells had held. "Barak and Niel said they could just about see them, and it was a half-hearted attempt only. I'm hoping they won't bother again."

"I think there must have been a dozen here last night, as well as the ones at my place earlier. How the hell many are there?"

Gabe grunted in his usual, non-committal way. "Hard to say. Depends what your ancestors got up to, doesn't it?"

"Yes, it does," Caspian conceded. "No injuries, then?"

"None. They sent the regular staff inside, so all good there." Gabe fell silent a moment, and then asked, "Is there anything we should know about Estelle?"

"No, why?" Caspian answered quickly. *What had she said now?*

"Nothing, she's just a bit, er, *crankier* than usual."

"Well, that's Estelle for you." He refused to elaborate. He couldn't, anyway. *Who the hell knew what she was thinking right now?*

Caspian heard Reuben enter the room, and he turned to see him head for the fridge, nodding at him in greeting. Caspian nodded back. Gabe continued to update him, telling him how he and Shadow had found a spriggan, as well. Caspian paused in front of the patio doors, not really noticing the fine drizzle starting to fall as he absorbed the news, and then they chatted about the business for a few more minutes before hanging up.

Reuben looked none the worse for his late night, and was busying himself getting bacon and eggs from the fridge. He glanced up at Caspian. "Breakfast?"

Caspian didn't normally have breakfast, preferring only coffee before heading to the office, but this morning it appealed to him. Perhaps it was the overcast weather, or the odd, bunkered-down mood he found himself in, sharing Reuben's house. He nodded. "Yes, please. Sounds great, actually."

"Bacon and eggs always does. Did I hear you mention spriggans?"

He nodded and updated him on Shadow's success with fey treasure.

Reuben paused, about to put the bacon in the frying pan. "Is she telling El?"

"Apparently, although she headed to Avery's first."

It was strange; he found himself reluctant to say Avery's name, as if he might give his feelings away, but Reuben was too worried about El. And besides, he didn't strike Caspian as the type to discuss love lives—or the lack of them. He doubted Reuben had ever had a lack of love life, ever. He watched his easy, laidback attitude, and noted he was like that with everyone, a subtle but supreme confidence in himself. Caspian exuded confidence too, and a tinge of arrogance—he'd been accused of it often enough—but he also knew that he didn't always feel that way, and he doubted Reuben did, too.

Reuben just nodded and continued to cook. "Good. I'm worried about El, but she's headstrong, and magically strong, so I have to trust her."

"Have to?"

Reuben laughed. "Yes. But I do, anyway. Those bloody mines are dark and damp and treacherous though, so I'm glad Shadow can help."

"I take it El and Briar are already at work?"

"Yeah." Reuben sighed and met Caspian's eyes, looking grim. "We have to find out what our ancestors did!"

Caspian refreshed his coffee cup and sat down at the wooden table in the corner of the room. "But what if we can't? Does it matter?"

Reuben turned around, half an eye on the bacon, and slung a tea towel over his shoulder. "I suppose it depends on what we want to do, or can do." He shifted his weight, leaning against the counter and waving the spatula as he spoke. "Virginia and Serephina cast a spell together to stop the Dane—we know that much. We assume that it was either to protect their businesses, the towns, or both."

"Or could it be revenge for something? Someone who was hurt, or a business that was damaged?"

Reuben nodded. "Maybe, but whatever the motive, they acted together, in an unusual show of trust."

"Unless, of course, at that point in our history, they actually were friends," Caspian countered, amused by the thought.

Reuben gave a wry smile. "It's possible." And then his

expression sobered. "But why not go to the Witch Council? That would be their obvious support, right?"

"Actually, I don't think the council existed then. And remember, it was harder to communicate between towns far away. Penzance would have meant hours of travel, unless they went by boat. The roads were probably awful. Closer would have been better." He tried to recall what his father had told him. "I don't think the council existed until later on in the 1900s...not like it is now, anyway."

"I guess it doesn't matter," Reuben reasoned. "But I do think the spell is important. It was designed to get rid of Coppinger, and it worked. He disappeared, and it looks like his men went with him. Piecing it together, they must have wrecked the ship he was trying to escape in. Some of his men would have been on that, but others would have been here, surely, continuing the business."

Caspian nodded. "That would make sense. He had a big operation, was ruthless, and surely energetic, when you consider he was moving down from the north of Cornwall."

Reuben turned to flip the bacon. "But Bodmin was the central hub. A network carried smuggled goods there from all over Cornwall, and then on to the rest of England. They would have all known each other—or of each other, at least."

"And would have probably divided Cornwall between them."

Reuben laughed. "But there's clearly no honour among thieves, is there, if Coppinger was moving into other areas."

"I would imagine he was universally disliked. Actually, *hated* is more likely. He terrified people." Caspian had also been reading the books about smuggling that El and Avery had bought in Bodmin.

"You happy to have your bacon and eggs in a sandwich?" Reuben asked, already slicing crusty bread.

"Absolutely."

Reuben plated their breakfast up and carried them to the table, where he took a seat, too. He had a large bite, sighing with satisfaction as he swallowed. "Awesome. So, I suggest we head up to my attic where my spell books are, take yours there too, and search them thoroughly. I honestly think the key to understanding what's happening now is to understand what happened then."

Caspian wiped crumbs from his mouth. "I'm not so sure it will help, but what else are we going to do, locked up in here all day?"

Reuben looked at him, surprised. "I really want to know what we did that was so bad we're being targeted all these years later. It must have been the mother of all spells! Big juju! And frankly, I don't want to be stuck in here for months."

"Don't worry, I'm in. Your hospitality is great, but I prefer my own bed."

"Then let's do this, Caspian. Come on, before we even go up there, in an exercise in narrowing down our search, if you were to stop a murderous madman who was terrorising the country and risking your business right now, what would you do?"

"What would *you* do?" Caspian asked, slightly affronted. "I'm not the only one with magic."

"But I'm charming and guileless," Reuben said, his blue eyes wide and a huge smirk on his face. "I haven't got a mean bone in my body. You're the sneaky shit here, with the family history of making curses and holding momentous grudges."

Okay, so they were at this stage in their strange truce.

"Fair point," he grudgingly conceded. He took another bite of his sandwich and leaned back in his chair, running through his options while he chewed. The word *truce* resonated, and an idea struck him. "Okay, I'm a rich busi-nessman who needs to bring my shipments in, but the damn pirates are trying to scuttle my ships and steal my goods. The man at the root of all my troubles is also threatening the locals, forcing them to work for him, and generally making the place hell. So, rather than plan an outright attack, because he has a *lot* of men, I decide to make a truce. In exchange for a cut of my profits, he allows my ships free passage. But," Caspian gave a victorious smile, "I double-cross him. But not just him…his gang, too. I invite him and his men to a neutral venue, and spring the trap—with your help."

"Why not just kill him, or curse him from a distance?"

"Because I want to do this in one big hit," Caspian countered. "And I want to know that it worked. I want to *see* it!"

Reuben nodded. "I like it. It's logical. But what do you do to trap them?"

"I use a cave, a smuggling cave, or a storage place somewhere. It has to be close—for both of us. When they're trapped, I either kill them immediately, or leave them to a horrible, slow death. As you observed," Caspian said, cutting his eyes at Reuben, "I'm a vindictive bastard, so it will be some kind of curse-inflicted agony."

"That would be far more likely," Reuben agreed. "You are mean."

"Well, you helped me! You have a lot to lose too, remember. White Haven is overrun with smugglers, and you're losing money!"

"But the stories say that Coppinger was seen rowing out to sea in a storm. No, hold on, rowing out from *an island* in a storm, to his big ship, where he was never seen again."

Caspian nodded. "True, but it could just be a fanciful story."

"Or—" Reuben leapt to his feet and started pacing, and Caspian almost spilled his coffee in surprise. "That's exactly what happened! Why come to Harecombe, across country?

I'd bring my ship, Black Prince, and weigh anchor off the coast, bringing some of my men ashore. But not all of them, because, frankly, rumours have reached me that you are a sneaky, not-to-be-trusted-businessman. That's kind of why I like you—we're the same."

"Thanks, I think."

"*Or*, maybe I think this is a sign of weakness, and I decide to pounce." He rounded on Caspian and pointed at him. "You are offering a truce, but I want it all. I am Cruel Coppinger, the demon smuggler, used to having my own way. I decide to attack *you*!"

Caspian had to admit he was enjoying this ridiculous role play. It was fun, and actually productive. Clearly Reuben thought so too, as he strode about his kitchen, swishing his spatula like a sword. Caspian pointed back to Reuben. "But you, Cruel Coppinger, don't know that I've enlisted the support of my neighbours, the do-gooding, simpering, too-terrified-to-say-boo, Jacksons."

"Ha! You may think that's an insult, but it's to my advantage! I lure people in with charm, and then, *a-ha*, I attack like a ninja assassin! I flank the Cruel Gang, and add to your curse to overcome them."

"I thought *you* were Cruel Coppinger?"

Reuben looked startled. "Oh yes, I am. Okay." He paced again. "I come ashore to meet at the agreed *rendezvous* point, but some of my men have arrived before me and are laying in wait to attack you and your family…or whoever you bring with you. When you arrive, we go through the motions, until I feel the time is right, and then attack."

"But I'm prepared, and at a given signal, the Jacksons attack, too."

"Furious, and knowing I'm out-manoeuvred—but not out-gunned, because I have backup—I abandon my men, because I care more about me than them, and retreat."

Caspian continued, "I go after you, but am delayed because of your men. We manage to kill or curse some of them, and then as soon as I can, I pursue you!"

"But I'm way ahead by now, though I daren't take my boat…I'm a sitting duck, it's too obvious. So, I flee into the tunnels." Reuben looked at Caspian. "So this is where it gets murky."

Caspian roared with laughter. "*This* is where it gets murky? I think the whole thing is bloody murky!"

"Oh, ye of little faith!" Reuben strode across the kitchen again. "I head down the nearest tunnels, because I know them all by now. I am a cunning pirate, the biggest badass of the sea, and I flee to where I don't think anyone can find me…right under the sneaky Jacksons' nose! Their own tunnels!"

Reuben stopped dramatising and turned to Caspian. "We *were* smugglers—in some way. I'm not sure why or how. I mean, you're right…we were in trade. Maybe we thought we'd get better profits. Maybe we were coerced by Coppinger."

Caspian shook his head. "You're witches. You wouldn't have been coerced. You might have thought it was a good deal—at first—and then realised that you got in bed with the devil."

"No. That doesn't work. We'd have still done something about it."

Caspian looked at him thoughtfully. "You had your own smuggling business. Just some local-level stuff. You're the lord of the manor, the simpering, do-gooding, look-after-your-own, look-after-the-village kind of family. Maybe Coppinger was moving in on you. Maybe he had something on you. And remember, you don't do curses. You're trying to manage it. You want my help."

"You know, I think we're close with this. Our reasoning is good."

"I agree. And it could be that he fled to Gull Island. The stories talk about Gull Rock, but it might not be."

"But we've both seen the caves on Gull Island," Reuben said. "There are no rotting bones there, or treasure."

Caspian met Reuben's gaze, knowing they were both thinking of the fateful night of Gil's death. "No, there weren't. But there were a lot of old chests and crates in there. What if there's a hidden tunnel under all that? Did you ever check?"

Reuben sat down as if all his energy had left him. "No. I only went back for the first time the other day." Caspian felt as if the whole room had closed down around them and his heart raced as Reuben continued. "I still didn't search it. I was there for some space, actually, after I learned that Alex had spoken to Gil in the spirit world."

Caspian was suddenly unsure of what to say. He'd apologised before, but it had been short, in passing, something he was embarrassed to talk about. He was also scared of breaking whatever strange accommodation they had arrived at between them. And then he frowned. "Was that where you were attacked?"

"Yes, in the cave leading to the beach."

"I didn't see that one."

"It's just beyond the big one."

Reuben's face was carefully schooled, but Caspian was sure there was a lot going on beyond that calm exterior. He had another thought. "Where else has a lot of tunnels and is neutral ground?"

Reuben looked puzzled, and then said, "West Haven."

"We didn't explore all of those tunnels."

"But the police did."

"Did they? What if there was another disguised doorway,

or access to another section. What if there's another tunnel that leads to Gull island? Another cave?"

"Lupescu's cave wasn't it, that's for sure," Reuben pointed out.

Caspian remembered the attack from the night before. "I saw those spirits emerging from your glasshouse last night. What if the place where Cruel Coppinger was finally defeated was on Gull Island all along?"

They both looked out of the window to the small isle that lay draped in mist and drizzle.

Reuben spoke first. "Another cave." He nodded and sighed. "We know goods were smuggled ashore there. The big cliff on the far side shelters the beach from the mainland. It's possible."

Caspian turned away from the view and focussed on Reuben again. "I would chase him down and finish him straight away. I wouldn't allow him to regroup and strike back. And when I was done, I would hunt down his remaining men. Or just extend the curse to the rest of them."

"And I'd be with you. Once we'd started this thing, there would be no going back. We had effectively started a war."

"And if I couldn't track down all of his men, which would be tricky," Caspian admitted, "even with magic, I would curse his treasure, ensuring that anyone who tried to move it would die. Or something of the sort."

"If we cursed the treasure, wouldn't that mean it would *still* be cursed?" Reuben asked, looking through the door and into the snug where the old chests still sat.

Caspian eyed them warily too, and unable to detect anything remotely like magic coming from them said, "Maybe not the treasure, then. Just the men."

"What about the ship? Did it get away, or did we sink it? Or did the storm do it?"

"Or did we summon the storm, and bring the ship down?" Caspian asked.

Reuben huffed out a deep breath and leaned back in his chair. "Wow. Double-crossing him and cursing his gang would be a very good reason to come after us now."

"But don't forget they've been enhanced somehow, probably by Mariah, who has to be the witch Gil detected walking in the spirit world. Maybe her family was involved all those years ago, and this is her chance to have her revenge on us?"

"Or maybe this is just opportunistic. They found out the connection to us, and decided to have fun." Reuben sighed. "Whatever. We need to stop them—for good. They're strong, in the spirit world, too. They've captured Helena."

Caspian nodded. "So I gather, and set Gil in action. Of course, the other option is that the curse tied them to the treasure, or their bones, meaning they couldn't rest." He frowned. "Seems short-sighted though. You'd want them gone forever." He stood and carried his plate to the sink. "Come on, Reuben. Enough maybes. Let's find this damn spell and work out what they did. You're right, it's the key. Then, I think we need to head out there."

His gaze lingered on the island in the mist, sure that somewhere under it lay the answers to Coppinger's doom.

CHAPTER 23

*A*fter thirty minutes of slow progress through narrow tunnels, El wondered again why she'd volunteered to come with Newton.

Wheal Droskyn, which was the name of the tin mine at Droskyn Point in Perranporth, was one of the oldest in Cornwall, parts of it estimated to be 2,000 years old. Fortunately, the oldest workings were shallow, but that didn't make the experience any better. The newer parts went much deeper, with shafts that dropped deep into the earth, one leading into a cave that was known to have been used for smuggling in the past.

El was dressed in jeans and boots, complete with a hard hat, for which she was very grateful. The tunnel was low in places, and they had to duck and squirm through tight passages, watching their every step. In the end only the four of them had gone in, and Newton had left two constables outside the entrance to stop anyone from following. Jethro Carter, their guide through the mines, was at the front, followed by Newton, and Moore was behind her.

El's headlamp illuminated the stonework, some of which was stained blue from thin seams of copper deposits, although this was mined predominantly for tin. She wished she could use a witch-light, but Jethro's presence made it impossible. Jethro had expressed disbelief that anything was hidden in here, explaining that because the oldest mines were easily accessed by the narrow path along the cliffs, many people had explored here over the years. The newer, deeper sections were sealed off on the whole. Although, he did say there were a couple of access points through narrow shafts. All of the mine workings above ground had long since been pulled down, and major shafts had been capped for safety.

They reached an intersection of tunnels and Jethro paused to pull out his map, addressing them as he did so. "The way to the left is where our particular adit accesses, but as I said, I doubt you'll find anything there. This area has been explored countless times, and there are certainly no remnants of treasure." He frowned at them. "I've been down here, admittedly years ago now, and I never saw anything, either. Unless, of course, someone hid something more recently."

Newton shook his head. "No, I doubt that. But whether anything's there or not, I do want to try and find where the girl could have been."

Before they entered the mine, Newton had told Jethro some very basic information, but the lack of clarity was obviously very frustrating for him. While they talked, El extended her magic, trying to sense a supernatural presence, but so far all she could feel was cold, damp air, and the metals that were layered through the earth. In the pockets of her coat were a piece of Shadow's fey armour and a few fey coins, for bribery purposes, but she hoped she wouldn't have to use them. It struck her that mines would be a natural place for spriggans to be, considering the metals that were all around them.

Moore was silent, as usual, just staring around the space suspiciously. He looked as tired as Newton. Both of them had thick stubble and shadows under their eyes as if they hadn't slept for days, and El was sure that Moore had been as affected by Inez's death as Newton.

"Keep going left," Newton said, finally ending their discussion, and Jethro turned and led the way again.

They passed dark entrances—crawl spaces, really, that El peered down nervously—but Jethro ignored them, leading them deeper and deeper as he explained that they had reached a newer section of the mine. The tunnels were shored up in places with huge wooden beams, but they bulged alarmingly at some points, while other areas dripped with moisture.

"You're lucky," he said to them as they walked. "Many newer areas are inaccessible, unless you have climbing equipment. These hills are riddled with shafts." They entered a large cave, the deeper parts running to their right, and he took out a flare and lit it, hurling it into the darkness where it illuminated a pool of water and a dark exit at the end. "Through there are shafts filled with water. It's treacherous. The part we're heading to is dry." He looked at all three of them. "Are you sure you want to go on?"

"A woman has died," Newton said abruptly. "Yes, I do."

They eventually reached a big, barred gate that lead to another area of the mine, and Jethro swore.

"Someone has broken the padlock."

"*What?*" Newton pushed him aside.

The gate was rudimentary, set into the rock wall to block the narrow tunnel that led deeper into the earth. A chain and padlock had secured it, but it now hung loose, the chain cut cleanly through.

Newton turned to El, his expression saying everything before he nodded at Jethro. "It means we're on the right track, then. Go on, but slowly!"

Jethro was a man in his fifties, with grey hair, a grizzled beard, and a gruff manner. He wielded a heavy, handheld torch as well as his headlamp, and he hefted the former like a weapon before heading down the passage. El glanced at Moore, but as usual he looked inscrutable and just waved El ahead of him.

"Do you want me to go first, Newton?" she asked him.

He shook his head. "No, but stay sharp."

They progressed deeper, passing other passageways, and El quickly lost her way. This was terrifying. If something happened to Jethro, who was clearly very comfortable with finding his way down here, they could be lost forever.

Eventually, he called over his shoulder, "We're nearly there. The adit runs off this tunnel."

The tunnel widened and the roof lifted, finally bringing them to a larger area. However, when they reached it, Jethro swore again. "What the bloody hell?" He trailed off, looking dumbstruck at a hole in the rock face. "That's new."

"It is?" Newton asked, excited.

"Absolutely. I haven't seen it before. Look at the edges where the stone has been broken, and the new rock fall."

He was right. Although rocks of various sizes were strewn across the ground, some of them had edges that weren't discoloured by age, and the border of the new hole in the wall looked fresh, too.

Jethro pointed to the dark, low tunnel to the side and crouched, shining his torch down it. "You can see daylight down there. That's the beach. It carries water out of here. As you can see from the damp ground, it can get very wet in here. We're lucky it's only drizzling."

El crouched, spying a tiny pinprick of light at the far end. *This is where it happened. Jasmine was killed here.*

She stood quickly, extending her magic perception, again searching for something supernatural, or the ancient magic that Avery said she'd felt, but nothing seemed out of place, and she shook her head at Newton, who watched her carefully. He nodded, directing Jethro to keep to the side, and after flashing his torch light across the ground, stuck his head through the newly-made hole. El stood next to him. Their torchlight illuminated another cave beyond, and at the far side, on a rudimentary rock shelf, were the remnants of old, wooden chests.

"Bingo," Newton said softly.

Jethro squeezed next to them, looking in too. "Incredible. Are you telling me that those have been in there all this time?" He stepped back and examined the rock face. "I have *never* noticed anything abnormal about this wall."

Newton was already clambering over the lip and stepping into the cave. El followed, her power pulsing at her fingertips, and as soon as she entered the cave, she felt it. An ancient presence that watched them. She threw out her arm to block Newton, but before she could assess what was going on, a creature exploded out of the darkness, throwing Newton against the wall and sending her rolling across the floor before *something* landed on her chest.

Alex groaned as he exited the kitchen of The Wayward Son, hearing Jago laughing loudly at the terrible joke he'd just told him. The other kitchen staff groaned as well, but Jago didn't care; the worse the joke, the more he laughed. As the door swung shut behind him, Jago's laughter was replaced by the chatter and music in the pub.

Friday lunchtime was often busy in the pub. Everyone was winding down for the weekend, and despite the grey drizzle and mist that had set in outside, everyone seemed determined to have fun. A few lights were on to alleviate the gloom, and the low music added to the atmosphere. Alex served a few customers and took some food orders, and then noting Zee was restocking the glasses, headed to his side to help.

"I hear you had an interesting night," Zee said, absently polishing a glass.

"That's one word for it. I take it Ash updated you?"

He nodded. "Did you know Caspian's warehouse was attacked, too?"

"No!" Alex said, alarmed. "Anyone hurt?"

"Fortunately not. Caspian's protection spell held." Zee looked worried. "They seem to be scaling up their activities."

"I agree. I just wonder what set them off in the first place. It has to be the fact that their treasure has been disturbed."

"Seems logical," Zee agreed. He looked across the pub. "Your ghost hunters are here."

Alex turned to see Cassie, Ben, and Dylan take seats at the corner of the bar, and he hurried over to them. "Is everything okay?" He looked them up and down, but they didn't seem to be injured.

"We're fine," Cassie assured him. "Why so worried? You've got a line between your eyes."

His hand flew to his forehead. "Have I?"

She sniggered. "Don't worry. I'm sure it's not permanent."

"I bet it will be," he grumbled. "We're having a nightmare at the moment."

"So I gather," Dylan said. He was distracted, eyeing the menu in his hand. "Let's get a pint and some food and then we'll tell you what we've found."

Alex nodded, quickly sorting their drinks and taking their

order, and then Ben lowered his voice and leaned forward. "We decided to take some general readings in the areas that have been affected by current events."

"Newton told us."

"Fowey, Looe, here, and Perranporth," Dylan explained. "And we noticed something odd."

"Odder than spirit activity?"

"Yes," Cassie answered, sipping her cider. "We've calibrated our instruments, based on what we've learned over the last year, so that we're more specific in our searches."

Alex was confused. "Isn't that counterintuitive? Won't you fail to pick up on stuff?"

Ben shook his head, impatient. "No. We search wide and then narrow it down. And we position ourselves above towns too, which is pretty easy in a lot of Cornish coastal towns. We can set ourselves up on the hill, and take readings for the whole place."

"Especially at night," Dylan added, "using the thermal imaging camera."

All three of them were looking very excited as they started explaining, and Alex was intrigued.

"We've been taking base readings over the last year," Ben said, "as a matter of course, and knowing how interesting Cornwall can be, and we've definitely found changes."

"Hold on!" Alex looked at them, amazed. "You took readings across Cornwall? Wasn't that a huge amount of work?"

They all shrugged, and Cassie, said, "Sure it was. But we did it over months, more as data-gathering, really, for our website."

Dylan's eyes widened. "You'd be amazed at the sort of supernatural energy that's out there. We're going to study some of the old sites next—you know, dolmens, stone circles, remains of old forts—and put all that on our website, too."

He grinned. "We're kind of making a map of the spookiest places in Cornwall!"

"Wow." Alex was impressed. "That's great advertising for you. And very useful for us!"

"Exactly," Ben said. "So all of this work is valuable all around. Anyway, considering the recent events, we went back to the places where the deaths occurred and noticed another type of energy. *Your* type."

"What do you mean, my type?" Alex asked, confused.

"Witch-type!"

"You can differentiate?"

"Sure," Cassie nodded. "We took your readings, remember? Your energy signature is different. Well, when you do magic."

"I guess that confirms what we suspected, especially after last night," he told them, and quickly updated them on spotting Mariah leaving Ethan's house.

Dylan looked pleased. "Great, so that corroborates us too, not that we really doubted that."

"So where is *our* type of energy?" Alex asked.

"Well, we see it in the centres where you witches are based. The coven members, I mean," Ben said. "Obviously there was a big cloud of magic over White Haven, but that's gone now. Looe and Fowey are hotspots, and that's to be expected. But," he faltered, glancing at the others, "there's some over Gull Island, too."

Alex gripped the counter in alarm, and then tried to calm himself. "I guess that sort of makes sense. Reuben's house was attacked last night, too. And he was attacked in the caves there."

"It's big, Alex," Cassie said, eyeing him nervously. "The energy pouring off that place is very strong."

Alex started to feel very uneasy. It may be an island, but there was a path running from it to Reuben's house. *Was last night's attack the start of something bigger?* He should phone Reuben, just to check on him. And then he thought of El and Newton heading down Wheal Droskyn. Unpleasant images of them lying dead and broken in a mineshaft filled his head.

"Did you see anything over Perranporth? El and Newton are there today."

"Oh, yeah," Dylan said, huffing. "We've saved the best 'til last. We saw a really old energy signature there! We even went on to the beach to check. Not too close, because of that girl's death, but close enough. It's enormous. Giant-sized."

El slammed her power against the creature on her chest, sending it flying, and then lashed at it with a wave of fire, throwing it back against the rock face. She dropped the fire, but used air like a battering ram to hold it in position, and staggered to her feet. She could feel seams of metal behind the spriggan, and decided she could use it.

Her magic was particularly attuned to metals, especially after years of working them, and she reached for them now. Tendrils of tin emerged from the earth, and she fashioned them quickly into a cage, securing the spriggan in place and enhancing its prison with magic.

Out of the corner of her eye, she saw Moore wrestle with Jethro, trying to keep him from entering the cave. Moore couldn't see Newton, and El heard the panic in his voice as he shouted his name. Wow. He actually spoke.

"I'm okay," Newton shouted back. Well, groaned would be the better word. "Stay back."

He dragged himself to his feet, and checking that El was okay, they both advanced on the furious spriggan.

"Nice reflexes," he said to El admiringly, but without taking his eyes off the creature.

"I should have been quicker." She was annoyed with herself. She had known they would likely be attacked, and had still ended up on her back.

Newton was pre-occupied with their prisoner. "That's an ugly little thing. Like some bloody deformed baby." He grimaced. "So this is a spriggan!"

"It seems so," El murmured, taking in its odd appearance.

She pulled the fey metal out of her pocket, waving it in front of the spriggan's eyes. It immediately watched it with ill-concealed greed.

"This is yours, little man," she said, "if you promise to behave."

It shot her a calculating look as it grasped the bars of its cage.

"Understand me?" she asked, studying it. "Or I can do worse than pin you to the wall." She hated to threaten it. It was like Shadow had said. It acted on instinct, but that's what made it even more dangerous.

"Wait," Newton said. "Do you think it can answer questions?"

"You can try."

She continued to hold the fey armour in front of it as a reward, as Newton said, "This is yours if you tell me who came here."

It hissed, looking at Newton malevolently, and for a second El didn't think it either could or would answer, and then with a horribly grating voice it said, "Four humans came, three left. One death for one death."

El and Newton glanced at each other, puzzled.

"What do you mean?" Newton asked.

It snarled and then pointed to the far end of the cave, lost in darkness. Newton flashed his torch that way, lighting up the tiny, lifeless form of another spriggan.

El felt rage build within her. Someone had killed it! Logically she knew that spriggans were violent, but still, it was sad, and it had obviously retaliated, killing Jasmine.

Newton pressed on. "Men or women?"

"Two men, two women." It flicked its angry, beady eyes at El. "Hair like that one."

"Blonde?" Newton asked.

"Like silver. Much power."

"What did they take?"

"All the gold, all the gold, all the gold." It kept repeating it over and over again in its rasping little voice, making El's skin crawl. "Give me the fey treasure!" Its hands flexed with greed.

Newton looked balefully at El. "I doubt it can tell me anything else."

"I have a question." She turned to the creature. "Why are you still here?"

"More gold. More gold. More gold."

Again it glanced nervously to the side, and in the light of Newton's torch, they saw a few spilled coins.

"Okay," Newton said. "We're going to give you this, and then you leave, for good. More men are coming, and I don't want to hurt you. And you need to take your friend."

It looked as if it was about to argue, but it clearly understood what Newton was saying, because it nodded. El released her magic, dismantled the cage, and handed it the armour. In seconds it scampered across the ground, grabbed the other body, and disappeared through a barely there crack in the wall.

El kept her magic readied, just in case. "What now?"

"Now I get a team in here to examine every inch of this place, to see if we can find some evidence of who was here." He shook his head, frustrated, as he looked around. "They must have found an old map with this hidden cave, and worked out how to get to it. They're determined, I'll give them that."

"It has to be Mariah!"

"I agree. And I think it must be Ethan, too. Like you guys, I don't believe in coincidences, and there are too many connections."

"And there's someone else. Another man."

"He has a brother. It could be him, or maybe a colleague." He patted El's shoulder and gave her a weak smile. "Thank you for coming."

"My pleasure." She hesitated, and then said, "Well done for not wanting to kill it—even after what one of them did to Inez."

"Yeah, well, like you said, it acts on instinct. I'll save my revenge for those who started this whole thing."

El smiled. "Fair enough, but I'll hang around here, just in case." Despite the fact that the spriggan had vanished, she didn't want to take any chances. "If you can explain me being here."

"The team were okay in Looe. I think the crowds put it off attacking again."

She shrugged. "I'm here now. Let me be useful."

"All right. I'll think of something."

"When are you going to interview Ethan?"

"This afternoon. I'll leave SOCO to it here, if you're okay with that?"

"Absolutely. Catch us up with a pint later? My treat."

"You're on." He nodded to Jethro, where he stood looking at both of them wide-eyed with shock. "And you might want to glamour that one. Make it good."

⁓

Alex stared at the three investigators. "When you say *giant*, do you mean just a big wave of energy?"

"No." Dylan looked excited, the complete opposite of Alex's feelings. "We mean an energy field in the shape of a giant was visible on the cliff top. Just briefly, and then it vanished."

"A giant? An actual giant!"

"Yes," Ben nodded, also grinning. "That piece of footage may actually get us on the news. It must have something to do with those spriggan-creatures you mentioned."

"Fuck it! El and Newton are there today." Alex tried to be logical. They knew this might happen, but at least Alex had faced a spriggan with another witch. Alex reached for his phone, anxiously watched by his three friends who no longer looked so excited, and called El and then Newton. Neither of them answered. "Crap."

"But they're down a mine, right?" Dylan pointed out. "They wouldn't get the call, anyway."

At that point, Avery walked in and sat on a stool, her broad smile disappearing as she looked at their expressions. "What's going on?"

Alex quickly updated her, half expecting to see Avery race out of there, but she nodded calmly instead.

"She'll be okay," she reassured him. "Shadow popped into the shop this morning with a tip and a present—fey metal and coins. She gave them to El. They worked well as bribery, apparently, when she and Gabe found the one at Looe."

"Yeah, but you have to get it to stop bashing your brains in first!" Alex reminded her. "You're very blasé about this. Inez died because of one of those!"

"I haven't forgotten that," she said, infuriatingly calm. "But El is forewarned, and we weren't. She'll be okay. Can I have a wine, please?"

He shot her an annoyed look and then grabbed a glass,

wishing he could have a pint, too. "When did you get so Zen all of a sudden?" he asked as he poured her drink. "That's normally my job."

"Of course I'm worried, but I trust El. She's a strong witch."

"Agreed," Cassie chimed in. "Sorry we alarmed you, Alex." She told Avery what they'd seen on the Perranporth cliff top, stunning her into momentary silence.

Avery took a large sip of wine as if to fortify herself, and when she finally spoke, she said, "Proof of giants! That's amazing. Actual Cornish giants! Just that one, or are there more?"

"Isn't one enough?" Alex asked. What was the matter with them all?

"Only one so far," Ben answered. "But now that we've seen one, I think we should check other areas that folklore tell us had giants. Their spirits could still be there, striding the landscape."

Alex groaned. "They could be, but I really hope you don't find any more, and that this little spate of attacks has been stirred up by these events." He studied Ben, Cassie, and Dylan's faces, each one pleased with their success, and felt bad that he couldn't be more enthusiastic. He knew they were upset about the recent deaths, they weren't monsters, but he also understood how important this was to them. "You didn't see one in Fowey or Looe?"

"No, just Perranporth," Dylan said. "But, like we said, it vanished in seconds. We could have missed the others."

Cassie looked apologetic. "Sorry, but just because we've seen it won't make things worse."

"Of course it won't, and it is amazing," Avery said, shooting Alex a warning look that told him to be nicer. "I can't wait to tell Dan and Sally. In fact, you must bring your footage to show us. We really should all see it, too!"

"That's partly why we're here," Ben said. "To see if we can arrange a time."

Avery nodded. "I think we're heading to Reuben's tonight. I'll check. You should come if you're free. Just be aware that they're under a lockdown up there, all sealed up with protection spells."

All three nodded immediately.

"Just check with Reuben, and we'll be there," Ben agreed.

"So, Avery," Alex said, "did you have success this morning?"

Her face fell. "No. A complete bust at St Catherine's Castle, as expected. But the good news is that everything seemed settled up there. No weird findings or magical happenings. I thought I'd pop in, have some lunch, and then head back to the shop. But I have another suggestion for tonight. I think you should scry to watch Mariah. We're on the back foot on all this, and I'm sick of it. We need to get ahead."

Alex nodded. "All right. That's probably a good idea."

He paused when Anna approached carrying a couple of bowls of fries, and she placed them on the counter with a cheery, "Here you go, guys," before heading back to the kitchen.

Dylan reached for a chip. "I've just thought of something else we should do, too. Set the camera up to point at Gull Island again. That could prove very interesting!"

"Excellent," Avery said, reaching for her phone. "I'll ring Reuben and organise it all."

CHAPTER 24

*R*euben ended the call with Avery and said to Caspian, "Well, that's sorted, then. Everyone's coming around tonight."

Caspian looked up from his grimoire. "Who's everyone?"

"The witches, plus Ben, Dylan, and Cassie. They have thermal imaging footage they want to show us."

Caspian studied him for a moment, an almost unreadable expression on his face, and then he asked, "Do you all do this a lot?"

"Catch up for drinks and watch weird thermal imaging footage? Yes to the first, not really to the second," he answered, sitting again at the old wooden table in the attic spell room. "Why?"

Caspian had a sort of lost look on his face, which was a weird word to use, but it suddenly made Reuben feel very sorry for him. "No reason," he answered. "It just seems you have a busy social life. You're very close, your coven."

"We are. We get together in each other's houses, and in Alex's pub. It's what friends do, right?" Even as he was saying it, Reuben got the distinct impression it wasn't what Caspian did. Before he could consider whether it was an okay question to ask, he said, "You must catch up with your friends a lot. Or your family, at least. They're your coven, aren't they?"

Caspian gave a dry laugh. "No, we do not. We discuss business, mainly."

"But you have non-business friends?" he asked, starting to turn the pages of his grimoire in an effort to keep the conversation light. For some reason, he felt he was on unstable ground.

"My business friends are my friends," Caspian said, "and we socialise in fancy restaurants or over boardroom tables."

Caspian's voice had taken on an edge, and Reuben risked a glance at him, but Caspian was studying his grimoire, too.

Regret. That's what Reuben heard in his voice and saw on his face.

"And Estelle? She must be a riot at Christmas!" Reuben's tone was cheeky, hoping to get something positive from Caspian.

Caspian looked him straight in the eye. "Now I know you're taking the piss."

Reuben leaned back, all pretence at reading his grimoire gone. "I'm not taking the piss. She is your sister, and for all you bicker, I'm sure you must get on, really."

"We tolerate each other, and I think that might have just run its course, too." He shrugged. "So be it. I'm sure we'll muddle together for the business." He nodded over at Reuben's end of the table, and the grimoires open in front of him. "Anyway, have you found anything useful?"

"No. But I'm sure I will. You?"

"No, and it's beginning to piss me off."

"Me too."

Once he and Caspian finished their breakfast, Reuben had taken him up to what had once been the hidden attic. Since Gil and Alicia died, Reuben had decided to take out the brick wall that divided his spell room from the main attic, and now it could be accessed without having to use the hidden passageway in the walls. He'd debated whether it was wise to take Caspian there, and then laughed at his paranoia. Caspian knew he was a witch. He wouldn't give a crap where his spell room was, and no casual visitor would ever see the attic. And if he ever split up with El, there was no way he would become involved with someone who didn't know he was a witch. Life was far too complicated for that. For the last few hours they had once again examined the grimoires for potential spells used on Coppinger, but all Reuben had achieved was a headache. They even used witch-light to reveal invisible spells, and had then tried finding spells, but still hadn't discovered anything their ancestors may have used. They'd debated a couple that might be plausible, and then dismissed them just as quickly.

Reuben pointed to the stack of papers he had found in Caspian's attic, just before he'd been attacked. "What about those?"

He shrugged. "Interesting letters, but nothing that suggests what the spell could be, or where it was finally executed."

Reuben looked around the attic, distracted. "I guess any of these spells that we've found could be adapted, but I just have a feeling I'm missing something. I think Virginia would have been keen to hide any evidence…like in their letters, really. The contents were kept deliberately vague. I suspect the spell is either right under our noses and we've missed it, or it's hidden in this house somewhere—or at yours. I know there are hidden passages all around this place."

Caspian laughed. "I once found an entire secret room in Harecombe Manor."

"A torture chamber?"

"No! I don't think we were that bad, thanks Reuben."

"Just kidding." He sighed. "Virginia wouldn't have been proud of cursing a load of men, even if it saved the town. She'd have hidden the spell really well."

Caspian shook his head. "We're thinking about this all wrong. This was Serephina's suggestion. It's our family's spell, not yours. It has to be in my grimoire. And although I'm sure Serephina wouldn't give a crap about cursing a whole load of smugglers, I doubt she'd have wanted to shout about it, either." He smiled. "You said the spell would be under our noses."

"Yes, but how does that help?"

"There's a spell on it, something to hide it."

"But we've already used witch-lights and finding spells! I don't get it."

"I think the entire page has been hidden, and that requires a different spell to find it."

Reuben was still confused. How many layers of subterfuge could you use to hide a spell? But Caspian started to look very excited and grabbed the letters, making a pile of them on the table.

"Have you got a silver bowl, Reuben?"

"Sure." He stood to take one off the shelf. "Are you doing another finding spell?"

"No, an unveiling spell. Where are your letters?"

Reuben picked them up from the corner of the table, and watched Caspian add them to his own stack and place them all in the bowl. "I hope you're not attached to them, because I need to burn them."

"Wait. Let's take photos of them first, just in case." If Reuben had learnt anything from the other witches, it was to take notes and have backup plans.

"While you do that, I'll get the herbs I need—if you don't mind."

He looked at Reuben uncertainly, and Reuben wished

he'd stop standing on ceremony. "Stop asking, Caspian. Assume it's yours."

Caspian gave a small smile and started to prepare his ingredients while Reuben took photos of all the letters with his phone.

Five minutes later, they were both seated opposite each other, with one solitary candle in front of them, the bowl of letters mixed with herbs, and Caspian's grimoire. Reuben eyed it warily. Caspian's grimoire had a very different feel than his own. Some spells exuded an undercurrent of menace, and while there were some spells in his that gave a prickle of unease because of the power and intent within them, the spells within Caspian's gave him the shivers. Pushing his misgivings aside, he clasped Caspian's outstretched hands, struck by how odd this unlikely pairing was.

"My reasoning," Caspian explained, "as I said, is that you're right. This spell is in here, and we can't see it because it has been thoroughly hidden. I have a few unveiling spells I've used before, but this one should be the best for this purpose. I'm trusting our bloodlines and magical heritage will help."

"Do I need to do anything?"

"Just lend your energy to mine."

Silence fell as Caspian took several deep breaths, and then he intoned the spell. The letters in the bowl burst into flames, and the smoke wafted over the table. A light breeze sprang up, and the candle flickered as Reuben felt Caspian's power extend. Reuben offered up his own, and Caspian weaved them together, and then directed the smoke over the grimoire. It wrapped sinuously around it, teasing the pages apart. For a moment, the smoke hesitated as if meeting resistance, but Caspian raised his voice, and with it his magic, and the spell strengthened.

Suddenly pages flickered violently, from one end of the book to the other, so quickly it seemed the book might tear apart. Then a wave of power blasted from it, throwing Reuben out of his chair and against the wall as raucous cries filled the room.

Everything went black.

As Briar exited her old Mini on Reuben's drive, an explosion resounded from above, glass showering around her as a wave of magic sent her crashing to the ground.

Flat on her back, she stared horrified at the upper level of Reuben's house, seeing an oily, green vapour pouring from the attic windows. Even from down here she could feel the power of the spell; it reeked of lost souls.

Scrambling to her feet, she raced to the front door, spelled it open, and ran up the broad flight of stairs. The spell was stronger inside, and she could hear screams from above that made her skin crawl. Shit. Was that Reuben or Caspian?

Horrified, she ran even faster, her heart slamming in her chest, trying to reason through what she could feel. Desperately trying to contain her panic, she shouted, "Reuben! Caspian!"

There was no response.

The first and second floor were being pounded with waves of magic, and the thick green vapour that had poured from the upper windows eddied around her, filling her lungs and seeping into her hair and her clothes. She summoned the Green Man from deep within her, then blasted rich, earthy magic around her like a shield, filling her instead with a clean spring power. But her heart was in her mouth as she reached the door to the attic. It had blown off its hinges and was lying on the floor.

Briar slowed, her hand on the doorframe as she peered up the narrow stairs into the gloom, wary of being attacked by spirits. Nothing moved, and the cries were ebbing away.

Throwing caution aside, she ran up and immediately felt as if she'd been plunged underwater. The attic was bathed in a murky green light that rippled across the walls and old, disused furniture, and everything seemed muffled. She heard the faint crash of the surf upon a distant shore, and inhaled the strong smell of the sea.

The green light was denser at the far end where Reuben's spell room was. Cautiously, she walked across the room, feeling the damp air swirl around her and settle on her skin, and desperate to dispel the strange sensation, forced the murk out of the broken windows, leaving the smell of blossoms in its place.

She finally halted on the spell room's threshold, unable to see anything in the gloom. The watery quality was thickest there, and a murmur of voices twisted around her; she felt anger, and the thick stench of vengeance. She tried to enter, but the magic pushed her back.

What had they done?

Briar was terrified now, and called out, "Reuben! Caspian!"

There was no answer. Screw this. She had to get in there. She focussed, trying to work out what magic she could feel and how to dispel it. She slowed her breathing, easing her panic. The voices were distracting, but she ignored them, concentrating only on the magic. Elemental water was strong here, entwined within the binding curse, and it was old, made with strangely familiar magic.

Briar pulled her earth magic from deep within her, feeling the Green Man rise again. "I need your help," she muttered to him, pleased when she felt his power ripple through her veins. She slipped her shoes off, feeling the wooden floor beneath her bare feet, warm and grounding, and forcing through the resistance, started to absorb the water into her earth magic like a sponge.

Briar resisted the urge to run in, knowing she had to contain the curse first. She would be useless to them if she got caught up in it, too. She caught a glimpse of Reuben and Caspian, each on either side of the room, their chairs upended, and the more she saw, the more horrified she became. This part of the attic was a wreck—shelves blasted off the walls, magical paraphernalia strewn across the room, and Reuben's grimoires in a heap in the corner. But Caspian's grimoire was in the centre of the wooden table, green light radiating from its open pages, words writhing in the air above it.

They must have found the curse used to bind Coppinger and his men, and what an ugly curse it was. Briar had no idea what exactly it contained, but she could feel its malevolence, and she had no doubt that the voices that still murmured in her ears were the souls of smugglers. She used a protection spell to contain Caspian's grimoire and the curse pouring from its pages, and then ran to Reuben's side.

Reuben was unconscious and partially upright, his shoulders and head propped against the wall. His breath was shallow and uneven, and he was horribly pale, but at least he was alive. Briar turned her attention to Caspian, and to her relief found he was alive too, but also unconscious, lying in a twisted heap under collapsed shelving. She rolled him gently over, checking his stab wound. Blood was trickling from it once more, but there were no new visible injuries, other than head wounds from where they had both struck the wall.

Briar shook Caspian gently, but although his eyes flickered beneath their lids, he didn't stir. She ran her hands inches above his body, familiar now with his energy, but something was horribly wrong. His life signs were low, and his magic a shadow of what it had once been. She reached for the nearest rug, wrapping it around him, and then returned to Reuben.

Briar had never felt so overwhelmed as she gazed at her friend. Reuben was vibrant, full of life and boundless energy, but now he was like a rag doll. Forcing herself to examine him dispassionately, she came to the same conclusion she had with Caspian. She rocked back on her heels, staring between them both. Whatever had happened had taken them both unawares, and had occurred within seconds of her arrival.

She needed to call the others.

CHAPTER 25

*A*very stood next to Alex, gazing in horror at their friends' motionless bodies, and then at the malevolent curse that struggled to free itself from the pages of the grimoire, as if it was alive.

Briar had waited for them on the threshold of Reuben's spell room, but she had been busy. She had already set her bag up that contained all of her herbs and gems for healing spells, and was going through it methodically, muttering to herself as she worked on the most appropriate spell to help.

"I think we should take them downstairs," she suggested, breaking in on Avery's thoughts. "Either a bedroom or the snug, where I can keep a close eye on them. Can you use witch-flight to take them?"

"I'm not sure that will be a good idea," she said. "They're unconscious, their magic is subdued, and I don't know how the flight might affect them. It probably won't, but I'm terrified of making things worse."

"That's fine," Alex reassured her. "Use air to cushion them, and we'll float them down the stairs." He turned to

Briar. "I think you're right. The snug is the best bet, rather than us all being spread out across this huge house."

He'd barely finished his sentence when El raced through the attic door, smeared with dirt and looking exhausted. She paused at the sight before her, and then tried to push past Alex, but he held her back.

"Just wait, El. The curse is still in that room, and we don't really know what it's done. We don't want you affected, too."

She glared at him. "Alex! That's Reuben lying there! I need to get to him."

"And you will. Let's just think this through, first."

Briar squeezed El's arm, trying to calm her down. "He's right. I've been in there and put a rudimentary protection around that grimoire, but the room feels weird, and so do they."

"Well, leaving them in there isn't going to do them any good!" El shot back, her blue eyes like ice.

"We're not going to," Avery said quickly. "But we need to be logical. We have no idea what's going on, and frankly, if Briar had arrived only five minutes earlier, she might have been caught up in this, too."

El took a deep breath, rubbing her hands over her face and smearing more dirt across her cheeks. "Sorry, you're right. I'm just worried. Look at him! Look at them both. They look so helpless. Is this what I looked like when I was cursed?"

Alex nodded. "I'm afraid so. But I don't think they *are* cursed. I think they've just been caught in the remnants of it!"

Avery summoned air, needing to do something, and she whisked it around the main attic, dispelling the rest of the green, watery quality that still lingered in the corners, and then directed the wind to Reuben. It wasn't easy to lift and cushion a body, even as skilled as she now was with air, but she worked slowly and patiently, and when Reuben was lifted sufficiently high enough, she brought him out of the room.

As soon as he was next to her, El took his hands. "He's so cold!"

"His spirit is buried deep within him," Briar explained. "So is Caspian's, and their energy is low. I'm planning a healing spell that should stabilise them."

Avery could tell Briar was very worried, and had a feeling things were worse than she was saying, but she concentrated on taking Reuben downstairs. "El, run ahead please. Grab blankets and sheets, and we'll make them comfortable on either the floor or the sofas."

El nodded, looking relieved at having something useful to do, and leaving Briar and Alex to talk about their options, left them to it.

It was fifteen minutes later when they all met again in the snug, with Caspian and Reuben laid next to each other in the corner of the room. El and Avery had made them as comfortable as possible, and Briar set up her herbs and potions.

"Can we help?" Alex asked her, watching anxiously.

"No," Briar said, shaking her head. "I'm going to stabilise their energies first. They're all over the place, and their magic is ebbing and flowing like the tide. It's so weird." She was on the floor, resting back on her heels, perplexed. "When I first arrived, I heard shouts…screams, really. I think I was hearing the smugglers' last moments." She shuddered, her dark hair tumbling around her face. "Now that I've had a chance to think about this, I believe the spell blasted out from the book, catching them completely unawares. Not only were they knocked unconscious, but the curse buried their spirits. It sounds weird, I know, but I think that's what I sense. I'm sure I can draw them back."

Alex studied them, arms across his chest. "That makes

sense." He glanced at Avery. "Come on. Let's head up there and try to work out what happened."

"Let's also cleanse the house while we're at it," she said. "Have you got any sage, Briar?"

"Sure." She rummaged in her bag and thrust a bundle of dried herbs at Avery. "It's my own blend, similar to what we used at Beltane."

Avery lit the smudge stick with a spark of magic, and as she and Alex made their way back to the attic, they worked a cleansing spell, flushing the remaining toxic energies away, and saving the last of it to purify Reuben's attic. They eyed Caspian's grimoire warily, edging as close as they could around the protection spell.

"I have never seen a spell like that before," Alex said, half admiringly, half fearful.

"It reminds me a bit of your rune spell," Avery admitted, thinking of how the runes lit up the air and wrapped around their victim.

The words were whirling above the pages, the lines of text writhing around each other and showing no signs of slowing down.

"True." He leaned closer, squinting at the spell.

"Can you make out any words?" she asked Alex.

"It's old, I know that. The English is old-fashioned from the odd word I can make out, but the page itself is blank—as if the words have lifted clean off it. And I think I can see water swirling around, too. Briar was telling me the whole attic felt like it was underwater when she arrived."

Avery stared into the words, mesmerised, seeing dark blues mixed in with the green at its heart, the spell pulsing and throwing off sparks. "It's like the *spell* is underwater."

Alex met her eyes briefly. "I think you're right. I'm going to see if I can make out a few lines," he said, settling himself onto a chair.

Avery examined the room while Alex studied the spell, looking for clues among the mess on the floor. She crouched next to a silver bowl, the remnants of ashes in it. She sniffed it carefully, smelling paper and the faint whiff of burnt herbs. "I think they were doing some kind of revealing spell, Alex." She frowned. "Where are the letters?"

Alex only grunted, so she searched on her own, righting objects as she went and restoring order to the room, but the letters had gone. They must have used them to find the spell; it was logical, after all.

She told Alex what she'd found and he grunted absently again, finally saying, "So, not only did their ancestors veil their intent in cryptic letters, but they hid the spell, too. It was either because they were ashamed of it, or it was too powerful to share." He leaned even closer, the green light illuminating his face.

"Or," Avery added, "they knew it had a tendency to backfire."

Alex shook his head. "No, I don't think that's it. Maybe they hid it as a means of stopping someone from reversing it?" He frowned, rubbing his stubble as he stared at the grimoire. "None of this makes sense!"

"What if their spirits are so low that Briar can't get them? Would you have to?"

"I don't want to, but if that's our only option, of course I will."

"I think we should summon Gil, instead. Tonight."

"We said we'd never do that."

"But there's still no sign of Helena! And," she added, "tomorrow is the anniversary of Coppinger's disappearance. Anything could happen!"

"All right, I'll think on it. But now, I just want to study this. And perhaps we should call Estelle."

"I suppose we should." She could already hear Estelle's

sharp, accusatory tone, and knew the reality would be so much worse.

"She's Caspian's sister, and will be well-versed with curse spells," Alex pointed out, but then he hesitated, too. "Let's see how far I get with this on my own."

"You're not studying it alone! I'll help, as soon as I've sealed the windows in some way," she said, moving to his side and squeezing his hand. "Two witches are better than one."

"That's what Serephina and Virginia thought, and look what they did!"

"They rid the world of Coppinger and his Cruel Gang! That's a plus, right?"

"*Was*," he said, turning back to the book. "Until now."

Newton studied Ethan James, and although they had barely started the interview, Newton was already annoyed with him. Moore stood at his side watching dispassionately, but he knew he was taking everything in.

They were in the corner of the large exhibition room at White Haven Museum, where half a dozen staff were putting the finishing touches on the displays. There was an atmosphere of controlled panic mixed with the buzz of anticipation and excitement. Newton had to admit that the exhibit looked impressive. Spotless glass cabinets displayed smuggling curios, and there were interactive displays too. There was a loud discussion at the far end of the room about what should be displayed more prominently. It seemed a little late for such discussions, but what did he know about how museums worked?

He tried to block the noise out as he again addressed Ethan. "As I said, Mr James, we do need your advice on the gold coins found at the scene of all three crimes. I'd also like to ask your opinion on the wooden chests that were found in Looe, and the human remains that were next to them. We feel you can offer us great insight, considering your speciality."

Ethan was a slim man in his forties, dressed in jeans and a shirt, attempting to look casually trendy. He was well-groomed and clean-shaven, and Newton was disappointed. He'd half expected him to look like Indiana Jones.

Ethan's lips narrowed. "This is a terrible time, I'm afraid. I am far too busy. As you can see, the exhibition opens tomorrow. I can recommend a couple of colleagues who can help."

"But I don't want to speak to your colleagues. I want to speak to *you*. You see, there's also the matter of your cousin, Jasmine, who was found in a mangled heap on Perranporth Beach."

Ethan blinked and swallowed. "Ah, yes. That was quite awful."

"Yes, it was. Were you close?"

He shook his head quickly. "No, not at all. I barely saw her."

"Oh, really? Even though she works at Charlestown with you? Her mother said that Jasmine had seen you recently, and seemed excited about something," Newton told him, an image of the crying, distraught woman filling his mind. "Any idea what that was?"

Ethan kept his expression carefully neutral. "No idea. I've been spending my time here, rather than Charlestown. I'd run into her briefly in Carlyon Bay, but that was all. It was so quick, I'd forgotten about it."

"She obviously had a passion for smuggling, like you."

Ethan was looking pale, but he was trying his best to bluster on. "Many of us do. That's not a crime. Er," he glanced around at his colleagues, who despite their busyness were watching them surreptitiously. "Should we go into my office?"

Now, he wanted his office! "Certainly. Lead the way."

He led them down a narrow set of stairs into the basement and opened the door to a windowless office, crammed with furniture and files, and by the time he sat behind his desk, gesturing Moore and Newton to sit too, he seemed to have composed himself.

"Right, you were saying?"

Newton threw the coins wrapped in evidence bags onto the desk. "These were found in the victims' mouths. What can you tell me about them?"

He looked reluctant to pick them up, but when he did, he examined them carefully. "Well, this one is a Spanish Doubloon, seventeenth century, and the other two are English Guineas. One is eighteenth and one nineteenth century." He put them back on the desk quickly, as if they might burn his fingers. "Not terribly uncommon, or particularly valuable."

"But if they were part of a hoard they would be, surely?"

"Well, that depends on how big the hoard was. It would be more valuable for historical purposes."

"It would also make an amazing display."

"Fascinating!" Ethan agreed. "But the chance of finding a hoard is incredibly low."

"I guess so." Newton studied him. Ethan looked uncomfortable now, his eyes darting around the room, and Newton said, "However, we believe the broken chests found in the cave in Looe contained treasure that was stolen recently, and we found evidence of more today in Wheal Droskyn. A few coins were left behind. We believe the thieves fled in panic. It was where Jasmine died."

"Wheal Droskyn?" Ethan's eyes were wide now, although

he was desperately trying to maintain a calm façade. He started to stutter. "Er, what led you there?"

"The adit that Jasmine's body was forced through. She had a horrible death. Violent. Painful." Newton leaned forward, arms resting on the desk. "Are you okay, Mr James? You look unwell. Would you like some water?"

"No! I'm okay. Obviously, I'm upset at the manner of my cousin's death. Any idea who did this?"

"We have our suspicions." Newton decided to push him further. He'd put money on Ethan being involved. He was pale and sweating now, shuffling uncomfortably in his seat. "And we also believe that Jasmine's deceased boyfriend, Miles, was involved, too. I suspect they were behind the theft in Looe. This is what she must have been so excited about. And we believe there are accomplices."

Ethan pulled himself together. "Why on Earth would you think that?"

"Well, there's no evidence of the treasure in the house they shared together. No maps or papers that indicate how they knew where to go. And of course, the treasure in Wheal Droskyn is gone. If Jasmine was on her own, the treasure would still be there, surely."

"I suppose that's logical. But," he laughed incredulously, "I think your imagination is running away with you. I doubt they found a hoard of any kind. There would have been remnants only, the rest stolen long ago."

"The broken locks happened very recently. And the cave in the mine was also a recent find. Was Jasmine involved in this exhibit? Could she have found an old map in the new material that was discovered here?"

Ethan laughed, but there a calculating expression behind his eyes. "Treasure maps! Please, Detective, I think that's a little far-fetched. No, she wasn't involved here, and everything we've found is upstairs, on display." He stood abruptly, his chair scraping against the floor. "Now, if you'll excuse me, I have an exhibition to finish. We open tomorrow, and I'm anxious that it should be perfect."

Newton and Moore stood too, and as Ethan came around the desk, they shook hands. "Thank you for your time, Mr James, but if you do think of anything else, please let us know."

"Of course!" He hustled them out of the door and up the stairs, and Newton watched him enter the exhibition, amused.

He turned to Moore. "Verdict?"

"Guilty. He's in it up to his neck."

"Let's have him watched tonight. I bet he'll be scurrying off somewhere as soon as he's able to."

CHAPTER 26

Caspian was lost in a sea of green-blue mist.

He was formless, unable to discern arms from legs, or fingers from toes. He couldn't even feel any sensations, and for the first time in days, was free from the pain of his stab wound and bruises. With growing horror, he realised his spirit had left his body.

But he wasn't spirit-walking. There was no silver cord tying him to his body. He was somewhere else, and he had a horrible feeling he was in the spirit world. If the spirits of the smugglers found him, they would surely kill him, severing his spirit forever from his body, trapping him here.

Unless he was already dead.

He tried not to panic and concentrated on his surroundings, finally hearing distant voices. They were familiar. *Were they voices of the dead? No.* It was Briar, and then Avery and Alex, but he couldn't make out what they said.

That meant he couldn't be dead. He was hovering somewhere in between.

What the hell had happened? Trying to think was hard.

He couldn't focus, and his thoughts drifted randomly. He'd been working a spell, but something else had happened.

Reuben! He'd been working with Reuben, and something had exploded from the pages of the grimoire. The voices of his friends were reassuring, grounding him, but he needed to know if Reuben was here. *But was this really the spirit world, or something different? Why did he feel as if he was drifting on a tide?* Drawing on the voices from above like an anchor, he cast around for Reuben's magical signature, and finally felt it. Relieved, he drifted towards it like a leaf on a current, shocked to hear Reuben's voice in his head.

"Caspian?"

"Reuben! Are you okay?"

"I'm great, except for the fact that I can't feel my body."

Great? Great was odd…

Caspian continued, regardless. *"We've left them behind. That bloody spell."* Now that he was talking to Reuben, he had a sense of his shape and being, which helped ground him even further as he found his footing in this strange place. *"We need to get back to our bodies before we're discovered."*

"By who?"

"The smugglers' ghosts, you idiot! We're in their world—I think."

Even in the spirit world, he could discern Reuben's dry scepticism. *"Pull the other one, Caspian."*

"Look around! Where the hell else do you think we are?"

"I'm on a beach."

"What?" Caspian looked around him, confused. *"No, you're not. We're in the middle of nothingness!"*

"No, I'm on a tropical beach. It's so warm! I'm watching the sea right now."

"I thought you said you couldn't feel your body?"

"I can't, but I know I'm on a beach."

"That doesn't make sense."

"*Neither do you.*"

Of all the people to be stuck in some sodding limbo-land with, he was with Reuben-bloody-surf-mad-Jackson! "*Reuben! Focus! How can you be on a beach when we were in your attic only minutes ago?*"

"*You were in my attic? Weird.*"

"*We were looking for the curse that killed Coppinger!*"

Silence fell, and then he said, "*Oh yeah, I thought that was a dream.*"

"*No! That is reality. Your beach is a dream.*"

"*Come and look at it, then you'll see.*"

Reuben's voice seemed to be drifting away from him, and Caspian realised that Reuben could be dying. Or was he already dead? Was that why he was on a beach and Caspian wasn't?

Perhaps, Caspian reflected, he should be grateful for the weird, green mist rather than being in his happy place. Where would that even be? Avery's arms, that's where. He could feel her now, her softness, her slim body within his hold, her lips that tasted like honey. He'd drown in her, and he'd die happy.

Alex's eyes burned with fatigue, and he sat back in his chair, frustrated.

"I can make out a couple of lines of this spell, at best!"

"More than I can," Avery confessed, leaning back in the chair and stretching. "I think we have to admit that we can't do this."

"I hate being defeated by a spell."

"We're not good at curses, and there's a lot of elemental water in this. That's one of my weakest elements."

Alex exhaled heavily. "Mine, too. At least we've got a feel for the shape of it, even if we don't know the details."

"Come on," Avery said, rising to her feet. "I'm starving, and I want a glass of wine. No, *need* a glass of wine. And we should update the others on our lack of progress."

Alex glanced at his watch, groaning when he saw the time. "Shit, it's after seven. No wonder we're knackered and starving. Let's go downstairs and see who else has arrived." He looked around at the attic, properly focussing on it for the first time in the last couple of hours, and realised the malevolence and despair he'd felt earlier had vanished. "You did a good job of cleansing this, Avery."

"I had to. It felt toxic."

So many things here reminded him of Gil. "This must be weird for Reuben, being surrounded by Gil's stuff."

"*Their* stuff."

"Yeah, but still." He looked at Avery's tired and frustrated expression, her wild red hair soft on her shoulders. "I'm not sure I could stand to see all your stuff around me if anything happened to you. I think the memories would be too painful."

She stepped forward into his arms, snuggling against his chest. "I know what you mean, but I'd find it comforting, too."

He inhaled her fresh scent of musk and roses, and nuzzled her neck. "You make all this worthwhile."

She leaned back to look up at him, puzzled. "What do you mean?"

"Magic is great, but it's nothing without someone to share it with." His fingers trailed across her cheek. "I'm lucky. Seeing Gil's spirit again reminded me of him and Alicia, and it still burns me how awful that was—her deception. Their lies to each other."

"I agree. But we won't do that."

She sounded so certain, and yet she had kissed Caspian and kept that from him. His doubt must have showed, because she tightened her grip around him.

"Caspian kissed *me*," she reminded him forcefully, "just in case that's going through your head, and I told you about it! And I guarantee it won't happen again!"

"I know. I trust you, but it still niggles me. Especially since I've come to realise that Caspian isn't going anywhere. He's one of us now, in some weird annoying way." He wanted to say he was like a bad rash, but he decided Avery wouldn't appreciate that.

"And we're stronger for having him as a friend."

"As long as we don't have to put up with Estelle, too."

"Oh, she hates us, so we won't." She stretched up to kiss him. "Come on, mister. Food time."

When they reached the bottom of the stairs, El was just closing the front door, and white plastic bags were on the floor around her, filled with cartons.

"El! You bloody superstar. I smell curry!" Alex hurried forward and picked up a couple of bags as she turned to smile at him. She looked tired, but seemed a little less bleak than she had earlier. And cleaner. "You've showered!"

"I had to. I stank of Wheal Droskyn," she said, picking up two bags and handing them to Avery, and then another two for herself before walking down the hall. "Have you had success?"

Avery shook her head. "No, other than identifying a couple of lines. We'll update you when we're all together." She gestured to the bags. "Why have we got so much food?"

"Because *everyone* is here! Ash is down in the billiard room, so I'll take some down to him."

They stopped in the kitchen, finding beer for Alex and wine for Avery, and when they entered the snug, they found that Ben, Cassie, and Dylan had just arrived, the room full of chatter. Alex glanced at Reuben and Caspian, but they were still lying unconscious under the blankets.

He greeted the others, and then said to Briar, "No luck, then?"

"Not yet." She gestured to the gemstones she'd used on various points of their bodies, and the herbs burning steadily in bowls around them, their fragrance scenting the room. "I'm drawing out their spirit, and stabilising their energies, but they're slow to respond. Did you have luck with the spell?"

Alex rolled his eyes. "No. But from the couple of lines I could read, it's a doozy. Let's hope Caspian can decipher it. Before we get into it, let's eat."

After a flurry of activity they all settled themselves into the snug, plates perched on laps, with the various naan breads and accompaniments spread across the coffee table. A low fire was burning in the grate, and Alex looked outside for the first time in hours, seeing that rain was falling heavily now, and a sea mist had rolled in, obscuring the grounds from view.

He settled in his chair and started to eat, listening to El update them on her day.

Ben groaned. "I can't believe we missed another spriggan!"

"But it sounds like you've recorded the essence of one," Briar pointed out. She was still seated next to the two unconscious witches, keeping a close eye on them while she ate what seemed to Alex like a tiny portion of food. "I can't wait to see the footage."

Dylan mumbled through a mouthful of curry, "I'll put it on in a minute."

Alex turned to El. "Did SOCO find anything while you were there?"

She frowned and shrugged as she tore a piece of naan.

"They certainly searched the place thoroughly, and they took my footprints and fingerprints to rule me out, but I don't know. I certainly couldn't see anything obvious."

"Did you pick up any magic signatures you might recognise again?" Avery asked.

"No. The place felt swept clean. It was only the news from the spriggan himself that told us anything."

Cassie put her empty plate on the table, and said, "So there were two men and two women, one of whom was Jasmine—who is now dead."

El nodded. "Yep, and we have no idea who the others are, except for the fact that the woman was blonde. Silver-haired as the spriggan said." She shrugged again. "I'm presuming Mariah, but I hate to jump to conclusions. Newton hopes to come by later, so we'll see if he has any updates. He was going to interview Ethan. Now your turn," she said to Alex and Avery.

Alex said, "The spell is complex, heavily rooted in elemental water that harnesses the power of the sea, and it's definitely a curse. I can understand why Serephina needed help to execute it."

"But why has it affected Caspian and Reuben?" El asked.

"They hid the curse with the aid of another spell—obviously a strong one. We think," he glanced at Avery, "that they did a kind of unveiling spell, and when that lifted, it knocked them out." A thought struck him. "Maybe they had to veil the spell because it was so strong, rather than hide it just for the sake of it. It's struggling to get off the page now, like it's alive."

He wasn't sure he'd explained it very well, but the others nodded anyway, and Cassie asked, "Is that common, for a spell to try to escape like a living thing?"

"Bloody hell, no!" Avery exclaimed, horrified. "I can't imagine anything worse. I can only think that it was a regular spell that they embellished, and it just became too much to control. Hence, the spell to contain it." She sipped her wine, looking thoughtful. "I couldn't make out any of the text, but Alex could—just a couple of lines. Enough so that we know it's a very ugly curse." She referred to the notes that she pulled from her jeans pocket. "It's quite chilling. It says, 'As your spirit leaves your body, it will be forever bound to the object of your desire.' We're presuming their desire is gold."

"Seriously?" Cassie exclaimed. "Chilling doesn't cover it *at all*!"

"I guess that explains why the spirits want vengeance," El pointed out. She had settled into an armchair next to the fire, and was sipping her beer, all the while keeping an eye on Reuben. "I would, after that!"

Briar leaned forward, her elbows on her knees. "Was it directed at Coppinger and all his men?"

"Hard to say. The only other line I could make out was, 'To all who have lost and failed to grow old, thou shall know their pain a thousand fold.'"

"A thousand fold?" Cassie repeated. "If that's all you can read, what else is in that horrible spell?"

A silence fell on the room as they absorbed the enormity of the curse, and Ben nodded slowly. "So what now?"

"Great question," Alex admitted. "We know there's a curse, we assume it involves Coppinger, and we know it's horrible, which helps us understand some of what's happening. Potentially, when they found the first of Coppinger's treasure in Looe, they disturbed the spriggan, and maybe the spirits of the three dead men. This could have been the trigger event for the other spirits to rise, maybe accidentally at first—"

"And then Mariah decided to strengthen the ghosts," Avery cut in. She shook her head. "I still don't understand how she knew this was related to Reuben and Caspian. I mean, did she decide that making the ghosts stronger would be fun, just for the sake of it? Or was it a calculated move to have her revenge on us? She's never liked us, and feels Caspian has let her down."

"Like Caspian said," Alex reminded her, "she's like me. She can commune with spirits. She must have talked to Coppinger...or his men. They would have told her what happened."

"Which means they would have known who cursed them," Briar said. "It must have happened up close and personal. But there's still much we don't know."

"Like what Mariah did to make the ghosts stronger," Alex admitted. "I'm not sure how she's done that." Alex glanced across to Reuben and Caspian. "What's worrying me most is that we haven't encountered Coppinger's spirit yet. He could be stronger than all the others. And the anniversary of his death is tomorrow. But this doesn't answer your question, Ben." He turned to face him. "Now, we need to stop the spirits and send them back to where they belong. And that means dealing with Mariah."

Dylan stirred. "Time for some light relief, I think." He plugged his USB into the TV and in a few seconds had found the file. "I haven't brought it all. I'm sure seeing big, magical clouds above certain places doesn't interest you much, but this is Perranporth earlier this week."

The film was shot on the beach, looking up towards the cliff top. Initially all it showed was a hazy blue glow along the cliffs, brighter at certain points. Then a flare of light flashed across the screen, leaving the image of a giant on the cliff top, two arms and two legs clearly visible. It seemed to watch the sea, and then as it turned they saw that it carried what appeared to be a club in its hands. It strode inland, taking gigantic strides, and then vanished into nothing again.

Alex could scarcely believe his eyes. "Holy shit."

Dylan was grinning from ear to ear. "Impressive, right? You wait until we put this up on the website!"

Avery was still looking at the screen. "By the Gods! Are you telling me that *thing* is contained within that little spriggan that attacked us?"

"And me!" El said, half horrified, half impressed. "Amazing." And then she stopped laughing and said, "The enemy of my enemy is my friend…right?"

"It's too late to be philosophical," Ben groaned.

"No, it's not. The spriggans killed Jasmine because another spriggan died. It loathed 'the silver one,' which I took to mean that Mariah killed the spriggan. Maybe we could use its anger to help us?"

"I'm not sure," Alex said warily. "The ones we met didn't seem that bright or willing to listen to reason."

"I'd forgotten you encountered *two*!" El said. "Maybe they were mated? To lose your mate, or even a friend, is good motivation." Her face fell. "Mind you, I wouldn't—no, *couldn't* —go back down that mine again. It was a maze! A bloody death trap."

"You might not need to," Dylan suggested. "The creature clearly comes to the surface sometimes. Something to think about, I guess."

"I thought you were going to film Gull Island again?" Alex asked.

Dylan looked doubtful. "I will, but it's cold and wet out there now, and I'm not sure if we'll pick up anything."

A groan disturbed their conversation, and they all turned to look anxiously at Reuben and Caspian. Both of them now displayed a sheen of sweat on their pale faces, and Briar dropped to her knees next to them, running her hands above their bodies.

"We're losing them, I can feel it. It's like their spirits are sinking. We need to help them."

"How?" Alex asked, already moving to her side.

"We lend them our strength." She glanced around the room. "Quick! Circle, everyone. Now!"

～

Caspian's thoughts were suddenly pierced by Briar's sharp voice, and the notion of Avery's body disappeared. Briar was calling to him, and he could feel his body again, sort of.

Part of him hated it. He'd never felt so happy, so content or complete. He tried to dive back into his dream state again, but Briar's voice became louder, more insistent, and he felt a tug on his body as his aches and pains started to return.

As quickly as Avery disappeared, he thought of Reuben and shouted his name, hearing a faint cry in return. He had the feeling that if he followed Briar's voice right now, he'd be back in his body, but then he'd lose Reuben, and he didn't know if he could hear her, too.

Deciding to ignore her voice, he focussed on Reuben, and as if he was washed up by an incoming tide, he found himself on Reuben's beach, blinking in the sun.

Reuben was standing on golden sand, surveying the sea, and he grinned at Caspian. "*You made it!*"

"*We have to leave!*"

"*Caspian, you're such a killjoy. Let me teach you to surf.*"

"*I don't want to learn to fucking surf! You're dying!*"

Caspian's exasperation fuelled him. He was losing Reuben; *El* would lose Reuben. He was not going to be responsible for another Jackson's death. Rage filled him, and without knowing quite how he did it, he tackled Reuben, knocking him to the sand, instantly feeling his own body become more real as he sat on Reuben's chest and stared down at his shocked face.

"*Dude?*"

"*Reuben, listen to Briar!*"

"*You're hallucinating!*"

And then Briar's voice broke through to them both, clear and commanding, and Reuben looked around, shocked.

"*How did you do that?*"

"*I didn't!*"

Caspian knew he was in danger of slipping from the beach again, while Reuben just lay there, like a grinning idiot. He needed to anger him into action.

"*You know why I killed your brother? Because he was weak! And you are weak! Your whole family is weak, just like your friends.*"

Reuben suddenly focussed. "*What did you say?*"

"*I said, I killed Gil deliberately, and would do it again in a heartbeat.*"

Caspian was still kneeling on Reuben, but now Reuben reared up beneath him, throwing him to the side, and then punched him, again and again. "*You bastard.*"

Inexplicably, Caspian felt his lip split and his head thud against the sand, but he sneered at Reuben. "*You bet I am!*" And for good measure, he punched him back.

The beach vanished instantly, and so did Reuben.

"*Reuben! Where are you?*"

"*Where are you, you shit?*"

"*Right here! Can't you find me, you idiot?*"

Caspian could feel Reuben's rage, and also confusion, but before he could say anything else, Briar's voice resounded around them as she summoned them. Voices cradled him, and then Caspian was sharply aware of feeling his aching wound, the warmth of indoors, and a hard surface beneath him.

His eyes flew open, and he took a sharp breath in, shooting upright. "Reuben!"

For a moment, Caspian couldn't focus, and then he became aware of a circle of people around him. But it wasn't them he was looking for. He twisted in panic, and then saw Reuben lying next to him, still out cold. *Pain.* That was what Reuben needed.

Without thinking, he punched Reuben's wounded shoulder, and heard a gasp run around the watching circle. But he ignored them, holding his breath until Reuben's eyes flew open and he shouted out, "That fucking hurt!"

Caspian started laughing hysterically, and fell back on the floor. *Job done.*

CHAPTER 27

Reuben looked at Briar, and then at the drink in her hand. "I said I want a bloody whiskey, not some hideous herbal tea!"

She looked outraged. "I've just saved your bloody life, you ungrateful shit. You need tea to strengthen you!"

He took a deep breath. "I'm not ungrateful, but I am in shock, and whiskey helps shock. And for the Gods' sake, give Caspian some, too. Look at his face. He couldn't look more disgusted with that horrific concoction."

They were in the snug, and he and Caspian were sitting in the big, comfy armchairs on either side of the blazing fire, while their friends sat around them watching the exchange. Outside, rain was pouring down, and night had fallen.

Caspian cradled his cup, the steam rising around his face, but he was openly laughing at Reuben. "Maybe you should listen to Briar. This tea is actually quite good."

"Thank you, Caspian," Briar said, throwing him a beaming smile, before glaring at Reuben. "You were nearly dead! This tea that I have so lovingly made for you is restorative."

"But whiskey would be better."

"If you drink the tea, I will get you a whiskey."

"Blackmail?"

"You bet. And you won't get curry, either, until it's gone."

He looked across the room, seeing everyone looking amused. "You all think this is so funny, don't you?"

"No, actually," El said, the smile slipping from her face. "You scared the crap out of us. Drink the tea, and I will bring you whiskey. And curry."

He grunted with annoyance and stuck his hand out. "All right. Give me the cup, and while I make my eyes bleed with this stuff, you can tell us what the hell's going on."

Cassie was tittering. "You're so funny."

"Don't encourage him," El told her crossly, before turning back to him. "Listen closely while we explain."

Ten minutes later, Reuben's confusion had vanished, and with a whiskey in hand he felt more like his normal self, although his shoulder really ached. He remembered the lead up to the spell, although that was more like a dream now.

"Elemental water, you say? That might explain why I was on a beach."

"And why I felt underwater," Caspian added. "It was so odd, like I was floating in some vast ocean. And you're a water witch, Reuben. You probably felt comfortable in it, in some weird way—hence, the beach."

"Your energies were ebbing and flowing," Briar told them, "just like a tide. You definitely were caught in the edges of that curse."

Reuben looked at Caspian, who now had his own whiskey, and was staring into the fire. "Sorry I hit you on the beach."

He lifted his gaze and shrugged. "Sorry I provoked you. It seemed my only option. I'm sorry I punched your shoulder, too."

Reuben grimaced as he gingerly felt his wound. "It really aches. But I guess it worked." He winced as he realised his head ached too, and he patted it, feeling for a wound. "Why does my head hurt?"

"You whacked the wall," Alex said. "We found you in a crumpled heap in the attic."

"Oh, that explains it." He sighed heavily. "At least we succeeded. We found the curse. So, what now?"

"Well," Avery said, "we need to decide on our next plan. Tomorrow is the anniversary of the curse. The spirits are getting stronger. We've been discussing the options, and essentially we'll have to send the spirits back to where they belong. Which could mean facing Mariah."

"And where do we do that?" Reuben asked.

"Well," Alex said, "it seems like there's a lot of activity on Gull Island. I think that's where we need to go." He nodded towards the three parapsychologists. "They've picked up a lot of energy over there."

"Reuben and I have already discussed this," Caspian said, "and I think there could well be another passageway leading from the main cave, under the crates. And last night, the spirits came from the glasshouse."

Reuben nodded. "He's right. We never fully explored under there. Unless, of course, there's a whole separate cave and entrance, which is possible, but unlikely."

"Why unlikely?" El asked. "There could have been a rock fall over the years, which would have disguised any cave entrance, or filled a previously useable cove. And they could have been linked, regardless. This whole country is riddled with caves and tunnels for smuggling—the islands, more so! They were perfect pirate hangouts."

"We should go and check," Dylan suggested, clearly getting excited. "We could end this tonight!"

"We?" Caspian asked. "How are you going to help?"

Dylan folded his arms across his chest as he looked belligerently at Caspian. "I may not have magic, but I can help!"

"Whoa!" Alex said. "Of course you can, but slow down. We're not just marching down there until we have a plan. We need to banish the spirits, and try to stop Ethan and Mariah. Ethan should be easy, but Mariah? That's a different matter."

"And of course, if there's more treasure, spriggans may be there, too," Briar reminded them.

"This morning," Reuben told his friends, "we walked through the possibilities, and think that when Coppinger tried to escape from what he realised was a trap, the spell extended to his ship." He nodded towards the window and the darkness outside. "They could have run the ship aground on Gull Island."

"Surely the wreckage and their bodies would have been found," El said.

"Depends how big the storm was, and if no one went there for days... Well, the remains could have been swept out to sea."

Briar was kneeling on the floor in front of the fire, and she said, "So any treasure that's there now would have been there before the night they cast the curse?"

"Why not?" Reuben said. "Coppinger was clearly in the habit of stashing his treasure in out of the way places, as security."

"But Gull Island? That seems crazy," Dylan pointed out. "Your family or smugglers working with you could have found it."

"I don't know." He rubbed his face, suddenly weary. "It seems deviously genius to me. You hide it right under your enemies' noses. And it's accessible for an easy getaway when you have your own ship—Black Prince."

Avery grimaced. "I've got a headache, and I'm tired, but I feel we should be doing *something*!"

Ben asked, "Can't you just do a spell now to end it all?"

Avery looked nervous. "It's possible, but that would entail doing something big—like the curse, but not a curse—and I'm not sure it would work."

"Why not?" Dylan asked.

Alex answered. "There are many components. The spirits, the spriggans, Mariah… And we still don't really know how the curse works. A couple of lines isn't enough to understand it."

A knock at the door interrupted them, and El hurried to answer, quickly returning with Newton, who looked surprisingly cheerful.

"Good news?" Briar asked him, as he found a seat on the sofa.

"Very. Ethan is shifty as hell, and we're following him." He grinned broadly. "He's just turned up at Mariah's place in Looe. I think they'll be on the move again soon."

"What makes you say that?" Alex asked.

"Because in our interview today, I told him we suspected Jasmine and Miles were involved in stealing treasure and had accomplices, and I think he won't wait. If there's more to find, he'll go after it tonight. Or try to hide what they have. My officers will call if they stir. In the meantime," he sniffed, "can I smell curry?"

Avery paced the attic room, watching Alex attempt to see Mariah using his scrying bowl. He'd been trying for well over fifteen minutes, and he hadn't moved a muscle.

She shivered inside Reuben's borrowed sweatshirt. It was

cool in the attic, the sound of the rain loud on the roof and through the windows that had no glass in them. She had sealed them with a protection spell, but it wasn't really designed to insulate against weather.

At the other end of the attic, Dylan had set up his thermal imaging camera, focussing on Gull Island. He too was locked in his own world, and she was grateful for it. It was dark and quiet up here, and it gave her time to think. All the others were still downstairs, no doubt discussing their options. She eyed Caspian's grimoire warily. The book lay open, the curse still circling above the page in its ghoulish green light, and again she tried to work out why.

They'd discussed many possibilities, so many that her head hurt. But the only one that really made sense, to her at least, was that the curse was still active, and although it didn't seem tied to the treasure they had already found, she had a feeling it was still affecting Gull Island in some way. She was also convinced that Mariah had made the smugglers' ghosts stronger, and that Helena had become aware of that and in her effort to intervene had been captured.

But what were they doing now?

She walked to the window and looked towards Gull Island in the distance. The mist had cleared a little, and the dark bulk of the island could just be seen through the drizzle. It looked so innocuous, and she hoped that whatever Dylan had seen before had gone. She glanced across to him, but he was transfixed with the image, a pair of headphones clamped to his ears, oblivious to her presence.

A groan drew her attention to Alex and she turned to him, seeing him flex his shoulders, finally looking up with a sigh. "Nothing."

She headed to his side. "Nothing at all?"

He rubbed his forehead and leaned back in the chair, his expression hard to read in the subdued light. "Nope. I searched over Looe looking for magical signatures, but there's nothing, and I was focussing on the area she lives, too. She has a veil of protection over her, much like us. Either that or they've already left, but I'm sure Newton would have been told."

"Okay. So we don't know what they might be planning, but I guess that shouldn't stop us. Dylan is right. We have to go to Gull Island, tonight."

"I agree. If Coppinger's power is growing and he's planning on attacking Reuben and Caspian again—and maybe the town—I'd rather stop it now."

"Even if we find nothing, at least we'll have ruled it out," Avery reasoned.

"I'll eat my shorts if you find nothing!" Dylan appeared next to her, as silent as a cat, and Avery jumped.

"Bloody hell! What are you, some kind of ninja?"

Dylan slid his hand around her arm and tugged her. "Come and see this. You too, Alex." He led them back across the attic and showed them the screen attached to his camera. "Look at that! That's even bigger than it was last night!"

Avery stared at the image, trying to understand what she was looking at. "What's that thing that looks like a thundercloud?"

"A build-up of psychic energy, and it's over the entire island." He pointed at the screen. "Look. It doesn't bleed over the sea, so I know it's not to do with the weather. The sea itself is cold, that's why it's blue."

"Crap," Alex said. "You say it's getting bigger?"

"Yep, and denser. But don't ask me what that means. Nothing good, I'm sure." He frowned. "If I was to hazard a guess, I'd say it meant the presence of many spirits, but I'll check with Ben."

Alarmed, Avery asked, "Alex, is there any way to banish these ghosts from here?"

"Nope. I have to be there."

Avery looked at the curse spell again, pulsing at the far end of the room. "That thing is still going, and I think while it did its job well back then, I don't think it's helping us now. It's keeping the spirits active, somehow."

"Ably assisted by Mariah," Alex said. "She's obviously reached some kind of compromise with them."

"Yeah, she's promised them Reuben and Caspian," Avery huffed.

"Oh, crap! Look," Dylan said, pointing at the screen again. He directed their attention to a point on the right of the island where a shape was coming into view. "If I'm not mistaken, that looks like the bow of a ship."

He was right. The image was blurry, but it did look like a ship, and within a few seconds, they could see a sail too, as the whole thing slid into view.

"Please tell me that's a regular ship just cruising past," Alex said, his voice strained.

Avery blinked as if to clear her vision, and looked from the camera out of the window and back again. "Er, I don't think it is, Alex."

His voice rose with alarm. "Are you saying that's a ghost pirate ship?"

Dylan tried to sound horrified, but he wasn't really. He could barely disguise his glee. "Yes, yes it really is!"

Caspian stood in the attic with everyone else, including Ash, and like the others, was watching the screen with a mixture of amazement and horror.

"Well, that settles it," Briar said, determination radiating from her small frame. "We have to go there now."

"And do what, exactly?" Newton asked.

"Get rid of them!"

"Armed with cutlasses and your own bloody pirate ship? This isn't the Pirates of the bloody Caribbean!"

"Not even the *Pirates of Penzance*?" Dylan asked cheekily.

"No!" he shot back.

Briar glared at Newton. "I know that! I don't mean I'm going to get on the phantasm ghost ship. I mean the island. We have the Empusa's swords, one Nephilim, a witch who's good at banishing spells, and the rest of us who wield elemental magic!" She rolled her shoulders and jutted her chin out. "We are more than a match for Mariah!"

"Actually," Caspian said, hating to admit it, "I can't fight with my wound. It's much better than it was, thanks to you, but I'm not at full strength. I think I should tackle that thing." He nodded to his grimoire.

"I'm not sure that's a good idea. Finding it nearly killed you!"

He smiled at her affectionately. He had started to think of Briar as a little sister, a much more pleasant version than his real one. "I'm good at curses, remember? I'll be fine."

"What are you planning to do?" Avery asked him, turning her back on the window.

"Like you said, it's active, and still has something to do with what's going on now. If I can break it, or reverse it, then it will help you banish them." He directed this at Alex, and then looked at Ash and El. "I know you have the swords, but you can't dispatch them all."

Ash stirred, his hand on the Empusa's hilt. "I'd ask my brothers to come, but Shadow, Gabe, Nahum, and Niel are in London. They left today. Barak and Eli are at the warehouse, and Zee is in the pub."

"And that's where I want him to stay," Alex said, eyeing the ship across the bay. So far it seemed anchored in deep water, but they had wondered if it might attack White Haven. "Having a Nephilim in town might be useful."

"We'll obviously come with you," Ben said, his tone brooking no argument. "You taught us simple banishing spells, and we have some of your other portable spells with us in the van."

"You carry them with you?" Reuben asked.

"Of course. We never know when we might need them."

"While I don't want to leave you alone," Reuben said to Caspian, "I'm not staying here! My shoulder is fine!" he said to Briar, before she could complain.

"Actually, Reuben," Caspian said, "I think I'll need you."

His eyes flashed belligerently. "Why?"

"Because our ancestors fashioned this curse together. There's a lot of elemental water in it, and you're the water witch. I think if they cast it together, we need to break it together."

Reuben fell silent, his mouth working, before he finally said, "But you're the curse expert."

It seemed to Caspian that Reuben looked suddenly uncertain, some of his natural confidence shaken and a wariness behind his eyes, but Caspian pressed on. "Yes, but I'm an air witch and one of my weakest elements is water. I need you." He nodded at the others. "They need you. Here."

Reuben glanced at El, and she nodded encouragingly. "I think he's right. Besides, one bad fall on your dodgy shoulder could mean you're vulnerable. And Caspian shouldn't be alone here."

Reuben swung his gaze back to Caspian, resentment oozing from him. "Okay. If I have to."

Caspian thought they had achieved a new level of friendship today, but now he doubted that. However, this wasn't the time to be second-guessing. "Thank you." He addressed the others. "What will you do if Mariah and Ethan turn up?

Potentially, there's more treasure there that they have probably left until last because of the curse. Like you said, Newton, you've forced their hand. If they don't get it now, they might lose out."

Avery didn't hesitate. "We'll deal with them, too."

CHAPTER 28

*A*very stood in the large cave under Gull Island, currently illuminated by a dozen witch-lights, and wondered if they'd got it wrong.

She was there with El, Briar, Alex, Newton, Ash, and the three investigators, all armed to varying degrees. Newton and Ben held shotguns, El and Ash had the Empusa's swords, and Dylan carried the bag of portable spells that she and the other witches had made. They had proceeded cautiously down the tunnel, Ash leading the way, all of them wary of meeting vengeful ghosts, but so far everything was quiet.

Too quiet.

"If we can't find this mysterious passage that we think exists but have no proof of, then we're stuck!" Newton said, annoyed.

They had already pulled a large portion of the old wooden boxes out of the way, and so far the ground underneath was solid earth.

Alex looked up from the area he'd been searching. "Can you save the frustration until we've finished, Newton?"

"We're losing time! Ethan could be up to anything right

now, and I'd never know because there's no bloody coverage in this godforsaken pit!"

Newton's team hadn't seen any movement before they entered the tunnels, and everyone knew he was frustrated.

"Have you got any better leads?"

Newton scowled. "No."

"So stop whining, and help us search!"

Avery suppressed a grin and also returned to moving the boxes out of the way, directing them over the heads of the searchers using a current of air and on to the area that they'd already searched. The magical energy was strong in here, building in pressure around them, so despite Newton's complaints and Avery's own doubts, they were in the right place...or thereabouts.

"Maybe we need to get on the beach," El suggested, her hands on her back as she arched backwards to ease the kinks.

"Good idea," Avery agreed. "We might be able to detect a kind of magical path to the centre of the energy."

Alex straightened up, looking doubtful. "I'm not sure we should split up."

"We'd save time," Ben said.

Briar marched decisively to the middle of the cave, closed her eyes, and wiggled her bare feet into the ground. "I'm going to feel for changes in the earth, to see if I can detect another tunnel or something. Just ignore me while I work."

"And I," El said, ignoring Alex's doubts, "am going to head to the beach."

Avery nodded and headed to her side. "Great. I'll come with you."

"Wait," Dylan called over. "I'll come, too. We can use my thermal camera again. It's picking up nothing significant here."

Avery could hear Alex muttering under his breath about headstrong women as she left with El, and a few minutes later they were in the smaller cave where Reuben had been attacked. The sounds of the rain and the sea crashing on the beach were loud as they edged through the scrubby bushes that veiled the cave. As soon as they were in the open, the wind hit them, as did spray from the thundering surf and the heavy rain. They were drenched in seconds.

"Shit!" El exclaimed, raising her voice to be heard. She looked at Dylan. "It's wild out here. Can you use that thing in the wet?"

"Not this bloody wet," he said, rain dripping off the end of his nose. "I'll head to the entrance, in the shelter."

"Wait!" Avery pulled a current of air around them, using it like a shield, and combined it with a protection spell, remembering that Eve had used something similar when she was conjuring the storm. All of a sudden, they were in a protected bubble, while the elements raged around them.

Dylan looked around, startled. "Wow! That's super cool!"

Avery smiled, feeling incredibly smug. "Yes, it is. I have actually never tried that before!"

"In that case, super brain," El said, "Is there some kind of spell we can use that can show us magic in a thermal way like Dylan can do?"

"You're the fire witch, you tell me!"

"Fair point," she said, slicking her wet hair away from her face, and issuing a little warmth from her palm to take the worst of the water out of it. "Challenge accepted. Just let me think a moment."

Giving El a few minutes of silence, Avery moved to Dylan's side. He was panning the camera over the rocks and beach to either side, and then he swept it up to the cliffs behind them.

"Bloody hell, you can see it more clearly from here," he said, pointing up and to the right. "The epicentre appears to be over there."

Avery nodded. "Further inland. Have you checked the sea for the ship?"

"Ooh, no." He turned around, panning across the ocean, and within seconds they could see it. Avery's heart faltered.

The ship had two long masts and was fully rigged with sails, and its long, spar-like bow protruded from the front of the ship. It sat steadily in the sea, unmoved by the strong winds and the high waves.

"Shit! That's big!" Avery squeaked out.

"Very. I believe that's a sloop." He squinted at the image. "I wonder if that's Black Prince."

"I don't care what it is, as long as it stays there."

"You know, I think I can see figures on it."

"Please don't say that." Avery squinted into the spray. "What do you think it might do?"

"I don't know. But it's a ghost ship. Surely it can't do much!"

"Did you see the hole in Reuben's wall? Does it have cannons?"

"They modified them for all sorts of things," Dylan told her. "They would originally have been merchant ships that were stolen and refitted for smuggling purposes."

Avery huffed. "Okay, there's nothing we can do about that right now, and it doesn't look like there's a way to the centre of the energy from here. The cliffs are too steep. I think we should head inside, see if they've found a tunnel."

Dylan folded his camera away. "It was worth a shot. El? Any luck?"

El was staring at the cliffs in fierce concentration, saying what Avery presumed to be a spell. Before she could answer, a boom sounded above the noise of the storm and a cloud of dust and debris carried on a wave of magical energy blew through the opening of the rock and billowed around them, held at bay by the protection spell. The ground rocked beneath their feet and Avery staggered, almost falling, until Dylan pulled her upright.

Avery didn't hesitate. She ran back to the cave entrance, getting pelted by rain again, but she could barely get in. The cave had completely collapsed.

~

Reuben watched Caspian working, utterly frustrated. He should be with his friends, not here, trying to undo some complicated, knotty spell that was completely beyond his abilities.

"Reuben," Caspian said, not taking his eyes from the spell. "I can feel your annoyance. Help me!"

"I don't know how!"

"That's because you're not focussing!"

"Because I'm worried about my girlfriend and our friends out there!"

Caspian lifted his head and stared at him, and Reuben felt pinned beneath the intensity of his gaze. "*Water*. I want you to focus on water!"

Reuben clenched his fists and with a deep breath, counted to five and released them again. "Okay. I'll level with you. I don't do this type of thing. I don't know how to unpick a spell."

"But you know how to make one?"

"Er, yes, I guess so."

"What do you mean, guess? You have a grimoire full of spells, a good chunk of which are based around elemental water, and I've seen you work water magic, so what is wrong?"

Reuben wrestled with how much to say. He hated to confess he was useless, but Caspian should know he couldn't rely on him. "I'm not that good a witch, Caspian. I use my magic more instinctively, and sporadically. The others, and you, seem to use it all the time. I don't. Sorry. You've got the dud one."

Caspian had been leaning on the table, but now he straightened. "That's bullshit."

"No, it's not. It's the truth." He stared back at Caspian, unflinching, and waited to see the disappointment and derision he was due.

"I get it. You were late to the party. You ignored your magic, pretended it didn't exist, and now you're still doing it."

"I'm not ignoring it. It's just not there."

"Of course it's bloody there. I've seen you use it, and I can feel it now! You used it on us in my home last year! And on those bloody vampires. And at the Crossroads Circus," he said, reminding him of what El had pointed out.

"It was a fluke."

Caspian looked up at the ceiling. "The Goddess give me strength." He levelled his gaze at Reuben again. "Water elemental magic is malleable, moody. It flows, seeping through cracks and finding ways through all sorts of things, much like water itself does. It wears things down over time. And, in large quantities, like the sea or raging rivers or masses of rain," he threw his arms out, indicating the rain they could hear falling on the roof, "it is immensely powerful! But it is also intuitive, like you."

"I'm not intuitive."

"Yes, you are. You are one of the most intuitive witches I know. You feel every one of your friends, I can tell. You tune into them, their moods, their doubts, their happiness. That's why you're the joker. You like to put them at their ease, massaging the mood of the group, picking them up when they're down, celebrating with them when they're happy. You do it so instinctively you don't even know you're doing it."

Reuben fell silent, debating whether Caspian was taking the piss, and then cast his mind back to when he was with them. *Did he do that?*

Caspian continued, "They like spending time with you, everyone does. You're popular because you flow with people. You roll with your moods—or rather, *their* moods. Water is the most emotional element, more so than the psyche. We're made of water. Water is life-giving, which means you have some healing abilities, too. And bodies of water—rivers, springs, lakes—are considered sacred spaces. And of course, you surf. You'll use your magic then too, as I'm sure you know, but again because it's so instinctive, you don't even question it. Am I right?"

"You might be right about the surfing," he grudgingly admitted.

Caspian smirked. "I'm right about it all. And that elemental magic is deep within you, like a well at your centre, and you have barely begun to tap it."

Shadow had said a similar thing when he'd first met her, so had Oswald once, but this was the first time anyone had picked up on some of the things he did and hadn't even noticed. He began to feel just the slightest bit more positive. "Perhaps."

"The trouble with elemental water is that it is so malleable, so…well, watery. You think you've got it, and then it's gone again, but you have to remember it's still always there, and it flows through your veins, rich and full of life."

"And how is that going to help me now?"

"I need you to be at your most instinctive. Let your emotional awareness flow around this spell. Water is a big part of it." Caspian stared into the spinning words. "I think they used it because this is about cursing pirates, who are at their most comfortable at sea. And like I said, water in a mass is incredibly destructive. It sweeps away everything before it.

But," Caspian studied the spell from different angles, "this is structured differently to any spell I've seen before. The words are tangled together, like a knot, and we need to find the end of it to untangle it and read it fully. That's what we're looking for."

"The end of the thread." Reuben looked at the spell again, trying to let his instincts take over. He took a deep breath, and then addressing the spell rather than Caspian, said, "Thanks."

"I didn't do anything."

"Yes, you did."

"Thank me when we've cracked this thing. And by the way, don't do anything too dramatic. We don't want to end up unconscious again."

Briar was covered in a layer of sand and earth, the ground hard beneath her, a dull ringing in her ears.

For a moment she was stunned, and then as reality filtered in, she leapt to her feet, brushing earth from her eyes and blinking rapidly to clear her vision. She was on the far side of the cave and the air was filled with dust, clogging her nose and throat. She reached for her t-shirt, pulling the hem over her nose and mouth as she tried to see the others.

Ash was circling overhead, the beat of his huge wings helping to clear the air. Around her, the others staggered to their feet, Ben pulling Cassie free from a mound of earth, and Newton cocking his shotgun.

But where was Alex, and what had happened?

"Alex!" she shouted, running to where she had last seen him.

He had been searching the final area they had uncovered. She scrambled over the debris, horrible memories of Gil's death flooding back. They had found him behind the boxes, his neck broken, his eyes vacant.

For a second, grief overcame her and she couldn't breathe. *If Alex was dead...*

In seconds, Newton had ran past her, throwing the remnants of boxes out of the way with surprising strength. He was quickly followed by Ben and Cassie, while she just stood there, unable to move.

What was the matter with her? She needed to focus. She needed to find Alex.

A blur of wings above her made her look up, and Ash streaked to where the mound of rubble and earth was biggest, grabbed something that was sticking out of the surface, and hauled a limp body out.

Briar collapsed, her eyes filling with tears. No. *No.*

Avery stared at the wall of rock, desperately trying to move it with her magic, but it stayed firmly put, and she could feel tears threatening to fall. She blinked them back, furious with herself.

"There's no way past that," Dylan said to Avery, his hand on her shoulder. "And if you succeed in some way, you might bring more down in the process." He nodded up to where a huge crack ran across the rocky roof of the cave, and pulled her back with him so they were well away from the cave entrance and any potential rock fall.

"I have to get through." Water streamed down her face as the raging weather buffeted them, and she shook his hand off. "Our friends are through there."

"We need to find another way," he said calmly, holding her gaze with his own.

She took a deep breath. He was right. She had to focus.

But all she could think of was Alex. "What if they're injured, or…" She couldn't bring herself to say the word.

"And what if they're not? What if this debris has just fallen between us, not in the main cave? Come on; let's get back to shelter and El."

He pulled her across the stony beach and into the bubble of protection, where El was still focussing on the cliffs. As they entered she started to smile, and then she saw their faces. "What's wrong?"

"A rock fall has blocked the cave," Dylan said quickly, shooting a nervous glance at Avery. "We have no idea how big it is, but we can't get through."

El was stunned into silence, her shoulders sagging, and she looked towards the entrance. "How bad?"

"Very," Avery said, finding her voice. "I couldn't move it with magic."

A portion of rock suddenly sheared off with a rumble, completely occluding the entrance, and Avery was suddenly grateful for Dylan's calm advice.

"Thanks," she said to him. "I wasn't thinking straight."

"You're worried about Alex, it's understandable. El, any luck?"

"Yes. I've been focussing on energy and heat signatures, and I can see a section up there that's emitting an energy similar to what's above us." She pointed halfway up the cliff face over on the right. "I think it's the entrance to a passage, or another cave."

Dylan grabbed his camera and focussed on the area, magnifying the image, and Avery saw that El was right. It was like a flame, flickering within the cliff.

Pushing her fear about Alex aside, Avery took a deep breath. "I can fly up there. Give me a moment, and I'll check it out. If it's clear, I'll come back for both of you."

And before any of them could complain, she summoned air and vanished.

~

As Reuben teased the last of the elemental water away, the words of the spell floated free, lining up into orderly sentences, still hovering over the page.

"Well done," Caspian muttered. "Let's see what this says."

Reuben had been working on the opposite side of the table, but now he moved around and sat next to Caspian, studying the words with him. It had taken a good hour to unravel the spell, and the start had been the hardest. Essentially, the tendril of elemental water was as sinuous and undulating as a stream, and grasping it was like trying to pick up water between your finger and thumb. But as he'd relaxed into it, he'd finally made the connection.

As he worked on his part, Caspian untangled the other. It felt like they were performing surgery together, and was certainly weird, but oddly satisfying. And Caspian, surprisingly, had been incredibly patient and utterly focussed.

As he studied the words, Reuben realised it wasn't just an incantation; it listed the ingredients, too. Salt water, dried and ground kelp, sea holly, thrift, and sea kale, as well as dragon's blood, cinnamon, camomile, and sandalwood. Right at the beginning was Coppinger's name.

"Bloody hell, Reuben, this is a horrible spell," Caspian said, raising an eyebrow in masterful understatement. "The strength of it lies in the fact that it directs the evil of Coppinger and his gang back at them." He pointed to a line of script. "'And by your hand, all that walk with you shall suffer your fate. By wealth, by stealth, each raid by blade, to all who have lost and failed to grow old, thou shall know their pain a thousand fold.'"

"It does extend to his men, then."

"Absolutely. The spell turns the offenders' ill deeds back on them 'a thousand fold.' Then it uses their greed to bind them to the treasure, ensuring it acts as a poison, rendering a slow and painful death. Their spirits are then denied rest. It says, 'As your spirit leaves your body it will be forever bound to the object of your desire, and ye shall never rest. Not by night, by day, by dark or full of moon, by sunshine, rain, or snow. Thou shall always be a slave to that which wrought your doom.'"

"The ingredients are water-based plants or seaside plants, too," Reuben noted. "I guess that explains why the water element is so strong. How do we break it?"

"Good question."

While Caspian stared at the words, Reuben stood and stretched his legs, heading over to the thermal imaging camera still trained on the island. He frowned and squinted at the image. "Er, Caspian. There's been a development."

"What?" He was at his side in seconds.

"The ship. It's heading back to Gull Island, and there seems to be some big plume of energy rising even higher. Like an explosion."

The ship had almost disappeared again, only the stern visible.

They stared at each other bleakly, and without another word, returned to the spell.

CHAPTER 29

*A*lex heard voices shouting his name, and felt someone gripping his shoulders, shaking him. His eyes jolted open. "Herne's horns! What the hell's going on?" he groaned.

"You scared the shit out of us, that's what!" Newton said, looming over him.

"I did? What did I do?" He struggled to sit up, and Newton extended a hand, helping to pull him upright.

Alex's head pounded, and he rubbed his face, feeling it covered with dust and grit. He blinked, the black spots in his vision finally clearing, and he saw Briar sitting next to him, pale and silent. "Briar, are you okay?"

"I am now! For one horrible moment…"

Memories of the explosion flooded back, and he suddenly remembered finding a trapdoor covered by layers of earth, alerted to its presence by the seal of magic.

"I think I found the passage!" He looked around him, realising he was sitting on a mound of dirt a short distance from where he'd originally been. Ash, Cassie, and Ben were there now, peering into a hole in the ground and talking quietly.

"I remember now. I released the door, and felt a surge of power. I tried to deflect it." He looked behind him. "That way."

Newton nodded. "You successfully deflected it, but you've also brought the next cave's roof down."

"*Shit*! Avery!" He'd reacted so instinctively that he'd had no time to think about where to direct the blast. "What if they were in there?"

Briar regarded him steadily. "Hopefully they've thrown up a protective shield, or were on the beach, but it would be good to know for sure. Any chance you could try to connect to them? I mean," she glanced to where the hole in the floor beckoned, "we need to go, but it would be good to see if they're okay first."

"Sure." He nodded wishing the ringing in his ears would stop.

Newton stood up. "I'm going to join the others. Make it quick, Alex. We need to get moving."

As he trudged over to the others, Briar said, "Are you sure you're okay?"

"I'm fine. Sorry I gave you a shock." He knew exactly what she'd been fearing…and remembering.

"I'll forgive you." She stood, too. "I'll give you some privacy and see you over there."

Alex took a few deep breaths and then reached out his awareness, feeling for Avery with his subconscious. He'd done this before, and because of their strong connection he could normally find her quickly, but now…nothing. Frustrated, he kept trying, but it was as if something was blocking him, and he realised it was probably the strong magic that was pouring through the trap door. He rose to his feet and joined the others, staring at the steps leading downwards.

"Any luck?" Briar asked.

"Nope. Too much energy buzzing around." He tried to sound more confident than he felt. "I'm sure they're fine."

"I agree," Ash said, turning to him. The Nephilim looked as dusty as the rest of them, but his eyes burned with intrigue. "Glad to see you're back on your feet." He gestured to the passage. "Quick question before we head down there. You say this was sealed?"

Alex nodded. "Yeah, with magic. Nothing complex. I didn't expect that surge of power to come out of it."

"Well," Briar said, "unpleasant though that was, I think it confirms we're heading in the right direction. The centre of Virginia and Serephina's spell is through there."

Ben's EMF meter was issuing a high-pitched, steady whine, and he said, "There's some serious psychic energy in there—*lots*! I think this is spirit central."

"Why do I have the feeling we're entering a crypt?" Cassie asked.

Ash swept the Empusa's sword from its scabbard. "Unfortunately, I think that's exactly what this is. Ready?"

"Ready," Alex answered, already taking the first step downwards. "Let's finish this."

Avery led Dylan and El down the tunnel that cut into the cliff, a witch-light bobbing ahead of them.

When she'd used witch-flight to fly to the tunnel's entrance, she found a series of shallow steps carved into the rock, leading up to the headland above, and she'd wondered if it was an escape route. Confirming the tunnel was clear, she'd fetched the others, and they'd now been walking inland for several minutes, on a steady downward trajectory. She quickened as she heard the boom of surf, and seeing a glow of green light ahead, extinguished the witch-light. Feeling the light was ominously familiar, she cautiously edged forward before coming to a sudden stop, the others clustering around her.

"What's going on?" El asked.

"Herne's bollocks," Dylan muttered as they took in the space in front of them. "It's a bloody pirate lair!"

They were at the side of a large cavern that glowed with a green and blue light. It emanated from a spectral, blazing fire on a beach edging a deep-water cove. The light made it seem as if the whole place was underwater, just like Reuben's attic. The bay was cut off from the sea by a massive wall of fractured rock that had sheered a ship in the bay in half. The rotten timbers wallowed in the deep water, leaving only the bowsprit, masts, and tattered sails visible.

Tiers of rock led up from the beach, filled with wooden barrels bound with iron, old wooden boxes, and chests. Rough tables and chairs, mostly decomposing, were grouped on the far side, behind which was a dark archway that Avery presumed led to another cave or tunnel. The upper levels of the cave were cloaked in shadow.

Even more chilling were the bones of dozens of men spread across the levels.

This was definitely the centre of the curse. Avery could feel it drenching the air around them.

Before Avery could even begin to work out what to do, there was a slow handclap from the top tier, and a glowering figure materialised out of the shadows, fire gleaming where there should be eyes. It was a broad shouldered, powerfully built man, wearing old-fashioned clothing and knee-length boots. He laughed, the sound booming out around them.

In seconds, dozens of other figures appeared, and Avery froze as a blade was pressed to her throat, a weather-beaten, ghoulish face leering into her own.

Alex heard shots, shouts, and the sounds of clashing metal. He ran, heedless of the uneven floor and poor light, until he saw a whirling blade slicing through the air.

He batted it away, and yelled, "Something's coming!"

A spectral hand grabbed his shirt beneath his throat and lifted him up, smashing him against the roof. Alex twisted, narrowly avoiding smacking his head, and punched out a blast of pure energy on instinct.

The ghost vanished, and Alex crashed to the floor, but another spectre emerged as Alex struggled to his feet, furious at having been caught out. The gathering energy was completely throwing him, leaving him unable to detect anything remotely magical or supernatural around him.

But Ash was already thundering past him, the Empusa's sword swinging to dispatch the spirit, and then he charged onwards. Newton hauled Alex to his feet and they raced after him, finally emerging onto a narrow shelf of rock at the back of a large cave.

For a bewildering moment, Alex thought he was under-water, as green light rippled around him, and then he saw Avery, El, and Dylan below, furiously fighting a dozen spirits that surrounded them. Magic flashed, swords clashed, and Dylan blasted his shotgun.

Alex had a moment of pure relief at seeing them alive, and then horror at their predicament. But Ash, wings outstretched, was already soaring down to assist them. Alex felt a sharp sting across his ear and the shattering of stone as a bullet ricocheted past. A spirit sneered at him, only feet away, with an old-fashioned musket in his hand. Before he could fire again, Alex uttered a banishing spell, satisfied as the spirit vanished with a howl.

His relief was short-lived, however, as other spirits manifested around them. Before he could attack again, he was aware of Cassie, Ben, Briar, and Newton lining up next to him, advancing as one.

The next few minutes were bewildering.

Alex hesitated to think of their attackers as ghosts. They may have an Otherworldly shimmer to them, and could pop in and out of vision, but they had a startlingly strong physical form, capable of touch. He and his friends were weaving in and out, ducking, diving, throwing spells and desperately trying to avoid the quick stab of blades. He was vaguely aware of Ben pulling bottled spells out of his pocket, and felt a blast of fire race past him as Cassie hurled a globe at the nearest spirit.

"Whoa!" he shouted, rolling to avoid the blast. "Careful where you throw that!"

"Sorry!" she yelled, breathless, and then out of nowhere, a spirit appeared and threw her down the tiers of rock like a rag doll. Fortunately, she rolled athletically, leaping to her feet again.

Alex turned away, a flash of movement distracting him.

A giant man grabbed Alex around the throat and pinned him to the wall. His breath was rancid, and Alex recoiled. Fire burned where his eyes should be, and he rasped in his face. "You made a mistake today, boy! You'll all die. No outsider breaches my cave and lives."

Boy?

"Screw you!" Alex yelled, convinced he was now fighting Coppinger.

He pressed his palm to Coppinger's face, scorching him with elemental fire, and his clammy skin started to slip from his features, revealing the bone beneath. But Coppinger tightened his grip around Alex's throat. He was horribly strong, fuelled by rage and hate, and his spirit was powerful.

A resounding blast caused Coppinger to drop him and

vanish, and Newton appeared to his right, already reloading his shotgun. "You okay?"

"Not really," Alex said, bewildered and breathless. "I think they're toying with us."

"And someone else has just turned up," Newton said with a scowl, and he pointed to a flurry of activity below.

Ethan had just entered the cave from another entrance below, closely followed by Mariah and Zane. As Alex stared down at them, Mariah lifted her gaze and smiled at him triumphantly.

⁓

Caspian took a deep breath and looked up at Reuben's anxious face, willing himself to be patient. "Have you got a way to break this?"

"No. We're taking too long," Reuben said to him.

"Shut up and keep trying."

But he was right, Caspian reflected. They had untangled the spell a good half an hour ago, and he was still no closer to working out how to break it. He'd glared at it, and paced around it, but it refused to give up its inner workings. He'd had one interesting idea, but was worried about the repercussions on his friends.

That word brought him up short. *Friends*. He'd never viewed the White Haven witches as that before. Well, Briar maybe, and certainly Avery. But Alex, El, Reuben, or Newton? Never. He blinked and rubbed his brow. He was getting soft in his old age.

Or maybe loneliness was driving him to it.

He'd never thought of himself as lonely, ever. But being around Reuben these last few days had made him realise how few true friendships he really had. *How sad did that make him?*

Could he even count Gabe as a friend? Or Shadow? He employed them, so maybe not.

Annoyed with his sentimental internal waffling, he focussed on the spell, starting to talk it through.

"Focus, Reuben. This is a big spell, encompassing all of Coppinger's men, his treasure, his ship, and the deep ocean. Elemental power at its strongest. It uses their greed against them. It has tied their spirits to the treasure, making them forever restless, and Mariah has used that, fuelling their spirits somehow."

"Are the spriggans a side effect?" Reuben asked, leaning back in his chair, his hands behind his head. "Or are they part of this spell?"

"They're not mentioned, so they are not part of the spell, no. They're drawn to the treasure, and as natural Other-worldly creatures, they are unaffected by the curse. Anyway, forget the spriggans." He stared at the spell again, the words shimmering in the air before him. "Curses are hard to break. It took all of us to lift the spell from El. If you remember, that was an earth-based spell."

Reuben nodded. "Yes. It suffocated her spirit, burying her alive."

"This one uses water in a similar way. It's like the curse is *suspended* in deep water. I can sense its weight. You untangled a stream of it from the words, but water is still an integral part of it. I'm wondering, if we can get rid of the water, will the curse crack?"

Reuben sat forward, leaning his arms on the table. "You're saying the water is protecting the curse, like a bubble. Which is why my attic felt like it was underwater earlier."

"Yes."

"But what about the words of the spell? Won't Coppinger's spirit still be bound to his treasure?"

"I don't think so. Once the water's gone, so are they! In

theory, at least." Caspian struggled to find the right words. "It's like letting the bathwater down a plug hole. It will take the cursed spirits with it."

"So we need to create a plug hole?" He looked alarmed, his voice rising. "Like a bloody great whirlpool? That's insane!"

"I know." He worried his lips with his fingers, staring into Reuben's wide blue eyes. "Where would we siphon it to?"

Reuben was silent for a moment, his gaze drifting to the spell again. "I've got a better idea! We freeze and shatter it."

Caspian blinked with surprise. "I like that idea better. Although, we run the risk of freezing everyone to death."

"I think that option is better than sucking them into some great whirlpool of doom."

"Of course, we could also superheat the water, turning it into steam and evaporate it."

"And boil them to death instead?"

Caspian grimaced. "Let's go with the ice thing. I think it's the lesser of the three evils."

"Ya think?" Reuben said sarcastically. He flexed his fingers and glared at the spell. "Let's get this shit-show on the road."

CHAPTER 30

*N*ewton scrambled down the rocks towards Ethan, but Ethan had cast him one long, hard look and then ignored him, racing with the witches to the treasure chests stacked at the side of the beach.

A ghost manifested directly in front of Newton and he shot it, satisfied to see it explode and vanish. He marched through it, firing at another one that appeared right behind it.

Mariah was focussing on bagging up the treasure with Ethan, but Zane, the weasly-faced witch who Newton had a vague recollection of from All Hallows' Eve, had paused and faced them. Even from a distance, Newton could see his mouth moving.

Briar was next to Newton, and she threw a blazing fire-ball at Zane, but he deflected it and threw one back, causing them both to dive to the floor.

Then something very peculiar started to happen. The skeletons lying across the cave began to twitch, and as Newton regained his feet, so did they. Every single one of them. And they weren't animated by the spirits, who, although dwindling in number, were still fighting furiously. Newton could barely keep track of his friends, lost in the melee.

"What the actual—"

"Holy shit!" Briar exclaimed. "He's animated the skeletons."

"I can see that!" Newton said, reloading quickly. "How?"

"Let's worry about that later."

Briar stamped her foot, and a ragged crack split the ground from her feet to Zane's. Zane was holding another ball of fire in his hands, ready to hurl it, but Briar's magic caught him off guard. He staggered backwards and the fireball shot into the roof, sending shards of rock flying like shrapnel.

Distracted, Newton didn't see the charging skeleton coming at him until it was too late, and the next thing he knew, he was flat on his back.

El fought her way free of the immediate group of spirits that had ambushed them and stood next to the water's edge, buying herself a few moments to assess what was happening and where she should go next.

Ash was still fighting his own battle, his huge wings sweeping back and forth as he laid waste to the spirits and skeletons that were clambering from the wreck. He balanced on the bowsprit, incredibly agile, and El was lost for a moment as she admired his skill. A shout distracted her, and she turned to see Avery struggle under another onslaught, Dylan right next to her. El was about to abandon her position to help them, when a familiar figure appeared out of nowhere with a whirl of magic that scattered the spirits.

Helena.

El grinned. She had escaped and now wanted revenge.

Did that mean...

El scanned the cave, hoping to see Gil, and to her relief saw him helping Alex fight the hulking spirit of Coppinger on the upper level. A few tiers down Cassie and Ben fought back to back, and on the far side of the cave Briar was hauling Newton to his feet as she threw a skeleton against the wall. Despite the madness of the situation, El felt herself relax slightly.

The very fact that the spirits had so much physical substance was helping them. Everyone seemed to see them, and although they vanished and reappeared bewilderingly quickly, her friends seemed to be keeping one step ahead. But Alex clearly had no time to banish them, and that was a major problem—especially now that the skeletons were on the move.

Zane and Mariah's arrival had further complicated things, and El wondered how best to thwart them. Mariah was gathering the gold coins with Ethan, Zane protecting them more than attacking anyone, and for a fleeting moment, El wondered what they thought they would do with it. They couldn't possibly think they could get away with it? There were too many people here, witnessing their actions.

And then she realised there was only one reason for their confidence. *They were planning to kill them all.* They either thought the spirits would do it, or they had another plan.

A spriggan suddenly exploded out of one of the chests, showering gold everywhere, and Mariah shrieked as it sent her sprawling. In a split-second its shadow grew, swelling until it was towering above them. It swung its enormous club, catching Ethan in the chest and throwing him into the rotting ship, where he landed with a splintering crash.

Everyone froze—including the spirits.

The spriggan didn't, however, and as the club swung towards her, El ran.

Avery grabbed Dylan, and without warning used witch-flight to take him to the edge of the cave and the entrance to the tunnel they had entered in.

He collapsed on hands and knees, retching. "Herne's balls, Avery! That's bloody horrible!"

"Would you rather your brains be bashed in?"

"Er, no." He staggered to his feet and then stopped, trans-fixed as he watched the spriggan sweep his enormous club back and forth.

Their friends were running and ducking as old barrels and boxes went flying, and Ash flew around the spriggan, trying to distract it. Sensibly, everyone else was scurrying to the edges of the cave, and El appeared next to Avery, breath-less from her scramble.

But something else was distracting Avery.

It was starting to feel very cold. She could see her breath in front of her, and the green, underwater quality of the cave was turning a glacial blue. Alarmed, she looked at the water, and saw ice forming where it met the beach. In mere seconds it spread across the bay and towards the wrecked ship.

"Guys, I think Caspian and Reuben are doing something. It's freezing in here."

Looking back to the cave, she saw fingers of ice clawing up the rock walls, across the ground, and over the barrels and splintered wood.

They needed to leave, quickly. Avery turned to Dylan. "You stay here and guard this exit. This is our only way out. Have you got any salt shells left?"

He patted his pocket, and immediately reloaded. "Yep. No problem."

"Good." She turned to El. "We need to get everyone out of here—right now!"

El didn't wait, and ran towards Briar and Newton, shouting loudly.

Avery manifested next to Ben and Cassie, halfway up the tiers of rock that were now sheer ice, appearing in front of them so unexpectedly that Cassie yelled in shock. Avery pointed to where Dylan stood at the side of the natural amphitheatre. "Join Dylan, and make your way to the end of the tunnel. There's a set of steps cut into the cliff face. It leads upwards to safety."

"But—" Ben started to object.

"Look around, Ben! This place is turning into one giant ice cube." As if to punctuate her point, snow started to fall, and an icy stalactite crashed to the floor next to them, along with Ash.

"She's right," Ash said, and without waiting for Cassie's permission, he wrapped his arms around her and soared across the cave.

"You too, Ben!" Avery shouted. "*Go!*"

She watched him scramble away, and then looked up to where Alex and Gil were still fighting Coppinger. She grabbed the icy stalactite and flew to Alex's side, catching all of them unawares, especially Coppinger. She hefted her weapon like a spear, plunging it straight through his chest, and he flew backwards.

"Alex! Time to leave!"

He looked at her with a mixture of relief and bewilderment on his face. "But I haven't banished them yet!"

"I don't think you'll need to. Look around! We'll end up an ice exhibit if we don't move."

Snow was falling thicker now, stinging their skin as it

hardened into hail. But it seemed Coppinger had no intention of letting them leave. He charged them like an enraged bull, and just as Avery was about to respond, Helena joined Gil and they both shielded Alex and Avery as they faced down Coppinger together.

Helena extended her arms and flames flickered along her entire body, thick black smoke pouring from her, creating a barrier that Coppinger couldn't pass.

Gil turned to them. "We've got this. Helena has a lot of anger to burn off."

Avery stepped towards him, wishing she could hug him. "Gil! I wish we had more time. Will we ever see you again?"

He gave her a weak smile. "I'm aiming to retire after this, so I hope not."

"But you can't stay! You'll be caught up in whatever's happening here!"

He winked as Helena screamed like a banshee and launched herself at Coppinger. "We'll be just fine."

He ran to join Helena, and all three of them vanished from sight in the thickening blizzard.

Alex's hands were already around her waist, and without waiting another second Avery transported them to the tunnel's entrance.

Only El was waiting there, and she sighed with relief at their arrival. "Come on, everyone else is out."

"Ethan?" Avery said, catching sight of his twisted body now partially consumed by ice.

"Already dead."

The ice was already spreading down the tunnel, so with one final look at the icy maelstrom, they raced to join the others.

∼

Reuben stared into the heart of the block of ice, continuing to lower the temperature.

The pool of elemental water that he'd connected to deep within him was powerful, and he closed it like a fist around the spell, his hands on either side of it as it turned slowly above the pages.

Little by little he'd lowered the temperature, seeing the ice form first around the outside and then thicken, moving ever towards the centre, where the words of the spell were now trapped. Caspian had offered him some power, but he found that he didn't need it. Once he'd tapped into his own, it was like he'd released a dam. It was actually a struggle to slow it down.

He glanced up at Caspian, who was unmoving, opposite him. "One more push and it will be frozen solid. What do you think?"

"It's been a good fifteen minutes already. That should have given them plenty of warning. Hold on." Caspian ran back to the thermal imaging camera, and then returned within seconds. "It's an icy blue over the island now, but I can see odd heat spots right on the top of the cliff. I'm no expert on thermal imaging, but I think they're human signals. Go for it."

Reuben lowered the temperature again, watching the ice become cloudy and more dense, the words within it disappearing entirely. Reuben knew it was now solid all the way through. Minute crystals formed over the surface, building up and creating starburst patterns, and Reuben accelerated the growth, until the cube was contained within a giant, beautiful snowflake.

Reuben smiled at his handiwork. "Call me Picasso. I could make money out of this."

Caspian's lips twitched. "Maybe in another life."

"What now?"

"Now, we break it. May I?"

"Be my guest."

"You might want to lean back," he warned.

Caspian uttered a short phrase that Reuben couldn't quite catch. Instantly fractures ripped through the ice, the cube exploding outwards with such force that Reuben shielded his eyes. The words of the curse flew up and out, letters tumbling over each other, throwing Caspian and Reuben off their chairs with a resounding crash. Reuben lay on his back and stared up at the ceiling, seeing letters still whirling before they dissolved into nothing.

Winded, he shouted, "Caspian? Are you still alive?"

He groaned. "Yes. But I'll have a serious headache."

"When you tell me to lean back, you may want to specify an area next time."

"Sure, Reuben. The next time we crack an evil curse, I'll bear that in mind."

The second Avery reached the cliff face, she realised just how precarious the steps were, and it didn't help that the rain was steadily falling, making them treacherously slippery.

But Ash was hovering in the air in front of them, his enormous wings protecting them from falling, and although Avery wasn't worried for her own safety, she was relieved for everyone else. She could have used witch-flight, but she wanted to be with her friends, escaping together, and as soon as she reached the grassy cliff top, she saw them clustered a short distance from the edge.

"Is that everyone?" she asked, quickly scanning the group.

They were a bedraggled bunch, shivering and soaked from the rain, and Newton hustled them into action, shouting to be heard above the wind. "That's it, we're all here. Head down the slope to the beach. The police launch is on the way."

They raced across the grassy headland, and then down the long slope to the shore that faced White Haven, slipping and sliding on the slick grass, and it was only when they reached the beach that they stopped and caught their breath. The rain finally fizzled out, but a damp wind buffeted them, catching their hair and ruffling their clothes. Across the waves the town glittered, its warm yellow lights clustered around the harbour and scattered across the hills like stars. A lone engine broke the silence of the night, and they saw a boat streaking towards the shore.

"That must be Mariah and Zane," Briar speculated. "I saw them race out of the cave, but there was no way I could follow them."

Newton was watching them with narrowed eyes, his lips tight. "I've called Moore and told him to back off in case they get violent. The police will have no defence against their magic, and right now, I'm not sure what they're capable of."

"I agree," El said. "I honestly think they were planning to kill all of us in there. Otherwise, why be so brazen?"

That was a horrible thought, but El was right, and Newton nodded. "We'll catch up with them eventually."

"That reminds me," El said, reaching for her phone, but it rang before she could dial and she smiled as she answered. "Reuben!"

Even from a distance, Avery could hear his voice and El drifted away to talk to him in private, reassuring him of their wellbeing.

Ben, Dylan, and Cassie had caught their breath and were grinning from ear to ear, Ben asking, "Did you see that bloody spriggan? Even the spirits were scared of it!"

"I'm not surprised!" Cassie said. "We just came face to face with the ghost of a Cornish giant!" Her eyes took on a faraway glaze.

Dylan snorted. "And the ghosts of many, many murderous pirates!"

"Like I'd forget that! It will give me nightmares!"

"At least," Alex said, brushing his hair away from his face, "you weren't face to face with Coppinger. He was determined to kill me."

Avery slid her arm around his waist. "But he failed. Are you okay?" she asked, drawing him away from the others as they continued their excited chat.

"I'm fine. A bit shocked from seeing Gil, but it was good, too."

"At least we know Helena is free!"

Alex stared down at her. "Remind me not to piss her off. She's mean."

"But she helped us!"

"I'm just glad she's on our side."

Newton joined in again. "I'm going to have to come back here tomorrow, to see if we can get any evidence." He looked inland uneasily, as if he was staring through the ground and into the cave. "I'm giving it overnight in the hope that it will be safe tomorrow."

"We should come with you," Alex immediately said. "Just in case. Will you have a drink with us tonight? We're heading to Reuben's."

"Unfortunately not. I have many things to do, including contacting Ethan's relatives."

Avery's good mood immediately vanished. "You saw his body, then?"

"Flying across the cave like a broken doll? Yes, I saw it. We'll collect that, too." He hesitated a moment. "Do you think the treasure will still be there now that the curse has been broken?"

"Probably," Alex said cautiously. "Why?"

"I was just thinking that it would be an excellent addition to the White Haven exhibition. It would be nice to salvage *something* from this bloody mess."

CHAPTER 31

*A*very leaned back in her chair and sipped her tea, listening to the chatter in Reuben's snug.

They had all arrived about an hour ago, and had finally dried out. El was looking proudly at Reuben, who was sitting in front of the fire on the rug, and she said to him and Caspian, "You two are so clever! What an ingenious way to break the spell!"

"It was all Reuben, not me," Caspian said softly. He was sitting in an armchair, and he raised his glass in a silent salute.

"Yeah," Reuben said, shaking his head. "He had some crazy whirlpool idea that would have seen you all sucked into oblivion. And let's not forget the steam!"

Caspian just smiled at him. "Yes, so don't give me your bullshit stories again."

Avery frowned, and then realised what Caspian must be referring to. *Reuben's self doubt.* It seemed they weren't the only ones to share interesting experiences that night.

"Hold on a minute," Alex said, leaning forward from his spot on the sofa. "Are you telling me that I didn't need to banish hordes of angry spirits, and we could have sat by the fire all night while you two worked upstairs?"

Reuben laughed and looked slightly sheepish. "Ah, my friend! That might be the case, but wouldn't you have regretted missing all that fun?"

"No. Coppinger tried to kill me, on multiple occasions!"

"I would have missed it!" Ben cut in. "That was amazing. I just wish we could have recorded some of it."

Dylan gave an abrupt laugh. "Ha! I was too busy fending off spirits to film it! At least we have the other footage. I'll start editing it tomorrow."

"You guys showed some impressive fighting skills today," El told them.

Cassie smiled at her. "Thanks. We've been practising, although with our exams and everything we've been neglecting it lately. No excuses anymore."

"Have you got a team name yet?" Reuben asked.

"Yes, we have!" Dylan said, excited. "After much argument," he shot Ben an annoyed look, "we are called Ghost OPS, which stands for Objective Paranormal Studies."

"I like it," Reuben said, nodding his approval. He gave a sly grin. "I can call you GOPS, as in *'help, help, call the GOPS, I'm being attacked!'*"

"If you have to," Ben said, groaning, as they all laughed. He turned to El, probably just to shut Reuben up. "Hey El, your sword fighting looked pretty good tonight."

"Well, that's thanks to Shadow. She's been giving me private lessons."

"Has she?" Ash said, surprised. He was sitting on the floor too, leaning back against the sofa and sipping a beer. "She kept that quiet, and that's unusual, because she loves to brag!"

"Interesting housemate?" Alex asked, laughing.

"You could say that."

"Why have they gone to London?" Avery asked him, remembering what he'd said earlier.

He shrugged. "No idea, yet. I'll call Gabe later."

Avery wondered how true that was, and what they were now involved with, but she didn't say anything else. With luck, Shadow would update them eventually.

"I have a question," Ben said, looking at Reuben and Caspian. "Did your ancestors seal that cave? Because Alex had to use magic to open it, and when he did, energy exploded out of it."

"I believe so," Caspian said, but he looked uncertain. "The details of what they did remain murky, and even though we deciphered the whole spell, we can only conjecture how it really happened. I suspect it didn't play out quite as they planned, but once they had Coppinger cornered with most of his men, they used the curse. From what you've said, there were multiple entrances into the cave, and I guess they must have sealed them all."

"They sheered the cliff face off too, crushing the ship and splitting it in half," Avery said. "The bay looked to be a natural deep water harbour that allowed the ship to enter the cave. Amazing, really. It was a proper pirate hangout!"

Briar had been sipping her tea as she listened, but now she roused. "I think that's why Mariah left that place until last. They knew it was cursed, and knew it would be the trickiest to access, despite their magic and her compromise with the spirits. I wonder what she'll do now?"

"She and Zane will have to hide, surely?" Reuben said. "They attacked me and Caspian, stole treasure, and although they're not responsible for the deaths, they were very much involved."

Caspian's eyes hardened as he looked at Reuben. "I agree, but it will be hard for the police. I wonder what Genevieve will say."

"And what about their other coven members?" Alex asked. "Are they involved?"

"I guess we'll soon find out," he answered ominously.

Caspian stood on Reuben's porch the next morning, looking across the gravelled drive to Briar's Mini. She had turned it around, and was now waiting for him with the engine running.

He shook Reuben's hand. "Thanks for your hospitality. It's been…interesting."

Reuben laughed. "That's one word for it. You could stay another day or two, until your wound is healed."

"I'm fine now—well, apart from the odd twinge. And I don't have to fear attack by ghosts again."

"What about Mariah or Zane?"

"I think they'll leave well enough alone. And my protection spells will be strong. Make sure yours are, too." He stepped onto the drive, and Reuben followed him as Caspian looked up at the attic's shattered windows. "Are you sure you don't want help with those?"

"I'm going to do it the old-fashioned way and get glaziers in, and hire a builder for the wall." Reuben hesitated, and then said, "Thanks for all your help, with everything." He shuffled, looking suddenly uncomfortable. "I know I struggled a bit."

"You did just fine. Better than fine." Caspian was feeling unexpectedly sad to be leaving. He'd found that he was very comfortable around Reuben and the rest of the White Haven Coven, and it was a strange feeling, one that had been growing for a while. It was a feeling he'd buried, but couldn't anymore, and didn't actually want to. He debated just turning away and getting in Briar's car, but there was one more thing he needed to say. He looked Reuben directly in the eye. "I really am sorry about Gil. I'm responsible. I caused it, even though it wasn't my intention. You have been incredibly forgiving, and I don't know if I could have done the same in your shoes."

Reuben's gaze dropped to the ground, and Caspian hoped he hadn't said the wrong thing, but then he looked up again, as if he'd mastered his emotions. "It's been hard, I won't lie, but thank you. I appreciate it. And now you need to move on, and so do I...from all sorts of things." Caspian heard Avery and Alex's voices coming down the hall, and Reuben spoke quickly. "And you need to move on from her, too."

"Easier said than done," he confessed, and having said it, he already felt lighter.

Reuben just nodded, and then Avery and Alex were with them, Avery saying, "There you are! I thought I'd missed you." She stepped forward, enveloping him in a hug. "Thanks so much for your help, again. It's becoming a habit. You're on team White Haven now!" She stepped back and smiled at him, leaving him feeling bereft, but once again grateful for her kindness.

Caspian laughed. "Don't let Estelle hear you say that." *Something else he needed to deal with.* He quickly reached forward and shook Alex's hand, aware of his cool glance that said everything. "Alex. I'll see you soon."

And not wanting to linger, he headed quickly to Briar's car.

≈

Reuben stood next to Newton and Alex, watching Moore and another couple of officers examine the cave.

They had set up huge lights and a generator, after accessing the cave via the tunnel from Reuben's glasshouse, and Reuben tried to imagine how it would have looked the previous evening in the watery green light.

"Wow," he said, spotting the splintered remnants of the ship. "That's incredible. It's all incredible!"

Alex grunted. "It looks a damn sight better today than when it was full of bloody ghosts and animated skeletons. Although the pressure of the ice has crushed all the wood."

"Yes!" Newton exclaimed, hurrying across to the ruined chests and piles of gold. "The treasure is still here!"

"Slow down." Alex said, rushing to follow him. "The spriggan might still be here, too!"

"Oh come on," Newton scoffed. "This place turned into solid ice. It would have surely killed it! We're probably surrounded by tiny little pieces of it."

Reuben listened to their banter as he followed them with his easy stride, taking in the abandoned weapons, the skeletal remains, and the piles of shattered wood. It was cold and damp, with water dripping down the walls and forming pools across the tiers. It was hard to believe his magic had filled this place with ice. There was certainly no curse remaining, or any palpable psychic energy. It just felt very empty. He could hear the surf pounding outside, but the only evidence of it inside were the gentle waves that splashed on the now inland beach.

Ethan's body was still lying twisted on the spar, and once Newton was happy that the place was safe, the coroner would be called in, as would SOCO. Reuben wondered what the ice had done to his body, and shuddered. *Turned his innards to mush, probably.*

Newton's shout broke through his thoughts. "Hey Reuben, do you mind if the police set up on your grounds by the glasshouse? It could take days to process in here."

He walked over to join them. "It's fine, as long as they don't mind me being incredibly nosey!"

"It will be out of bounds until they've finished, you pillock."

"Thanks, Newton. You're always so nice." In the harsh white lights that illuminated the cave, Newton looked very tired, and he thought he'd trade an insult. "Are you sure you slept last night? You look like shit."

"Barely." He watched Moore and the other two officers exploring the tiers of rock. "I called Maggie Milne this morning. I thought I should let her know about Mariah and Zane. We had officers watching their houses, but there's been no movement, and their cars are gone." He turned to Alex and Reuben. "I've never had to chase witches before, so I'm not exactly sure what I should do next in regard to safety and magic."

"What did she say?" Alex asked.

"To tread carefully, and involve other witches." He gave them a long, questioning look.

Reuben tried to laugh and failed. "Are you saying you need *us* to find them?"

"You're the only ones I trust."

Reuben looked at Alex's bleak expression, and knew he was thinking the same as him. He didn't want to fight other witches, or hunt them down, but if they were a danger—and they probably were—they'd have no choice.

Avery ended her call with Genevieve and walked back to the counter to join Dan and Sally.

It was late morning in Happenstance Books, and because it was a Saturday, the place was busy. All three were capitalising on a lull and taking a quick coffee break. Sally had opened a packet of chocolate digestives, and she dunked one in her coffee as Avery leaned on the counter.

"What's the verdict?" Dan asked. He'd decided to celebrate the museum's smuggling exhibition that—despite Ethan's death—was still opening that day, by wearing a t-shirt that said, *All the best pirates smuggle books.*

Avery had already updated them on the events of the night before, and there had been a mixture of emotions from them both—excitement, horror, wonder, amazement, and now worry at the thought of Zane and Mariah's disappearance.

"Genevieve is furious, but she doesn't want to jump to any conclusions or make rash decisions. And I agree. We have time."

"But won't that give *them* time?" Sally asked. "They could be planning anything!"

"They're not bloody Voldemort activating his dark mark," Dan said. "And I'm pretty sure Genevieve won't need to unleash any Dementors, either."

Avery giggled, but Sally glared at him. "I know that! But they've been very underhanded, and were behind Reuben's attack. He could have been killed! Caspian, too. All of you, really," she added, turning her attention to Avery. "And Zane has never liked you, Avery. He could blame you for needing to flee!"

Avery sobered. "I know, and we're not taking this lightly, but we need a plan. It's Litha next week, and we'll all be gathering to celebrate at Rasmus's place, so that's when we'll decide on a plan, too." She sipped her drink, thinking about her conversation. "Genevieve is going to visit the Looe and Bodmin Coven members if they're around, and also let the other covens know today, just in case Zane or Mariah contact someone for help. Personally, I think they're a long way from here by now."

"Good." Sally took another biscuit. "Well, I'm just glad

you're safe, and despite everything, I will still be going to that exhibition. Do you think they'll add the treasure, too?"

"Maybe. Surely at least some of it, once they've assessed it."

"And what about the chests you found and took to Reuben's?" Dan asked.

"I took those back to the big cave first thing this morning, once I knew it was safe." She had risen early and flown there with Alex. "It'll be easier to pretend it was part of that treasure than tell anyone about the room beneath St Catherine's Castle. It also means we can leave those spriggans well alone."

Dan looked confused. "Why was Miles killed if he didn't even get in there? You said there was no way he could have entered the place."

"I've been thinking on that, and I can only presume he got too close and triggered them somehow. It's odd, though. It's close to a popular walking spot, and I imagine lots of people are around there all the time. They haven't attacked any of them."

"Unless, of course," Dan suggested, slightly tentatively, "Mariah orchestrated it to get him out of the way. And then let them attack Jasmine. You mentioned that you and Alex had managed to control them, and El also did, and I know you said they were strong, but why couldn't Zane and Mariah stop them?"

A chill rushed through Avery as she considered Dan's words, and realised that actually made a lot of sense. Her legs went weak, and she sagged against the counter. "Shit. You might be right."

He stared back at her, Sally watching them wide-eyed. "Maybe," he said, "they intended for Ethan to never leave there, either."

"And the man walking his dog!" Sally added. "Maybe he

saw something, because he was nowhere near the cave in Looe, either!"

Avery staggered to the stool behind the counter. All the odd things that had happened made a lot of sense if Dan was right, which meant Mariah and Zane were far more dangerous than they thought. She took a deep breath, deciding to think on it and discuss it with the others later.

"Thanks, guys. I have a horrible feeling you might be right, Dan. Now, let's do something positive, because this is depressing me."

"Of course," Sally said, visibly gathering herself and giving Avery a beaming smile. "We have new stock in, shelves to fill, and I need to decorate the shop for the solstice! It's time for another witchy celebration in White Haven!"

"And I think it's also time for some pirate music," Dan said, quickly changing the track that had been playing.

Avery groaned as she heard the booming, jaunty words, "I am the very model of a modern major general."

"*The Pirates of Penzance*!" She looked at him, aghast. "In my shop!"

She tried to wrestle the controls from Dan, but he just laughed maniacally and scooted after Sally, tugging her hair and making her squeal as he did a silly jig. Despite her mood, Avery giggled, and once again thanked her lucky stars for her shop and her friends, because she was pretty sure the coming weeks were going to be hard.

Thanks for reading *Vengeful Magic*. Please make an author happy and leave a review.

I have also written a spinoff series called White Haven Hunters. The first book is called *Spirit of the Fallen*, and you can buy it here.

If you enjoyed this book and would like to read more of my stories, please subscribe to my newsletter at www.tjgreen.nz. You will get two free short stories, *Excalibur Rises* and *Jack's Encounter*, and will also receive free character sheets of all the main White Haven witches.

AUTHOR'S NOTE

Thank you for reading *Vengeful Magic*, the eighth book in the White Haven Witches series.

I'm sure you've noticed that this book was told from multiple points of view. I was encouraged to do this by all of my fantastic readers who said they would love to have more insight into the other characters.

I must admit, I'd wanted to, especially after doing this with White Haven Hunters, but wondered how well this would be received, considering this is the eighth book! Hopefully you have loved the opportunity to get in the heads of the other witches, and of course Newton. I feel it's given the characters and stories a new lease of life, and I'm fizzing to get started on the next novel in the series.

I had a lot of fun writing about pirates. Cornwall is awash with pirate tales, and many of the places I refer to do exist, such as the Charlestown Shipwreck Treasure Museum and Jamaica Inn Smuggling Museum. Obviously the characters associated with them do not exist, and I'm sure there's no skulduggery among the archives! Wheal Droskyn in Perranporth exists too, and in fact there are hundreds of mines all across Cornwall.

Cruel Coppinger was a real pirate who landed on the north Cornish coast during a storm, and he became notorious for his cruelty. His story was embellished by the Reverend Robert Stephen Hawker, who collected legends. Zephaniah Job was also a real person who kept the financial records for pirates, and his ledgers were burnt following his death.

If you'd like to read a bit more background to the stories, please head to my website, www.tjgreen.nz, where I blog about the books I've read and the research I've done on the series. In fact, there's lots of stuff on there about my other series, Rise of the King, as well.

Now for the thanks I owe everyone who helped me produce this book.

I decided to run a competition in my newsletter and Facebook Inner Circle for a name for the parapsychologists. I had some fantastic suggestions and ended up narrowing it down to eight that had the final vote. Ghost OPS won by a big margin! Thank you Margaret Meyer for your awesome suggestion!

Thanks again to Fiona Jayde Media for my awesome cover, and thanks to Kyla Stein at Missed Period Editing for applying her fabulous editing skills.

Thanks also to my beta readers, glad you enjoyed it; your feedback, as always, is very helpful!

Finally, thank you to my launch team, who give valuable feedback on typos and are happy to review on release. It's lovely to hear from them—you know who you are! You're amazing! I also love hearing from all my readers, so I welcome you to get in touch.

If you'd like to read more of my writing, please join my mailing list at www.tjgreen.nz. You can get a free short story called Jack's Encounter, describing how Jack met Fahey—a longer version of the prologue in Call of the King—by subscribing to my newsletter. You'll also get a free copy of Excalibur Rises, a short story prequel. You will also receive free character sheets on all of my main characters in White Haven Witches—exclusive to my email list!

By staying on my mailing list you'll receive free excerpts of my new books, updates on new releases, as well as short stories and news of giveaways. I'll also be sharing information about other books in this genre you might enjoy.

You can also follow my Facebook page, T J Green. I post there reasonably frequently. In addition, I have a Facebook group called TJ's Inner Circle. It's a fab little group where I run giveaways and post teasers, so come and join us. https://www.facebook.com/groups/696140834516292

ABOUT THE AUTHOR

I grew up in England and now live in the Hutt Valley, near Wellington, New Zealand, with my partner, Jason, and my cats, Sacha and Leia. When I'm not writing, you'll find me with my head in a book, gardening, or doing yoga. And maybe getting some retail therapy!

In a previous life I've been a singer in a band, and have done some acting with a theatre company—both of which were lots of fun.

Please follow me on social media to keep up to date with my news, or join my mailing list—I promise I don't spam! Join my mailing list here.

For more information, please visit my website, as well as Facebook, Pinterest, Goodreads, BookBub, TikTok, and Instagram.

facebook.com/tjgreenauthor

twitter.com/tjay_green

instagram.com/tjgreenauthor

Rise of the King Series

A Young Adult series about a teen called Tom who is summoned to wake King Arthur. It's a fun adventure about King Arthur in the Otherworld!

Call of the King #1

King Arthur is destined to return, and Tom is destined to wake him.

When sixteen-year old Tom's grandfather mysteriously disappears, Tom will stop at nothing to find him, even if that means crossing over into a mysterious and unknown world.

When he gets there, Tom discovers that everything he thought he knew about himself and his life was wrong. Vivian, the Lady of the Lake, has been watching over him and manipulating his life since his birth. And now she needs his help.

The Silver Tower #2

Merlin disappeared over a thousand years ago. Now Tom will risk everything to find him.

Vivian needs King Arthur's help. Nimue, a powerful witch and priestess who lives on Avalon, has disappeared.

King Arthur, Tom, and his friends set off across the Otherworld to find her. Nimue seems to have a quest of her own, one she's deliberately hiding. Arthur is convinced it's about Merlin, and he's determined to find them both.

The Cursed Sword #3

An ancient sword. A dark secret. A new enemy.

Tom loves his new life in the Otherworld. He lives with Arthur in New Camelot, and Arthur is hosting a tournament. Eager to test his sword-fighting skills, Tom is competing.

But while the games are being played, his friends are attacked, and everything he loves is threatened. Tom has to find the intruder before anyone else gets hurt.

Tom's sword seems to be the focus of these attacks. Their investigations uncover its dark history, and a terrible betrayal that a family has kept secret for generations.

White Haven Hunters

The fun-filled spinoff to the White Haven Witches series! Featuring Fey, Nephilim, and the hunt for the occult.

Spirit of the Fallen #1

Kill the ghost, save the host.

Shadow is an overconfident fey stranded in White Haven after the Wild Hunt is defeated on Samhain.

Gabe is a Nephilim, newly arrived from the spirit world, along with six of his companions. He has a violent history that haunts him, and a father he wants answers from—if he ever finds him.

When they get into business together with The Orphic Guild, they're expecting adventure, intrigue, and easy money.

But their first job is more complicated than they imagined.

When they break fey magic that seals an old tomb, they discover that it contains more than they bargained for. Now they're hunting for a rogue spirit, and he always seems one step ahead.

The fight leads them in a direction they never expected.

Gabe can leave his past behind, or he could delve into the darkest secrets of mankind.

Shadow has no intention of being left out.

Shadow's Edge #2

As Shadow and Gabe become more involved with The Orphic Guild, they find out that the occult world is full of intrigue and far more complicated than they realised.

Especially when it seems that someone wants the same thing that they do — The Trinity of the Seeker.

Cause for concern?

Absolutely not. If anything, Shadow is more committed than ever, and relishes pitting her wits against an unpredictable enemy.

And Gabe? When they find instructions that could enable him to speak to his father, he and the Nephilim are more than ready to fight.

Join Shadow, Gabe, and Harlan as they race against an occult organisation that is as underhand as they are.

Printed in Great Britain
by Amazon